PENGUIN  CLASSICS

WOMEN IN POWER

STEPHANIE McCARTER is a professor of classics at the University of the South in Sewanee, Tennessee. She has published translations of Horace and Ovid and has written for *The Sewanee Review*, *Eidolon*, Electric Literature, *The Millions*, and elsewhere.

T0182279

Women in Power

CLASSICAL MYTHS AND STORIES, FROM THE AMAZONS TO CLEOPATRA

Edited by
STEPHANIE McCARTER

PENGUIN BOOKS

PENGUIN BOOKS
An imprint of Penguin Random House LLC
penguinrandomhouse.com

LIBRARY OF CONGRESS CATALOGING-IN-PUBLICATION DATA
Names: McCarter, Stephanie, editor.
Title: Women in power : classical myths and stories, from the Amazons to
Cleopatra / edited by Stephanie A. McCarter.
Description: 1st edition. | New York : Penguin Books, [2024] |
Includes bibliographical references.
Identifiers: LCCN 2023048423 (print) | LCCN 2023048424 (ebook) |
ISBN 9780143136361 (paperback) | ISBN 9780525507888 (ebook)
Subjects: LCSH: Leadership in women—Case studies. | Women—History.
Classification: LCC HQ1233 .W5965 2024 (print) |
LCC HQ1233 (ebook) | DDC305.42—dc23/eng/20240116
LC record available at https://lccn.loc.gov/2023048423
LC ebook record available at https://lccn.loc.gov/2023048424

Printed in the United States of America
1st Printing

Set in Sabon LT Pro

Contents

Introduction

Power takes many forms, and the ancient Greeks and Romans, unsurprisingly, had many words to denote it. In Greek, *dynamis, rhômê, sthenos, kratos, archê, exousia, dynasteia,* and *megethos* are just some of the words that might be translated as "power." These words, moreover, can take on specific nuances, such as raw "ability" (*dynamis*), physical "strength" (*rhômê, sthenos*), governmental "authority" (*archê*), "mastery" over others (*kratos*), and "grandeur" (*megethos*). Possessing such power regularly brought further rewards such as "honor" (*timê*), "glory" (*kleos, kydos*), and "renown" (*doxa, onoma*). The Romans called "power" *potestas* or *potentia,* but further delineated physical "strength" (*vires, robur*), "capability" (*facultas*), financial "resources" (*opes*), "legal authority" (*manus*), and "domination" (*dominatio*). Other types of power were rarely wielded by individual humans but by gods (*numen*) or states (*maiestas*). Those who held power enjoyed concomitant attributes such as *auctoritas* ("influence") or *gravitas* ("importance"). Power can of course also be exercised through softer methods—for instance, through craft or persuasion. Such unofficial forms of power, however, usually fall to those denied the imprimatur of sanctioned authority.

Official power in classical antiquity was a man's game, which might make the title of this book seem like an oxymoron to a Greek or Roman. Not all men, however, exercised power equally, or at all. Greece and Rome were both enslaver societies that built up their own power by denying it to others, and an enslaved man was not considered fully a "man" in Greek or Roman thought; he was instead a *pais* or a *puer* ("boy"). Noncitizens, immigrants, and freed people, moreover, existed in an in-between category, one that allowed them to enjoy a degree of freedom and perhaps own property (or, in the case of a freedman, to vote) but that banned them from holding power through political office. Such power was restricted to freeborn men who held full citizenship. In Greece and Rome, this political liberty was manifested in several ways, from the power to control one's own body (including sexually) to the power to speak in public. To employ the intersectional framework developed by Kimberlé Crenshaw, power and disempowerment depended not only on one's gender but also on a host of other factors such as class, marital status, sexuality, language, age, and ethnicity.[1]

Though much of what we call "power" would have been off-limits to women, many women would indeed have had access to varying degrees of influence or authority, particularly within the home.[2] A Greek wife would have been expected to run the household, thus wielding power over the enslaved persons of all genders who toiled for it, and even the unfree women dwelling within the home might have held varying levels of authority over others. Indeed, one key motive for a man to empower a woman within the domestic sphere was to shore up his own patriarchal power. To quote philosopher Kate Manne, "Women's power, strength, and agency may be highly valued, when she is standing behind a great man as the 'great woman' in the background."[3] Going all the way back to the *Odyssey*, Homer describes how Laertes, Odysseus's father, "honored" (1.432) key women within the household, including the enslaved woman Eurycleia, giving her as much honor as his own wife, thus ensuring her faithful service. Similarly, in Xenophon's *Oeconomicus* (7.42), the Athenian Ischomachus promises his (unnamed) wife so much honor (*timê*) that even he will seem to be her slave within the home. Of course, in giving her such authority, Ischomachus himself is freed from domestic responsibilities and able to participate in the political and social life of the city. Even a goddess like Athena regularly uses her considerable power to uphold masculine authority. In the *Odyssey*, for instance, she helps Odysseus reestablish himself as the *kyrios* ("lord" or "master") within his home, a feat that necessitates ridding the house of any unfaithful or self-serving women. She was regularly the helper of other powerful male heroes, such as Hercules, Perseus, Bellerophon, and Jason.

In the Roman world, free women would have been under the *potestas* of the male head of household and after marriage would have remained under his legal authority (*manus*) or (though less frequently in the late Republic and Empire) transferred to the *manus* of their husbands. They could own wealth, including in the form of enslaved persons, but were normally required to be under the guardianship (*tutela*) of a man who would have to approve of how they transacted that wealth. When Augustus came to power, he instituted the *ius trium liberorum*, which released freeborn women who had given birth to three children, or freedwomen who had given birth to four, from *tutela*. Despite these restrictions, many elite women exercised considerable influence in the public sphere through benefactions.[4] In early first-century CE Pompeii, for example, the wealthy woman Eumachia was a patron of the guild of fullers, who honored her with a statue, and she funded an enormous colonnaded building adjacent to the forum. Even non-elite women, such as the purveyors of *tabernae* ("taverns") in Pompeii, wielded what political influence they could by adorning the building's exterior walls with campaign endorsements.[5]

Throughout Greco-Roman antiquity, religion gave women key roles of public power and influence. Eumachia, for instance, held an important religious role as the priestess of Venus Pompeiana. The priestess of Athena Polias in classical Athens enjoyed an unusual amount of prominence. One woman named Lysimache held that position for over six decades and upon her death was honored with a public statue. She may even have served as the inspiration for the title character of Aristophanes's *Lysistrata*.[6] In Rome, the Vestal Virgins were granted exceptional prestige.[7] They had special seats at public events, were freed from male guardianship, and even were attended by the lictors who otherwise escorted male magistrates. Yet the Vestal Virgins were also harshly subjected to patriarchal control. Their virginal bodies, meant to symbolize the impenetrability of the Roman state, were stringently policed, and a priestess who broke her vow of chastity was subject to being buried alive. The power the Vestals enjoyed was thus ultimately aimed at serving the state's patriarchal status quo. The same can be said for the powerful and influential empresses who have often been portrayed in ancient sources, and often in our own modern media, as stereotypes of manipulative and dangerous women plotting to exercise power through their husbands, sons, and fathers. In their own portraiture, however, these empresses, such as Augustus's wife Livia, emphasize their role as providers, nourishers, and supporters of the patriarchal state.[8] By being good, devoted wives, they promote the moral order of Rome and ensure the gods' continued support of Roman domination. The image of Livia, in particular, was carefully fashioned to stand in opposition to Cleopatra, the ultimate exemplar of female domination, at least according to Augustan propaganda.

The present book takes as its focus stories not of women who use their power to support men, but those who actively challenge male power by exercising it themselves. These are tales of women who wield *official* power by stepping out of the traditional roles of women and into those of men. They command armies, exercise sexual autonomy and even dominance, speak in public, issue laws, and subject others (even masculine heroes and citizen men) to their control. All of these stories were written by men, and most of them have a clear pro-Greek or pro-Roman bias, with gender prejudices difficult to disentangle from ethnic ones. Indeed, none of these tales can be read as affirmations or celebrations of women in power. They are instead misogynistic tales that aim to shore up masculine authority by exposing the consequences when women rather than men wield it, and in doing so these tales subscribe to a range of sexist beliefs justifying women's exclusion. Ancient misogyny, like its modern counterpart, has a clear agenda—to put women back into their socially acceptable place. The words of Kate Manne, writing about misogyny in modern America, apply equally well to these ancient tales: "Women who reverse gendered hierarchies and aspire to masculine-coded social roles are . . . liable to provoke misogyny. One can think of few more obvious triggers than seeking political office—especially when it would come at the expense of rival male politicians."[9] By reading these stories, we can understand the logic that led to the barring of women from public authority, and we can see how seeds planted so long ago continue to take root and flourish in our contemporary world.

It is because the Greeks and Romans conceived of "power" as a masculine prerogative that their stories of *women* in power paint a world that is often absurdly topsy-turvy and inverted. These old stories almost invariably depict power as a zero-sum game that bestows masculinity on the winners and femininity on the losers. Such power is asymmetrical and hierarchical, stokes division, and reinforces simple definitions of "us" and "them." A state run by a woman becomes something of an imaginary, even comical, thought exercise. The woman who runs such a state is constructed as the ultimate "Other," the anti-Greek or anti-Roman masculinized woman who in holding power denies it to a man who should wield it, thus feminizing him. Such a gender inversion is readily apparent in the tales of Hercules and Omphale, which portray the (significantly Eastern) queen not only as ruling the manliest of Greek heroes but also as donning his lion skin and club as he wears her clothes and spins thread, a gender inversion that visual artists, both ancient and modern, have frequently delighted in depicting.[10] In this myth, there is a comical antithesis between the manly brawn of the hero's hypermasculine body and the utter subjugation he experiences in his enslavement by—and erotic desire for—the Lydian queen. Omphale's domination of the Greek hero is a temporary suspension of the ideal scenario in which physical, political, and domestic power converged on the same male body, a body that (in the case of Hercules) normally thwarted female power rather than succumbing to it.

Like Omphale, the Amazons are Eastern "Others" who invert the expected customs of the Greeks and Romans. Although there is ample evidence for horsewomen dwelling on the Scythian steppes, the Amazons as depicted by the Greeks and Romans are mythical fantasy.[11] In many of these tales, the expected gender roles are simply reversed: men stay in the home and weave while women go to war. In others, the men are disposed of altogether, or are used by the Amazons only for sex and pregnancy. The gender role occupied by the Amazons, however, is quite complex, as the seemingly antithetical designation "warrior women" would suggest. In some ways, they conform to the behavior expected of men—they make war, are skilled equestrians, and excel at archery and hunting. Yet they also conform to many feminine stereotypes, especially sexual ones. The Greeks and Romans regularly represented women as hypersexual and thus lacking in the natural self-control that qualified men to rule. Such insatiability is clear in Quintus Curtius's tale of Alexander and Thalestris, in which it takes the Greek king thirteen days to satisfy the sexual desire of the Amazon queen. The ancient belief that Amazons cauterized their right breast yet kept their left one intact nicely demonstrates their gender ambiguity. The idea for this body modification, which is never depicted in ancient art, comes from a false Greek etymology for their name (a + mazon suggests "breastless" in Greek), and its repeated appearance in the tales illustrates how the Amazons display on their very bodies the contested gender that marks their way of life more broadly.

The stories of the Amazons are not simply about female power—they are even more emphatically about male correction of such power, and thus a reassertion of the appropriate hierarchical order. Such "correction" often came in the form of an Amazonomachy, a battle between Greek men and Amazons, in which an important male hero, such as Heracles or Theseus, would defeat an Amazon. This indeed was a story motif that adorned the (now greatly damaged) western metopes of the Parthenon in Athens, while the other metopes presented the Centauromachy (southern), the Trojan War (northern), and the Gigantomachy (eastern). In each of these myths, Greek heroes or gods overcome threatening monstrous hybrids or Eastern Others and thereby reestablish Greek masculine superiority. Indeed, it became almost a rite of passage for Greek heroes to defeat Amazons. To quote Helen Morales, "Killing Amazons was part of what made Greek heroes, heroes."[12]

Such male "correction" of powerful women also involved asserting sexual dominance over them. Theseus, for instance, does not kill the Amazon queen Antiope (also called Hippolyta)—he instead marries her, thus placing her under his patriarchal control. In the case of Achilles, his killing of Penthesilea often takes on highly sexual overtones. In Quintus of Smyrna's *Posthomerica*, for example, his violent penetration of her with his spear has clear phallic imagery, and in her dying moments he imagines leading her back to his home in Phthia as his bride. In art, sexual and military defeat are again yoked in the figure of conquered Amazons who are depicted partially nude, with one or both breasts exposed.[13]

Other Greek heroes encounter not Amazons but Amazon-like women, over whom they must gain the sexual upper hand to prevent them from hindering their quests. In Apollonius's *Argonautica*, for instance, it is not through military might but through sexual prowess that Jason is able to ensure his stay in Lemnos remains safe—and the threat is not small, given that the women of the island have just massacred its male inhabitants and instituted a female-run state. In Statius's *Thebaid*, the Lemnian women are repeatedly compared to Amazons as they undertake the murder of the island's men. Dido too is likened to an Amazon in Vergil's *Aeneid*, appearing to Aeneas for the first time as he is looking at the depiction of Penthesilea on the frieze sculptures of Juno's temple in Carthage. The comparison underscores Dido's potential danger and invites us to see Aeneas's eventual sexual relationship with and abandonment of her, as well as her subsequent suicide, as something of a martial defeat that anticipates Rome's eventual destruction of Carthage. After all, Venus's motives in having her *other* son, Cupid, shoot Dido are as much about the future expansion of the Roman Empire as they are about the safety of Aeneas.

Closely related to these tales of mythical heroes subduing powerful women are those of *historical* men doing likewise, tales that are given a sheen of mythology by those who record them. No historical queen has been as mythologized as Cleopatra, and much of what we know about her comes from the writings of Roman men who were eager to present her in the guise of a monstrous or dangerously seductive female who threatens male heroes. Like Circe or Calypso, for instance, she offers perilous hospitality to the men she encounters, easily getting the best of Lucan's Julius Caesar or Plutarch's Antony by hosting lavish banquets that soften the men's masculine resolve and allow her to gain mastery over them. In Horace's *Ode* 1.37,

xvi   INTRODUCTION

celebrating Cleopatra's death, she finally meets her match in Augustus, who makes a dramatic entrance right in the middle of the poem to vanquish the female "monster" (*monstrum*), much like Hercules killing the Chimaera or Perseus the Gorgon Medusa. In Vergil's *Aeneid*, Augustus's defeat of Cleopatra at Actium is right at the center of the shield that the god Vulcan crafts for Aeneas, and the battle is depicted as a cosmic clash that marshals human and divine forces of Roman order against those of Egyptian chaos, much as the Amazonomachy is portrayed on the Parthenon. The elegiac lover of Propertius 3.11, on the other hand, is far from being an Aeneas or Augustus. Rather than resist the temptations of a dangerously powerful woman, he becomes her slave. Where the hero is masculine and dominant, the elegiac lover is effeminate and submissive—like Antony enthralled to Cleopatra. Yet even as these writers condemn Cleopatra, they often display open admiration for her, making it clear that she was a worthy foe to Rome and Augustus.

A similar figure is Zenobia, queen of Palmyra, whose reign is recorded in the late-antique *Historia Augusta*. This Eastern queen, at least according to the text, purposefully models herself on earlier female foes of Rome, tracing her ancestry back to Cleopatra and dressing like Dido. Her rise is attributed to a vacuum of male leadership not only in Palmyra, where she is regent for her underage sons after the death of her husband, but also in Rome, where the emperor Gallienus fails to exercise male imperial dominance in the East. The "correction" comes in the form of the new Roman emperor Aurelian, who defeats Zenobia and leads her in triumph. This account exposes an undercurrent of concern, however, that to defeat a woman is no manly achievement at all but an act that is itself "unmanly" (*non virile*). The author of the *Historia Augusta* tries to allay this concern by endowing Zenobia with a host of masculine qualities that counterbalance her feminine ones. She enjoys all the beauty and luxury of a Cleopatra, but also possesses the wise counsel, the austerity, the sexual moderation, and even the voice of a man.

Repeatedly in these stories there is a sense that women are able to take control of realms inappropriate to them, such as sex and war, not necessarily because they are strong but because the men around them are weak, foolish, and themselves in need of correction. Surrounded by such men, it seems inevitable for the women to become more masculine—and often more admirable—than their husbands, fathers, sons, and even their enemies. These stories take frequent aim especially at Eastern masculinity and subscribe to a host of stereotypes presenting Eastern men as effeminate and enervated, the sort of men that a woman could easily dominate. In Cassius Dio, for instance, Cleopatra fills her court with eunuchs and easily places Antony among them. In Herodotus's *History*, the Carian queen Artemisia I is portrayed in a surprisingly positive light, even though she is a Greek who fights against the Greek alliance. This is perhaps due to the fact that she ruled Herodotus's own Halicarnassus, but it is more likely because her chief interactions are with Eastern men rather than Greek ones. She is meant to be a foil not only to the advisors of Xerxes, the Persian despot, but also to Xerxes himself, whose rule over the Persian forces is repeatedly likened to an enslaver over the enslaved. Artemisia, in contrast to Xerxes's male advisors, exercises frank speech and offers wise counsel that Xerxes repeatedly ignores. The failure of Persian masculinity thus becomes a key factor in the defeat of Xerxes's invasion. Even Greek women, Herodotus seems to suggest, have more masculine virtues than Eastern men.

Sometimes Greek and Roman writers use these stories of powerful women to cast aspersions not on the masculinity of foreign "Others" but on their own male weakness, which they thereby argue is in need of correction. This is the case in Aristophanes's comedy *Assemblywomen*, which presents us with an Athens seemingly in such a bad state that the women have no choice but to intervene and effect a gender reversal. The women, led by an Athenian wife named Praxagora, don their husbands' clothes and enter the all-male space of the Assembly, while Praxagora's husband, Blepyrus, is left at home with only his wife's clothes to wear. These clothes symbolize both the feminized position she has put him in as well as the masculine impotence that has led her to take over government of the city. Interestingly, the wives of *Assemblywomen* do not abandon their female roles by entering the male sphere—they instead enter this sphere in order to obliterate it. They argue that they should take over the city on the basis of their skillful management of the home, and thereupon they proceed to turn the city into one big household with wives running the show. Unlike in Aristophanes's other play about female revolution, *Lysistrata*, the women of *Assemblywomen* never hand back the reins of power to the men; their task is not to save patriarchy from itself but to destroy it. They take and keep control, leaving their husbands to dine and dance and carouse in a way that befits their enervation. The play is thus deeply interwoven with Athenian gender ideology that conceived of the city as a locus of male power and the home as one of female management. Aristophanes's play is of course a comedy, but the Athenian men watching it may have detected in it a real accusation hurled against them by the poet—it would be better simply to get rid of male public life than for men to continue to conduct it so ineffectively.

Similarly, Tacitus's *Annals* records a Julio-Claudian Rome that has become feminized by the excessive power of emperors, particularly Nero, whom Tacitus perceives as effete and lacking in self-control even as he strips those beneath him of freedom. In Tacitus's writings it is often so-called "barbarians" (especially northern barbarians) who invoke Roman ideals such as liberty and virtue, and by doing so they expose Rome's lost morality under its "bad" emperors.[14] Boudicca, the British queen who leads an uprising after Roman soldiers whip her and rape her daughters, becomes in Tacitus something of a noble figure fighting for independence against a dominating Rome that has no respect for the bodily autonomy of its subjects, even the family members of its client kings.[15] But Boudicca ultimately emerges as a highly complex figure. Though she displays traits a Roman man might admire, both Tacitus and Cassius Dio also portray her as exercising violence that discredits her. Even as she condemns the Romans for treating their subjects as slaves, her retaliation in Tacitus's *Annals* employs punishments that were reserved for the enslaved, such as crucifixion. In the *Agricola*, Tacitus accuses her and her troops of the *saevitia*, "savagery," he views as characteristic of barbarians. Cassius Dio describes in vivid horror how her British forces mutilate the bodies of Roman women in a way that answers and magnifies the violence she and her daughters experienced—they cut off their breasts, sew them to their mouths, and then impale their bodies. Neither Tacitus nor Cassius Dio present a Boudicca that reflects historical reality, and therefore we can read their descriptions of her as mirrors for male anxieties about the destructive vengefulness of female power, whether wielded by feminized emperors or barbarian queens. The solution seems to be a "good" emperor who can reassert male control.

Female violence is indeed a running theme in these tales. Hypsipyle, queen of Lemnos, comes to power in a brutal act of carnage when the women kill their husbands, brothers, sons, and fathers. In Statius's *Thebaid*, the force driving such women is *furor*, "madness," a force to which women seem particularly susceptible. In other stories, *furor* drives Vergil's Dido to curse Aeneas's line and Horace's Cleopatra to make war on Rome. Yet Statius's Hypsipyle does not herself succumb to such madness, instead saving her father. In doing so, she is a stark contrast not only with the women she comes to rule but also with the men to whom she tells her tale, driven as they are by *furor* to make war on Thebes. Statius's Hypsipyle is also an exemplar of *pietas*, the "dutifulness" for which other male heroes, especially Vergil's Aeneas, were celebrated, while the male heroes of the *Thebaid* positively revel in *impietas* as brother fights brother. There is again a sense that a woman must take on masculine traits because the men in the tale have abnegated their own masculinity, yet the final solution is *not* female rule. Instead, the final books of the *Thebaid* have the male Athenian hero Theseus enter Thebes to set matters right at last.

Another source of male anxiety in these stories is the belief that women were dangerously prone to deceit and cunning, and this served as a primary motivation for checking female power. Going back to the earliest Greek poetry, especially Hesiod's *Theogony*, "cunning intelligence" (*mêtis*) was personified as a female goddess. Fearing that she would bear children that would threaten his supremacy, Zeus simply ate her, whereupon he himself gave birth to their daughter Athena, a virgin warrior who employs her keen intelligence to serve him loyally. Again and again, female rulers acquire and wield power through trickery. In Aristophanes's *Assemblywomen*, it is through deceit and disguise that the wives infiltrate the Assembly, while the men are all too easily duped. When Herodotus's Artemisia finds herself hemmed in between friendly and enemy ships at the Battle of Salamis, she employs a clever trick to escape and even win glory, not caring about the collateral damage to her own side. In Statius's *Thebaid*, the women of Lemnos trick their husbands into believing they are being welcomed home to a feast, then offer up a massacre instead. The Babylonian queen Semiramis, in the account of Diodorus Siculus, concocts a highly clever deception to overcome her lack of war elephants—she simply constructs fake elephant costumes out of the slaughtered skins and meat of three hundred thousand oxen and puts them on camels!

Another source of female power, one closely related to cunning intelligence, is cunning speech. One repeated refrain in our ancient sources is that men who aspire to power must silence women and cordon off public speech as a male-only sphere. This link between silencing women and masculine power is as old as Homer's *Odyssey*. As Telemachus tells his mother, Penelope, at 1.359–60, "speech will be men's concern, especially mine—for the power in the house belongs to me." As Mary Beard puts it in a landmark essay on speech, gender, and power in antiquity:[16]

> There is something faintly ridiculous about this wet-behind-the ears lad shutting up the savvy, middle-aged Penelope. But it is a nice demonstration that right where written evidence for Western culture starts, women's voices are not being heard in the public sphere. More than that, as Homer has it, an integral part of growing up, as a man, is learning to take control of public utterance and to silence the female of the species.

In classical Athens, such "public utterance" was termed *parrhesia*, a word that denoted the right of male citizens to express themselves freely in the city, especially in the Assembly. In Rome, the word *libertas* similarly connotes both "freedom" and "free speech." For a woman to exercise such speech constitutes an abnegation of her femininity and an unacceptable intrusion in the male sphere.

Speech therefore becomes one key way the powerful women of these stories exercise control. Plutarch's Cleopatra, for instance, learns many languages so that she can speak directly to varying groups of people without relying on interpreters. He compares her voice to a musical instrument that could overcome men with its sweetness, thus producing a Siren-like song hard to resist. Taking over public speech is crucial to the wives of Aristophanes's *Assemblywomen*, who beat Athenian men at their own game by using the Assembly as a site for clever persuasion. In doing so, they best the women of *Lysistrata*, who assert control over male spheres such as money and sex but never gain a legal backing for their radical action. Apollonius's *Argonautica* likewise presents us with an all-female assembly as the women deliberate about the best way to deal with the Greek heroes who have arrived on the *Argo*. Apollonius's version of the tale ends in an offer of hospitality, but the assembly presented in Statius's version of this myth gives rise to the plan to murder all the men. In the *Aeneid*, Dido's speech likewise varies from helpful to threatening. She initially speaks publicly in order to grant hospitality to the Trojans, but soon she is uttering curses against Aeneas and his whole line. When Aeneas later encounters her in the Underworld in Book Six, she opts instead for silence as a way to assert her agency. In Ovid's *Heroides*, Dido reclaims her speech through writing, using her voice to respond to and question Vergil's "authorial" account. For Dido, therefore, choosing what to say, how to speak, and whether to speak becomes a key way she asserts power. Boudicca too uses speech to achieve her goals, and her address to her troops, in both Tacitus and Cassius Dio, parallels the battlefield speeches normally delivered by famous male generals. Though much of what Boudicca says sounds admirable, the fact that a woman is saying it makes it immediately suspicious.

The accounts of powerful women given by these ancient

male writers are an interesting mixture of condemnation and awe. In some ways a powerful woman is what the Greeks would call a *thauma*, a "marvel" that defies belief. The legendary Babylonian queen Semiramis, for instance, never comes into direct conflict with Greece or Rome, and so Diodorus Siculus is free to fill his readers with wonder for her as she achieves superhuman architectural and military feats. She ultimately ends her life in a divine metamorphosis, "like one transforming into a god," (2.20.2) and takes the form of a dove, the same bird that Diodorus claims nurtured her in the equally marvelous story of her birth. Yet Diodorus also carefully curbs his reader's awe by describing how her army is routed not by a Greek warrior or hero but by an Eastern king, Stabrobates, ruler of India. She continues to rule after this defeat, but eventually her own son, aided (significantly) by a eunuch, conspires against her. In the end, it does not take a hypermasculine Heracles to bring down this most awe-inspiring of women. We must also bear in mind that *admiration* of powerful women does not equate to an *endorsement* of them. In the end, a woman like Semiramis is an Eastern curiosity whose threat is neutralized by time, distance, and her own lack of moderation.

These stories of women in power are largely meant to discredit the idea of women in power. They highlight the danger, or perhaps the absurdity, of women taking charge, pinpointing the very areas from which it was thought necessary to bar them. One key exception included in this book is Lavinia, who, according to the Roman historian Livy, was regent in Lavinium, the Italian town founded by Aeneas, her husband. After Aeneas dies, and then again after his son Ascanius comes of age and departs to found Alba Longa, Lavinia wields power— and she does so in Roman territory. This is the one powerful woman in this book who seems to receive no condemnation at all from the man who tells her story, but she is also the one who intrudes upon the male sphere the least. She displays no ambition for herself but looks out for the political interests of her husband and (step)son. We never see her lead armies or even hear her speak—as in Vergil's *Aeneid*, she remains totally silent. She is a model for female power precisely because she uses her talents to support rather than threaten the patriarchal state.

She is also, incidentally, one of the least famous women included in this volume (though her story has, thankfully, received a beautiful novelization by Ursula K. Le Guin).

Indeed, not all of the women in this volume occupy our modern imagination equally. Cleopatra is unrivaled in her later fame, largely because she played such an outsized role in the Roman imagination and her tale was later taken up by influential writers such as Shakespeare. I have therefore included some women whose stories are not often told when considering powerful women from classical antiquity. Salome Alexandra, for instance, was the sole queen of Judea during the period of Hasmonean rule. Her reign is recorded by the Romano-Jewish historian Josephus, and his depiction of her is clearly influenced by hostile Roman portraits of women in power. Although he admires her administrative capabilities, Josephus simultaneously presents her reign as an explanation for the weakening and eventual collapse of the Hasmonean dynasty, and the ensuing takeover of Judea by Rome. Another queen who has received scarce notice by scholars of Greece and Rome is Amanirenas, who was the queen of the African kingdom of Kush at the same time that Augustus came to power.[17] Like Boudicca, she is a warrior queen who opposes Rome, and her uprising against them was also quelled. Yet Amanirenas also enjoyed an undeniable measure of success, negotiating a treaty with the Romans that set a firm limit on Roman expansion into the African continent, and she herself was neither killed nor deposed. She did not, like Cleopatra, offer the Romans a narrative that could easily be mythologized to conform to ideas of male domination and female defeat. It is interesting as well that Salome Alexandra and Amanirenas bookend Cleopatra both geographically and temporally and seem almost to have been swallowed up by her legacy. My hope is that their inclusion here will invite us to consider how many other stories have been left untold by our sources. There have no doubt been other powerful women whose lives are under-recorded, but there is also much more about *these* women's lives that has been left unsaid.

Despite the rampant misogyny of many of these tales, they can give empowering lessons to those who read them with a careful, critical eye. To trace the links between the present and past exclusion of women from power can be galvanizing, offering us answers to the baffling question of *why* power continues to be bound to masculinity in the minds of so many, including many women. Not only do these stories help us pinpoint the specific arenas of power from which women were barred—sex, government, speech, etc.—they also illustrate that women can and indeed must claim power for themselves by stepping into these very arenas. There is no separate-but-equal sphere in which women can be content to exercise power. Studying how power was formulated in the past may also help us envision alternatives for the future. By constantly falling back on the same familiar frameworks, these stories expose how often our imaginations have failed us when it comes to thinking about power, especially when we simply switch out the male face at the top of the hierarchy with a female one and call that equality. These stories expose the intersectional nature of disempowerment, and they thus illuminate how empowerment too must be intersectional, or else be doomed to reconstruct the same hierarchies again and again.

These powerful women from the classical past continue to fascinate us, but likely not in the same way, or for the same reasons, that they fascinated the men who first authored their tales. Despite the fear and suspicion the male sources direct their way, we can find much to endorse, and even admire, in the women described in this book, from the coordinated action of the women of Aristophanes's *Assemblywomen*, to Dido's questioning of the male value system that leads Aeneas to abandon her, to the righteous anger of Boudicca against sexual violence by men in power, to the successful resistance of Amanirenas against Rome's colonial expansion. This means reading these stories differently, by resisting the meanings originally inscribed on them by the men who wrote them down. And if Plutarch or Ovid or Lucan or Shakespeare can invent these women as they see fit in order to reinforce their society's gendered values, then we can reinvent them as *we* see fit in new retellings. After all, "women in power" is only an oxymoron if we ourselves believe it to be one.

STEPHANIE McCARTER

INTRODUCTION

1. **intersectional framework developed:** See Kimberlé Crenshaw, "Demarginalizing the Intersection of Race and Sex: A Black Feminist Critique of Antidiscrimination Doctrine, Feminist Theory and Antiracist Politics," *University of Chicago Legal Forum* 1989, no. 1 (1989): 139–67.
2. **within the home:** For an intersectional look at the Greek house, see Birgitta L. Sjöberg, "More than Just Gender: The Classical *Oikos* as a Site of Intersectionality," in *Families in the Greco-Roman World*, eds. Ray Laurence and Agneta Strömberg (London: Continuum, 2012), 48–59. For the gendered composition of the Roman household, see, in the same volume, Lindsay Penner, "Gender, Household Structure and Slavery: Re-interpreting the Aristocratic *Columbaria* of Early Imperial Rome," 143–59.
3. **philosopher Kate Manne:** See *Down Girl: The Logic of Misogyny* (Oxford: Oxford University Press, 2018), 118.
4. **public sphere through benefactions:** On elite Roman women in public life, see especially Emily A. Hemelrijk, *Hidden Lives, Public Personae: Women and Civic Life in the Roman West* (Oxford: Oxford University Press, 2015).
5. **with campaign endorsements:** See, for instance, Liisa Savunen, "Women and Elections in Pompeii," in *Women in Antiquity: New Assessments*, eds. Richard Hawley and Barbara Levick (London: Routledge, 1995), 194–206.
6. **of Aristophanes's *Lysistrata*:** On the Lysimache/Lysistrata connection, see, for instance, Peter Thonemann, "Lysimache and Lysistrata," *Journal of Hellenic Studies* 140 (2020): 128–42.
7. **exceptional prestige:** The bibliography on the Vestals is substantial. A good place to start, both on the Vestals and women in Roman religion more generally, is Meghan J. DiLuzio, *A Place at the Altar: Priestesses in Republican Rome* (Princeton: Princeton University Press, 2016).
8. **supporters of the patriarchal state:** For Livia's portraiture, see especially Rolf Winks, "Livia: Portrait and Propaganda," in *I Claudia II: Women in Roman Art and Society*, eds. Diana E. E. Kleiner and Susan B. Matheson (Austin: University of Texas Press, 2000), 29–42. On the power of imperial women, see especially Mary T. Boatwright, *Imperial Women of Rome: Power, Gender, Context* (Oxford: Oxford University Press, 2021).
9. **"rival male politicians":** Manne, *Down Girl*, 102.
10. **delighted in depicting:** A third-century mosaic now in the National Archaeological Museum of Spain in Madrid (Madrid

38315BIS) depicts all twelve of Hercules's labors surrounded by a larger central image of the hero and Omphale. Hercules wears women's clothing and holds a distaff and spindle for spinning thread, while the queen holds his club and dons only his lion skin. Later examples in painting include Bartholomaeus Spranger, *Hercules and Omphale* (ca. 1585) and Édouard Joseph Dantan, *Hercules at the Feet of Omphale* (1874).

11. **are mythical fantasy:** For a study that nicely considers both the archaeological evidence for and mythical accounts of ancient warrior women, see Adrienne Mayor, *The Amazons: Lives and Legends of Warrior Women across the Ancient World* (Princeton: Princeton University Press, 2014).

12. **To quote Helen Morales:** See *Antigone Rising: The Subversive Power of the Ancient Myths* (New York: Bold Type Books, 2021), 3.

13. **both breasts exposed:** For the Amazons' exposed breasts as a sign of defeat, see Beth Cohen, "Divesting the Female Breast of Clothes in Classical Sculpture," in *Naked Truths: Women, Sexuality, and Gender in Classical Art and Archaeology*, eds. Ann Olga Koloski-Ostrow and Claire L. Lyons (London: Routledge, 1997), 66–92. A good example of such a depiction is the statue of a wounded Amazon (1st/2nd c. CE) at the Metropolitan Museum of Art in New York City (32.11.4).

14. **under its "bad" emperors:** On northern barbarians in Tacitus, see, for example, Aske Damtoft Poulsen, *Accounts of Northern Barbarians in Tacitus' Annales: A Contextual Analysis*, *Studia Graeca et Latina Lundensia*, Volume 24 (Lund: Faculty of Humanities and Theology, Centre for Languages and Literature, Lund University, 2018).

15. **member of its client kings:** For Rome figured as an imperial enslaver of the provinces, see, for example, Myles Lavan, *Slaves to Rome: Paradigms of Empire in Roman Culture* (Cambridge: Cambridge University Press, 2013). For Boudicca's appeals to freedom, see Michael Roberts, "The Revolt of Boudicca (Tacitus, *Annals* 14.29–39) and the Assertion of *Libertas* in Neronian Rome," *American Journal of Philology* 109, no. 1 (1988): 118–32. For another British "barbarian" represented as invoking freedom against Roman imperial enslavement, see the speech of Calgacus in Tacitus's *Agricola*.

16. **landmark essay on speech:** Mary Beard, "The Public Voice of Women," *London Review of Books* 36, no. 6 (2014): 11–14. This essay was later incorporated into her book *Women and Power: A Manifesto* (New York: Liveright, 2017).

17. **African kingdom of Kush:** For Greek and Roman ideas about Kush, see Stanley M. Burstein, "Greek and Roman Views of Ancient Nubia," in *The Oxford Handbook of Ancient Nubia*, eds. Geoff Emberling and Bruce Beyer Williams (Oxford: Oxford University Press, 2021), 697–712.

Suggestions for Further Reading

The bibliography on women in the ancient Mediterranean world has been growing exponentially in recent decades. The following bibliography is therefore highly selective.

WOMEN, GENDER, AND POWER IN THE ANCIENT MEDITERRANEAN

Bauman, Richard A. *Women and Politics in Ancient Rome*. London: Routledge, 1992.

Beard, Mary. *Women and Power: A Manifesto*. New York: Liveright, 2017.

Budin, Stephanie Lynn, and Jean Macintosh Turfa, eds. *Women in Antiquity: Real Women across the Ancient World*. London: Routledge, 2016.

Blundell, Sue. *Women in Ancient Greece*. Cambridge, MA: Harvard University Press, 1995.

Boatwright, Mary T. *Imperial Women of Rome: Power, Gender, Context*. Oxford: Oxford University Press, 2021.

Carlà-Uhink, Filippo, and Anja Wieber, eds. *Orientalism and the Reception of Powerful Women from the Ancient World*. London: Bloomsbury, 2020.

Carney, Elizabeth D., and Sabine Müller, eds. *The Routledge Companion to Women and Monarchy in the Ancient Mediterranean World*. London: Routledge, 2021.

Coşkun, Altay, and Alex McAuley, eds. *Seleukid Royal Women: Creation, Representation and Distortion of Hellenistic Queenship in the Seleukid Empire*. Stuttgart: Franz Steiner Verlag, 2016.

Cussini, Eleonora. "Beyond the Spindle: Investigating the Role of Palmyrene Women." In *A Journey to Palmyra*, edited by Eleonora Cussini, 26–43. Leiden: Brill, 2005.

Dixon, Suzanne. *Reading Roman Women*. London: Duckworth, 2001.

Fabre-Serris, Jacqueline, and Alison Keith, eds. *Women and War in Antiquity*. Baltimore: Johns Hopkins University Press, 2015.

Hallett, Judith P. *Fathers and Daughters in Roman Society: Women and the Elite Family*. Princeton: Princeton University Press, 1984.

Hemelrijk, Emily. *Hidden Lives, Public Personae: Women and Civic Life in the Roman West*. Oxford: Oxford University Press, 2015.

Hemelrijk, Emily, and Greg Woolf, eds. *Women and the Roman City in the Latin West*. Leiden: Brill, 2013.

Holmes, Brooke. *Gender: Antiquity and Its Legacy*. Oxford: Oxford University Press, 2012.

James, Sharon L., and Sheila Dillon, eds. *A Companion to Women in the Ancient World*. Chichester: Blackwell, 2012.

Lefkowitz, Mary R., and Maureen B. Fant. *Women's Life in Greece and Rome: A Source Book in Translation*. 4th ed. Baltimore: Johns Hopkins University Press, 2016.

Llewellyn-Jones, Lloyd, and Alex McAuley. *Sister-Queens in the High Hellenistic Period: Kleopatra Thea and Kleopatra III*. London: Routledge, 2023.

Middleton, Guy D. *Women in the Ancient Mediterranean World*. Cambridge: Cambridge University Press, 2023.

Parks, Sara, Shayna Sheinfeld, and Meredith J. C. Warren. *Jewish and Christian Women in the Ancient Mediterranean*. London: Routledge, 2021.

Pomeroy, Sarah B. *Goddesses, Whores, Wives, and Slaves: Women in Classical Antiquity*. 2nd ed. New York: Schocken Books, 1995.

Pomeroy, Sarah B. *Women in Hellenistic Egypt: From Alexander to Cleopatra*. Detroit: Wayne State University Press, 1990.

Salisbury, Joyce. *Encyclopedia of Women in the Ancient World*. Santa Barbara, CA: ABC-CLIO, 2001.

Siekierka, Przemysław, Krystyna Stebnicka, and Aleksander Wolicki. *Women and the Polis: Public Honorific Inscriptions for Women in the Greek Cities from the Late Classical to the Roman Period*. Berlin: De Gruyter, 2021.

Sherratt, Melanie, and Alison Moore. "Gender in Roman Britain." In *The Oxford Handbook of Roman Britain*, edited by Martin Millett, Louise Revell, and Alison Moore, 363–80. Oxford: Oxford University Press, 2016.

Stol, Marten. *Women in the Ancient Near East*. Translated by Helen and Mervyn Richardson. Berlin: De Gruyter, 2016.

Tsakiropoulou-Summers, Tatiana, and Katerina Kitsi-Mitakou, eds. *Women and the Ideology of Political Exclusion: From Classical Antiquity to the Modern Era*. London: Routledge, 2019.

WOMEN AND GENDER IN CLASSICAL MYTHOLOGY

Haynes, Natalie. *Pandora's Jar: Women in the Greek Myths.* New York: Harper Perennial, 2022.
Lefkowitz, Mary R. *Women in Greek Myth.* 2nd ed. Baltimore: Johns Hopkins University Press, 2007.
Morales, Helen. *Antigone Rising: The Subversive Power of the Ancient Myths.* New York: Bold Type Books, 2021.
Roberts, Ellen Mackin. *Heroines of Olympus: The Women of Greek Mythology.* London: Welbeck, 2020.

THE AMAZONS

Blok, Josine H. *The Early Amazons: Modern and Ancient Perspectives on a Persistent Myth.* Leiden: Brill, 1995.
DuBois, Page. *Centaurs and Amazons: Women and the Pre-History of the Great Chain of Being.* Ann Arbor: University of Michigan Press, 1991.
Hardwick, Lorna. "Ancient Amazons—Heroes, Outsiders or Women?" *Greece and Rome* 37, no. 1 (1990): 14–36.
Mayor, Adrienne. *The Amazons: Lives and Legends of Warrior Women across the Ancient World.* Princeton: Princeton University Press, 2014.
Penrose, Walter Duvall, Jr. *Postcolonial Amazons: Female Masculinity and Courage in Ancient Greek and Sanskrit Literature.* Oxford: Oxford University Press, 2016.
Stewart, Andrew. "Imag(in)ing the Other: Amazons and Ethnicity in Fifth-Century Athens." *Poetics Today* 16, no. 4 (1995): 571–97.

ARISTOPHANES'S *ASSEMBLYWOMEN*

De Luca, Kenneth M. *Aristophanes' Male and Female Revolutions: A Reading of Aristophanes'* Knights *and* Assemblywomen. Lanham, MD: Lexington Books, 2005.
Foley, Helene P. "The 'Female Intruder' Reconsidered: Women in Aristophanes' *Lysistrata* and *Ecclesiazusae*." *Classical Philology* 77, no. 1 (January 1982): 1–21.
Nichols, Peter. "The Comedy of the Just City: Aristophanes' *Assemblywomen* and Plato's *Republic*." In *The Political Theory of Aristophanes: Explorations in Poetic Wisdom*, edited by Jeremy

J. Mhire and Bryan-Paul Frost, 259–74. Albany: State University of New York Press, 2014.

Slater, Niall W. "Waiting in the Wings: Aristophanes' *Ecclesiazusae*." *Arion* 5 no. 1 (1997) 97–129.

Taaffe, Lauren. *Aristophanes and Women*. London: Routledge, 1993.

Tsoumpra, Natalia. "Sex Can Kill: Gender Inversion and the Politics of Subversion in Aristophanes' *Ecclesiazvsae*." *Classical Quarterly* 69, no. 2 (December 2019): 528–44.

SEMIRAMIS

Asher-Greve, Julia M. "From 'Semiramis of Babylon' to 'Semiramis of Hammersmith.'" In *Orientalism, Assyriology and the Bible*, edited by S. W. Holloway, 322–73. Sheffield: Sheffield Phoenix Press, 2006.

Beringer, Alison L. *The Sight of Semiramis: Medieval and Early Modern Narratives of the Babylonian Queen*. Tempe: Arizona Center for Medieval and Renaissance Studies, 2016.

Dalley, Stephanie. "Semiramis in History and Legend." In *Cultural Borrowing and Ethnic Appropriation in Antiquity*, edited by Erich S. Gruen, 11–22. Stuttgart: Franz Steiner Verlag, 2005.

Stronk, Jan P. *Semiramis' Legacy: The History of Persia According to Diodorus of Sicily*. Edinburgh: Edinburgh University Press, 2017.

OMPHALE

Cyrino, Monica S. "Heroes in D(u)ress: Transvestism and Power in the Myths of Herakles and Achilles." *Arethusa* 31, no. 2 (Spring 1998): 207–41.

Eppinger, Alexandra. "*Hercules Cinaedus?* The Effeminate Hero in Christian Polemic." In *TransAntiquity: Cross-Dressing and Transgender Dynamics in the Ancient World*, edited by Domitilla Campanile, Filippo Carlà-Uhink, and Margherita Facella, 202–14. London: Routledge, 2017.

Fantham, Elaine. "Sexual Comedy in Ovid's *Fasti*: Sources and Motivation." *Harvard Studies in Classical Philology* 87 (1983): 185–216.

HYPSIPYLE

Asso, Paolo. "Statius' Argonautic Background." *Classical Philology* 115, no. 4 (October 2020): 659–76.

Augoustakis, Antony. *Motherhood and the Other: Fashioning Female Power in Flavian Epic.* Oxford: Oxford University Press, 2010.

Clauss, James J. *The Best of the Argonauts: The Redefinition of the Epic Hero in Book One of Apollonius's* Argonautica. Berkeley: University of California Press, 1993.

Finkmann, Simone. "Polyxo and the Lemnian Episode—An Inter- and Intratextual Study of Apollonius Rhodius, Valerius Flaccus, and Statius." *Dictynna* 12 (December 2015).

Ganiban, Randall T. *Statius and Virgil: The* Thebaid *and Reinterpretation of the* Aeneid. Cambridge: Cambridge University Press, 2007.

Holmberg, Ingrid E. "Μῆτις and Gender in Apollonius Rhodius' *Argonautica.*" *Transactions of the American Philological Association* 128 (1998): 135–59.

Nugent, S. Georgia. "Statius' Hypsipyle: Following in the Footsteps of the *Aeneid.*" *Scholia* 5, no. 1 (January 1996): 46–71.

DIDO

Bertman, Stephen. "Cleopatra and Antony as Models for Dido and Aeneas." *Echos du Monde Classique: Classical News and Views* 44, no. 3 (2000): 395–98.

Casali, Sergio. "Further Voices in Ovid *Heroides* 7." *Hermathena* 177/178 (2004): 147–64.

Drinkwater, Megan O. *Ovid's* Heroides *and the Augustan Principate.* Madison: University of Wisconsin Press, 2022.

Harrison, Stephen J., ed. *Oxford Readings in Vergil's* Aeneid. Oxford: Oxford University Press, 1990.

Giusti, Elena. "Rac(ializ)ing Dido." *Proceedings of the Virgil Society* 31 (2023): 53–85.

Krevans, Nita. "Dido, Hypsipyle, and the Bedclothes." *Hermathena* 173/174 (2002/2003): 175–83.

Lovatt, Helen. "The Eloquence of Dido: Exploring Speech and Gender in Virgil's *Aeneid.*" *Dictynna* 10 (2013).

Nelis, Damien. *Vergil's* Aeneid *and the* Argonautica *of Apollonius Rhodius.* Leeds: Francis Cairns, 2001.

Perkell, Christine G. "On Creusa, Dido, and the Quality of Victory in Virgil's *Aeneid.*" In *Reflections of Women in Antiquity,* edited by Helene P. Foley, 355–77. New York: Gordon and Breach, 1981.

Perkell, Christine. "Creusa and Dido Revisited." *Vergilius* 67 (2021): 117–38.

Perkell, Christine, ed. *Reading Vergil's* Aeneid: *An Interpretive Guide.* Norman: University of Oklahoma Press, 1999.

Segal, Charles. "Dido's Hesitation in *Aeneid* 4." *Classical World* 84, no. 1 (1990): 1–12.

LAVINIA

Keegan, Peter. *Livy's Women: Crisis, Resolution, and the Female in Rome's Foundation History.* London: Routledge, 2021.

Stevenson, Tom. "Women of Early Rome as *Exempla* in Livy, *Ab Urbe Condita*, Book 1." *Classical World* 104, no. 2 (Winter 2011): 175–89.

ARTEMISIA I

Harrell, Sarah E. "Marvelous *Andreia*: Politics, Geography, and Ethnicity in Herodotus' *Histories*." In *Andreia: Studies in Manliness and Courage in Classical Antiquity*, edited by Ralph M. Rosen and Ineke Sluiter, 77–94. Leiden: Brill, 2003.

McCoskey, Denise Eileen. "The Great Escape: Reading Artemisia in Herodotus' *Histories* and *300: Rise of an Empire*." In *Exploring Gender Diversity in the Ancient World*, edited by Allison Surtees and Jennifer Dyer, 209–21. Edinburgh: Edinburgh University Press, 2020.

Munson, Rosario Vignolo. "Artemisia in Herodotus." *Classical Antiquity* 7, no. 1 (April 1988): 91–106.

Sissa, Giulia. "What Artemisia Knew: The Political Intelligence of Artemisia of Halicarnassus." In *Identities, Ethnicities and Gender in Antiquity*, edited by Jacqueline Fabre-Serris, Alison Keith, and Florence Klein, 49–68. Berlin: De Gruyter, 2021.

SALOME ALEXANDRA

Atkinson, Kenneth. *Queen Salome: Jerusalem's Warrior Monarch of the First Century B.C.E.* Jefferson, NC: McFarland & Co., 2012.

Liebowitz, Etka. "Josephus's Ambivalent Attitude towards Women and Power: The Case of Queen Alexandra." *Journal of Ancient Judaism* 6, no. 2 (December 2015) 182–205.

Liebowitz, Etka. "A New Perspective on Two Jewish Queens in the Second Temple Period: Alexandra of Judaea and Helene of Adiabene." In *Sources and Interpretation in Ancient Judaism*, edited by Meron M. Piotrkowski, Geoffrey Hermon, and Saskia Dönitz, 41–65. Leiden: Brill, 2018.

Scales, Joseph, and Cat Quine. "Athaliah and Alexandra: Gender and Queenship in Josephus." *Journal of Ancient Judaism* 11, no. 2 (2020): 233–50.

Sievers, Joseph. "The Role of Women in the Hasmonean Dynasty." In *Josephus, the Bible, and History*, edited by Louis H. Feldman and Gohei Hata, 132–46. Detroit: Wayne State University Press, 1989.

CLEOPATRA VII

Burstein, Stanley. *The Reign of Cleopatra*. Norman: University of Oklahoma Press, 2007.

Gruen, Erich. S. "Cleopatra in Rome: Facts and Fantasies." In *Myth, History, and Culture in Republican Rome*, edited by David Braund and Christopher Gill, 258–74. Exeter: Exeter University Press, 2003.

Jones, Prudence J. *Cleopatra: The Last Pharoah*. London: Haus Publishing, 2006.

Jones, Prudence J. *Cleopatra: A Sourcebook*. Norman: University of Oklahoma Press, 2006.

Kleiner, Diana E. E. *Cleopatra and Rome*. Cambridge, MA: Harvard University Press, 2005.

Miles, Margaret M., ed. *Cleopatra: A Sphinx Revisited*. Berkeley: University of California Press, 2011.

Roller, Duane W. *Cleopatra: A Biography*. Oxford: Oxford University Press, 2010.

Schiff, Stacy. *Cleopatra: A Life*. New York: Little, Brown and Co., 2010

Tronson, Adrian. "Vergil, the Augustans, and the Invention of Cleopatra's Suicide—One Asp or Two?" *Vergilius* 44 (1998): 31–50.

Wyke, Maria. *The Roman Mistress: Ancient and Modern Representations*. Oxford: Oxford University Press, 2002.

AMANIRENAS/WOMEN IN KUSH

Ashby, Solange. "Priestess, Queen, Goddess: The Divine Feminine in the Kingdom of Kush." In *The Routledge Companion to Black*

Women's Cultural Histories, edited by Janell Hobson, 23–34. London: Routledge, 2021.

Lohwasser, Angelika. "Queenship in Kush: Status, Role and Ideology of Royal Women." *Journal of the American Research Center in Egypt* 38 (2001): 61–76.

Lohwasser, Angelika, and Jacke Phillips. "Women in Ancient Kush." In *The Oxford Handbook of Ancient Nubia*, edited by Geoff Emberling and Bruce Beyer Williams, 1015–32. Oxford: Oxford University Press, 2020.

BOUDICCA

Adler, Eric. *Valorizing the Barbarians: Enemy Speeches in Roman Historiography.* Austin: University of Texas Press, 2011.

Gillespie, Caitlin. *Boudica: Warrior Woman of Roman Britain.* Oxford: Oxford University Press, 2018.

Johnson, Marguerite. *Boudicca.* London: Bloomsbury, 2012.

Williams, Carolyn D. *Boudica and Her Stories: Narrative Transformations of a Warrior Queen.* Newark: University of Delaware Press, 2009.

ZENOBIA

Andrade, Nathanael J. *Zenobia: Shooting Star of Palmyra.* Oxford: Oxford University Press, 2018.

Bergstein, Mary. "Palmyra and Palmyra: Look on These Stones, Ye Mighty, and Despair." *Arion* 24, no. 2 (Fall 2016): 13–38.

Jones, Prudence. "Rewriting Power: Zenobia, Aurelian, and the *Historia Augusta.*" *Classical World* 109, no. 2 (Winter 2016): 221–33.

Southern, Pat. *Empress Zenobia: Palmyra's Rebel Queen.* London: Continuum, 2008.

Stoneman, Richard. *Palmyra and Its Empire: Zenobia's Revolt against Rome.* Ann Arbor: University of Michigan Press, 1992.

Women in Power

PART ONE

THE WOMAN-RUN STATE

THE AMAZONS

The legend of the Amazons still resonates in our modern mythology, as attested by the success of a figure such as Wonder Woman. In Greco-Roman antiquity, the Amazons were a curious combination of fact and fantasy. They were connected to the historical women of the Eurasian steppes of Scythia, whose tombs have left us ample evidence of bow-and-arrow-wielding horsewomen. Yet the Amazons of the Greco-Roman imagination are largely a fabrication, a male fantasy of the woman warrior who challenges Greek gender norms and must therefore be either vanquished or put in her place. To quote Ken Dowan, "Amazons exist in order to be fought, and ultimately defeated, by men."[1]

STRABO,
GEOGRAPHY

11.5.1–4

Translated from the Greek by
Daniel Holmes

Strabo (64 BCE–24 CE) was a geographer and historian from Amasia, Pontus (in modern Turkey). His travels took him across the ancient Mediterranean world, including Egypt and Rome. Strabo's Geography *describes not just the land features of the inhabited world but also the ethnographic features of its inhabitants.*

They say the Amazons too live in the mountains above Albania. In fact, Theophanes,[1] who visited the Albanians while campaigning with Pompey, says that the Gelae and the Legae, Scythian peoples, live between the Amazons and the Albanians; and that the Mermadalis River flows through the middle of these peoples and the Amazons. But others, among whom are Metrodorus of Scepsis and Hypsicrates[2]—who themselves were not without knowledge of these areas—say that the Amazons share a border with the Gargarians and live in the foothills on the north of the Caucasian mountains where they are called the Ceraunian mountains.

They say, too, that the Amazons spend most of the year by themselves busy with their own various, particular works: plowing, planting, pasturing, and especially tending the horses, though the strongest women spend the majority of their time hunting and training in warfare. All of them have their right breast cauterized as infants so that they can have use of their right arm for any purpose, especially for the javelin; but they also use the bow, the long hammer,[3] and the light shield;[4] they also turn the skins of wild animals into headgear, protective clothing, and belts.

But they have two months marked out in the spring during which they go up into the nearby mountain that separates them from the Gargarians. The Gargarian men go up there too, in accordance with ancient custom, to join the women in sacrifice and in sexual intercourse for the reproduction of children—concealed and in darkness, as one male and one female chance upon each other. Once the men have made them pregnant, they then send the women away.

The women keep for themselves any female they bear, but bring the males back to the men to rear. Each Gargarian man then adopts any one of the boys into his family and regards him as his own son because he cannot know for sure whether he is or not.

The Mermadalis River crashes down from the mountains and through the land of the Amazons as well as Siracena and all the desert in between, and then flows out into Lake Maeotis. It is said that the Gargarians went up to this area from Themiscyra[5] together with the Amazons and then revolted from them, waging war against them with the help of certain Thracians and Euboeans who had come that distance in their wanderings. Then later, when the Gargarians had ceased warring with the Amazons, they came to an agreement with them on the terms stated above, so that they only associated with each other for offspring, but otherwise lived separately.

There is something exceptional about the account of the Amazons—namely, in all other accounts the mythic and the historic are kept distinct. Those things which are ancient and false and outlandish are called myths, but history (whether ancient or recent) wants truth and either omits what is outlandish or includes it only rarely. But, as regards the Amazons, reports have been consistent both now and in ancient times even though they are outlandish and beyond belief. For who could believe that an army or city or nation of women could ever properly exist without men, and not just exist, but also invade foreign territory, not only defeating neighboring peoples as far as what is now known as Ionia, but even sending an army over the sea to Attica? For this is the equivalent of saying that the men at that time were women and the women men. But even today these very same things are said about them. What is doubly strange about the account of the Amazons is that what is ancient is more believed than what is modern.

In any event, the Amazons are credited with the founding and naming of cities, such as Ephesus, Smyrna, Cyme, and Myrina,[6] as well as with tombs and other monuments. Everyone calls Themiscyra and the hills and plains around the Thermodon the work of the Amazons. And it was from here, as the account goes, that they were expelled.

Only a few writers report on where the Amazons are now, but none can be proven or believed. For example, they say Thalestria consorted and had sex with Alexander to produce offspring while she ruled the Amazons. Yet there is no consensus on this. Indeed, although many historians have written about this, those who have striven most for the truth have denied it; those who are most trustworthy have not mentioned it; and those who have affirmed it offer differing accounts. Cleitarchus says that[7] Thalestria came to Alexander after setting out from the Caspian gates and Thermodon. Yet the distance between Caspia and Thermodon is around six hundred and seventy miles.

DIODORUS SICULUS,
LIBRARY OF HISTORY

2.45–46

Translated from the Greek by
Stephanie McCarter

Diodorus Siculus (1st c. BCE) was the author of the Library
of History, *a massive Greek prose work that consisted of
a universal history from mythical time to the mid-first century BCE. Fifteen of the original forty books survive. In the
following selection, Diodorus describes the founding mothers of the Amazons and gives an account of their customs
and military accomplishments.*

There was a nation beside the Thermodon River where women
held power, and where women conducted the business of war
just like the men. They say that one of these women, who held
the office of monarch, possessed extraordinary strength and
prowess and that, organizing and training an army of women,
she conquered some of the neighboring peoples. As her valor
and reputation grew, she marched against the bordering nations, one after another. Her fortune flourished, filling her with
pride—she even gave herself the title Daughter of Ares. To the
men she assigned the spinning of wool and the domestic tasks
of women. She made laws whereby the women would go forth
to the contests of war, but on the men she imposed degradation
and servitude. When males were born, they mutilated their arms

and legs, making them useless for the business of war, and they cauterized the right breast of the females so that, when their bodies matured, it would not swell up and become a nuisance. And from this it happened that the nation of the Amazons acquired its name.[1]

This woman, who on the whole was outstanding in her intellect and in her skill at being a general, founded a city beside the mouth of the Thermodon River, called Themiscyra, where she built a famous palace. In her campaigns, she especially focused on discipline, and initially she conquered all her neighbors as far as the river Tanais.[2] She accomplished all this, they say, and then, while fighting brilliantly in battle, ended her life heroically.

She was succeeded by her daughter, who emulated her mother's valor and to some extent even surpassed her accomplishments. She trained girls from childhood in the chase and made them do daily military exercises, and she also introduced magnificent rites to Ares and to Artemis Tauropolos.[3] Marching beyond the territory of the Tanais River, she conquered, one after another, all the nations as far as Thrace. Returning home with many spoils, she built magnificent temples to the aforementioned gods. Because she ruled her subjects capably, she received their greatest approval. Her campaigns widened, and she won much of Asia, extending her power all the way to Syria. After her death, women of her family always inherited the queenship and ruled with distinction, boosting the nation of the Amazons in power and reputation.

Many years later, after the valor of these women had been proclaimed throughout the inhabited world, they say that Heracles, the son of Alcmena and Zeus, was tasked by Eurystheus with acquiring the war belt of the Amazon Hippolyta. And so, he set out on campaign, winning a great battle in which he decimated the camp of the Amazons. Capturing Hippolyta along with her belt, he utterly crushed that nation. For this reason, the neighboring barbarians grew to despise their weakness, and, remembering their past sufferings at their hands, they made such unrelenting war on that nation that they left behind not even the name of Amazons.

HERODOTUS, *HISTORIES*

4.110–118

Translated from the Greek by
Daniel Holmes

The Sauromatae, or Sarmatians, were a nomadic group in Scythia that Herodotus connects to the Amazons in order to explain why their women ride on horseback, fight in war, and wear clothing like the men. As is common in the myths associated with them, the Amazons are treated as sexually insatiable, and thus lacking the restraint that the ancient Greeks associated with masculinity. Herodotus's Amazons are akin to wild animals that are gradually "tamed" through sexual intercourse with Scythian men—but not entirely, since neither group ultimately conforms to the clearly defined gender roles that the Greeks assigned to men and women.

Here is what is said of the Sauromatae: When the Greeks fought the Amazons[1] (and the Scythians call the Amazons "Oeorpata;" this word has the meaning "man-killers" in Greek, since "oeor" is their word for "man" and "pata" for "kill"), as the story goes, the Greeks defeated them at the battle by the Thermodon River and, in three ships, sailed off with all of the Amazons they were able to capture alive. Once at sea the women slaughtered the men. The women, however, knew nothing of boats—neither how to use rudders, nor sails, nor oars. So after they had slaughtered the men, they floated wherever the waves or wind took them, and arrived at Cremni on Lake Maeotis, which is part of the territory of the free Scythians.

Here the Amazons disembarked and walked to a developed area. There, they first came upon a herd of horses which they stole and mounted, and then set about pillaging the Scythian territory. The Scythians could not work out what was going on, because they could recognize neither their speech nor clothing nor ethnicity and were wondering where they had come from. They thought they were men, though in early adulthood, and so engaged them in battle. The Scythians recovered some of their bodies from the battle and so realized they were women.

After some deliberation the Scythians decided not to keep killing them but to send out their youngest men—about the same number as they guessed the women were. These were to set up camp near the women and were to do whatever the women were doing. If they attacked them, they were not to fight, but to withdraw a little, and whenever the women stopped their pursuit, they were to go and camp near them again. The Scythians adopted these plans because they wanted to beget children from them.

The young men were sent out and did what they were ordered. When the Amazons worked out that they were not there to harm them, they let them be, and so day by day the two armies kept coming closer to one another. The young men, just like the women, had nothing except weapons and horses, and so they both passed their time in the same way, by hunting and plundering. At midday the Amazons would do the following: they would spread out in ones or twos and, at a distance from one another, would relieve themselves. When the Scythians learned of this, they started to do the same thing. Then one of the young men advanced upon one of the women while she was alone. The Amazon did not rebuff him, but allowed him to have her. She could not speak to him because they didn't understand one another, but with her hands she indicated to him to come to the same place on the next day and to bring

another, signaling that there had to be two and that she would
bring a second woman. The young man went away and told
the others. On the next day he went with a second and found
the Amazon also waiting with a second. When the rest of the
young men learned of this, they likewise tamed the rest of
the Amazons.

After this, the two camps joined and lived together, each
young man having the woman with whom he first had intercourse. The men were not able to learn the women's language,
but the women comprehended the men's. Now that they were
able to understand one another, the men said to the Amazons:
"We have parents and possessions, so let's not keep living like
this, but go and live among our population. We will keep you
as wives and take no others." But in response, the Amazons
said: "But we couldn't live among your women. We do not
practice the same ways of life. We use bows and spears, and
ride horses; we haven't learned women's work. Your women do
none of these things, but remain in their wagons doing wom-
en's work, not going into the hunt or anywhere else. So we
could not agreeably co-exist with them. But if you wish to keep
us as wives and to be seen to be honest men, go to your parents
and take your proper share of possessions, then let's go and live
by ourselves." The young men were persuaded and did what
they said.

When they got their proper share of possessions and returned to the Amazons, the women said to them: "We dread
and fear having to settle in this land because we have robbed
you of your fathers and have greatly despoiled your land. So
since you have seen fit to have us as wives, join us in quitting
this land and living on the other side of the Tanais River." The
young men were persuaded by these words also. They crossed
the Tanais and traveled east for three days, and then north
from Lake Maeotis for three days. Then they arrived at and
settled in the same place that they have inhabited until this day.

From that time on, the women of the Sauromatae have practiced the same way of life: they go into the hunt on horseback
(both with the men and without the men), they regularly go
into war, and they wear the same clothes as the men. The Sauromatae use the Scythian language, though from the beginning

have spoken it incorrectly, because the Amazons did not ade-
quately learn it. They have this law concerning marriage: a girl
cannot be married until she kills a man in battle. Some of their
women grow old and die unmarried because they cannot fulfill
this law.

DIODORUS SICULUS, *LIBRARY OF HISTORY*

4.16

Translated from the Greek by
Daniel Holmes

Diodorus describes how Hercules dispatches the foremost of the Amazons during his quest for Hippolyta's war belt. The excerpt combines the features of an "aristeia" (a moment of glory on the battlefield) with those of a catalogue or list, both of which were features of epic going back to Homer's Iliad.

Heracles was ordered to get the war belt of Hippolyta, the Amazon, and so made his campaign against the Amazons. He sailed into the Black Sea—which he named the Euxine—and sailed all the way up to the mouth of the Thermodon River. He camped near the city of Themiscyra, where the Amazons' palace lay. First, he asked for the war belt that had been ordered of him. When the Amazons ignored him, he joined battle. Now the rest of the Amazonian troops were lined up against Heracles' rank and file, but the preeminent women were drawn up against Heracles himself and put up a fierce contest. Aëlla was the first[1] to join battle with him—she got this name because of her speed—but she soon discovered that he was swifter than she was. Philippis was the second, but at the first encounter she was felled by a fatal blow. Thereafter he joined battle with Prothoë, who, they said, prior to this had challenged and defeated seven opponents. But she too fell.

The fourth he defeated was called Eriboea. She was full of manliness in contests of war and boasted that she needed no one's help. But this assertion was shown to be false when she encountered someone stronger. After these came Celaeno, Eurybia, and Phoebe, companions of Artemis in the hunt, whose spears always hit their targets—though on this occasion, they did not hit even their one target. Standing shield to shield, they were all cut down. After these, he defeated Deianeira, Asteria, and Marpe, then Tecmessa and Alcippe. This last had sworn to remain a virgin—she protected her oath, but did not secure her life.

The general of the Amazons, Melanippe, who was particularly awe-inspiring for her manly courage, now lost her leadership. Thus did Heracles dispatch the most outstanding of the Amazons and compelled the rest to flight. He destroyed so very many that their race was completely wiped out. Of the prisoners he gave Antiope to Theseus, but set Melanippe free in exchange for the war belt.

PLUTARCH, *THESEUS*

26–28

Translated from the Greek by Daniel Holmes

Plutarch (46–119 CE) was a philosopher as well as a biographer of both mythical and historical figures. In this selection from his Theseus, *he tells how the Greek hero took captive the Amazon queen known as Antiope, who in other accounts is conflated with the Amazon Hippolyta. The kidnapping of Antiope, according to Plutarch, becomes the motive for the Amazons' attack on Athens, a mythical event commemorated on the western metopes of the Parthenon in Athens. One ancient phenomenon that Plutarch uses as evidence for this Amazonomachy is the proliferation of so-called Amazon graves in cities throughout Greece, recorded also by writers such as Pausanias. This was probably a particular grave type that came to be associated with the warrior women, reinforcing the tale of the Amazons' attack on Greece.*

As Philochorus and certain others tell us, it was when Theseus was sailing to the Euxine Sea with Heracles on his campaign against the Amazons that he took Antiope as his war prize. But the majority of writers—notably Pherecydes, Hellanicus, and Herodorus—say that it was after the time of Heracles, and with his own crew, that he took this Amazon woman as his captive. This is the more plausible, because, in the various histories, none of the others who participated in Heracles' campaign are said to have taken an Amazon as captive. Bion even says that Theseus took this Amazon duplicitously; for, as he tells us, the Amazons by nature tend to love what is male and did not flee Theseus when he attacked their land, but even sent him gifts of hospitality. Then he invited Antiope with her gifts onto the ship, and, once she was onboard, he put to sea.

A certain Menecrates, who has published a history of the city of Nicaea in Bithynia, says that Theseus spent some time in the region while he was with Antiope. Three young men, brothers from Athens, happened to be on this campaign with him—Euneos, Thoas, and Soloïs. This last fell in love with Antiope but kept it to himself except for a single close companion to whom he confessed it. This companion then met with Antiope on his behalf, but she vigorously rejected his advances. Nevertheless, she dealt with the incident in a prudent and kindly way, and did not denounce him to Theseus. When Soloïs learned of this, he threw himself into a river and died. As soon as Theseus learned the source of the young man's suffering, he grew deeply distressed and, in his anguish, remembered an oracle he received from Apollo. For at Delphi the Pythian priestess had once commanded that whenever, in a foreign land, he felt most distressed and saddened, he should found a city there and leave behind some of his own as rulers. It was for this reason that the city he founded there was called Pythopolis, after Pythian Apollo. The nearby river he called Soloïs in honor of the young man, and he also left there the brothers of Soloïs as rulers and law givers, as well as a man called Hermus—one of the Eupatrids in Athens.[1] It is from this man that the Pythopolitans call a certain place the "house of Hermes," though they incorrectly lengthen the second syllable and thereby shift the glory from a man onto a god.

The capture of Antiope was the motive for the war of the Amazons against Athens, and it was clearly no petty or womanish campaign. For they could not have set up camp right in the city nor could they have joined in close battle around the Pnyx and the temple of the Muses, if they had not first taken control of the adjacent countryside and penetrated the city without fear of harm. It is scarcely believable that, as Hellanicus reports, they traversed and crossed over the Cimmerian Bosporus while its waters were frozen to ice. But that they encamped virtually within the city is testified to by the very names given to certain places and by the graves of the fallen.

For a long time both sides hesitated and delayed in their attack, but finally Theseus, following an oracle, slaughtered an animal to the god Fear and joined battle with the women. The battle occurred in the month of Boëdromion[2] on the day on which, still today, the Athenians celebrate the Boëdromia.[3] Cleidemus—in his desire to be accurate and detailed—reports that the left wing of the Amazons curved around to what is now called the Amazoneum, and on their right they reached the Pnyx near the Chrysa statue. It was against this left wing, he goes on, that the Athenians, attacking from the temple of the Muses, did battle with the Amazons; and the graves of the Amazons who fell are situated about the street that leads to the gate by the shrine of Chalcodon—the one now called the Peiraïc Gate. Here the Athenians were forced back as far as the shrine of the Eumenides as they tried to escape the women.

But on the right wing, the Athenians who attacked from the Palladion and the Ardettus Hill and the Lyceum pushed the Amazons back as far as their camp and cut down many. After three months the Amazons made a peace treaty through Hippolyta—for Cleidemus says that Hippolyta was the name of Theseus' consort, not Antiope.

But some say that this woman fell fighting beside Theseus, struck by Molpadia's spear[4] and that the pillar by the temple of Olympian Earth was set up for her. It is no surprise that the historical inquiry into such ancient events should be so divergent, because some also say the wounded Amazons were secretly conveyed across to Chalcis[5] by Antiope and there received treatment; and a few were buried there near what is now called the Amazoneum.[6]

At any rate, there is evidence that the war was concluded by way of a peace treaty. Firstly, the place beside the temple of Theseus is called the "Horcomosium," the "place of the oath"; furthermore, there was an ancient sacrificial ceremony performed for the Amazons just before the festival of Theseus.

The Megarians, too, can point to Amazonian graves in their own country—where the Rhomboid is located, on the road from the marketplace to what they call Rhus. It is also said that other Amazons died around Chaeronea[7] and were buried beside the stream which in ancient times seems to have been called Thermodon, but now Haemon. I wrote about these things in my *Life of Demosthenes*. It is clear that the Amazons passed not even through Thessaly without a disturbance, for still, even today, their graves are pointed out around Scotussa and Cynoscephalae.

These are the reports that are worth mentioning about the Amazons. As for the *Uprising of the Amazons* that the author of the *Theseïd* wrote, in which Antiope attacks Theseus because of his marriage to Phaedra, the Amazons together with Antiope take vengeance on him, and then Heracles kills them— all of this is manifestly a fictional story. He did, however, marry Phaedra after Antiope's death and have a son, Hippolytus (or as Pindar says, Demophoön), with Antiope. As for the unfortunate events surrounding Phaedra and this son,[8] since there are no contradictions between the historians' and the tragic poets' accounts, we ought to assume that these things occurred just as all the poets have written.

QUINTUS OF SMYRNA, *POSTHOMERICA*

1.574–674

Translated from the Greek by
Stephanie McCarter

Penthesilea was an Amazon queen who allied with the Tro-
jans and led a troop of Amazons against the Greeks in the
legendary Trojan War. This tale would have been featured
in the Aethiopis, *one of the poems of the lost Epic Cycle*
(7th–6th c. BCE), a series of epic poems that covered the
parts of the Trojan War left unnarrated by Homer. The ver-
sions of the Penthesilea story we now have come from later
writers, such as Quintus of Smyrna (3rd c. CE), who deals
with her extensively in Book One of his Posthomerica, *a*
fifteen-book epic that covers much of the same material as
the Epic Cycle. The following selection presents us with
Penthesilea's death, which traditionally involves the Homeric
warrior Achilles falling in love with her as he slaughters her.
The scene picks up just as Penthesilea has unsuccessfully at-
tacked Ajax, who was second only to Achilles among the
Greeks.

Taunting, the son of Peleus[1] addressed her:
"Woman, like one who vaunts with hollow words   575
you came against us in your lust for war.
We are the greatest heroes on the earth,

who boast to be the stock of Cronus'
loud-thundering son.[2] Even swift Hector quaked
with fear if even from afar he saw us   580
bolt to the painful clash. My own spear killed him,
though he was strong. You are insane to be
so brazen, threatening both of us[3] with ruin
today. Your own last day is close at hand.
Nor will your father Ares save you from me—   585
you'll pay an awful death, as when a fawn
meets an ox-slaying lion in the mountains.
You've not yet heard of all those men whose knees
crumpled beneath my hands near flowing Xanthus,[4]
or else you have, but heaven snatched your wits   590
so unforgiving Death might gulp you down."
     He spoke, then swooped, his mighty hand extending
the long, death-dealing spear that Chiron forged.[5]
Swiftly, he struck the fierce Penthesilea
beneath her right-hand breast; her dark blood spilled   595
in streams, and straightaway her knees went weak.
The giant ax fell from her hand as night
darkened her eyes and sorrow filled her heart.
Yet she revived and saw the man, her foe,
now poised to drag her from her nimble horse.   600
She weighed two options: either draw her sword
and wait for swift Achilles to attack,
or swiftly leap from that most nimble horse
and beg the godlike man with promises
of lavish bronze and gold, which melt the hearts   605
of mortal men, even a very brash one—
this just might curb Achilles' deadly force,
or else he might revere a girl his age,
who yearns to flee, and let her go back home.
     She weighed this, but the gods had other plans.   610
As she drew near, the son of Peleus seethed
and skewered her—her *and* her storm-swift horse,
as one might skewer meat on spits above
a blazing flame to make a hurried dinner,
or as a hunter casts a painful lance   615
on mountains, cutting cleanly through a deer

in haste, and, flying on, the mighty spear
pierces a trunk, a lofty oak or pine.
In just this way the son of Peleus cut
his raging sword clean through Penthesilea   620
and her fine horse. She joined with dust and doom,
falling to earth with grace; no shame debased
her noble flesh. Stretched long and prone, she quivered
around the spear, reclined on her swift horse.
Just like a fir cold Boreas has downed,   625
the tallest in the stretching glens and woods—
Earth fed it by a spring, her pride and joy—
so Penthesilea fell from her swift horse.
She still was dazzling, but her strength was crushed.

        The Trojans, when they saw her slain in battle,   630
trembled in fear and hastened to the city;
no words could voice the grief inside their hearts,
as when a cyclone falls on the wide sea
and sailors lose their ship but flee destruction—
a few who struggle in the woeful brine.   635
Land and a town appear close by at last!
Weary through all their limbs from painful toil,
they struggle from the brine, their minds in mourning
for friends the wave drove off to dreadful gloom.
Like this, the Trojans fled from war to city,   640
all grieving for relentless Ares' daughter
and the troops who perished in that painful war.
   Above her, the gloating son of Peleus boasted:
"Lie in the dust now, food for dogs and birds,
you wretch. Who tricked you into facing me?   645
Did you suppose you would return from battle
and win uncounted gifts from aged Priam
for slaying Argives?[6] But the gods did not
fulfill your purpose, since we are the greatest
heroes, a light to Greeks, a bane to Trojans   650
and you as well, destroyed since murky Death
and your own mind spurred you from women's work
to war, which causes even men to shudder."
   The son of Peleus spoke, then drew his lance
from the swift horse and grim Penthesilea.   655

Both writhed, cut down beneath a single spear.
He took the helmet from her head; it glittered
like rays of sunlight or the gleam of Zeus.
Fallen upon the dirt and blood, her face
shone beautifully beneath her lovely brow,   660
slain though she was. Surrounding them, the Argives
were awed to see her—she was like a goddess.
She lay armed on the ground like undefiled
Artemis, Zeus' daughter, tired and sleeping
after a hillside hunt for speedy lions.   665
For well-crowned Cypris,[7] mighty Ares' consort,
had made her wondrous even in her death,
so even fine Achilles would lament her.
And many prayed that, when they got back home,
they'd pass their nights in bed with such a wife.   670
Achilles, in his heart, felt endless sadness
for slaying her—he should have led her back
to horse-rich Phthia as his noble wife,
faultless in height and looks, so like a goddess.

QUINTUS CURTIUS, *HISTORY OF ALEXANDER*

6.5.24–32

Translated from the Latin by Stephanie McCarter

Quintus Curtius was a Roman historian of the first or second century CE. The following excerpt is from his ten-book account of Alexander the Great (356–323 BCE); in it, Curtius describes Alexander's legendary liaison with the Amazon queen Thalestris. The tale assimilates Alexander with Greek heroes such as Hercules, Theseus, and Achilles, who also had encounters (often sexualized) with Amazons.

As I said above, bordering Hyrcania[1] there was a race of Amazons inhabiting the fields of Themiscyra around the Thermodon River. Their queen was Thalestris, who ruled everyone around Mount Caucasus and the Phasis River. Inflamed with desire to see the king, she left the borders of her own realm and, when she was not far off, sent messengers ahead to announce that a queen had come and was eager to approach the king and make his acquaintance. Permission was granted immediately. She brought three hundred women to accompany her, telling the rest to stay behind, and, as soon as the king was in sight, she jumped from her horse, carrying two spears in her right hand.

The clothing of Amazons does not cover their whole body,

for the left side of the chest is left bare, but the other parts are covered. Nor does the fold of their clothing, which they tie in a knot, fall below the knee. One breast is kept intact, and with it they nourish their female children. The right is cauterized, so that they can stretch the bow and launch spears more easily.

Thalestris gazed at the king, her face undaunted, scrutinizing his appearance, which by no means equaled the fame of his exploits. Indeed, all barbarian peoples hold magnificent bodies in reverence, considering capable of great deeds only those whom nature has thought fit to endow with an outstanding appearance.

Yet when asked if she wished to make a request, she confessed, without hesitation, that she had come to have children with the king, that she was worthy to produce heirs to his kingdom. She would keep any female child but give any male to his father. Alexander asked if she would be willing to fight alongside him, but she declined, explaining that she had left her realm unguarded. She kept asking that he not send her away with her hopes dashed. The woman's sexual desire, which was more intense than that of the king, forced him to stop there for several days—thirteen days were spent in service to her passion. She then sought her own realm; and he, Parthia.

FEMALE REVOLUTION

The idea that women might revolt and try to acquire official power for themselves was largely, to the average Greco-Roman mind, the stuff of myth and fantasy. Yet the specter of female revolution did not fail to elicit anxiety within our male sources. Women indeed were often stereotyped as having precisely those qualities that might lend themselves to rebellion—they were considered sneaky, shrewd, conspiratorial, good at clever speaking, and desirous of power. The Athenians recognized, moreover, that their own gender norms were not universal; in Sparta, for instance, women may have had more public visibility, and to Athenian men Spartan women seemed to exercise an uncomfortable amount of authority. Some sources furthermore indicate that, amid the turmoil that ensued in Athens in the wake of the Peloponnesian War (431–404 BCE), women—and not just the disenfranchised who were normally expected to work outside the home—became increasingly visible in the public sphere. For instance, Demosthenes, writing in the fourth century BCE, states: "As I hear, many women—citizen ones—became wetnurses and laborers and fruit-gatherers due to the city's misfortunes during those times. And many women who used to be poor are now wealthy" (*Against Eubulides* 45). It is in this context that comedic playwrights, particularly Aristophanes, began to entertain the thought: What would the world—or, more specifically, Athens—be like if it were taken over by women?

ARISTOPHANES,
ASSEMBLYWOMEN

Translated from the Greek by
Stephanie McCarter

*In this play, a group of Athenian wives, led by Praxagora,
dress up as men and infiltrate the Assembly, the chief governing body of Athens, which met on the Pnyx Hill overlooking
the Acropolis. The women thereupon enact a revolution,
voting to hand the reins of government over to themselves.
In effect, they infiltrate the public sphere in order to obliterate it, reorganizing Athens as one large household managed
by women. Along the way, they also take control of and
regulate another male-dominated sphere: sex. This is among
the later plays of Aristophanes, who was writing a form of
drama now known as "Old Comedy." Such comedies take
up real political problems, laying the blame for them on
named individuals and proposing fantastical solutions to
solve them.*

Assemblywomen *was produced most likely in 391 BCE
amid the Corinthian War (395–387 BCE), which was fought
between Sparta and a Persia-backed alliance of Athens,
Thebes, Corinth, and Argos. This war came on the heels of
a long period of conflict and instability for Athens, including its defeat in the Peloponnesian War in 404 BCE and the
brief but violent rule of the Thirty Tyrants that ensued. The
Corinthian War would also see Athens's surrender after Persia switched sides and threw its support behind Sparta.*

*The play would have been performed at a religious festi-
val to Dionysus, such as the City Dionysia or the Lenaea.
Five comedies would have been performed, and we know*

from the play's closing lines that Assemblywomen *was allotted to be the first play of the day. We do not know, however, how it fared in the judging. Modern judgment of the play has been somewhat lukewarm, especially in comparison with Aristophanes's other women-centered plays,* Thesmophoria *and* Lysistrata, *produced two decades earlier. But* Assemblywomen *offers a potent reminder that within the Athenian household, unlike the city, it was expected that women—and especially wives—would play a key managerial role.*

The play's pronounced obscenity and sexual content may surprise, or even shock, modern audiences, but such content is tied to its religious and political contexts. Dionysus was the god of wine and ecstasy, and thus festivals in his honor brought a release from normal expectations of social decorum. Freedom of speech, parrhesia, *was also a crucial element of the Athenian democracy, in which each citizen had the liberty to speak his mind with frankness. By using obscene and sexual language, and by making personal political attacks, the women of the play claim this democratic privilege for themselves.*

Characters

Praxagora (an Athenian woman)
Blepyrus (Praxagora's husband)
Woman A
Woman B
Neighbor
Citizen Man
Chremes (an old man)
Female Herald
Old Woman A
Old Woman B
Old Woman C
Young Woman
Young Man
Slave Woman
Chorus of Women

PROLOGUE

*(The skenê building behind Praxagora has three doors,
each the entrance to a house. Praxagora stands alone onstage, holding an oil lamp in her hands.)*

PRAXAGORA

O splendid brilliance[1] of this wheel-wrought lamp,
most excellent invention of the shrewd,
for I shall now reveal your birth and fortunes:[2]
Begotten on a whirling potter's wheel,
you hold the sun's bright glory on your snout.   5
Kindle your flame, the signal we approved.
Our revelations are for you alone—
rightly, for in our chambers when we practice
techniques of Aphrodite, you stand by us.
None of us, as we arch our bodies back,   10
ever locks out your supervising eye.
It's you alone who light our thighs' forbidden
crevices when you singe our blooming hair.
You aid us when in secret we unlock
storehouses filled with food and Bacchic wine.   15
Abetting us, you never blab to neighbors,
and in exchange you'll learn our current plans,
the ones my friends agreed to at the Skira.[3]
But none of those supposed to come are here!
Yet it is nearly dawn, the starting time   20
for the Assembly, and we "bedfellows"
(to quote Pyromachus, if you recall)[4]
must take our seats and not arouse attention.
What could be keeping them? Do they not have
the crocheted beards that they were told to wear?   25
Was it too hard to steal their husbands' cloaks
and not get caught? But look! I see a lamp
approaching. Now let me step back again
in case it is by chance a man who comes.

CHORUS LEADER

We must keep moving, for as we set out   30
just now, the herald crowed his second crow.

(*The chorus enters the orchestra via the parodos.*)

PRAXAGORA

Well, I have been awake expecting you
the whole night long. But, come and let me call
my neighbor with a tap upon her door—
her husband mustn't notice.

(*Woman A emerges from one of the skenê doors.*)

WOMAN A

                    I could hear   35
your fingers scratching as I put my shoes on
since I was not asleep. The man I live with,
my dear, comes from the isle of Salamis,
and all night long he *rowed* me on the bed.[5]
I only now could snatch this cloak of his.   40

PRAXAGORA

I can see Cleinareta and Sostrata
approaching now, as well as Philaineta.

CHORUS LEADER

Let's get a move on! Glyce swore on oath
that the last woman there would have to pay
nine quarts of wine as well as one of chickpeas.   45

PRAXAGORA

See Melisticha, Smicythion's wife,
running in men's shoes? I think she alone
could slip away, at leisure, from her husband.[6]

WOMAN A

See Geusistrata, the tavern-keeper's wife,
who's carrying a torch in her right hand?   50

PRAXAGORA

Here come the wives of Philodoretos
and of Chaeretades—and many more,
all those with any standing in the city.

WOMAN B

I had a world of trouble slipping out
unnoticed, dear. My husband snored all night—   55
he stuffed himself with anchovies at dinner!

PRAXAGORA

Now come and take a seat. I'd like to ask,
now that you all are here, if you've completed
everything we agreed on at the Skira.

WOMAN A

Well, I have! First of all, I've grown my armpits   60
thick as a bush, just as we planned. And when
my husband went off to the Agora,
I'd slather my whole body down in oil
and sunbathe all day long to get a tan.

WOMAN B

Well I have too! But first I threw my razor   65
out of the house so I'd grow hair all over
and not look like a woman anymore.

PRAXAGORA

Does everybody have the beards that you
were told to bring when we convened today?

WOMAN A

Here's mine, by Hecate,[7] and it's a nice one.   70

WOMAN B

Mine's even nicer than Epicrates'![8]

PRAXAGORA

And all the rest of you?

WOMAN A

                         They do! They're nodding.

PRAXAGORA

And you've done all the rest, as I can see:
you're donning Spartan shoes and walking sticks
and, as agreed, you brought your husbands' cloaks.   75

WOMAN A

Well, I have Lamius' club with me—
I sneaked it off as he was fast asleep.

WOMAN B

That is the club he holds onto to fart!

PRAXAGORA

By Zeus the savior, if he wore the coat
of the all-seeing Argos, he'd be perfect   80
to keep . . . the executioner in business![9]
But come—we have to get through our to-do list
while there are stars still shining in the sky,
since the Assembly that we have prepared
to infiltrate will start at break of day.   85

WOMAN A

That's right, by Zeus, so we must take our seats
beneath the platform, facing the Presiders.

WOMAN B

By Zeus, I brought these things, you see, to get
some woolwork done[10] while the Assembly fills.

PRAXAGORA

You nitwit, while it fills?

WOMAN B

> By Artemis,   90
I did indeed! Can I not listen while
I'm working wool? My babies have no clothes!

PRAXAGORA

Woolwork! Good grief! How, when it's critical
not to bare any skin to the attendees?[11]
We'd be in one fine mess if it were crowded   95
and someone, as she climbed across, hitched up
her clothes, exposing her Phormisius.[12]
But if we sit down first, our cloaks wrapped tight,
no one will notice us! And while we're there,
we'll tie our beards on, letting them hang down.   100
Who, when they see us, won't assume we're men?
Agyrrhius sports Pronomus' beard
with none the wiser—he was once a woman.[13]
Now look at him—top fucker in the city!
Because of *him* (I swear on dawning day)   105
we have to dare a deed of such great daring:
take up the city's management ourselves
and try to help the city if we can—
since, as it is, we're going nowhere fast.

WOMAN A

How can a group of female-minded women   110
address the people?

PRAXAGORA

We'll be great, I think!
It's common knowledge that the young men screwed
the most become the cleverest at speaking.
We get screwed all the time, as luck would have it!

WOMAN A

I'm not sure. We are dreadfully unpracticed.   115

PRAXAGORA

Haven't we gathered here for just this reason,
for a rehearsal of what we must say?
Now tie your beard on, pronto! You do likewise,
all of you no doubt well rehearsed in talk.

WOMAN A

My friend, who here is not an expert talker?   120

PRAXAGORA

Tie on your beards—you'll be a man in no time!
I'll put these garlands down[14] and wear mine too,
in case there's something I should like to say.

WOMAN B

Darling Praxagora, come here, poor dear,
so you can see how silly these things look.   125

PRAXAGORA

How are they silly?

WOMAN B

It's as if somebody
were tying beards on roasted cuttlefish.[15]

PRAXAGORA

O Purifier, carry round the cat.[16]
Come to the front. Ariphrades, stop talking!
Come and sit down. Who'd like to give a speech?   130

WOMAN A

I would!

PRAXAGORA

Put on the garland, and good luck!

WOMAN A
(Putting on the garland)

Voilà!

PRAXAGORA

Well, speak.

WOMAN A

Before I have a drink?

PRAXAGORA

A drink? Good grief!

WOMAN A

Well, why else wear this garland?[17]

PRAXAGORA

Sit down now! Move! Is this what you'd have done
there too?

WOMAN A

What? Don't they drink in the Assembly?   135

PRAXAGORA

Drink? Bloody hell!

WOMAN A

They do, by Artemis,
strong wine! At any rate, when you consider
all of the resolutions they enact,
these seem to be the crazy talk of drunks.
What's more, by Zeus, they pour libations. Why   140
else would they pray so much if there weren't wine?
They argue like they've had a few. If someone
is in a wine-fueled rage, the archers oust him.

PRAXAGORA

Get down and take a seat. You're clearly hopeless.

WOMAN A

By Zeus, why did I even wear this beard?   145
I think I'll soon dehydrate from my thirst.

PRAXAGORA

Who else would like to give a speech?

WOMAN B

I would!

PRAXAGORA

Come put this garland on. We can't turn back.
You must speak like a man, with eloquence,
propping your walking stick between your legs.[18]   150

WOMAN B
(Imitating the language of oratory)

I'd rather someone else more qualified
tell you what's best, so I could sit in silence.
I can't allow, at least with my one vote,
barrels of water to be placed in taverns.
By the two goddesses, I am opposed.   155

PRAXAGORA

Two goddesses, you nitwit? Where's your brain?

WOMAN B

What is it? I did not request a drink!

PRAXAGORA

Men do not swear on the two goddesses!
But otherwise you spoke most skillfully.

WOMAN B

Right, by Apollo!

PRAXAGORA

                 Well, then, cut it out.   160
I will not take another single step
toward the Assembly till we get this perfect.

WOMAN B

Give me the garland. I will speak again—
I reckon now I've practiced really well:
As I think, women in the audience . . .   165

PRAXAGORA

Again, you dolt, addressing men as women?

WOMAN B

Because I saw Epigones right there—
I just assumed I was addressing women!

PRAXAGORA

Step aside too and take a seat right there.
I think for our sake I will need to speak.   170
Give me the garland. To the gods I pray
that we succeed in all we have resolved:

(Beginning her speech)

I have an interest in this land that's equal
to all of yours. The city's management
distresses me, and I can hardly bear it.   175
I see it being run by worthless leaders
invariably. If for a single day
one became useful, he'd spend ten more worthless.
Entrust it to another? He'd do worse!
It's hard to give advice to cranky men   180
that fear whoever wants to be their friend
yet ever fawn all over those who don't.
Back in the day,[19] we hardly ever held
Assemblies, but we knew Agyrrhius
was worthless. Now, we hold them all the time—   185
whoever gets their money praises him,
whoever doesn't says that those who seek
a wage for the Assembly merit death.

WOMAN A

By Aphrodite, you're a splendid speaker!

PRAXAGORA

By Aphrodite, twit? It'd be just great   190
if you should make that oath in the Assembly.

WOMAN A

I wouldn't there.

PRAXAGORA

Then break the habit now.

(*Resuming her speech*)

What's more, this League:[20] when we debated it,
they said the city would be lost without it.
But when it happened, there was so much grief   195
the speaker who endorsed it fled at once!
Suppose we must launch ships: the poor man wants to,
and yet the rich and farmers do not want to.
You're mad at the Corinthians; they, you.
But now they're nice, so you must be nice too.   200
Argives are fools; Hieronymus is wise.[21]
We glimpse salvation, yet Thrasybulus
gets angry[22] that he's not been put in charge.

WOMAN A

This man is brilliant!

PRAXAGORA

That's the way to praise me!

(*Resuming her speech*)

People of Athens, this is all your fault.   205
Each of you takes your pay from public funds,
then only cares about your private gain.
Like Aesimus, the common interest flails.[23]
If you take my advice, then you'll be saved.
I say that we must let the women run   210
the city. For already we employ them
as household managers and treasurers.

WOMAN B

Hear! Hear! By Zeus!

WOMAN A

Speak on, speak on, good sir!

PRAXAGORA

How their ways are superior to ours,
I now shall teach you. First, they dip their wool   215
into warm water, as per ancient custom—
without exception. You would never see
them revolutionizing. Meanwhile, Athens,
if something functioned well, would not maintain it,
since it must try its hand at each new thing.   220
They sit and do the cooking, as of yore.
They use their heads to tote things, as of yore.
They hold the Thesmophoria, as of yore.   223a
They bake their honeyed flat cakes, as of yore.   223b
They aggravate their husbands, as of yore.
They fill their homes with lovers, as of yore.   225
They treat themselves to goodies, as of yore.
They love their wine unwatered, as of yore.
They relish a good fucking, as of yore.
So, gentlemen, entrust them with the city.
Don't talk it out at length or question them   230
about what they intend. We simply need
to let them rule, considering only this:
as mothers, their supreme concern would be
the soldiers' safety. Plus, who would send more
provisions to them than the one who bore them?   235
A woman is unmatched at making money
and, as our ruler, never would be swindled—
they are the ones who do the swindling!
I won't list all the rest. Take my advice,
and you will live a life of happiness.   240

WOMAN B

Darling Praxagora, well done! So clever!
Good grief, where did you learn to speak so well?

PRAXAGORA

In the displacements[24] I lived with my husband
atop the Pnyx. I learned by hearing speeches.

WOMAN A

No wonder, dear, you were so terribly clever!   245
We women on the spot will choose you as
our general if you achieve your purpose.
But what if Cephalus[25] runs up to scold you,
how will you counter him in the Assembly?

PRAXAGORA

I'll say he's losing it.

WOMAN A

                         But everyone   250
knows that!

PRAXAGORA

          Well, then, I'll say he's batshit crazy.

WOMAN A

They know!

PRAXAGORA

          I'll say he sucks at sculpting pots
but shines at making Athens go to pot![26]

WOMAN A

But what if rheum-eyed Neocleides scolds you?[27]

PRAXAGORA

I'll say, "Go stare into a dog's rear end!"   255

WOMAN A

And if they try to bonk you?

PRAXAGORA

                    I'll jump *them*—
I've got experience with lots of bonking.

WOMAN A

One final worry: if the archers come
to drag you off, what then?

PRAXAGORA

                    I'll elbow them,
like this! They'll never get ahold of me!   260

CHORUS LEADER

And if they lift you, we'll say, "Let him go!"

WOMAN A

Well, then, we've got it all planned out superbly—
but haven't thought of this: how will we ever
remember to lift up our hands to vote
when we're so used to lifting up our legs?   265

PRAXAGORA

That's tricky! Still, we'll have to raise our hands,
uncovering one arm up to the shoulder.
But now come on and gird your tunic up.
Quick as you can, put on your Spartan shoes,
as you have watched your husband do each time   270
he heads to the Assembly or outdoors.
After you've done all this successfully,

it's time to put your beards on. Then, whenever
you've got them tied to you exactly right,
pick up your husbands' cloaks, the ones you stole,   275
and throw them round you. Now you'll lean against
your walking stick and shuffle off, while singing
an old man's ditty, mimicking the style
of rustic folks.

CHORUS LEADER

Well spoken!

PRAXAGORA

          But let's go
ahead, since I believe the other women   280
will make their way directly from the country
to the Pnyx. Quick! It's the practice there
that anyone not present right at dawn
must bugger off, and not one knob the richer.[28]

CHORUS

CHORUS LEADER

It's time to go now, *gentlemen*. Remember   285
always to use this word—don't ever make
a slip. There's no small danger if we're caught
attempting such a daring deed in darkness.

CHORUS

To the Assembly, gentlemen, because—

    The lawgiver has made this vow:[29]   290a
    Whoever doesn't get there now,   290b
    dust-caked, before the break of day,   291a
    content with garlic consommé,   291b
    his looks as hot as pepper sauce,   292a
    can reckon his three obols lost.   292b

But Charitimides, hey you!   293a
And Smicythus and Draces too!   293b
We really need to hurry there,   294a
but don't forget to be aware: 294b
there must be nothing badly played   295a
as we perform this masquerade.   295b
Do not forget to get your pass,   296a
then all of us in one big mass   296b
must sit together in the stands   297a
and vote by lifting up our hands   297b
for each proposal that seems good   298a
to this, our allied sisterhood—   298b
Oh no! I'm such a knucklehead!   299a
Our "brotherhood," I should have said.   299b

Now shove aside those coming from the town—   300

however many, formerly,   301a
when an Assembly-attendee   301b
could earn one obol (that is all!),   302a
would sit down in a flower stall   302b
and pass the day in conversation.   303a
Now what a source of aggravation!   303b
It did not used to be this way   304a
when good Myronides held sway.   304b
Back then, nobody would have dared   305a
administer the town's affairs   305b
to get his hands on cold hard cash.   306a
No, people got there in a flash!   306b
Each one would bring a bag of lunch: 307a
a baguette and a flask of punch.   307b
There'd be two onions packed in neat,   308a
an olive trio for a treat.   308b
But now they all demand their pay   309a
of three whole obols every day   309b
when laboring for the common good,   310a
just as a lowly worker would!   310b

(*The women and the chorus exit.*)

EPISODE ONE

BLEPYRUS

What's going on? Where has my wife gone off to?
It's nearly sunrise—she has disappeared!
I couldn't sleep. I need to take a shit,
but in the dark I couldn't find my shoes
or else my cloak. I groped around for them,   315
but had no luck. Yet Mr. Poopington
kept knocking at my door, and so I grabbed
this little yellow nightgown of my wife's,
then scooted on her Persian sandals too.
Where can I have some privacy to shit?   320
But in the darkness anywhere will do—
no one is gonna see me shit right now.
What in the hell possessed me to get married
in my old age? I really should be flogged!
She must be up to something pretty bad.   325
But, anyhow, I really gotta crap.

NEIGHBOR

Who is that? Not my neighbor, Blepyrus?
By Zeus, it is the man himself! But tell me,
why all the yellow? Did Cinesias
happen to have the runs[30] all over you?   330

BLEPYRUS

No way! I had to come outside just now
and grabbed this yellow nightie—it's my wife's.

NEIGHBOR

Where in the world's your cloak?

BLEPYRUS

                         I couldn't say.
I looked, but it was nowhere on the bed.

NEIGHBOR

You didn't ask your wife where it would be?   335

BLEPYRUS

By Zeus, I couldn't. She is not at home!
She sneaked away without me noticing.
I fear she's up to something radical.

NEIGHBOR

Well, by Poseidon! That's exactly what
I'm going through as well! The one I live with   340
is gone, and took the cloak I usually wear.
What's more annoying, she has got my shoes.
I couldn't find them anywhere at all!

BLEPYRUS

By Dionysus, I can't find my Spartans
either! But since I really had to shit,   345
I put these sandals on my feet real fast.
I didn't want to soil our nice clean blanket.

NEIGHBOR

What could it be? Perhaps one of her girlfriends
invited her for breakfast?

BLEPYRUS

                    I suppose.
She's not a wicked sort, as far as I know.   350

NEIGHBOR

That's one long turd you're shitting! But it's time
for me to get myself to the Assembly,
if I can find a cloak—it just was here!

BLEPYRUS

I'll head off too, as soon as I'm done shitting.
But now some pear has got my food all clogged.   355

NEIGHBOR

The pear Thrasybulus mentioned to the Spartans?[31]

(*Neighbor exits.*)

BLEPYRUS

Yes, Dionysus, I'm completely blocked!
But what am I to do? My current plight
is not my only worry—when I eat
from this point on, where will the shit all go?   360
For right now Mr. Pearington, whoever
he is, has firmly bolted up the door.
Who can go fetch a doctor, and which one?
Which anal specialist could take this case?
Perhaps Amynon? He'd no doubt refuse.   365
But someone, somehow, call Antisthenes!
Based on his grunts, he is the perfect man
to understand a straining asshole's needs!
O reverend Ilithyia,[32] don't ignore me!
I'm nearly split in two with constipation!   370
Don't let me turn into a comic toilet!

(*Chremes enters.*)

CHREMES

You there, what are you doing? Shitting?

BLEPYRUS

                                        Me?
Not anymore, by Zeus. I'm standing up now.

CHREMES

Have you got on a nightgown of your wife's?

BLEPYRUS

The house was dark, and this is what I grabbed.   375
Where are you coming from?

CHREMES

                    From the Assembly.

BLEPYRUS

It's out already?

CHREMES

                    It was out at dawn!
The red rope stirred up quite a laugh, by Jove,
when they were using it to mark the circle.[33]

BLEPYRUS

You did get your three obols, right?

CHREMES

                              I wish!   380
But I got there too late, and to my shame   381
I left there empty-handed.

BLEPYRUS

                    You have nothing?   381a

CHREMES

Nothing, by Zeus, except my shopping bag.

BLEPYRUS

But why?

CHREMES

There was a massive crowd of people
(unprecedented!) swarming to the Pnyx.
And, what is more, we thought that all of them   385
looked just like shoemakers.[34] How very strange
to see pale faces filling the Assembly!
So, I got nothing, nor did many others.

BLEPYRUS

I'd not get paid if I went now?

CHREMES

          No way!
Not even if you got there when the cock   390
crowed for the second time.

BLEPYRUS

          Poor wretched me!
"Antilochus, mourn not for my 'three obols,'
but that I live, for I've lost everything!"[35]
What business rallied this enormous swarm
at such an hour?

CHREMES

          Just that the Presiders   395
resolved to let the speakers give opinions
on how to save the city! First of all,
the rheum-eyed Neocleides crept right up.
But then the people yelled with all their might:
"How terrible that he would dare address us—   400
especially when the question is our safety.
He cannot even keep his eyelids safe!"
Then he looked all around and shouted out,
"Well, what am I to do?"

BLEPYRUS

                  "Crush up some garlic
with fig juice, throwing in some Spartan spurge,   405
then smear it on your eyelids in the evening!"
That's what I would have said if I had been there.

CHREMES

Well, after him, that very shrewd Euaion
came forward—naked, as it looked to most,
though he kept claiming that he had a cloak on.   410
The speech he gave was very democratic:
"See how I also need salvation—sixteen
drachmas should do the trick! Still, I'll tell how
to save the city and its citizens.
For if the clothing makers offer cloaks   415
to those who need them at the winter solstice,
no one would ever get a chest infection.
Whoever doesn't have a couch or bed
can have themselves a bath, then go to sleep
in tanners' shops. And if they lock their doors   420
in wintertime, then they'll be fined three blankets."

BLEPYRUS

Bravo, by Dionysus! If he'd added
this too, nobody would have voted "nay":
that the grain dealers must provide three quarts
to all the poor for dinner—or else suffer.   425
And Nausicydes could have funded this![36]

CHREMES

And then some good-looking young man leapt up
to speak. With his pale skin he was the image
of Nicias.[37] He ventured to propose
that we should let the women run the city!   430
The crowd of shoemakers applauded, shouting
approval of his speech. The rustic folks,
though, grumbled loudly.

BLEPYRUS

They're no fools, by Zeus!

CHREMES

They were outmanned. His shouting drowned them out
as he heaped compliments upon the women   435
but scorn on *you*.

BLEPYRUS

What did he say?

CHREMES

He first

called you a rascal.

BLEPYRUS

You as well?

CHREMES

Just wait—

and then a swindler.

BLEPYRUS

Only me?

CREMES

By Zeus,

and an informer!

BLEPYRUS

Only me?

CHREMES

By Zeus,

this crowd right here as well!

BLEPYRUS

Who'd disagree?   440

CHREMES

He said a woman is a clever thing,
a money-maker. They do not divulge
the secrets of the Thesmophoria,
as you and I do when we're on the Council.

BLEPYRUS

Indeed, by Hermes, that is *not* a lie.   445

CHREMES

He then said women lend each other cloaks
and jewelry and coins and drinking cups
in private, with no witnesses around,
then bring them back, and never pilfer them,
which he said lots of us are guilty of.   450

BLEPYRUS

Yes, by Poseidon—even with witnesses!

CHREMES

He said much more besides in praise of women:
They don't inform, they don't file suits, they don't
subvert the people, but they do much good.

BLEPYRUS

How did they vote?

CHREMES

To turn the city over   455
to them. This seemed the only thing the city
has not yet tried.

BLEPYRUS

So, it's decreed?

CHREMES

It is.

BLEPYRUS

So all the things male citizens attend to
have been assigned to them?

CHREMES

They have indeed.

BLEPYRUS

You mean my wife, not I, will sit on juries?   460

CHREMES

And she, not you, will now support the household.

BLEPYRUS

So I'll no longer have to groan at dawn?

CHREMES

The women now will see to all of this,
by Zeus! You'll stay at home and fart, not groan.

BLEPYRUS

But there's an awful risk for men our age: 465
that when they've taken up the city's reins,
they'll forcefully compel us . . .

CHREMES

To do what?

BLEPYRUS

To fuck them! And if we aren't able to,
they might not give us breakfast!

CHREMES

Then, by Zeus,
you'll need to eat your breakfast while you fuck.   470

BLEPYRUS

It's really awful to be forced.

CHREMES

But if
it helps the city, every man must do it.

BLEPYRUS

There is a saying of our ancestors:
"Whatever senseless, foolish things we plan
will all work out to help us in the end."   475

CHREMES

By Pallas and the gods, I hope this helps us.
But I am off. Goodbye now.

BLEPYRUS

Goodbye, Chremes.

(Blepyrus and Chremes exit.)

CHORUS

CHORUS LEADER

Move it! Advance!
Is there a man who could be following us lasses?
Now turn and glance!   480

But guard yourself with care, since creeps are out in
    masses,
and one might be behind us checking out our asses!

CHORUS

But as you walk, be sure to stomp your feet!

For it would be to our chagrin,
if in the presence of the men,   485
our escapade should be exposed.   486a
So wrap up tightly in your clothes   486b
and look around you left and right—   487a
keep all directions in your sight.   487b
We do not want our grand success   488a
to turn into a giant mess.   488b

CHORUS LEADER

Be quick, since we are almost back now to that site
where we set off for the Assembly in the night.   490
It's possible to see our general's house at last,
the one who made the plan the citizens have passed.

CHORUS

We do not need to loiter any longer.

Let's lose these beards and go away!
If someone saw us in the day,   495a
our enterprise might be betrayed!   495b
So, hurry over to the shade
provided by this house's wall,
and keep your eyes peeled, one and all.
Let's take the cloaks off that we wore,   499a
becoming who we were before.   499b

CHORUS LEADER

Don't dawdle! For I see our general coming back   500
from the Assembly. It is no time to be slack,

but get those whiskers off and let your cheeks be free
of the disguise they long have worn unwillingly.

EPISODE TWO

PRAXAGORA

Well, women, we have had good luck today!
Our stratagem has gone just as we planned.   505
Now, hastily, before someone can see us,
throw off your cloaks, and then take off your shoes
by "loosening the tightened Spartan reins,"[38]
and ditch your walking sticks. But I'll need you
to see to all of this, since I intend   510
to sneak inside before my husband sees me
and put this cloak of his back where I got it,
and all the other things I carried off.

CHORUS LEADER

All has been done[39] as you asked. Now your task is to
   teach us
what we can do to be useful and seem like good helpers.   515
I've not encountered a woman more awesome than you are!

PRAXAGORA

Stay by my side and advise me as I take the office
I was elected to hold. For back there how I thought that
you were most manly amid the great hubbub and danger!

(*Blepyrus enters.*)

BLEPYRUS

Praxagora! Where have you been?

PRAXAGORA

                              What's that   520
to you, my dear?

BLEPYRUS

What's that to me? What nonsense!

PRAXAGORA

Back from a lover, you will claim!

BLEPYRUS

                    Perhaps

not just from *one*!

PRAXAGORA

              Well, you can easily

test that.

BLEPYRUS

How?

PRAXAGORA

Does my head smell like perfume?

BLEPYRUS

A woman can't get fucked without perfume?   525

PRAXAGORA

I can't, regrettably.

BLEPYRUS

               Then why go out

without a word at dawn, and take my cloak?

PRAXAGORA

During the night a friend went into labor
and summoned me.

BLEPYRUS

So you could not have told me?

PRAXAGORA

You would not have me focus on my friend   530
in her great labor?

BLEPYRUS

Yes, *once you had told me*!
What mischief is this?

PRAXAGORA

By the goddesses,
I had to go at once! The messenger
was asking that I come by any means.

BLEPYRUS

Then shouldn't you have taken your own cloak,   535
not strip mine off and throw this thing around me?
You went, and left me like a corpse on view—
one without garlands or a flash of oil.

PRAXAGORA

That was because it's cold! I'm thin and weak.
I put it on in order to keep warm   540
and left you lying in your nice, snug bed,
my darling husband.

BLEPYRUS

Then why did you take
my Spartan shoes and walking stick with you?

PRAXAGORA

So that your cloak would not get robbed, I changed
to imitate you, then I stomped my feet   545
and struck the pavement with the walking stick.

BLEPYRUS

You've lost us all eight quarts of wheat I would
have gotten if I'd gone to the Assembly!

PRAXAGORA

Oh, do not fret! The baby was a boy.[40]

BLEPYRUS

Whose? The Assembly's?

PRAXAGORA

No, by Zeus! My friend's!   550

Was an Assembly held?

BLEPYRUS

Yes, don't you know?

I told you yesterday!

PRAXAGORA

Now I remember.

BLEPYRUS

Do you know the decree?

PRAXAGORA

I don't, by Zeus.

BLEPYRUS

Then take a seat and chew some cuttlefish.
They say you lot have been assigned the city.   555

PRAXAGORA

For what? For weaving?

BLEPYRUS

No, for governing!

PRAXAGORA

Governing what?

BLEPYRUS

All of the city's business!

PRAXAGORA

The city, then, will be forever blessed,
by Aphrodite!

BLEPYRUS

Why?

PRAXAGORA

For many reasons!
From now on brazen men won't be allowed   560
to treat it shamefully, to bear false witness,
to be informers . . .

BLEPYRUS

By the gods, don't do this!
You'll strip me of my livelihood completely!

(*The Neighbor enters.*)

NEIGHBOR

Now, sir, you need to let the woman speak!

PRAXAGORA

No one will pilfer clothes or envy neighbors.   565
No one will be undressed or indigent,
no one abused or dispossessed through debt.

NEIGHBOR

Great, by Poseidon—if these aren't all lies!

PRAXAGORA

I will explain, and you'll give your approval.
My husband here won't even speak against me!   570

CHORUS

Now you must rouse your mental keenness,
become a philosophic genius,
one who's attained the education   573a
to be our sisterhood's salvation.   573b
For it will bring a panacea   574a
if you lay out your big idea   574b
for how to help the populace   575
with gains that will be bottomless.   576a
It's time to show its true potential!   576b
To help our city, it's essential   577a
that we adopt this clever scheme.   577b
Describe in full this new regime   578a
unparalleled in days of yore,   578b
not even put in words before.
For they get angry when they watch
now hackneyed and recycled plots.   580

DEBATE

CHORUS LEADER

Off with delay![41] Now with speed you must launch your idea.
Briskness will win the approval of those who are watching.

PRAXAGORA

I am convinced that I'll teach something good. But those
    watching—
will they be open to newness, or will they keep doing
things that are tired and old fashioned? This is my worry.   585

NEIGHBOR

Newness should not be a worry! It's what we value
over all else! We don't care about anything ancient.

PRAXAGORA

No one should now contradict me or else interrupt me
till they have learned my idea and heard all my counsel.
I say we all share our assets in common as equals,   590
not letting someone be rich while another is wretched,
one have great farms, but one not enough for a tombstone,
one have a surplus of slaves, but one no attendant.
I'll make a shared way of life for us all that is equal.

BLEPYRUS

Shared by all *how*?

PRAXAGORA

You'd bite first in a shit-eating contest!   595

BLEPYRUS

Shit will be shared?

PRAXAGORA

By Zeus, *no*! I meant your interruption!
I was about to explain this. First, I'll make farmland
common to all, and then money—whatever's now private.
Then from the store we all share, we women will keep you,
managing this with frugality and our good judgment.   600

NEIGHBOR

What about those without land, with wealth less
            transparent—
things such as silver and gold?

PRAXAGORA

They will hand it all over.

BLEPYRUS

They could swear falsely! That's how they got it to start
  with!

PRAXAGORA

That would be totally useless!

BLEPYRUS

How *can* it be useless?

PRAXAGORA

No one will work out of need. It will all be communal: 605
bread, wine, and fish sticks, barley and garlands and
  chickpeas.
Why would they *not* hand it over? Give me a reason.

BLEPYRUS

Isn't it thieves even now who enjoy such possessions?

NEIGHBOR

That was the past, my good man, under laws now outdated.
Why, now that wealth will be shared, would they not hand
  it over?   610

BLEPYRUS

So, when a man sees a girl and desires to bone her,
can he withdraw from this fund for her fee, and then
  fuck her?
That is communal!

PRAXAGORA

Well, he can fuck her for nothing!
I'll make the girls held in common, and men can come
    fuck them,
and, if they want, make a baby.

BLEPYRUS

Won't all of the men just   615
rush to the prettiest girl in their longing to hump her?

PRAXAGORA

Lowly and snub-nosed women will sit by the chic ones.
If one desires the latter, he'll first bang a foul one.

BLEPYRUS

What of old men? Will we not, if we first fuck the foul ones,
dry out our cocks by the time we get round to the others?   620

PRAXAGORA

They will not fuss over you! Have no fears about fussing.

BLEPYRUS

Fuss about what?

PRAXAGORA

You not fucking! You're like that already.

BLEPYRUS

This makes some sense for you women since it's been
    decreed that
nobody's hole will be empty. But how will the men fare?
Women will run from the foul ones and flock to the
    hotties.   625

PRAXAGORA

Lowlier men will keep tabs on the hotties when heading
home from a dinner and monitor them out in public.
We won't let women be fucked by the tall ones or hotties
till they've obliged all the foul ones as well as the short ones.

BLEPYRUS

Now will Lysicrates stick up his nose with the hotties?   630

NEIGHBOR

Yes, by Apollo! The notion is most democratic.
We will all cackle whenever some man in cheap sandals
says to a signet-ringed noble, "Aside and be patient!
When I am finished I'll give her to you to have seconds."

BLEPYRUS

Since we will live in this manner, then how could a father   635
know his own children?

PRAXAGORA

                    Why does he need to? They'll reckon
all older men of a suitable age to be fathers.

BLEPYRUS

Will they not thoroughly choke each old man in succession
since they don't know? Now they know, and they all
    choke their fathers.
What will they do when they *don't* know? Shit on them
    also?   640

PRAXAGORA

No! For a witness will stop this. Once, no one cared when
fathers of others were beaten. But *now* when this happens,
he'll be concerned it's his father and fight the offenders.

BLEPYRUS

Most of your words are well spoken, but should Epicurus
or else Leucolophus greet me as "dad," it'd be awful.   645

NEIGHBOR

Something's more awful by far!

BLEPYRUS

                              What in the world is more awful?

NEIGHBOR

What if Aristyllus claimed you as father and kissed you?

BLEPYRUS

I'd make him shriek!

NEIGHBOR

                              But his poopermint scent[42] would perfume you!

PRAXAGORA

Yes, but his birthdate precedes the decree! There's no danger
that man would kiss you!

BLEPYRUS

                              Well, if he did he'd be sorry!   650
Who's gonna farm?

PRAXAGORA

                    The enslaved. All you'll do, when the shadows
grow to ten feet, is anoint yourself, then go to dinner.

BLEPYRUS

How will our cloaks be provided? This really needs asking.

PRAXAGORA

First, you will keep what you have, and then *we* will weave
  others.

BLEPYRUS

One final question: if somebody loses a lawsuit,   655
how will they pay? It's not fair if it comes from the shared
  fund.

PRAXAGORA

First, there won't *be* any lawsuits.

BLEPYRUS

Well, *that* will destroy you.

NEIGHBOR

That is my verdict as well!

PRAXAGORA

My poor man, for what reason?

BLEPYRUS

Reasons galore, by Apollo! First, what if someone
shirks on their debt?

PRAXAGORA

From what fund did the creditor lend it?   660
All things are shared, so it's clear that the creditor stole it!

NEIGHBOR

Nicely explained, by Demeter.

BLEPYRUS

Answer me this now:

How will assailants pay fines for assaults they've inflicted
after a party? I'm certain that this will confound you!

PRAXAGORA

Out of the barley they eat! For if rations get lessened,   665
they'll not be quick to assault once their stomachs have
     suffered!

BLEPYRUS

Thieves won't exist?

PRAXAGORA

                    How can somebody steal what they share in?

BLEPYRUS

Clothes won't be robbed in the night?

NEIGHBOR

                         If you're home and asleep, no!

PRAXAGORA

Nor if you're out as before! For all things will be furnished.
Somebody's clothing is robbed? Let him *give* it! Why
     struggle?   670
Then he can come get a better one out of the shared fund!

BLEPYRUS

People won't gamble at dice?

PRAXAGORA

                    Well, what stake could they wager?

BLEPYRUS

What about living arrangements?

PRAXAGORA

They'll be communal!
Let's reconfigure the city as *one* single household.
Everyone's home will be open.

BLEPYRUS

But where will you feed us?   675

PRAXAGORA

I'll reconfigure the law courts and stoas for banquets.[43]

BLEPYRUS

What of the speaker's stand?

PRAXAGORA

Storage for pitchers and wine bowls!
Plus, that is where we will let little boys recite poems
all about courage in war. And if any are cowards,
shame will prevent them from dining.

BLEPYRUS

Well done, by Apollo!   680
What of the urns that hold lots?

PRAXAGORA

They'll be put in the market
next to Harmodius. All will draw lots to determine
under what letter they'll dine. Then they'll go away happy.
Those with a "Rho" will be told to proceed to the Royal
Stoa for dinner, and those with a "Nu" to its neighbor.   685
Those with a "Pi" will proceed to the Mill-Workers' Stoa—

BLEPYRUS

Yes, for some pie!

PRAXAGORA

Well, by Zeus, that is where they'll have dinner!

BLEPYRUS

What about lots with no letter? Does that mean no dinner?

PRAXAGORA

We won't allow[44] this to happen!
We'll give to all in abundance!   690
Each will be drunk and in garlands,
holding a torch when he exits.
Lining the streets there'll be women
fawning on all after dinner,
telling them, "Come over our way!   695
Here is a girl who is lovely!"
"Here beside me there's another!"
someone will shout from a garret.
"She is a radiant beauty!
But—when it comes to the fucking,   700
I will go first, and she second!"
Foul-looking fellows will follow
all the young men who are handsome,
asking them, "Where are you rushing?
Run all you want, but it's useless!   705
Legally, snub-nosed and foul ones
get to go first in the fucking.
You can go jerk on the leafage
crowning your two-fruited fig tree!"

Now say if[45] you endorse my plan.

BLEPYRUS AND NEIGHBOR
                    We do!   710

PRAXAGORA

I must depart now for the Agora,
to go receive the goods as they come in

and find a heraldess whose voice rings out.
Since I'm in charge, I have to do these things,
as well as get the common meals set up   715
so you can have your first big feast today.

BLEPYRUS

The feasts will start already?

PRAXAGORA

                    Yes, they will!
And then I'll put an end to prostitution
entirely.

BLEPYRUS

            But why?

NEIGHBOR

                    Is this not clear?
So *these* can have the young men at their peak!   720

(He points to the women of the chorus.)

PRAXAGORA

Slavewomen too no longer can dress up
to pilfer from the sex lives of the free.
They only can be fucked by fellow slaves,
with pussies plucked to look like furry coats.

BLEPYRUS

Go on, and I will follow close behind,   725
so anyone who sees me will exclaim:
"Isn't our general's husband quite the stunner!"

NEIGHBOR

And I'll go inventory my belongings
so I can take them to the Agora.

(*The neighbor enters his house.*
A subsequent chorus is missing.)

EPISODE THREE

(*The Neighbor reemerges from his house.*)

NEIGHBOR

Come here, my sieve,[46] resplendently resplendent,   730
the foremost of my goods, come here outside,
so you can be my powdered basket-bearer,
for you've tipped over many bags of flour.
But where's the chair-bearer? Come, saucepan, come!
You're nice and black, as if you boiled the dye   735
that tinted Lysicrates' hair all black.
Stand by the sieve. Now, maid-in-waiting, come.
Come, pitcher-bearer, bring that pitcher here.
Now, you, come here outside, my lyre-player.
Your early song, before the sun comes up,   740
has often woken me for the Assembly.
Now let the bearer of the tray come forth,
conveying honeycombs and olive shoots.
Bring the two tripods and the flask of oil.
And now send forth the crowd of little cups!   745

CITIZEN MAN

Will I give up my things? Well, if I did,
I'd be a sad sack with a measly brain!
I'd never, by Poseidon, not before
I do a lot of testing and appraising!
I won't be throwing out my sweat and thrift   750
for nothing, in a brainless kind of way,
not till I've figured this whole matter out!
Hey you, what's up with all these pots and pans?
Have you brought all this out because you're moving,
or are you taking it to pawn?

NEIGHBOR
No way!   755

CITIZEN MAN
Why is it all lined up? It's not parading
off to the auctioneer Hieron, is it?

NEIGHBOR
I mean, by Zeus, to take it to the city,
the Agora, as was decreed by law.

CITIZEN MAN
You're taking it?

NEIGHBOR
Of course.

CITIZEN MAN
You're one sad sack,   760
by savior Zeus!

NEIGHBOR
How?

CITIZEN MAN
How? That's obvious.

NEIGHBOR
But how? Am I to disobey the law?

CITIZEN MAN
What laws are those, you schmuck?

NEIGHBOR

The kind decreed.

CITIZEN MAN

The kind decreed! How brainless can you be?

NEIGHBOR

Brainless?

CITIZEN MAN

You're not? You might just be the dumbest   765
of all!

NEIGHBOR

Because I do as I was told?

CITIZEN MAN

And so the wise must do as they are told?

NEIGHBOR

That's right!

CITIZEN MAN

No, that's what stupid people do!

NEIGHBOR

You'll not hand over all your stuff?

CITIZEN MAN

I'll wait
and see what the majority will do.   770

NEIGHBOR

What else are they prepared to do but take
their things?

CITIZEN MAN

I will believe it when I see it!

NEIGHBOR

They say so in the streets!

CITIZEN MAN

Yes, they will say so.

NEIGHBOR

They're promising to take them!

CITIZEN MAN

Yes, they'll promise.

NEIGHBOR

Your doubts are killing me!

CITIZEN MAN

Yes, they will doubt.   775

NEIGHBOR

May Zeus destroy you!

CITIZEN MAN

Yes, they will destroy.
Who with a brain will give up all their stuff?
That's not our way here!

NEIGHBOR

So we do not give,
but take?

CITIZEN MAN

That's right, by Zeus! Just like the gods!
For you can tell this from their statues' hands.   780
As we make prayers for them to grant us blessings,
they stand there, stretching out their upturned hand,
in order not to give, but to receive.

NEIGHBOR

You sad sack, let me do what I was doing.
This must be tied together. Where's my strap?   785

CITIZEN MAN

You'll take it, then?

NEIGHBOR

By Zeus, I will. That's why
I'm strapping these two tripods up.

CITIZEN MAN

How foolish
not to hold off and see what other people
will do, and then and only then—

NEIGHBOR

Do what?

CITIZEN MAN

Delay some more, and then stall even longer!   790

NEIGHBOR

What for?

CITIZEN MAN

Well, if an earthquake should occur,
or lightning, or a cat should cross their path,
they'd stop relinquishing their stuff, you nitwit.

NEIGHBOR

It'd be just great if there were no room left
for me to put this!

CITIZEN MAN

No room left to put it?   795
Fear not. There'll still be room two days from now.

NEIGHBOR

How so?

CITIZEN MAN

I know how fast these people vote,
then change their minds about what they decreed.

NEIGHBOR

They'll bring their stuff, my friend.

CITIZEN MAN

What if they don't?

NEIGHBOR

They'll bring it—have no doubt.

CITIZEN MAN

What if they don't?   800

NEIGHBOR

Then we will fight them!

CITIZEN MAN

What if they are stronger?

NEIGHBOR

I'll leave them be.

CITIZEN MAN

What if they sell your stuff?

NEIGHBOR

Oh, go to hell!

CITIZEN MAN

And if I go to hell?

NEIGHBOR

That'd be most kind.

CITIZEN MAN

Still wanna take your stuff?

NEIGHBOR

I do! And I can see my neighbors too   805
are taking theirs!

CITIZEN MAN

I'm sure Antisthenes
will take all his! But it would sooner suit him
to take a shit that lasts for thirty days!

NEIGHBOR

Fuck off!

CITIZEN MAN

Callimachus, the chorus-trainer—
will he bring something?

NEIGHBOR

More than Callias![47]   810

CITIZEN MAN
(Partly aside)

This guy is gonna lose all that he has.

NEIGHBOR

That's nonsense.

CITIZEN MAN

Nonsense how? As if we don't
see such decrees occurring all the time!
Don't you recall the one about the salt?

NEIGHBOR

I do.

CITIZEN MAN

And do you not recall the vote   815
to switch to copper coins?[48]

NEIGHBOR

Yes, and those coins
did not go well for me. I'd sold some grapes,
then filled my mouth with copper coins and went
to get some barley at the Agora.
And yet, as soon as I held out my sack,   820

the herald cried, "Nobody is to take
copper from here on out. We're using silver!"

CITIZEN MAN

And lately, when Heurippides imposed
two and a half percent in tax, we swore
the city would receive five hundred talents![49]   825
We all poured gold upon Heurippides.
But then when we examined it, it seemed
the same old crap—the tax was not enough.
Then all poured pitch upon Heurippides!

NEIGHBOR

It's not the same, friend! *We* were ruling then,   830
but now the women are.

CITIZEN MAN

And by Poseidon,
I'll make sure they don't piss all over me!

NEIGHBOR

I don't know why you're raving. Slave, get going.

(*Female Herald enters.*)

FEMALE HERALD

All citizens, for *all* are now invited:
Now go! Rush straight to where the general is,   835
so that the lot assigned to you can tell
you one by one where you will have your dinner,
because the tables now are all arranged,
and have been heaped with treats of every kind.
Couches are piled with coverlets and blankets.   840
The wine is being poured, and perfume girls
are all lined up. The fish are being grilled,
and hares are on the spit. Fritters are frying,
garlands are woven, and desserts are baking.

The younger women have the pea soup boiling.   845
Smoeus is with them, donning riding garb
as he is licking clean the women's bowls.[50]
Geron is there,[51] dressed in a nice, new cloak
and sandals, giggling with another youngster.
His tattered shoes and cloak have been thrown out.   850
Now get there too! Servers are standing by
with barley cakes. Just open up your mouths!

(*Female Herald exits.*)

CITIZEN MAN

Then I'll get going. Why keep standing here
when this is what the city has decreed?

NEIGHBOR

Get going where? You haven't turned your stuff in!   855

CITIZEN MAN

To dinner!

NEIGHBOR

            If the women have some sense,
not till you turn it in!

CITIZEN MAN
I will.

NEIGHBOR
                    But when?

CITIZEN MAN
I'm not the one who'll cause a problem!

NEIGHBOR

How?

CITIZEN MAN

I'm sure I won't be last to bring my stuff.

NEIGHBOR

You'll still go dine?

CITIZEN MAN

Of course! What choice is there?   860
All people of good will must aid the city
as they are able.

NEIGHBOR

What if they should stop you?

CITIZEN MAN

I'll tackle them!

NEIGHBOR

And what if they should whip you?

CITIZEN MAN

I'll sue them.

NEIGHBOR

What if they make fun of you?

CITIZEN MAN

I'll stand beside the door—

NEIGHBOR

Why? I'm all ears.   865

CITIZEN MAN

So when they bring the food by, I can snatch it.

NEIGHBOR

Well, get there after I do then! Parmenon
and Sicon, hoist all my belongings up.

CITIZEN MAN

Come now and let me help.

NEIGHBOR

Not on your life!
I fear that when I put these items down   870
beside the general, you will claim they're yours!

(Neighbor exits.)

CITIZEN MAN

By Zeus, I need some clever machination,
so I can keep all of my property
and also have my share of the confections.
I think I've got it! I must hurry off   875
to where the feast will be, and not delay!

*(The citizen man exits.
A subsequent chorus is missing.)*

EPISODE FOUR

OLD WOMAN A

Where are the men? They should have come long since!
I'm standing here, my makeup plastered on,
and decked out in a saffron-colored nightie.

I pass the time by humming to myself   880
while hunting ways to nab one of the youngsters
as he goes by. Come here, Muse, to my mouth!
Devise a ditty in Ionian style!

YOUNG WOMAN

You're on the prowl before me, you old hag!
You thought that in my absence you could strip   885
unguarded vineyards and entice someone
by singing! If you try, I'll sing in turn!
And though the audience may find this grating,
it's still a bit amusing and comedic!

OLD WOMAN A

Converse with *this*[52] and then get gone! But you,   890
my darling flute-player, pick up your flute
and play a tune that suits both me and you!

> If someone's set on feeling glee,
> he really should have sex with me,
> because young women are untried   895
> in arts we ripe have long since plied!
> Whereas I have it in my head
> to gratify my man in bed,
> she'd flit to someone else instead!

YOUNG WOMAN

> Don't let young women meet your scorn!   900
> For we have tenderness inborn
> in our soft thighs and in the breasts
> that bloom and blossom on our chests.
> *You* cake on blush and depilate
> only to be the Reaper's date!   905

OLD WOMAN A

I really hope your cunt falls out,
and that no mattress is about

when it is love you want to make,
and that in bed you grab a snake
when it's a kiss you want to take!   910

YOUNG WOMAN

Oh me! Oh my! I'm so upset!
My boyfriend hasn't got here yet,
and I've been left alone today
because my mother is away . . .
I don't need to elaborate!   915
But, ma'am, it's you I supplicate—
ask Mr. Dildo to come near   917a
so you can give your*self* some cheer.   917b

OLD WOMAN A

It seems, my dear, that it is you
who'd like a sex toy you can screw.
And I suspect that you're quite keen   920a
to be declared the blow job queen![53]   920b

YOUNG WOMAN

I'll never let you steal away
the boys with whom I like to play!
You cannot pilfer or suppress   923a
the blessings of my youthfulness!   923b

OLD WOMAN A

Sing all you want while prowling like a cat—
if someone visits, they'll come in here first!   925

YOUNG WOMAN

Visits a wake! Ooh, that's a new one, hag!

OLD WOMAN A

It's not.

YOUNG WOMAN

Well, who can tell the old new jokes?

OLD WOMAN A

It's not my age about to cause you pain!

YOUNG WOMAN

What will? That paint and powder on your face?

OLD WOMAN A

Why talk to me?

YOUNG WOMAN

Why are you on the prowl?   930

OLD WOMAN A

I'm humming to my love, Epigenes.

YOUNG WOMAN

Who could love you except for Mr. Oldman?[54]

OLD WOMAN A

Well, you will see! Soon he will come to me.
Look there! He's coming now!

YOUNG WOMAN

You pest, there's nothing
he wants from you!

OLD WOMAN A

By Zeus, there is, you beanpole!   935

YOUNG WOMAN

Soon he himself will show us. Now I'm off!

OLD WOMAN A

Me too. You'll see that I know more than you!

(Young Woman exits. Epigenes enters.)

EPIGENES

I wish the girl and I could shag,
but first they're forcing me to bag
a snub-nosed and an oldie too—   940
it's more than a free man can do!

OLD WOMAN A

You shag, by Zeus, and then you'll pay—
this isn't Charixene's day!
It's right to do this legally
if this is a democracy.   945

I'll watch from here to see what he will do.

(She hides behind her still open door.)

EPIGENES

Just let me have the pretty one! I'm drunk,
and here to have the girl I've long desired.

YOUNG WOMAN

I really duped that odious old woman.
She beat it, thinking I would stay inside.   950
But here he is, the one we were discussing.

Come here to me, come here to me!   952a
My darling boy, come here to me!   952b
Come forward, for it's only right
for you to sleep with me all night.   954a

Desire makes me quite insane   954b
for all those ringlets in your mane.
Some unfamiliar lust holds sway!
It grasps me, grinding me away!
Let go, Desire! That's my plea.   959a
Just make him come and sleep with me!   959b

EPIGENES

Come here to me! Come here to me!
Run down, my dear! Run down to me!
Come open up this door right here,
or I'll collapse and wallow near.
I'd rather lie upon your lap
and give your tush a playful slap!
Why, Aphrodite, madden me?
Let go, Desire, that's my plea!
Just make her come and sleep with me!

And yet these words cannot express
the full extent of my distress!   970a
But you, my dearest sweetie pie,   970b
(oh me! oh my!) please do comply: 971a
Open the door and welcome me—   971b
you're why I'm in such agony!

You gold-wrought masterpiece of mine,
scion from Aphrodite's line,
the Muses' bee, the Graces' treasure,   974a
the very paragon of Pleasure!   974b
Open the door and welcome me—   975a
you're why I'm in such agony!   975b

OLD WOMAN A

Hey, why the knocking? Seeking me?

EPIGENES

                            No way!

OLD WOMAN A

You really banged my door!

EPIGENES

Damned if I did!

OLD WOMAN A

Well, then, what are you here for, torch in hand?

EPIGENES

I'm looking for a man from Wanksville.

OLD WOMAN A

Who?

EPIGENES

Not Fucksville, as perhaps you were expecting.   980

OLD WOMAN A

Like it or not, you are, by Aphrodite!

EPIGENES

I'm not now prosecuting any cases
past sixty years of age. They are postponed.
I'm only litigating under-twenties.

OLD WOMAN A

My sweetie, that was under prior rule.   985
By law, you now must prosecute us first.

EPIGENES

But by the law of poker, one can pass.

OLD WOMAN A

You didn't have your feast by poker's laws.

EPIGENES

But *here's* the entrance[55] that I need to hammer.

OLD WOMAN A

You can, but you must hammer this one first.   990

EPIGENES

But I don't need a hammer at the moment.[56]

OLD WOMAN A

I know you love me—you are just surprised
that I'm outside. Come closer to my mouth.

EPIGENES

But I'm too frightened of your boyfriend!

OLD WOMAN A

                                                Who?

EPIGENES

The best of all the painters!

OLD WOMAN A

                                Yeah, who's that?   995

EPIGENES

The painter of the urns that hold the dead.[57]
But go! Don't let him see you in the doorway!

OLD WOMAN A

I know your wants.

EPIGENES

And I know yours as well!

OLD WOMAN A

By Aphrodite, my own patron goddess,
you won't escape.

EPIGENES

You're crazy, you old woman!   1000

OLD WOMAN A

Nonsense! I'm gonna take you to my bed.

EPIGENES

Why purchase hooks for lifting water buckets
when we could lower down a bent old woman
like her to fetch us water out of wells?

OLD WOMAN A

Don't mock me, jerk. But follow me inside.   1005

EPIGENES

I only have to if you've paid the city
two-tenths of a percent in tax on me.

OLD WOMAN A

By Aphrodite, it's not up to you.
And how I love to sleep with boys your age!

EPIGENES

And how I hate to sleep with women *your* age.   1010
I never will consent!

OLD WOMAN A

By Zeus, you have to—
and this is gonna force you.

(*She pulls out a scroll.*)

EPIGENES

What is that?

OLD WOMAN A

A law requiring you to come with me.

EPIGENES

Then read me what it says.

OLD WOMAN A

Okay, I'll read it.
"The women have decreed: If a young man   1015
wants a young woman, he is not to bang her
till he first fucks an old one. If he spurns
to fuck her first and yet still wants the young one,
the older woman with impunity
can grab the young man's cock and drag him off."   1020

EPIGENES

Oh no! Today I'm gonna be Procrustes!⁵⁸

OLD WOMAN A

It's necessary to obey our laws.

EPIGENES

What if one of my demesmen[59] or a friend
comes here to bail me out?

OLD WOMAN A

No man can enter
a contract that exceeds one bushel's value.[60]   1025

EPIGENES

I can't decline on oath?[61]

OLD WOMAN A

There'll be no dodging.

EPIGENES

I'll claim to be a merchant.[62]

OLD WOMAN A

You'd regret it!

EPIGENES

What *can* I do?

OLD WOMAN A

Come follow me inside.

EPIGENES

It is a must?

OLD WOMAN A

A Diomedean must.[63]

EPIGENES

Now first spread out a bed of marjoram,[64]   1030
then place four broken vine-twigs underneath it,
tie on some ribbons, put oil-flasks beside it,
and set a water jar outside the door.

OLD WOMAN A

No doubt you'll buy me a bouquet as well!

EPIGENES

By Zeus, as long as it's a funeral spray—[65]   1035
I think you'll fall apart once we're inside.

(The young woman reemerges from her door.)

YOUNG WOMAN

Where are you taking him?

OLD WOMAN A

Inside—he's mine!

YOUNG WOMAN

Well, that's not wise! He isn't the right age
to sleep with you, since he's so young. You'd make
more of a mother to him than a wife.   1040
If it is laws like this you will establish,
you'll fill the whole wide world with Oedipuses!

OLD WOMAN A

You fiend, you're jealous! That's why you concocted
that argument. But I'll get back at you!

(Old Woman A goes inside.)

EPIGENES

By Zeus the savior, you have really helped me,   1045
sweetie, by freeing me from that old woman!

And I'll repay your services tonight
by giving you a gift that's long and thick.

(Old Woman B comes outside.)

OLD WOMAN B

Hey you! Where are you taking him? You're breaking
the law that says in no uncertain terms   1050
that he must screw me first!

EPIGENES

            Poor wretched me!
You hideous nightmare, where did you pop out from?
This beast is even uglier than the last.

OLD WOMAN B

Come here.

EPIGENES

            Don't stand there watching as she drags
me off, I beg you!

OLD WOMAN B

            I'm not dragging you—   1055
the law is!

EPIGENES

            No it's not! It's an Empusa,
one covered in a giant blood blister.[66]

OLD WOMAN B

Come quick, you little wimp, and stop your talking.

EPIGENES

First let me pay a visit to the toilet
to give myself some confidence. If not,   1060
you'll see me doing something brown right here
from fear.

OLD WOMAN B

Cheer up. Come! You can shit inside.

EPIGENES

My worry is that I'll do more than shit!
But I can make two sizable deposits
for you.

OLD WOMAN B

No need.

(*Old Woman C comes out.*)

OLD WOMAN C

Hey you, where are you going   1065
with her?

EPIGENES

Not *going.* I am being dragged!
Whoever you are, bless you! You did not
ignore my grief. O Hercules! O Pan!
O Corybantes! O Dioscuri!
This beast is even uglier than the last!   1070
But, I implore, what sort of creature is this?
Is it an ape that's wearing too much makeup?
Or an old woman risen from the dead?

OLD WOMAN C

Don't mock me. Just get over here.

OLD WOMAN B
No, *here*!

OLD WOMAN C
I'll never let you go!

OLD WOMAN B
Neither will I!   1075

EPIGENES
You'll tear me limb from limb, you hideous nightmares!

OLD WOMAN B
The law states that you have to follow me!

OLD WOMAN C
Not if an uglier old woman comes!

EPIGENES
Tell me, if you two wear me out completely,
what will I have left over for the hot one?   1080

OLD WOMAN C
That's your concern. But *this* you have to do.

EPIGENES
So, who will I hump first to earn my discharge?

OLD WOMAN C
Don't know? Come here!

EPIGENES
Then this one must let go!

OLD WOMAN B

No way! Come here with me.

EPIGENES

If *she* lets go!

OLD WOMAN C

I won't be letting go, by Zeus!

OLD WOMAN B

Me neither!   1085

EPIGENES

You two would make rough ferrymen.

OLD WOMAN B

How so?

EPIGENES

You'd jerk your passengers till they're exhausted.

OLD WOMAN C

Come here—in silence.

OLD WOMAN B

No, by Zeus, come *here*.

EPIGENES

This is in keeping with Cannonus'
decree, no doubt. I'm bound and now must pound.[67]   1090
But how can I row both these boats at once?

OLD WOMAN B

It's fine—you'll eat a bowl of bearded oysters![68]

EPIGENES

Poor, cursed me! I'm dragged off to her door—
I'm almost there!

OLD WOMAN C

That won't do any good!
I'm coming in behind you!

EPIGENES

No, by the gods!   1095
It's best to fight one evil thing, not two.

OLD WOMAN C

Like it or not, you will, by Hecate!

EPIGENES

Oh, I am triple damned if I must fuck
a putrid woman all the day and night,
and then, once I have earned my discharge from her,   1100
embrace a toad with one foot in the grave!
Am I not triple damned? Indeed, a man
ill-starred, by Zeus the savior, and unlucky,
to be locked in with such enormous beasts!
But still, if I by chance should meet my end   1105
as I come into port with these two trollops,
then bury me right at the channel's mouth.
But that one there[69]—spill pitch all over her
while she still lives, and then pour molten lead
up to the ankles of her feet and stand her   1110
atop my tomb as though a funeral urn.

(*The old women drag Epigenes inside as
a slave woman comes onstage.*)

EPISODE FIVE

SLAVE WOMAN

O blessed people and this blessed land!
And the most blessed is my very mistress,
and all you women standing by these doors,
and all you neighbors and you demespeople!   1115
Along with these, I too, a slave, am blessed.
My head has been perfumed with lots of scents—
nice ones, by Zeus! But better still than this
are all those little jars of Thasian wine!
They stay inside your head a nice long time,   1120
but all the others fade and dissipate.
Yes, by the gods, these are the best by far.
Pour it unmixed. Your buzz will last all night!
Just choose the one that has the best bouquet.
But, women, tell me where my master is—   1125
I mean, where is the husband of my mistress?

CHORUS LEADER

I think you'll find him if you wait right there,
for here he is—he's on his way to dinner.

SLAVE WOMAN

O blessed master, triple fortunate!

BLEPYRUS

Me?

SLAVE WOMAN

      You, by Zeus! No other man's around.   1130
For who could be more fortunate than you?
From more than thirty thousand citizens,
you are the only one who's not yet dined!

CHORUS LEADER

You clearly think that he's a happy fellow.

SLAVE WOMAN

Where are you headed to?

BLEPYRUS

           I'm off to dinner.   1135

SLAVE WOMAN

You'll get there last of all, by Aphrodite!
But still, your wife told me to come and get you,
and with you all these girls right here as well.
There's still a lot left over—Chian wine
and other goodies. But don't get there slow!   1140
If there's a spectator out there who likes us,
or else a judge who does not favor others,
they can come too! We'll furnish everything.

BLEPYRUS

Why not be noble and address them all?
Do not leave anybody out, but freely   1145
invite the old, the teenaged, and the young.
For dinner's on the table now for each
and all of them—if they will scoot on home.
But presently I'm rushing off to dinner,
and luckily I have this torch right here.   1150

CHORUS LEADER

Well since you have it, don't waste time but take
these girls and lead them there. While you head down,
I'll sing a tune to kick the dinner off.
I'd briefly like to give the judges guidance:

Are you a brainiac? Recall the brainy bits and vote
    for me!   1155

You like a pleasant joke? This play was full of jokes,
    so vote for me!
It's clear that I am asking nearly everyone to vote for me!
And please recall that it was not my fault, but fell to me
    by lot
that I go first. Now, keeping all of this mind, you've
    really got
to keep your oath and judge the plays with fairness that
    is absolute!   1160
You must not imitate the habits of a naughty prostitute,
who only has a memory of those she saw most recently!

CHORUS

Hooray, hooray! It's time to eat!
Dear women, if what you intend is for this play to be
    complete,
we must steal off to dinner. Come on, you, you have to
    move your feet!   1165
And boogie like they do in Crete!

BLEPYRUS
                    I am! I am!

CHORUS
                              And these girls too!
They need to dance their lithe and lissome legs on down
    the avenue.
Here's what we're serving you:

        limpets and saltfish and shark bits and dogfish,
        mullet and fish sticks and tart pickle relish,   1170
        silphium and dressings and honey for pouring,
        thrushes and blackbirds and ringdoves and pigeons,
        rooster and stock doves and roast lark and wagtail,
        hare with a wine sauce reduction for dipping,   1174a
        finished with hot wings![70]   1174b

So hurry up and don't be late!
Go on and get yourself a plate!
It's time for you to move your feet
and get some stew for you to eat!

BLEPYRUS

They must be really chowing down!

CHORUS

So up you go! Hooray! Yippee!   1180
Let's go and eat! Yippee! Yippee!
It's time to toast our victory!
Yippee! Yippee! Yippee! Yippee!

PART TWO

MYTHICAL AND LEGENDARY QUEENS

SEMIRAMIS,
QUEEN OF BABYLON

Although Semiramis, the founder of Babylon, is probably to be traced back to the historical Assyrian queen Shammuramat, wife of the ninth-century BCE king Shamshi-Adad V, she had become a legend by the time the historian Diodorus Siculus wrote his account of her in the first century BCE. His is the longest and most significant narrative of the queen's life surviving from Greco-Roman antiquity, and it contains several fantastical elements, including the metamorphosis of both Semiramis and her mother, Derceto, into animals and the miraculous nursing of Semiramis by doves after she was exposed to die in infancy. The story might be compared to that of another legendary figure, Romulus, the founder of Rome. He too was suckled by an animal, a she-wolf, after being exposed as a baby, and he too simply disappeared at the end of his life and was thought to have been deified. Indeed, her adventures have much in common with those of other male figures such as Alexander the Great, who similarly marched his army eastward all the way to India.[1]

Semiramis is, according to Diodorus's introduction of her just prior to this selection, the "most renowned of women," so much so that she seems almost to transcend her sex. Yet there is something disquieting about this woman bent on domination over men, over cities, and even over the land itself. Her alterations to natural landscapes would have been particularly

eyebrow-raising to a Greco-Roman reader, since such transgressions of nature were usually marks of someone who refuses
to accept their human limitations and thus displays *hybris*. In
the end, Semiramis's imperial aims are checked by her own
unmitigated—and thus highly feminine—ambition.

DIODORUS SICULUS, *LIBRARY OF HISTORY*

2.4–20 (SELECTIONS)

Translated from the Greek by
Daniel Holmes

2.4.2–2.5.3

In the region of Syria there is a city, Ascalon.[1] Nearby is a large, deep lake, full of fish, and beside it lies a sanctuary of an eminent goddess the Syrians call Derceto.[2] She has the face of a woman, but the rest of her body takes the form of a fish, and the origins of this are as follows: the most learned men of the area relate the myth that Aphrodite had been offended by Derceto and so had aroused in her an overpowering desire for one of her young and handsome devotees. Derceto had sex with the Syrian youth and bore a daughter, but because she felt shame at her crime, she did away with the young man, exposed the child in a deserted, rocky place, and cast herself, in her shame and grief, into the lake, at which point her body was changed into the form of a fish. It is for this reason that, even to this day, the Syrians abstain from fish and honor them as gods.

A large number of doves made their nests around the place where the baby had been exposed. These birds incredibly and miraculously nurtured the child. Some enveloped the baby's body with their wings and kept it warm; others dripped between its lips milk that they brought from the nearby farms, keeping an eye out for when those who tended and herded the animals were absent. When the child was one year old and in need of more solid food, the doves pecked and brought tidbits of cheese for her survival. When the herdsmen returned and saw that their cheeses had been gnawed around the edges, they were astonished and could not figure out what was going on. They therefore kept a sharp lookout and learned what was happening; this is how they found the baby, which was extremely beautiful. They immediately brought the child to the farm house and handed it over to the overseer of the royal flocks, a man named Simmas. He was childless and brought up the child with all care as his own daughter. He gave her the name Semiramis, which is derived from the Syrian word for "doves." From that time onwards, all those in the Syrian region have continued to honor doves as goddesses.

This is, more or less, what is reported about the birth of Semiramis. When she was approaching the age of marriage and her beauty eclipsed all the other girls', an official came from the king to inspect the royal flocks. His name was Onnes—a preeminent person in the King's counsel who had been appointed governor over the whole of Syria. He lodged with Simmas, caught sight of Semiramis, and was assailed by her beauty. He begged Simmas to give him the girl so he could legally marry her. He then brought her to King Ninus, married her, and fathered two sons, Hyapates and Hydaspes. Everything about Semiramis—just like her physical beauty—was extraordinary, and so her husband was soon found to be totally enslaved to her. He did nothing without her advice and so prospered in everything.

At around this time, King Ninus had completed the construction of his eponymous city [Nineveh] and was beginning his campaign against the Bactrians.

Diodorus now discusses the incredible size and makeup of Ninus's army in this campaign. He goes on to tell how Ninus defeated all of the other cities in Bactria until finally only the capital city, Bactra, remained. This city could not be breached and so Ninus resorted to besieging it.

2.6.5–2.7.2

This siege had now lasted a long time, so Semiramis' husband, who was on the campaign with the king and desperately in love with his wife, sent for her. She—endowed with intelligence, boldness, and all the other qualities that lead to renown—took this opportunity to display her own particular greatness. First of all, because this was going to be a journey of many days, she had carefully crafted some clothing that made it impossible for any onlooker to distinguish whether she was a man or a woman. This garment was also functional as it both served to protect her skin in the heat of the journey and, because it was flexible yet strong, allowed her to move as she wished. In short, the garment had such charm that later the Medes, when they were in control of Asia, wore Semiramis' garment, and later so did the Persians.

When she arrived in Bactria and examined for herself how the siege was being prosecuted, she saw that Ninus' forces were making their raids in the plains and in places that were obvious to attack, but that, because of its defensive strength, no one was assaulting the acropolis. And she saw that the guards had accordingly left their post there to aid those under threat at the walls below. She therefore gathered soldiers experienced in rocky terrain and ascended with them through an arduous ravine. She captured a section of the acropolis and then signaled to those besieging the wall below. The Bactrians inside the walls were seized with panic at this breaching of the heights. They abandoned the walls and gave up any hope for their lives.

In this way the city was taken. The king marveled at the greatness of Semiramis. He first honored her with magnificent gifts, but then, because of the woman's beauty, he fell deeply in love with her and tried to persuade her husband to give her up to him of his own will, promising him the hand of his own daughter, Sosane, in return. When, however, Onnes took offense at this, the king threatened to strike out his eyes if he did not readily do what he was commanded. Onnes, both because he feared the king's threat and because of his passionate love for his wife, tied a noose around his neck and, in a deranged madness, hanged himself. This was how Semiramis first ascended to a royal position.

Ninus now took possession of the treasuries in Bactra, which contained much silver and gold. He likewise settled matters in Bactria and disbanded his forces. After fathering a son, Ninyas, with Semiramis, he died, leaving his wife as queen. Semiramis buried Ninus in the royal precinct and built up an enormous mound over him. It was, as Ctesias says, one mile high and just over a mile wide; and because the city was erected along the plain of the Euphrates, the mound could be seen from many miles away, like an acropolis. They say that it still exists to this day, even though Nineveh was completely destroyed by the Medes when they overthrew the Assyrian empire.

Semiramis, who by nature aimed at great achievements and was ambitious to surpass in fame the former king, now sought to found a city in Babylonia. She selected master-builders and craftsmen from the whole world, procured all of the required materials, and brought together from across her kingdom two million men to complete the job.

Diodorus describes in some detail the various structures, measurements, materials, and construction methods in the building of the awe-inspiring city of Babylon, with its famous brick walls, as well as some other cities she founded along the Euphrates and Tigris Rivers.

2.13.1–2.14.4

When Semiramis had brought her building activities to an end, she departed with a great military force toward Media. On reaching the mountain called Bagistan[3] and setting up camp nearby, she undertook the building of a pleasure garden[4] about a mile and a half in circumference. Lying at the foot of the mountain, the garden had a large spring for watering the plants. Mount Bagistan is sacred to Zeus. From the vantage of the park, its cliffs reach sheer up to a height of over a mile and a half. Semiramis scraped smooth a section at the bottom of this cliff and had etched upon it her own image with 100 spearmen standing by her.[5] In Syrian letters she inscribed: "Semiramis ordered the pack-saddles of the mules in her army to be heaped up, and she climbed this heap to the very top of the peak."

She left here and reached the city of Chauon, where she noticed atop a plateau a rock forbidding in its height and size. So here she built another garden, this one enormous. Positioning the rock in the middle of the park, she built very expensive and luxurious accommodations upon it. From these she could look down upon the plants in her garden and the whole of her army camped in the plain. She spent quite some time in this place and indulged in everything tailored to luxury. She did not wish to be lawfully married, making sure she might never lose any of her power, but she did choose the most exceptionally good-looking of her soldiers and had sex with them—only to make sure they all disappeared soon thereafter.

After this, as she journeyed toward Ecbatana, she reached the mountain called Zarcaeus.[6] This mountain extended for many miles and was full of cliffs and ravines, which made for a long and tortuous trek. She therefore ambitiously strove to leave behind an immortal monument of herself while at the same time cutting the length of the journey. And so, she cut through the cliffs, filled in the ravines, and thereby made a very expensive shortcut. To this day it is still called the Semiramis road.

When she reached Ecbatana, a city that lies in a plain, she built an expensive palace and spared no effort in her attention to the region. Since the city had a bad water supply and there were no nearby springs, she was able to irrigate the entire area by bringing in plentiful and very fresh water—though at great cost in labor and expense. About a mile and a half from Ecbatana is a mountain called Orontes, which is exceptional for its ruggedness and height—the path from bottom to top is a little under three miles. On the other side there is a large lake that issues into a river. So she dug through the base of the mountain to this river and thereby filled the city with water. The tunnel had a width of fifteen feet and a height of forty. These were her accomplishments in Media.

After this, she went to Persis and the remaining territory in Asia over which she ruled. Everywhere she cut down mountains and steep cliffs and built expensive roads; in the plains she heaped up mounds, preparing them as tombs for her generals that died or sometimes founding cities upon their summits. At each encampment of the army, she would also build smaller mounds so she could look down upon the camp from her private lodging on top. And throughout Asia many of the things she built still remain to this day and are called the works of Semiramis.

After this, she traversed the whole of Egypt and conquered most of Libya. She then reached Ammon, where she consulted the god about her own death.[7] It is said that the oracle told her that she would disappear from among human beings and gain immortal honor from certain nations in Asia, and that this would occur around the time when her son, Ninyas, conspires against her.

From here she went to Ethiopia, conquering most of it and surveying the wonders in that territory.

Diodorus next discusses some of the wonders in Ethiopia as well as the customs of its people.

2.16.1–2.20.2

After she had settled matters in Ethiopia and Egypt, Semiramis returned with her forces to Bactra in Asia. She now had a mighty military force and had established a long period of peace. So her ambition turned to achieving something glorious in war. Learning that the nation of the Indians was the greatest in the world and that they occupied the largest and finest land, she planned to march against India. Its king at this time was Stabrobates, who had a limitless supply of soldiers. He also had many elephants brightly decorated to sow terror in war.

India is a land of exceeding beauty. Because it is intersected by many rivers, it is everywhere well-watered and each year bears two harvests. The land provides such a great quantity of nutritional food that its inhabitants always enjoy an unstinting supply. It is said that, because the region has such a good climate, they have never had a famine or lost a harvest. India also has an incredible number of elephants, which are far superior to those in Africa due to their bravery and the strength of their bodies. Superior also is their gold, silver, iron, and copper. They have, in addition, a large quantity of valuable gems of every variety, as well as pretty much everything else that contributes to luxury and wealth.

On learning all of this, Semiramis was seduced into making war on the Indians, though she had no justifiable pretext. She realized that she would need an exceedingly large force and therefore sent messengers to all of her satrapies,[8] directing her generals to conscript the most talented youths—the number of troops was to be in proportion to the size of the respective nations. She ordered them all to bring new suits of armor and to arrive at Bactra, decked out magnificently in every detail, in three years' time. She sent for shipbuilders from Phoenicia, Syria, Cyprus, and every coastal land. She gave them a boundless supply of timber and told them to build river boats that could be dismantled. Because the Indus River was the largest in the surrounding area and acted as the boundary of her kingdom, many boats were needed to cross it and to provide protection from the Indians. The lack of any wood near the river also forced her to bring her boats from Bactra by land.

Semiramis was aware that she was at a great disadvantage because she lacked elephants. As a consequence, she contrived to construct fake elephants, with the hope that the Indians would be in shock, since they believed that there were no elephants at all outside of India. So, she selected 300,000 black oxen and distributed their meat to her skilled workers and to those who were assigned to construct the fakes. She then sewed the ox-hides together and filled them with straw, replicating in every possible way the outward appearance of elephants. Inside each of these was a man who controlled it, as well as a camel. This camel was able to make it move, thereby producing the impression—to those from afar—of a real elephant. The craftsmen who constructed these worked tirelessly in a walled enclosure that had gates so diligently guarded that none of the craftsmen inside could go out and no one from outside could come in. Semiramis wanted no one outside to see what was going on nor any word of it reaching the Indians.

The ships and beasts were all prepared within two years. In the third year, Semiramis sent for her extensive forces to gather in Bactra. As Ctesias of Cnidus[9] has recorded it, the size of her assembled force numbered 3,000,000 infantry, 200,000 horsemen, and 100,000 chariots. There were also 100,000 camel-riders who carried six-foot-long swords. She also had constructed

2,000 river boats that could be dismantled, and camels had been acquired to convey these by land. Camels also carried the fake elephants that I described above. Soldiers would bring their horses up to these "elephants" to try to condition them not to fear the beast's ferocity. Many years later, Perseus, the king of the Macedonians, did a similar thing when he was about to make a final stand against the Romans and their Libyan elephants.[10] But for all of his effort and ingenuity, Perseus did nothing to change the outcome of the battle, nor did Semiramis—as the following account will more precisely show.

When Stabrobates, the king of the Indians, learned of the size of the aforementioned forces and the great magnitude of Semiramis' military preparations, he strove to outdo her in every respect. First, he constructed 4,000 river boats out of reeds. India produces these reeds—so wide that no person could easily wrap their arms around them—along its rivers and marshes in abundance. Furthermore, because this material does not rot, these ships are said to be exceptionally practical. Stabrobates also put great energy into his procurement of arms and traveled throughout India to gather together a force far exceeding that of Semiramis. He additionally hunted out wild elephants and so added many times more to his existing elephant forces—and all of these he decorated to dazzle and sow panic in the enemy. It turned out that, when the animals approached the enemy, their very appearance gave the impression of being beyond human resistance—both because of their numbers and because of the towers erected on their backs.

When he had completed all of these preparations for war, Stabrobates sent messengers to Semiramis, already on the march. He charged her with beginning the war and without just cause. He strongly condemned her in his letter as a shameful hussy and swore by the gods that he would defeat her in the war and then crucify her. When Semiramis read the letter, she mocked his words and said that the Indian would learn of her greatness through deeds rather than words.

When, in her advance, she and her forces reached the Indus River, Semiramis came upon the enemies' boats ready for battle. She then quickly assembled her ships and manned them with her best soldiers. A naval battle ensued on the river, while the infantry, stationed along the river's edges, joined in with eager rivalry. Though the battle was drawn out for a long time and both sides fought with great spirit, Semiramis finally gained the victory. She destroyed around 1,000 boats and took very many captives. Elated by the victory, she enslaved the islands and the cities on the river and amassed more than 100,000 captives.

After this, the Indian king drew back his forces from the river, pretending to withdraw out of fear, but really wanting to draw the enemy into crossing the river. Now that things were progressing as Semiramis had intended, she spanned the river with a large and very expensive bridge. Once all her forces had crossed over, she left behind a garrison of 60,000 men to guard the bridge and led the rest of her army in pursuit of the Indians, bringing to the front her fake elephants so that the enemy spies might inform the king of their numbers. Her hope was not in vain. When the spies informed the Indians of their numbers, none could work out how the enemy could have so many elephants in their company. The ruse, however, did not remain a secret for long. One night, some of Semiramis' soldiers were discovered in the camp slacking off while on guard duty. Fearing the punishment that would be inflicted on them, they deserted to the enemy, where they informed them of their mistaken belief about the elephants. Encouraged by this, the Indian king told his forces about the fake elephants, turned his army around, and marshaled it into battle formation against the Assyrians.

Semiramis responded with her own preparations, and the two armies drew near one another. Stabrobates first sent out the cavalry and chariots far in advance of his infantry. The queen staunchly withstood this cavalry attack. Because the fake elephants had been stationed at equal intervals in front of the cavalry, it chanced that the enemy horses shied away from them. From afar the fakes had the appearance of real elephants, which the Indian horses were used to, and so they rushed against them without fear. But when they drew near, the odor that reached them was unfamiliar, and everything else about them was so enormously different that the horses were utterly confused. Some of the Indians were thrown to the ground, while others, whose horses no longer obeyed the reins, went flying—horses and all—at random among the enemy.

At this point, Semiramis, who was fighting with a select troop of soldiers, deftly took advantage of this turn of events and put the Indians to flight. But as the Indian cavalry fled back to the main body of soldiers, King Stabrobates did not panic but led his infantry line forward, with his elephants out in front. Stationed on the right wing, the king was fighting on the strongest of the elephants and so made a formidable sight as he charged, by chance, upon where the queen was stationed. The rest of his elephants followed his lead. For only a brief period did Semiramis and her forces withstand the beasts' attack— all of the elephants had remarkable courage and trusted in their own strength, and consequently easily destroyed any who stood in their way. The slaughter was great and manifold. Some were crushed under the elephants' feet, others torn apart by tusks, yet others flung aloft by their trunks. There was an enormous pile of corpses, and the visible danger roused panic and fear. No one was willing to stay in the line of battle.

Now that the entire body of the Assyrian army had turned in flight, the Indian king brought his force to bear upon Semiramis herself. First, he let fly an arrow that struck her in the upper arm, then he thrust a spear through the queen's back, but it did not pierce straight through. Neither proved to be deadly, so she quickly galloped off, easily outpacing the pursuing elephant. Now all were fleeing to the pontoon bridge. A giant mass was being forced into a single, narrow bottle-neck. The queen's troops were being killed by one another, trampled under-foot, soldiers and horsemen mixed up into an unnatural mash. As the Indians pressed forward, fear grew, and there was a violent push and crush on the bridge. Many were rammed to the edges of the bridge and pitched into the river. When the majority of the battle's survivors had crossed and reached safety, Semiramis cut the ropes supporting the bridge. When these were loosened, much of the pontoon bridge broke apart and was progressively destroyed by the violent current of the river. In the process, a great many Indians still in pursuit on the bridge died. But for Semiramis, this brought great security—no longer could the enemy cross.

After this, there appeared to the Indian king heavenly signs, which seers interpreted as prohibiting him from crossing the river, and he therefore remained inactive. Semiramis negotiated an exchange of prisoners and returned to Bactra having lost two thirds of her forces.

After some time, her son Ninyas, with the help of one of her eunuchs, conspired against her. Though she remembered the oracle of Ammon, she did not harm her conspirator. On the contrary, she gave him her kingdom and commanded her governors to obey him. Soon thereafter she simply disappeared, like one transforming into a god—just as the oracle said. Some turned it into a myth, saying that she became a dove, flying off with a number of birds after they descended upon her house. Consequently, the Assyrians honor the dove as divine, granting Semiramis immortal status. She was queen over the whole of Asia, apart from India, and met her end as I just related. She lived for 62 years, and ruled as queen for 42.

OMPHALE, QUEEN OF LYDIA

Omphale, the queen of Lydia in Asia Minor, is in many ways the prototype for various mythological women who threaten to gain the sexual upper hand over Greek male heroes. She is best known in our sources in connection with Hercules, who must become her slave for one year as retribution for killing a young prince named Iphitus, the son of the Oechalian king Eurytus. Hercules would later return to Oechalia and sack the city. Omphale traditionally compels the great hero to undergo a gender reversal, making him dress in women's clothing and perform women's tasks such as spinning and weaving while she dons his masculine garb. The relationship was regularly depicted as sexual, with the queen giving birth to a son named Lamus.

OVID, *HEROIDES*

9.53–118 (DEIANIRA TO HERCULES)

Translated from the Latin by
Stephanie McCarter

Ovid's Heroides *are a series of letters purportedly written by mythological heroines to the male heroes associated with them. In* Heroides *9, Deianira writes to her husband, the hero Hercules, after hearing a rumor that he has become enthralled by Iole, the daughter of Eurytus, the Oechalian king, whom Hercules has defeated. Deianira further reminds Hercules of his many infidelities in the course of his travels across the world. In the following excerpt, she complains especially about his relationship with Omphale as being beneath the glory he has won through his famous labors.*

I'll note just one of your affairs, a new misdeed
    that made me stepmother to Lydian Lamus.
Meander, frequent roamer[1] through the same terrain,   55
    who often twists his streams back on himself,
saw pendants hanging from the neck of Hercules—
    that neck that bore the sky with little effort!
Weren't you ashamed to bind your mighty arms with gold
    and to don gems upon your massive muscles?   60
Indeed, these crushed the life out of the Nemean fiend,
    which your left flank now wears as covering![2]
You dared to tie a headscarf round your shaggy hair—
    white poplar suits[3] the hair of Hercules!

Were you not mortified to bind a Lydian sash   65
    around your waist just like a lusty girl?
Didn't your mind remember bloody Diomedes,
    that brute who fed his mares with human flesh?[4]
But had Busiris[5] seen you dressed like that, he'd be
    appalled that such a victor vanquished him.   70
Antaeus would tear off the bows from your hard neck,
    shamed at submitting[6] to a man so soft.
They say you held a wool basket among Ionian
    girls as you cowered at your threatening mistress.
Hercules, don't you wince to touch a polished basket   75
    with hands that overcame a thousand labors?
Do you spin out rough woolen strings with your stout
thumb,
    then weigh back out your famous mistress' share?[7]
How often, as your fleshy fingers twisted threads,
    you crushed the spindle with your beefy hands!   80
You lay before[8] your mistress' feet . . .
    telling of deeds you ought to have concealed—   84
of how, no doubt, you choked the jaws of giant snakes   85
    as they were coiling round your infant hand,[9]
of how there lived on cypress-bearing Erymanthus
    Tegea's boar, whose great bulk mauled the earth.[10]
You do not leave untold the skulls nailed up[11] in Thrace's
    hall, or the mares kept fat on human slaughter,   90
or Geryon, that triple marvel,[12] rich in Spanish
    cattle, who had three bodies yet was one,
or Cerberus, his one trunk split into three dogs,
    whose fur is intertwined with hissing snakes,[13]
or else the fertile serpent who would multiply   95
    from fecund wounds, enriched by her own loss,[14]
or him whose weight, as you were strangling him,[15]
    hanged limp between your left flank and left arm.
or else the equine troop[16] you crushed in Thessaly's hills,
    too trusting in their feet and hybrid form.   100

Adorned in your Sidonian garb,[17] can you relate
    all this, your tongue not silenced by your clothes?

The nymph Omphale even dresses in your armor,
    taking famed trophies from a captive man.
Come now, rouse up your pride, recount your mighty
deeds.   105
    By rights, she was the man instead of you.
You're as inferior to her, you greatest hero,
    as you are greater than the ones you vanquished.
The measure of your exploits now redounds to her.
    Give up your goods, bequeath the girl your glory!   110
For shame! The rugged pelt you stripped off of the shaggy
    lion was wrapped around her tender flank!
You fool! Those spoils aren't from a lion but from you—
    you're the beast's vanquisher, but she is yours.
A woman won your arrows, dark with Lerna's poisons,[18]   115
    though she could scarcely lift the wool-packed distaff!
She bore your club, the beast-subduer, in her hand,
    and eyed my husband's armor in her mirror!

OVID,
FASTI

2.303–358

Translated from the Latin by
Stephanie McCarter

The Fasti *is a six-book elegiac poem inspired by the Roman calendar, especially its religious festivals and rites, the origins of which Ovid's poem records. This excerpt comes from Ovid's section on the Lupercalia, a festival held in mid-February to the rustic Italian god Faunus, during which naked priests would run through the city slapping women with goatskin straps, probably as a rite of expiation or fertility. Ovid seeks here to explain why the god prefers to be worshipped nude, tracing this back to an amusing encounter he had with Hercules and Omphale.*

Faunus especially declines to clothe himself,
    and there's a funny ancient story why.
While the Tirynthian youth attended to his mistress,[1]   305
    Faunus caught sight of both from a high hill.
And, burning at her sight, he said, "You mountain nymphs
    no longer are for me—here is my passion!"
The Lydian woman's scented hair streamed down her shoulders
    as she advanced, a sight in golden robes.   310
A golden parasol kept off the sun's hot rays,
    but it was Hercules who held it up.

She reached the grove of Bacchus and the vines of Tmolus[2]
    as dewy Hesperus rode his dusky steed.[3]
She came into a grotto roofed with tiles of tufa   315
    and living rock. A brook purled at its threshold.
And as the slaves lay out the feasts and wines to drink,
    she dresses Hercules in her own garments.
She gives him finespun tunics dyed Gaetulian purple[4]
    and the smooth breastband that she just had on.   320
The breastband does not fit his belly; he unpins
    the tunic so his big hands will fit through.
He breaks her bracelets, not produced for arms like those;
    his big feet rip her dainty shoes apart.
She meanwhile dons his heavy club and lion skin   325
    and totes his quiver filled with smaller weapons.
Like this, they dined; like this, they drifted off to sleep,
    though separately, in beds placed side-by-side,
since they planned rites at sunrise to the vine's inventor,[5]
    and these required them to abstain from sex.   330

Now it was midnight. What does naughty love not dare?
    Faunus comes to the dewy cave in darkness.
Seeing the retinue relaxed by wine and slumber,
    he hopes their masters too are fast asleep.
The heedless lover enters, roaming here and there,   335
    hands cautiously stretched out to feel his way.
Groping along, he reached the beds where they reclined
    and just was on the verge of getting lucky.
But when he touched the tawny lion's bristly pelt,
    he got an awful fright and stayed his hand.   340
He stepped back, struck by fear, as when a traveler
    has seen a snake and, startled, backs away.
He touches next the silky covers on the bed
    beside this and is tricked by the false clue.
He clambers up, reclining on this nearer bed,   345
    his swollen penis harder now than horn.
Meanwhile he raises up the tunic by its hem—
    the legs were hairy, thick with scratchy bristles.
He went to feel the rest, but the Tirynthian hero
    suddenly stopped him, hurled him off the bed.   350

There is a crash as the attendants scream. Omphale
  calls for a lamp, and light reveals the exploit.
Hurled from the lofty bed so roughly, Faunus groans
  and scarcely lifts his limbs from the hard ground.
Hercules laughs, along with all who see him sprawled there.   355
  The Lydian girl laughs at her lover too.
Deceived by clothes, the god despises clothes that trick
  the eye and calls the naked to his rites.

HYPSIPYLE,
QUEEN OF LEMNOS

Hypsipyle ruled a population of women on the Aegean island of Lemnos, which was sacred to the god Hephaestus. The Lemnian women are best known for two deeds: the slaughter of the island's men and a liaison with the Argonauts as they sail to retrieve the Golden Fleece from Colchis.

The first of these deeds springs from a spiral of vengeance. When the island's male inhabitants cease to honor Aphrodite (perhaps due to her infidelity to Hephaestus), she strikes them with repulsion toward their wives and lust for captive slave women. The wives retaliate in turn by killing every male on the island—except for Hypsipyle, who saves the life of her father, Thoas, the king, by putting him to sea in a makeshift boat. She pretends, however, to have killed Thoas and accedes to his throne.

A short time later, Jason and his crew approach on the *Argo*. The women welcome the young heroes into their bedrooms, eager for new offspring to replenish the island's population. The men eventually continue on their quest, and Hypsipyle bears twin sons, Euneas and Thoas.

The following selections give us two epic versions of the story, the first focusing primarily on the hosting of the Argonauts, and the second on the furious slaughter of the men. In each, Hypsipyle is a tantalizingly ambivalent character who skirts the line between truth and falsehood, safety and danger.

APOLLONIUS OF RHODES, *ARGONAUTICA*

1.607–914[1]

Translated from the Greek by
Aaron Poochigian

The Hypsipyle of Apollonius's Argonautica *(3rd c. BCE) plays a role similar to that of Calypso or Circe in Homer's* Odyssey: *she threatens to waylay the hero on his epic quest. She is ultimately much less dangerous than her other epic counterparts, offering Jason not violence but hospitality and an erotic interlude. She acts as a foil to the much more dangerous Medea, whom Jason encounters later in his journey. Jason, for his part, navigates this situation not with heroic brawn but with erotic appeal. Yet Hypsipyle has not been emptied entirely of dangerous potential—she clearly is crafty and duplicitous when needed, and the women's past slaughter of the men makes the Argonauts' stay on Lemnos not without risk.*

So the heroes rowed to rugged Lemnos,
land of the venerable Sintians.[2]

Here, in the previous year, the womenfolk   820
had mercilessly slaughtered all the menfolk—
inhuman massacre! The men, you see,
had come to loathe and shun their lawful wives
and suffer a persistent lust instead

for captive maidens they themselves had carried   825
home across the sea from raids in Thrace.
(This was the wrath of Cyprian Aphrodite
exacting vengeance on the men because,
for years, they had begrudged her any honors.)
Stricken with an insatiable resentment   830
that would destroy their way of life, the women
cut down not only their own wedded husbands
and all the battle brides who slept with them
but every other male as well, the whole
race of them, so that no one would survive   835
to make them pay for their atrocious slaughter.

Hypsipyle alone of all the women
thought to save her father—aged Thoas,
who, as it chanced, was ruler at the time.
She hid him in an empty chest and cast him   840
into the ocean, hoping he would live.
Fisherman caught him off an island called
Oenoa then but later on Sicinus
after the child Sicinus whom Oenoa
(a water nymph) conceived from her affair   845
with Thoas.
              Soon enough the women found
animal husbandry, the drills of war,
and labor in the wheat-producing fields
easier than the handcrafts of Athena[3]
to which they were accustomed. Often, though,   850
they scanned the level sea in grievous fear
that Thracian soldiers would descend upon them.
So, when they saw the *Argo* under oar
and heading toward their shore, they dressed in armor
and like a mob of Maenad cannibals[4]   855
dashed through Myrina Gate onto the beach.
They all assumed the Thracians were at hand.
Hypsipyle, the child of Thoas, joined them,
and she had donned the armor of her father.
There they mustered, mute in their dismay,   860
so great a menace had been swept against them.

Meanwhile the heroes had dispatched ashore
Aethalides, the posthaste messenger,
whose work included overtures and parleys.
He held the scepter of his father Hermes,[5]   865
and Hermes had bestowed on him undying
memory of whatever he was told.

Although Aethalides has long since sunk
under the silent tide of Acheron,[6]
forgetfulness has never seized his spirit—   870
no, he is doomed to change homes endlessly,[7]
now numbered with the ghosts beneath the earth,
now with the men who live and see the sun . . .
wait, why have I digressed so widely, talking
about Aethalides?
                        On this occasion   875
his overtures convinced Hypsipyle
to grant his comrades harbor for the night,
since it was getting on toward dusk. At dawn, though,
the heroes still had not unbound the hawsers
because a stiff north wind was blowing.
                                    Meanwhile   880
the Lemnian women all throughout the city
had left their homes and gathered for assembly.
Hypsipyle herself had summoned them.
When they had found their places, she proposed:

"Dear women, come now, let us give these men   885
sufficient gifts, the sorts of things that sailors
stow in the hold—provisions, honeyed wine—
so that they will remain outside our ramparts.
Otherwise, when they come to beg supplies,
they will discover what we've done, and thus   890
a bad report of us will travel far and wide.
Yes, we have done a horrid, horrid thing,
and knowing it would hardly warm their hearts.

This is the plan before us. If some woman
among you can propose a better one,   895

come, let her stand up and reveal it now—
that is the reason I convened this council."

So Hypsipyle proclaimed, then settled
again upon her father's marble throne,
and her beloved nurse Polyxo stood up,   900
using a cane to prop her palsied legs
and shriveled feet, since she was keen to speak.
Around her sat four women who, although
they still were maidens and had never married,
were garlanded with heads of pure-white hair.   905
Steady at last and facing the assembly,
Polyxo strained to lift her neck just slightly
above her stooping shoulders and proposed:

"Let us by all means send the strangers presents,
just as Hypsipyle has recommended.   910
It's best that way. But as for all of you,
what plan do you have to defend yourselves
if, say, a Thracian army or some other
enemy force invades? Out in the world
such raids are common. Witness, for example,   915
this group that has arrived out of the blue.

Furthermore, even if some blessed god
should drive them off, a thousand other troubles
worse than war await you in the future.
When all us older women pass away   920
and you, the younger ones, attain a childless
and cruel dotage, how will you get by?
Poor women. Will the oxen yoke themselves
as favors to you in the loamy fields?
Will they pull the furrow-cleaving harrow   925
over the acres of their own volition?
And who will reap the grain when summer ends?

My case is different. Though the gods of death
thus far have shuddered at the sight of me,

I'm certain that before the next year's out,   930
long, long before such troubles come about,
I will have drawn a gown of earth around me
and earned my share of reliquary honors.
Still, I entreat you girls to think ahead.
Right now a perfect means of upkeep lies   935
before your feet. All you must do is hand
your houses, property, and dazzling city
over to the strangers to maintain."

So she proposed. A murmur filled the assembly:
her speech made sense. As soon as she was finished,   940
Hypsipyle stood up again and answered:

"If all of you approve of this proposal,
I shall be so immodest as to send
an envoy to their ship at once."
                                                  So spoke she
and told Iphinoa, who was at hand: 945

"Please go and ask the man that leads their party
(whichever he might be) to come and visit
my royal palace so that I may make him
a proposition that will warm his heart.
Also, be sure to ask his comrades please   950
to come inside our land and city walls
without concern, provided they are friendly."

Once she had sent the message, she dissolved
the council and departed toward the palace.

Iphinoa sought out the Minyans,[8]   955
and, when they asked why she had come, she greeted
her questioners at once with this announcement:

"Queen Hypsipyle the heir of Thoas
has sent me here to summon your commander
(whichever he might be), so she can make him   960

a proposition that will warm his heart.
Also, she wishes to invite you others
to come inside our land and city walls
without concern, provided you are friendly."

So she announced, and all the men approved   965
of the auspicious overture. You see,
they all assumed Hypsipyle was queen
because she was the only child of Thoas
and he had passed on. So they sent her Jason
and started getting ready for their visit.   970

Over either shoulder Jason pinned
a double-woven, vivid-purple mantle,[9]
the handwork of Itonian Athena.
Pallas had given[10] it to him when first
she propped up trusses for the ship and taught   975
the men to measure out the beams by rule.
You could more comfortably stare upon
a sunrise than this mantle's rich resplendence.
The center was a fiery red, a violet
border ran around it, and embroidered   980
illustrations, subtly stitched vignettes,
stood side by side along its top and bottom:
The Cyclopes[11] were seated in it, plying
their endless trade. The stunning thunderbolt
that they were forging for Imperial Zeus   985
was all but finished, all but one last tip.
Their iron mallets pounded at it, giving
shape to a blast of molten, raging fire.

Antiope's twin sons were featured, too,
Zethus and Amphion,[12] and Thebes was there,   990
unfortified as yet, but they were raising
the circuit walls. While Zethus seemed to stagger
under the mountain peak upon his back,
Amphion simply strolled along behind him
and strummed his golden lyre, and a boulder   995
twice as gigantic followed in his footsteps.

Next appeared thickly braided Cytherea,[13]
the shield of Ares in her hand. Her gown
had come unfastened, tumbled from her shoulder
down to her forearm, and exposed a breast,   1000
and in the shield's polished bronze a mirror
image admired her, a true reflection.

Next, there were cattle on a tufted grange,
and Taphian marauders, Teleboans,
fighting the offspring of Electryon   1005
to win the herd.[14] The latter strove to fend off
the former, who were bent on taking plunder.
Dew dampened the enclosure, dew and blood,
and there were many brigands, few herdsmen.

A race came next, a pair of chariots,[15]   1010
and Pelops flicked the reins and held the lead,
Hippodameia standing at his side.
Myrtilus whipped his horses in pursuit.
Beside him Oenomaus rode in state,
his long spear pointed forward. But the axle   1015
snapped in his hub just as he lunged to pierce
Pelops' back, and he went tumbling sideways.

Apollo was embroidered in it, too,
a strong youth, not yet fully grown, and launching
a shaft at giant Tityus,[16] who was rashly   1020
tearing the veil from Apollo's mother—
Tityus whom divine Elara carried
but Earth brought forth and suckled like a
    midwife.

Phrixus the Minyan[17] was there as well,
depicted as if he were giving ear   1025
to what the ram was saying. Yes, the ram
seemed to be speaking. If you watched the scene
you would be mute with wonder, duped by art,
intent on overhearing something wise.
And you would gaze a long time waiting for it.   1030

Such was the gift of the Itonian goddess
Athena. In his right hand Jason gripped
the long-range throwing spear that Atalanta[18]
once gave him as a gift on Maenalus.
She had been pleased to meet him and was eager   1035
to undertake the quest, but he decided
against her in the end, because he feared
the ugly rivalries that lust provokes.

He strode on toward the city like the star
young brides who are confined to new-built chambers   1040
watch rising radiantly above their houses.
They stand adazzle as its twinkling crimson
shines through the dark-blue night and charms their eyes.
As it ascends, the virgin, too, delights
in longing for a youth, the groom for whom   1045
her parents have preserved her as a bride.
But he is off somewhere, some distant city,
dealing with strangers. Brilliant like that star,
Jason came marching in the envoy's tracks.

When they had passed the gates into the city,   1050
the females all came swarming up behind him,
admiring a strange new male. He fixed
his gaze steadfastly on the ground until
he reached Hypsipyle's sunlit abode.

At his approach, the serving women parted   1055
a pair of finely chiseled double doors.
Iphinoa then led him through a courtyard
and seated him upon a shining couch
facing her mistress, who, with eyes downcast,
released a blush across her maiden cheeks.   1060
For all her modesty, she told him lies:

"Why, stranger, have you sat so long outside
our circuit walls? As you can see, no males
inhabit here. They up and emigrated
and now are furrowing the harvest-bearing   1065

fields of the Thracian mainland. I shall tell
you truthfully all about our whole misfortune
so that you know the facts as well as I.

Back when my father Thoas ruled this city
our men would sail abroad and from their ships   1070
pillage the dwellings of the Thracian tribes
who hold the mainland opposite the island.
And when they sailed back home to us, they brought
countless spoils, including captive girls.

This was a plot, though, working toward fulfillment,   1075
a vicious plot of Cypris.[19] Yes, she struck them
with heart-corrupting madness. Husbands started
spurning their wedded wives and went so far,
once they had given way to the affliction,
to drive us from our homes and sleep instead   1080
with women captured by their spears. The fiends!
We let it go for quite some time indeed,
thinking they would come to change their minds,
but their diseased condition only worsened
and soon was twice as shameless as before.   1085

Legitimate descendants were compelled
to yield pride of place in their own homes.
A bastard populace was rising up.
Maidens and widowed housewives were abandoned
to walk the streets just as they were, disowned.   1090
A father never showed the least concern
for his own daughter, even if he saw
her brutalized by a merciless stepmother
before his very eyes, and sons no longer
avenged disgraceful slander of their mothers,   1095
and brothers cut the sisters from their hearts.
At home, at dances, feasts, and the assembly
the captive girls held sway, and so it went—
until a god inspired us to vengeance
and we barred the gates against our husbands   1100
when they returned from pillaging the Thracians.

We told them they must change their ways or pack up
their concubines and settle somewhere else.

After demanding all the children—all
the boys, that is—within our walls, they left   1105
and settled on the snowy plains of Thrace,
where they are living still. And that is why
you and your men should settle down with us.

If you are willing and would find it pleasant
to stay with us, you could assume the kingship   1110
and honors of my father Thoas. You
will not be disappointed in our soil,
I think. Ours is the richest, the most fruitful
of all the islands riding the Aegean.
Go now and tell your friends what I propose—   1115
and please do not remain outside the city."

So she proposed, with half-truths glossing over
the massacre that had been perpetrated
against the Lemnian males. Jason replied:

"Hypsipyle, we gratefully accept   1120
the heartfelt aid that you are offering
to ease our desperate need. After reporting
the details to my men, I will return here.
But let the royal scepter and the island
remain in your possession. I am not   1125
refusing them from scorn, no, but because
pressing adventures speed me on my way."

With this he clasped her right hand and at once
went back the way he came. Around him maidens
from all directions gathered in excitement,   1130
a swarm of them, until he passed the gate.
Later, once Jason had reported all
Hypsipyle had told him at the palace,
another company of girls arrived

in smooth-wheeled wagons, bearing countless tokens   1135
of friendship to the heroes on the shore.
Eagerly, then, the females led the males
into their homes for entertainment. Cypris,
you see, had roused them all with sweet desire—
she did this as a favor for Hephaestus,   1140
so that the isle of Lemnos might again
fill up with men and rest secure thereafter.

The son of Aeson[20] sought Hypsipyle's
royal estate, and his companions each
landed wherever chance received them—all   1145
but Heracles. He of his own free will
remained beside the Argo with a few
select companions. Soon the city turned
to dancing, banqueting, and pleasure. Incense
of offerings suffused the atmosphere,   1150
and all their songs and prayers celebrated,
before the other gods, famous Hephaestus
Hera's son and Cypris Queen of Love.

And so from day to day the journey languished.
The heroes would have idled there still longer   1155
had Heracles not called them all together,
without the women, and reproached them thus:

"Fools, what prevents us from returning home—
what, have we shed our kinsmen's blood? Have we
set sail to seek fiancées in contempt   1160
of ladies on the mainland? Are we planning
to divvy up the fertile fields of Lemnos
and settle here for good? We won't accrue
glory while cooped up here with foreign girls
for years on end. No deity is going   1165
to nab the fleece in answer to our prayers
and send it flying back to us. Come, then,
let's each go off and tend his own affairs.
And as for that one—leave him to enjoy

Hypsipyle's bedchamber day and night   1170
until he peoples Lemnos with his sons,
and deathless glory catches up with him."

So he condemned his comrades. None of them
dared meet his gaze or make excuses, no,
they hurried as they were from the assembly   1175
to get the Argo ready for departure.

The women ran to find them when they heard.
As bees swarm from a rocky hive and buzz
about the handsome lilies, and the dewy
meadow itself rejoices as they flit   1180
from bloom to bloom collecting sweet fruition,
so did the women press around the men
and weep as they embraced them one last time,
entreating all the blessed gods to grant them
safe passage home. So, too, Hypsipyle   1185
took Jason's hands in hers and prayed, and tears
were tumbling for her lover's loss:
                                              "Go now,
and may the gods protect you and your comrades
from harm, so that you live to give your king
the golden fleece. That is your heart's desire.   1190
This island and my father's royal scepter
will still be yours if, after you are home,
you ever wish to come back here again.
How easily you could amass a vast
following out of the surrounding cities!   1195
But you will not desire this future, no,
my heart foresees that it will not be so.
Promise that, both abroad and safe at home,
you will remember me from time to time—
Hypsipyle. But, please, what should I do   1200
if the immortals grace me with a child?
I shall obey your will with all my heart."

Stirred to esteem, the son of Aeson answered:

"Hypsipyle, I pray the blessed gods
accomplish everything as you desire it.   1205
Still, you must check your wild expectations
where I'm concerned, since it will be enough
for me to live again in my own land
at Pelias' mercy. All I ask
is that the gods preserve me on my quest.   1210

But if my fate forbid that I return,
after a lengthy journey, home to Greece,
and you have borne a son, hold on to him
until he comes of age and send him then
to Iolcus in Pelasgia to ease   1215
my parents' grief (if they are still alive),
so that they may be safe in their own home,
comfortable and far from Pelias."

He spoke these final words and was the first
to board the ship. The other heroes followed,   1220
took up their oars, and manned the benches. Argus
loosed the hawser from a sea-washed rock,
and soon the heroes were exuberantly
slapping the water with their lengthy oars.

STATIUS, *THEBAID*

5.1–498

Translated from the Latin by Stephanie McCarter

Statius's Thebaid *(ca. 93 CE) steeps us in a world of fury and madness. Its main narrative recounts the "Seven against Thebes," the myth of the Theban civil war fought between Polynices and Eteocles, sons of the infamous king Oedipus and his mother, Jocasta. The twin brothers agree to alternate rule in Thebes annually, but when Eteocles refuses to hand over the throne to Polynices, the latter leads an alliance of seven warriors (including himself) and their armies against him. While these Seven march to Thebes, they are afflicted with terrible thirst as Bacchus makes all the water dry up. At Nemea, they encounter a woman who leads them to a stream that still flows. The woman, it turns out, is Hypsipyle, who now is enslaved by Lycurgus, the Nemean king. Statius hands over narration to Hypsipyle for much of Book Five, letting her recount the women's massacre of the Lemnian men and the Argonauts' visit to the island. In many ways, Hypsipyle is a figure of piety and devotion that contrasts with the epic's many male characters who succumb to rage and slaughter. She is a viewer of violence rather than a direct participant in it. On the other hand, it is clear that, as in Apollonius's* Argonautica, *she carefully crafts her narration to present the best possible version of herself and her actions.*

The squadrons slaked their thirst, then left the banks,
the river's depths laid waste, its flow contracted.
Fiercer, the warhorse strides the plain. In joy,
the soldier packs the field. Strength, daring, menace,
and vows return, as if they'd drained war's fire   5
in draughts of blood, priming their minds for battle.
The troops, re-lined in strictly ordered ranks,
each in his former post behind his chieftain,
are told to march again. They drive up dust
that swells the earth as forests flash with weapons—   10
like loud flocks[1] that take refuge in warm Egypt
across the sea, then leave the Nile when brutal
winter abates. With fleeing peals they fly,
a shade on sea and fields. High heaven echoes.
North winds and rain now please them as they swim   15
in melted streams and summer on bare Haemus.[2]

Ringed by his noble peers, the chief Adrastus,[3]
standing by chance beneath an ancient ash,
leans on a spear held out by Polynices
and says, "Stranger, what glory you have won,   20
that countless troops, by fate, now owe you praise
that even heaven's ruler would not spurn.
Come, as we swiftly leave these streams, tell us
your home, your land, beneath what stars you breathe.
Tell us your father, for the gods are with you,   25
though Fortune has withdrawn. Your looks show noble
blood, and your stricken face inspires awe.
The Lemnian groaned. She paused for modest tears,
then spoke: "You bid me, ruler, to reopen
deep wounds: Furies and Lemnos, weapons brought   30
to narrow beds, males struck by shameful swords.
Behold! The crime returns, the rage that chills
my heart. Poor women brought to madness! Night!
Father! I'm she (your hostess need not shame you,
leaders)—I'm she, the only one who saved   35
and hid her father. Why weave lengthy preludes?
Arms call you too. Great plans are in your heart.

I'll say just this: I'm famous Thoas' daughter,
Hypsipyle, the captive slave of your Lycurgus."

This roused their interest—she seemed greater, noble,   40
equal to such a task. All yearned to know
her woes. Father Adrastus prods her first:
"Come, while we mobilize our broad front lines
(for Nemea does not suit wide-spreading forces,
veiled as it is with leaves and dense with shade),   45
reveal the crime, your fame, your people's groans,
how, driven from your realm, you labor here."

Wretches delight to speak of erstwhile sorrows.
She starts: "Aegean Nereus circles Lemnos,[4]
where Vulcan rests when tired of fiery Etna.[5]   50
Neighboring Athos drapes the land in massive
shadows. Its wooded outline shades the sea.
Across, the Thracians plow—the Thracian shores
that brought us death and crime. Our peopled land
bloomed, famed like Samos or resounding Delos,   55
the countless foam-flecked isles of the Aegean.
The gods resolved to raze our homes. Our minds
were guilty since we'd lit no fires for Venus,
built her no shrine. Heavenly hearts grieve too,
and Punishments, their squadron slow, sneak up.   60
She left her hundred shrines in ancient Paphos,[6]
her face and hair transformed. It's said she loosened
her nuptial sash and drove Idalia's birds[7]
far off. Some women claim the goddess, wielding
strange flames and greater weapons, flew at midnight   65
into their rooms with the infernal sisters.[8]
With tangled snakes she filled their homes' recesses,
their bridal thresholds with relentless dread,
pitiless toward her faithful husband's people.
At once, you tender Loves sped off from Lemnos.   70
Hymen grows hushed,[9] his torches turned. Desire
for lawful marriage beds grows cold. No nights
bring joys or sleep in an embrace. Fierce Hatred
and Rage and Discord sprawl across the cushions.

Our men desire to crush the haughty Thracians 75
on facing shores, to break that ruthless people
with war. Their homes and children wait across
the coast, yet they delight in Thracian cold,
the howling north, the crash of breaking torrents
when night is still at last, the battle done. 80
The mournful wives (carefree virginity
and youth protected me) weep night and day,
heartsick; they soothe themselves with conversation,
or gaze at ruthless Thrace across the sea.

"The noontime Sun loomed over high Olympus, 85
as if his steeds stood still. The clear sky thundered
four times, the caverns of the smoking god
vented their peaks four times, and the Aegean,
though windless, tossed and crashed into the shore.
Then suddenly Polyxo, ripe in years, 90
swept into awful rage, flies from her chamber,
a rare event. She's like a Theban Bacchant
seized by the raving god when called to rites
by Phrygian pipes and 'Euhan' heard on peaks.[10]
Like this, eyes open wide and pupils stained 95
with pulsing blood, she plagues the emptied city
with rabid cries. She pounds locked doors and thresholds,
calling a council. As she goes, her doomed
sons cling to her. No calmer, all the women
burst from their homes, urged to the citadel 100
of Pallas. Here, we crowd in disarray
until the crime's ringleader calls for silence,
sword drawn, and dares to speak as we surround her:

"'Widows of Lemnos, steel your hearts and banish
your sex! Spurred by the gods and rightful grief, 105
I'm primed to sanction drastic action. If
you're tired of keeping empty homes forever,
of foul neglect, though flush with youth, of barren
years passed in pain—I swear, I've found a way
(the gods won't fail us) to recover Venus. 110
Have strength to match your pain! Tell me: three winters

have now grown white. Who has had bridal bonds,
the bedroom's hidden praise? Whose spouse has warmed
her chest? Whose labors has Lucina witnessed?[11]
Whose prayers have swelled and kicked until their due date?   115
Even the birds and beasts have mating customs!
Indolent women! And yet one Greek father,[12]
pleased by his ruse, gave vengeful swords to virgins
to soak their bridegrooms' carefree sleep with blood?
Yet we are slow? To name a nearer feat,   120
take courage from the Thracian wife[13] whose hand
punished her husband as it fed him feasts.
Not free from crime nor care do I exhort you:
my house is full, my toil immense! These four,
their father's pride and joy, upon my lap—   125
though slowed by hugs and tears, I'll skewer them
together, blending brothers' wounds and gore,
then pile their father on them as they wheeze.
Who's bold enough to swear so many kills?'

"As she still spoke, sails gleamed upon the deep—   130
the Lemnian fleet! Polyxo, joyful, seized
this luck, resuming, 'Will we fail the gods
who summon us? A vengeful god, a god,
conveys them to our wrath and aids our task.
My dream was true—Venus stood by me, vivid,   135
sword drawn, no empty vision. "Why waste time?"
she asked me. "Cleanse your beds of hateful husbands!
I'll bring you other torches, greater bonds!"
She spoke, then laid this sword atop the blankets—
this sword, believe me! Heartsick women, plot   140
while there is time to act. Their firm arms churn
the sea, and Thracian brides perhaps come with them!'

"Her goads were sharp. Their loud shouts rolled star-high.
You'd think that Amazons made Scythia roar,
that crescent-shielded troops advanced, their father   145
thrilled[14] by their spears and shaking harsh war's gates.
No cries object. No clashing camps dispute,
as in the way of mobs. All rage as one.

All yearn as one to desolate their homes,
to cut the threads of young and old, to break   150
babes at the breast, to slash through every age.
Beside Minerva's height, a dark green grove
shadows the ground. Above it soars a peak,
and sunlight dwindles in the double darkness.
Here they swear oaths. You witness, Martial Enyo   155
and nether Ceres.[15] The Stygian goddesses
leave Acheron and come, uncalled. All round
mills Venus. Venus arms them, Venus riles them.
The blood was not by custom. Charops' wife
offered her son. The women gird themselves,   160
then split his startled chest with steel, their hands
an eager swarm. With his fresh blood they vow
sweet sin, his ghost aflutter round his mother.
What horror chilled my bones as I was watching!
How my complexion changed! Like this, a deer   165
hemmed in by bloody wolves, whose soft heart holds
no strength, her rapid legs her one small hope—
she speeds her flight, uncertain, every second
thinking she's caught. She hears the bites that miss her.

"The men have come. Their ships now strike the sand.   170
They vie to be the first to leap ashore.
Poor wretches, unsubdued by ghastly valor
in war with Thrace and by the sea's ill will!
They fill the holy shrines with smoke and drag
the promised flocks. All altar fires burn black.   175
No god unblemished breathes upon the entrails.

"Jove was late to cast down night from dewy
Olympus—as I think, he slowed the turning
sky with his tender care, though fate forbade him.
Never did sundown's twilight last so long.   180
Though late, the stars came to the world, reflected
by Paros, wooded Thasos, and the crowded
Cyclades. Only Lemnos hid behind
dense sky, beneath a shroud of gloomy clouds
and murky mist, unrecognized by sailors.   185

Stretched out at home or in dark, sacred groves,
the men feast lavishly and drain deep wine
from golden cups, idly recounting battles
near Strymon[16] or their sweaty toil on icy
Haemus or Rhodope. The wives recline   190
amid the wreathes and festive banquets, dressed
to kill. Venus had made their husbands tender
for one last night, a late and fleeting peace,
in vain, rousing doomed passion in the wretches.
Dances grew quiet. Feasts and wanton play   195
came to an end, and evening's murmurs faded.
Drenched in the darkness of his kinsman Death
and wet with Styx, Sleep clasps the ill-starred city
and pours deep ease from his ungentle horn—
just on the men. The wives and brides are restless   200
for sin. The Sisters, joyous,[17] hone fierce swords.

"They launch their crime, each heart ruled by a Fury.
Like this, Hyrcanian lionesses circle
the herds on Scythia's steppes when hunger stirs
at dawn and ravenous cubs demand their breasts.   205
Crime took a thousand forms, and I'm unsure
what deaths to tell. Bold Gorge towers over
Helymus, wreathed and on a pile of blankets,
the reek of wine increasing with his snores.
She parts his clothes to gaze upon his wounds,   210
but sad sleep leaves him as his death comes near.
Confused, eyes dull with slumber, he embraces
his foe, but just as quickly, as he holds her,
she stabs him from behind till iron pricks
her chest. Her crime is done. His face reclines   215
charmingly as he murmurs, quaking, looking
for Gorge, clinging to her worthless neck.
I'll not report the common deaths, though cruel,
but my own family's griefs. I saw you fall,
fair-headed Cydon and long-haired Crenaeus—   220
we shared a nurse, although our father had us
from different lines. Blood-stained Myrmidone
wounded brave Gyas, the betrothed I dreaded.

A barbarous mother stabbed her own Epopeus,
who played among the beds and wreaths. Lycaste,   225
disarmed, wept over Cydimus, her twin,
seeing a face like hers in his doomed body,
his blooming cheeks, the hair she'd bound with gold,
till her fierce mother, her own husband slain,
stood by her, threatening, handing her the sword.   230
As a wild beast tamed by a gentle trainer
is slow to strike, though often whipped and prodded,
and won't resume its ways, so she lies crumpled
atop him as his blood streams in her lap
and wipes his fresh wounds with her tattered hair.   235

"I saw Alcimede clutching her father's
still murmuring lopped head, sword barely bloodied.
My hair pricked up then truly. Horror chilled
my bones. That seemed my Thoas, my own dreadful
right hand! In shock, I sought my father's chamber.   240
He was awake, for what great ruler sleeps?
The house was far from town, and yet he pondered
the din, the murmurs of the night, the noisy
quiet. He quaked as I revealed their crime,
their grief, their nerve: 'No force can stop their rage.   245
Follow, poor man! If we delay, they'll strike,
and you might fall with me.' Moved by my words,
he rose from bed. Veiled in dark mist, we traveled
the emptied city's backroads. Everywhere
we saw the night's great piles of dead, all those   250
the cruel evening strewed in sacred groves.
Here faces pressed to couches, hilts protruding
from open chests, huge broken spearshafts, corpses
that donned sword-shredded clothes, overturned bowls,
and feasts afloat in gore could be observed,   255
and wine that refilled cups, cascading like
a river, mixed with blood from severed throats.
Here, young were heaped; there, old—a group no weapons
should harm. Atop their groaning fathers' faces
lay half-dead boys upon life's threshold, gasping   260
their quaking souls out. Lapith feasts on chilly

Ossa[18] are no more ruthless when strong wine
has warmed the Cloud-Born—faces pale with wrath,
they flip the tables and arise for battle.

"Then for the first time, as we quaked, Thyoneus   265
appeared to us,[19] bringing his son support
at last. He blazed with light as if from nowhere.
I recognized him, though his temples were
unwreathed, his hair undecked with golden grapes.
Gloomy, and weeping unbecomingly,   270
he spoke: 'While fates permitted, I kept Lemnos
mighty for you, my son, and feared by foreign
nations. I never shirked this righteous task.
The dismal Fates have cut their cruel threads.
I've poured out many words and tears in vain   275
while supplicating Jove, but none can stop
this grief. He grants his child this impious honor.
Hasten your flight! And you, my worthy grandchild,
virgin, direct him where the double wall
leads shoreward. At that gate, where all looks calm,   280
stands Venus—deadly, armed, and stoking rage.
(Where did the goddess get such strength, such martial
spirit?) Entrust your father to the deep,
and I will tend your cares.' He spoke, then vanished
into the air. Since shadows dimmed our sight,   285
he kindly lit the way with beaming flame.
This sign I follow, then entrust my father,
shut in a skiff, to sea-gods and to winds,
to the Aegean that rings the Cyclades.
Our shared tears flow till Lucifer drives off[20]   290
the eastern stars. Then on the crashing shore
I turn, afraid and scarcely trusting Bacchus.
My feet speed forward, my dismayed heart backward.
I cannot rest, but from each hill I gaze
upon the waves as winds swell up in heaven.   295

"Day rises, filled with shame. The Sun unveils
the sky but turns his rays from Lemnos, hiding
his headlong chariot with clouds. Night's rage

lays bare. In dread of this new light, they all,
though guilty all, feel sudden shame and bury   300
their impious crimes or burn them hastily.
Now sated, the Eumenides[21] and Venus
flee the seized town. The women realize
their daring, tear their hair, bathe eyes with tears.
An island full of fields, wealth, arms, and men,   305
famed for locale, enriched with Thracian triumph,
lost everyone—not by a sea attack
or foe or hostile sky. It was bereft,
split from the world. No men plow fields or waves.
Houses grow quiet. Blood is deep, all things   310
smeared red with curdled gore. In the great walls,
we are alone as fierce ghosts moan on rooftops.
Deep in the house I too construct a pyre
with mounting flames and pile it with my father's
scepter and arms and well-known kingly garb.   315
I stand there sorrowful, hair loose, sword bloodied,
and wail to hide the fraud and empty tomb.
In fear, I pray that this not curse my father
but scatter any fears that doubt his death.
My false crime was believed, and for my service   320
I won my father's city, realm, and scepter—
a punishment! Hard-pressed, could I refuse?
Yielding, I often called the gods to witness
my faith, my guiltless hands. Oh dreadful power!
My rule was weak, sad Lemnos leaderless.   325
Now more and more grief plagues their restless minds.
Groans echo as they come to loathe Polyxo.
They let themselves recall their crimes, raise altars
to ghosts, and swear upon the buried ash,
like quaking cows, shocked that their chief, the stable's   330
husband, who rules the groves, the horned race's
glory, lies crushed beneath his Libyan foe—
the herd goes maimed, disgraced. The field, the streams,
the silent orchards mourn for their lost king.

"But look! The Pelian ship![22] Its bronze prow cleaves   335
the waves, propelled by Argonauts, a stranger

on seas untouched. You'd think Ortygia moved,[23]
roots snapped, or that a broken peak surfed waves.
But when the surface stills and oars are raised,   340
a sweeter voice than ancient swans or the lyre
of Phoebus echoes from the stern. The seas
yield to the keel. As we learn later, Thracian
Orpheus leans[24] against the mast and sings
to make the rowers disregard their toil.   345
They sailed to Scythian Boreas and the mouth
of Pontus, blocked by Clashing Rocks.[25] We saw them
and, thinking Thrace attacked, rushed home in panic,
just like stampeding herds or fleeing birds.
Where are the Furies now? We mount the walls   350
that hug the port and shore, then from tall towers
we watch the water. Here the quaking women
haul rocks and lances and their men's sad armor
and bloodstained swords. They're not ashamed to wear
scale-covered breastplates or to helmet their   355
unbridled faces. Shocked by these bold troops,
Minerva blushed. Mars laughed on facing Haemus.
Then first did reckless madness leave their minds.
It seemed not that a ship at sea approached,
but the gods' justice, vengeance for their crimes.   360

"They were a Cretan dart-shot from the land,
when Jove amassed a raincloud, blue and bursting,
and stationed it atop the Greek ship's sails.
The water trembles. Day is robbed of sun
and dims into a darkness the same color   365
as waves. Winds strive to smash the hollow clouds,
to rend the deep. The wet earth reemerges
out of dark whirlpools. As the winds contend,
the whole sea swells. Its bowed back reaches heaven,
then breaks. The ship careens, momentum lost,   370
and sways, the Titan on its prow now sunken,
now in the sky. The strength of the heroic
demigods does no good. The frenzied mast
lashes the stern, and, leaning, weight unstable,
drags through the water. Oars strike chests, unhindered.   375

While the men toil, disdaining straits and winds,
we too, along the cliffs and from the ramparts,
cast wavering spears, weak-armed, at Telamon
and Peleus.[26] (What did our hands not dare?)
We even aimed our bows at Hercules!   380
As for the men toiling with war and water,
some brace the ship with shields, some bail the hold,
some fight, their bodies fumbling from the motion—
their strength is thrown off balance, ineffective.
Our spears keep flying, and their iron rain   385
vies with the storm. Burnt stakes and broken stones
and spears and flame-tipped arrows shower down
now on the sea, now on the ship. The covered
pine crashes as the hull's planks groan in echo.
Like this, Jove strikes Hyperborean fields   390
with snow, blanketing every kind of beast.
Birds, overtaken, fall. The grain lies flat
from piercing ice. Hills thunder, rivers rage.

"But when a cloud, twisted by Jove on high,
hurls lightning that lights up the mighty sailors,   395
our minds are petrified. Fear-slackened hands
drop their strange weapons. Hearts resume their sex.
We see the sons of Aeacus,[27] Ancaeus
threatening our walls, and Iphitus repelling
rocks with his lance. But most conspicuous   400
is Hercules, who strains the ship on one
side, then the other, yearning to dive in.
Yet Jason, still unknown to wretched me,
darts over benches, oars, men's trampled backs.
His voice and hand now spur great Meleager,   405
now Idas, Talaüs, Tyndareus' son,
dripping with spray, and Calaïs, who toils
inside his father's icy fog to tie
the sail onto the mast. Their oar-strikes shake
now sea, now walls, and yet the foamy surface   410
does not give way. Spears ricochet off towers.
The driver Tiphys wearies heavy waves
and the unhearing helm. His orders vary

as he directs, now left, now right, the prow
intent on pummeling ship-wrecking rocks,   415
till on the ship's bow Aeson's son raised up
boughs of Minervan olive worn by Mopsus
and sought a truce, although his crew held back
their comrade. Storming winds obscured his words.
The battle ceased, and wearied gales grew still.   420
Day looked once more from disarrayed Olympus.
The fifty duly moor the boat, then leap
down from its height, shaking the unknown shore,
tall grace of mighty fathers. Brows now calm,
their looks return, their faces free of rage   425
and wrath. Like this, the gods burst through a hidden
gate when they yearn for humbler feasts within
the sunkissed Ethiopians' homes and shores[28]—
streams and peaks yield, earth glories in their steps,
sky-bearing Atlas gets to catch his breath.   430

"Here we see Theseus, Marathon's proud savior;[29]
the Ismarian brothers, sons of Aquilo,[30]
each with bright wings that thrummed beside his
    temples;
Admetus, master of ungrudging Phoebus;[31]
Orpheus, not at all like rugged Thrace;   435
Calydon's heir befitting Nereus' son-in-law.[32]
The Spartan twins[33] confuse our eyes with error—
one wears a flaming cloak, as does the other,
each holds a spear, bare-shouldered. Both possess
smooth cheeks and hair that gleams with matching stars.   440
Young Hylas dares to march with Hercules,
but can't keep pace (not even if one runs
and one plods slowly); lifting Lerna's weapons,
he thrills to sweat beneath the mighty quiver.

"Venus returns. With stealthy flames, Love enters   445
the Lemnians' hard hearts. Queen Juno fixes
their thoughts upon the heroes' dress and armor,
marks of high birth. Doors one by one all vie
to welcome guests. Then for the first time fires

burn on the altars, dreadful cares forgotten. 450
Then feasts come, happy slumber, quiet nights,
and (willed by gods, I think) pleasing confessions.
You chiefs might ask what fate abates my blame—
I swear on my own people's ash and Furies:
I wed a stranger not through my own will 455
or crime[34]—as heaven knows!—though Jason's charm
does snare young virgins. Bloody Phasis has
its own laws. Colchis, you rouse different loves.[35]

"And now the stars, stripped of their ice, warm up
as days grow long. The speedy year returns. 460
Now come new offspring, births that answer prayers,
and unexpected nurslings' cries fill Lemnos.
I too bear twins, reminders of forced marriage,
and, made a mother by a heartless guest,
revive my father's name. I don't know what 465
befell them once I left. If fated, they're
now twenty—if, as asked, Lycaste raised them.

"The sea's rage wanes as calm winds beckon sails.
The ship disdains delay and quiet bays,
straining the mooring ropes. The Argonauts 470
prepare to flee, and Jason calls his men—
that beast! I wish he'd sailed straight past my shores!
His sons and sworn faith do not matter to him.
No doubt, he has won fame from distant realms
and fetched the fleece of ocean-going Phrixus. 475
The day to sail was set, and Tiphys augured
the weather. Setting Phoebus' bed blushed.
Again we grieve, again have one last night.
At daybreak, Jason mounts the ship and orders
them to depart. The first stroke pounds the sea. 480
From cliffs and peaks we trail them with our gaze,
as they cut through the wide main's foaming back,
until the light tires out our roving eyes,
seeming to weave the waves and sky together,
to press the deep against the heavens' edge. 485

"A rumor docks that Thoas crossed the waves
and rules his brother's Chios—I was guiltless
and burned an empty pyre. The impious throng
roars, stung by guilty goads, demanding crime,
and secret whispers also swiftly spread: 490
'Only she's pious, while we bask in death?
Was this not god and fate? Why rule us sinners?'
Such words scare me to death. Dire payback comes,
and rule is no avail. Alone, in secret,
leaving those deadly walls, I trace the shore   495
known by my father's flight—no Bacchus now.
A band of pirates snatched me (I kept silent!)
and brought me as a slave here to your shores."

DIDO, QUEEN OF CARTHAGE

Vergil's *Aeneid* (19 BCE) recounts the flight of Aeneas from the conquered city of Troy, his quest across the Mediterranean, and the war he must fight once he arrives in Italy before he can found what one day will become the Roman Empire. One chief obstacle comes in the figure of Dido, herself a refugee from the Phoenician city of Tyre and the founder of Carthage in North Africa. Aeneas lingers in Carthage for a year with Dido; she clearly considers them to be married, but it is unclear whether Aeneas himself believes the same. It is thus erotic passion that is the ultimate threat to the labor of founding Rome, a labor that has been handed to Aeneas by fate. His stay with Dido seems to be an exercise of his own free choice, yet he ultimately must forswear this relationship in obedience to the will of the gods.

For Dido too love is a destructive force, both for herself and for her city. Vergil's portrait of her is deeply ambivalent—she is at once a figure of immense sympathy and of intense fury. On the one hand, her struggles mirror Aeneas's own, and from them she has learned to show hospitality and kindness. She is moreover a victim of the gods, who seem little concerned with how their schemes will affect her. On the other hand, she is in many ways a doublet of Cleopatra, herself a North African queen and a figure vilified in Roman propaganda. Dido's rage leads her to curse the Carthaginians and Romans to perpetual enmity, a curse that gives a mythological cause for the historical series of wars fought between the two peoples, the Punic Wars, which ended in Carthage being razed to the ground in 146 BCE.

VERGIL, *AENEID*

(SELECTIONS)

Translated from the Latin by
Robert Fagles

*In the first half of Book One, Vergil introduces us to Aeneas
and to the gods helping and hindering him. At the book's
start, Juno, Aeneas's foremost divine adversary, causes a
storm to blow his ships off course, driving him to the shores
of Carthage. The goddess Venus, his mother, then goes to
Jupiter to receive his assurances that Aeneas's destiny to
become the founder of Rome remains unchanged. After Jupiter sends Mercury down to make Dido receptive to welcoming Aeneas, Venus speeds to Carthage herself to guide
her son, appearing to him in disguise while he is hunting.*

BOOK ONE (1.314–756)[1]

Suddenly, in the heart of the woods, his mother
crossed his path. She looked like a young girl,   380
a Spartan girl decked out in dress and gear
or Thracian Harpalyce[2] tiring out her mares,
outracing the Hebrus River's rapid tides.
Hung from a shoulder, a bow that fit her grip,
a huntress for all the world, she'd let her curls   385
go streaming free in the wind, her knees were bare,
her flowing skirts hitched up with a tight knot.

    She speaks out first: "You there, young soldiers,
did you by any chance see one of my sisters?

Which way did she go? Roaming the woods,   390
a quiver slung from her belt,
wearing a spotted lynx-skin, or in full cry,
hot on the track of some great frothing boar?"

    So Venus asked and the son of Venus answered:
"Not one of your sisters have I seen or heard . . .   395
but how should I greet a young girl like you?
Your face, your features—hardly a mortal's looks
and the tone of your voice is hardly human either.
Oh a goddess, without a doubt! What, are you
Apollo's sister? Or one of the breed of Nymphs?   400
Be kind, whoever you are, relieve our troubled hearts.
Under what skies and onto what coasts of the world
have we been driven? Tell us, please. Castaways,
we know nothing, not the people, not the place—
lost, hurled here by the gales and heavy seas.   405
Many a victim will fall before your altars,
we'll slaughter them for you!"
                                        But Venus replied:
"Now there's an honor I really don't deserve.
It's just the style for Tyrian girls to sport
a quiver and high-laced hunting boots[3] in crimson.   410
What you see is a Punic kingdom, people of Tyre
and Agenor's town, but the border's held by Libyans
hard to break in war. Phoenician Dido is in command,
she sailed from Tyre, in flight from her own brother.
Oh it's a long tale of crime, long, twisting, dark,   415
but I'll try to trace the high points in their order . . .

    "Dido was married to Sychaeus, the richest man in Tyre,
and she, poor girl, was consumed with love for him.
Her father gave her away, wed for the first time,
a virgin still, and these her first solemn rites.   420
But her brother held power in Tyre—Pygmalion,
a monster, the vilest man alive.
A murderous feud broke out between both men.
Pygmalion, catching Sychaeus off guard at the altar,
slaughtered him in blood. That unholy man, so blind   425

in his lust for gold he ran him through with a sword,
then hid the crime for months, deaf to his sister's love,
her heartbreak. Still he mocked her with wicked lies,
with empty hopes. But she had a dream one night.
The true ghost of her husband, not yet buried,   430
came and lifting his face—ashen, awesome in death—
showed her the cruel altar, the wounds that pierced his chest
and exposed the secret horror that lurked within the house.
He urged her on: 'Take flight from our homeland, quick!'
And then he revealed an unknown ancient treasure,   435
an untold weight of silver and gold, a comrade
to speed her on her way.
                              "Driven by all this,
Dido plans her escape, collects her followers
fired by savage hate of the tyrant or bitter fear.
They seize some galleys set to sail, load them with gold—   440
the wealth Pygmalion craved—and they bear it overseas
and a woman leads them all. Reaching this haven here,
where now you will see the steep ramparts rising,
the new city of Carthage—the Tyrians purchased land as
large as a bull's-hide could enclose but cut in strips for size   445
and called it Byrsa, the Hide,⁴ for the spread they'd bought.
But you, who are you? What shores do you come from?
Where are you headed now?"
                              He answered her questions,
drawing a labored sigh from deep within his chest:
"Goddess, if I'd retrace our story to its start,   450
if you had time to hear the saga of our ordeals,
before I finished the Evening Star would close
the gates of Olympus, put the day to sleep . . .
From old Troy we come—Troy it's called, perhaps
you've heard the name—sailing over the world's seas   455
until, by chance, some whim of the winds, some tempest
drove us onto Libyan shores. I am Aeneas, duty-bound.
I carry aboard my ships the gods of house and home
we seized from enemy hands. My fame goes past the skies.
I seek my homeland—Italy—born as I am from highest
    Jove.   460
I launched out on the Phrygian sea with twenty ships,

my goddess mother marking the way, and followed hard
on the course the Fates had charted. A mere seven,
battered by wind and wave, survived the worst.
I myself am a stranger, utterly at a loss,   465
trekking over this wild Libyan wasteland,
forced from Europe, Asia too, an exile—"

    Venus could bear no more of his laments
and broke in on his tale of endless hardship:
"Whoever you are, I scarcely think the Powers hate you: 470
you enjoy the breath of life, you've reached a Tyrian city.
So off you go now. Take this path to the queen's gates.
I have good news. Your friends are restored to you,
your fleet's reclaimed. The winds swerved from the North
and drove them safe to port. True, unless my parents   475
taught me to read the flight of birds for nothing.
Look at those dozen swans triumphant in formation!
The eagle of Jove had just swooped down on them all
from heaven's heights and scattered them into open sky,
but now you can see them flying trim in their long ranks,   480
landing or looking down where their friends have landed—
home, cavorting on ruffling wings and wheeling round
the sky in convoy, trumpeting in their glory.
So homeward bound, your ships and hardy shipmates
anchor in port now or approach the harbor's mouth,   485
full sail ahead. Now off you go, move on,
wherever the path leads you, steer your steps."
                                                      At that,
as she turned away her neck shone with a rosy glow,
her mane of hair gave off an ambrosial fragrance,
her skirt flowed loose, rippling down to her feet   490
and her stride alone revealed her as a goddess.
He knew her at once—his mother—
and called after her now as she sped away:
"Why, you too, cruel as the rest? So often
you ridicule your son with your disguises!   495
Why can't we clasp hands, embrace each other,
exchange some words, speak out, and tell the truth?"

Reproving her so, he makes his way toward
town but Venus screens the travelers off with a dense mist,
pouring round them a cloak of clouds with all her power,   500
so no one could see them, no one reach and hold them,
cause them to linger now or ask why they had come.
But she herself, lifting into the air, wings her way
toward Paphos, racing with joy to reach her home again
where her temples stand and a hundred altars steam   505
with Arabian incense, redolent with the scent
of fresh-cut wreaths.
                              Meanwhile the two men
are hurrying on their way as the path leads,
now climbing a steep hill arching over the city,
looking down on the facing walls and high towers.   510
Aeneas marvels at its mass—once a cluster of huts—
he marvels at gates and bustling hum and cobbled streets.
The Tyrians press on with the work, some aligning the walls,
struggling to raise the citadel, trundling stones up slopes;
some picking the building sites and plowing out their
      boundaries,   515
others drafting laws, electing judges, a senate held in awe.
Here they're dredging a harbor, there they lay foundations
deep for a theater, quarrying out of rock great columns
to form a fitting scene for stages still to come.
As hard at their tasks as bees in early summer,   520
that work the blooming meadows under the sun,
they escort a new brood out, young adults now,
or press the oozing honey into the combs, the nectar
brimming the bulging cells, or gather up the plunder
workers haul back in, or close ranks like an army,   525
driving the drones, that lazy crew, from home.
The hive seethes with life, exhaling the scent
of honey sweet with thyme.
                              "How lucky they are,"
Aeneas cries, gazing up at the city's heights,
"their walls are rising now!" And on he goes,   530
cloaked in cloud—remarkable—right in their midst
he blends in with the crowds, and no one sees him.

Now deep in the heart of Carthage stood a grove,
lavish with shade, where the Tyrians, making landfall,
still shaken by wind and breakers, first unearthed that sign: 535
Queen Juno had led their way to the fiery stallion's head
that signaled power in war and ease in life for ages.
Here Dido of Tyre was building Juno a mighty temple,
rich with gifts and the goddess' aura of power.
Bronze the threshold crowning a flight of stairs,   540
the doorposts sheathed in bronze, and the bronze doors
groaned deep on their hinges.
                                      Here in this grove
a strange sight met his eyes and calmed his fears
for the first time. Here, for the first time,
Aeneas dared to hope he had found some haven,   545
for all his hard straits, to trust in better days.
For awaiting the queen, beneath the great temple now,
exploring its features[5] one by one, amazed at it all,
the city's splendor, the work of rival workers' hands
and the vast scale of their labors—all at once he sees,   550
spread out from first to last, the battles fought at Troy,
the fame of the Trojan War now known throughout the
     world,
Atreus' sons and Priam—Achilles, savage to both at once.
Aeneas came to a halt and wept, and "Oh, Achates,"
he cried, "is there anywhere, any place on earth   555
not filled with our ordeals? There's Priam, look!
Even here, merit will have its true reward . . .
even here, the world is a world of tears
and the burdens of mortality touch the heart.
Dismiss your fears. Trust me, this fame of ours   560
will offer us some haven."
                              So Aeneas says,
feeding his spirit on empty, lifeless pictures,
groaning low, the tears rivering down his face
as he sees once more the fighters circling Troy.
Here Greeks in flight, routed by Troy's young ranks,   565
there Trojans routed by plumed Achilles in his chariot.
Just in range are the snow-white canvas tents of Rhesus—

he knows them at once, and sobs—Rhesus' men betrayed[6]
in their first slumber, droves of them slaughtered
by Diomedes splattered with their blood, lashing   570
back to the Greek camp their high-strung teams
before they could ever savor the grass of Troy
or drink at Xanthus' banks.
                              Next Aeneas sees
Troilus in flight,[7] his weapons flung aside,
unlucky boy, no match for Achilles' onslaught—   575
horses haul him on, tangled behind an empty war-car,
flat on his back, clinging still to the reins, his neck
and hair dragging along the ground, the butt of his javelin
scrawling zigzags in the dust.
                              And here the Trojan women[8]
are moving toward the temple of Pallas, their deadly foe,   580
their hair unbound as they bear the robe, their offering,
suppliants grieving, palms beating their breasts
but Pallas turns away, staring at the ground.
                              And Hector—
three times Achilles has hauled him round the walls of Troy
and now he's selling his lifeless body off for gold.[9]   585
Aeneas gives a groan, heaving up from his depths,
he sees the plundered armor, the car, the corpse
of his great friend, and Priam reaching out
with helpless hands . . .
                              He even sees himself
swept up in the melee, clashing with Greek captains,   590
sees the troops of the Dawn and swarthy Memnon's arms.
And Penthesilea leading her Amazons bearing half-moon
    shields—
she blazes with battle fury out in front of her army,
cinching a golden breastband under her bared breast,
a girl, a warrior queen who dares to battle men.
                              And now   595
as Trojan Aeneas, gazing in awe at all the scenes of Troy,
stood there, spellbound, eyes fixed on the war alone,
the queen aglow with beauty approached the temple,
Dido, with massed escorts marching in her wake.

Like Diana urging her dancing troupes along   600
the Eurotas' banks or up Mount Cynthus' ridge
as a thousand mountain-nymphs crowd in behind her,
left and right—with quiver slung from her shoulder,
taller than any other goddess as she goes striding on
and silent Latona[10] thrills with joy too deep for words.   605
Like Dido now, striding triumphant among her people,
spurring on the work of their kingdom still to come.
And then by Juno's doors beneath the vaulted dome,
flanked by an honor guard beside her lofty seat,
the queen assumed her throne. Here as she handed down   610
decrees and laws to her people, sharing labors fairly,
some by lot, some with her sense of justice, Aeneas
suddenly sees his men approaching through the crowds,
Antheus, Sergestus, gallant Cloanthus, other Trojans
the black gales had battered over the seas   615
and swept to far-flung coasts.

                                        Aeneas, Achates,
both were amazed, both struck with joy and fear.
They yearn to grasp their companions' hands in haste
but both men are unnerved by the mystery of it all.
So, cloaked in folds of mist, they hide their feelings,   620
waiting, hoping to see what luck their friends have found.
Where have they left their ships, what coast? Why have
    they come?
These picked men, still marching in from the whole armada,
pressing toward the temple amid the rising din
to plead for some good will.

                                    Once they had entered,   625
allowed to appeal before the queen—the eldest,
Prince Ilioneus, calm, composed, spoke out:
"Your majesty, empowered by Jove to found
your new city here and curb rebellious tribes
with your sense of justice—we poor Trojans,   630
castaways, tossed by storms over all the seas,
we beg you: keep the cursed fire off our ships!
Pity us, god-fearing men! Look on us kindly,
see the state we are in. We have not come

to put your Libyan gods and homes to the sword,   635
loot them and haul our plunder toward the beach.
No, such pride, such violence has no place
in the hearts of beaten men.
                              "There is a country—
the Greeks called it Hesperia, Land of the West,
an ancient land, mighty in war and rich in soil.   640
Oenotrians settled it; now we hear their descendants
call their kingdom Italy, after their leader, Italus.
Italy-bound we were when, surging with sudden breakers
stormy Orion drove us against blind shoals and from the
    South
came vicious gales to scatter us, whelmed by the sea,   645
across the murderous surf and rocky barrier reefs.
We few escaped and floated toward your coast.
What kind of men are these? What land is this,
that you can tolerate such barbaric ways?
We are denied the sailor's right to shore—   650
attacked, forbidden even a footing on your beach.
If you have no use for humankind and mortal armor,
at least respect the gods. They know right from wrong.
They don't forget.
                   "We once had a king, Aeneas . . .
none more just, none more devoted to duty, none   655
more brave in arms. If Fate has saved that man,
if he still draws strength from the air we breathe,
if he's not laid low, not yet with the heartless shades,
fear not, nor will you once regret the first step
you take to compete with him in kindness.   660
We have cities too, in the land of Sicily,
arms and a king, Acestes, born of Trojan blood.
Permit us to haul our storm-racked ships ashore,
trim new oars, hew timbers out of your woods, so that,
if we are fated to sail for Italy—king and crews restored—   665
to Italy, to Latium we will sail with buoyant hearts.
But if we have lost our haven there, if Libyan waters
hold you now, my captain, best of the men of Troy,
and all our hopes for Iulus have been dashed,

at least we can cross back over Sicilian seas,   670
the straits we came from, homes ready and waiting,
and seek out great Acestes for our king."

    So Ilioneus closed. And with one accord
the Trojans murmured Yes.
                      Her eyes lowered,
Dido replies with a few choice words of welcome: 675
"Cast fear to the winds, Trojans, free your minds.
Our kingdom is new. Our hard straits have forced me
to set defenses, station guards along our far frontiers.
Who has not heard of Aeneas' people, his city, Troy,
her men, her heroes, the flames of that horrendous war?   680
We are not so dull of mind, we Carthaginians here.
When he yokes his team, the Sun shines down on us as
    well.
Whatever you choose, great Hesperia—Saturn's fields—
or the shores of Eryx with Acestes as your king,
I will provide safe passage, escorts, and support   685
to speed you on your way. Or would you rather
settle here in my realm on equal terms with me?
This city I build—it's yours. Haul ships to shore.
Trojans, Tyrians: they will be all the same to me.
If only the storm that drove you drove your king   690
and Aeneas were here now! Indeed, I'll send out
trusty men to scour the coast of Libya far and wide.
Perhaps he's shipwrecked, lost in woods or towns."

    Spirits lifting at Dido's welcome, brave Achates
and captain Aeneas had long chafed to break free   695
of the mist, and now Achates spurs Aeneas on:
"Son of Venus, what feelings are rising in you now?
You see the coast is clear, our ships and friends restored.
Just one is lost. We saw him drown at sea ourselves.
All else is just as your mother promised."   700

    He'd barely ended when all at once the mist
around them parted, melting into the open air,
and there Aeneas stood, clear in the light of day,

his head, his shoulders, the man was like a god.
His own mother had breathed her beauty on her son,   705
a gloss on his flowing hair, and the ruddy glow of youth,
and radiant joy shone in his eyes. His beauty fine
as a craftsman's hand can add to ivory, or aglow
as silver or Parian marble ringed in glinting gold.

 Suddenly, surprising all, he tells the queen: 710
"Here I am before you, the man you are looking for.
Aeneas the Trojan, plucked from Libya's heavy seas.
You alone have pitied the long ordeals of Troy—
 unspeakable—
and here you would share your city and your home with us,
this remnant left by the Greeks. We who have drunk deep   715
of each and every disaster land and sea can offer.
Stripped of everything, now it's past our power
to reward you gift for gift, Dido, theirs as well,
whoever may survive of the Dardan people[11] still,
strewn over the wide world now. But may the gods,   720
if there are Powers who still respect the good and true,
if justice still exists on the face of the earth,
may they and their own sense of right and wrong
bring you your just rewards.
What age has been so blest to give you birth?   725
What noble parents produced so fine a daughter?
So long as rivers run to the sea, so long as shadows
travel the mountain slopes and the stars range the skies,
your honor, your name, your praise will live forever,
whatever lands may call me to their shores."
        With that,   730
he extends his right hand toward his friend Ilioneus,
greeting Serestus with his left, and then the others,
gallant Gyas, gallant Cloanthus.
       Tyrian Dido marveled,
first at the sight of him, next at all he'd suffered,
then she said aloud: "Born of a goddess, even so   735
what destiny hunts you down through such ordeals?
What violence lands you on this frightful coast?
Are you that Aeneas whom loving Venus bore

to Dardan Anchises on the Simois' banks at Troy?
Well I remember ... Teucer came to Sidon once,[12]   740
banished from native ground, searching for new realms,
and my father Belus helped him. Belus had sacked Cyprus,
plundered that rich island, ruled with a victor's hand.
From that day on I have known of Troy's disaster,
known your name, and all the kings of Greece.   745
Teucer, your enemy, often sang Troy's praises,
claiming his own descent from Teucer's ancient stock.
So come, young soldiers, welcome to our house.
My destiny, harrying me with trials hard as yours,
led me as well, at last, to anchor in this land.   750
Schooled in suffering, now I learn to comfort
those who suffer too."
                          With that greeting
she leads Aeneas into the royal halls, announcing
offerings in the gods' high temples as she goes.
Not forgetting to send his shipmates on the beaches   755
twenty bulls and a hundred huge, bristling razorbacks
and a hundred fatted lambs together with their mothers:
gifts to make this day a day of joy.
                                      Within the palace
all is decked with adornments, lavish, regal splendor.
In the central hall they are setting out a banquet,   760
draping the gorgeous purple, intricately worked,
heaping the board with grand displays of silver
and gold engraved with her fathers' valiant deeds,
a long, unending series of captains and commands,
traced through a line of heroes since her country's birth.   765

    Aeneas—a father's love would give the man no rest—
quickly sends Achates down to the ships to take
the news to Ascanius, bring him back to Carthage.
All his paternal care is focused on his son.
He tells Achates to fetch some gifts as well,   770
plucked from the ruins of Troy: a gown stiff
with figures stitched in gold, and a woven veil
with yellow sprays of acanthus round the border.
Helen's glory, gifts she carried out of Mycenae,

fleeing Argos for Troy to seal her wicked marriage—   775
the marvelous handiwork of Helen's mother, Leda.
Aeneas adds the scepter Ilione used to bear,
the eldest daughter of Priam; a necklace too,
strung with pearls, and a crown of double bands,
one studded with gems, the other, gold. Achates,   780
following orders, hurries toward the ships.

But now Venus is mulling over some new schemes,
new intrigues. Altered in face and figure, Cupid
would go in place of the captivating Ascanius,
using his gifts to fire the queen to madness,   785
weaving a lover's ardor through her bones.
No doubt Venus fears that treacherous house
and the Tyrians' forked tongues,
and brutal Juno inflames her anguish too
and her cares keep coming back as night draws on.   790
So Venus makes an appeal to Love, her winged son:
"You, my son, are my strength, my greatest power—
you alone, my son, can scoff at the lightning bolts
the high and mighty Father hurled against Typhoeus.[13]
Help me, I beg you. I need all your immortal force.   795
Your brother Aeneas is tossed round every coast on earth,
thanks to Juno's ruthless hatred, as you well know,
and time and again you've grieved to see my grief.
But now Phoenician Dido has him in her clutches,
holding him back with smooth, seductive words,   800
and I fear the outcome of Juno's welcome here . . .
She won't sit tight while Fate is turning on its hinge.
So I plan to forestall her with ruses of my own
and besiege the queen with flames,
and no goddess will change her mood—she's mine,   805
my ally-in-arms in my great love for Aeneas.

"Now how can you go about this? Hear my plan.
His dear father has just sent for the young prince—
he means the world to me—and he's bound for Carthage now,
bearing presents saved from the sea, the flames of Troy.   810
I'll lull him into a deep sleep and hide him far away

on Cythera's heights or high Idalium, my shrines,
so he cannot learn of my trap or spring it open
while it's being set. And you with your cunning,
forge his appearance—just one night, no more—put on   815
the familiar features of the boy, boy that you are,
so when the wine flows free at the royal board
and Dido, lost in joy, cradles you in her lap,
caressing, kissing you gently, you can breathe
your secret fire into her, poison the queen   820
and she will never know."
                              Cupid leaps at once
to his loving mother's orders. Shedding his wings
he masquerades as Iulus, prancing with his stride.
But now Venus distills a deep, soothing sleep
into Iulus' limbs, and warming him in her breast   825
the goddess spirits him off to her high Idalian grove
where beds of marjoram breathe and embrace him with
    aromatic
flowers and rustling shade.
                              Now Cupid is on the move,
under her orders, bringing the Tyrians royal gifts,
his spirits high as Achates leads him on.   830
Arriving, he finds the queen already poised
on a golden throne beneath the sumptuous hangings,
commanding the very center of her palace. Now Aeneas,
the good captain, enters, then the Trojan soldiers,
taking their seats on couches draped in purple.   835
Servants pour them water to rinse their hands,
quickly serving them bread from baskets, spreading
their laps with linens, napkins clipped and smooth.
In the kitchens are fifty serving-maids assigned
to lay out foods in a long line, course by course,   840
and honor the household gods by building fires high.
A hundred other maids and a hundred men, all matched
    in age,
are spreading the feast on trestles, setting out the cups.
And Tyrians join them, bustling through the doors,
filling the hall with joy, to take invited seats   845

on brocaded couches. They admire Aeneas' gifts,
admire Iulus now—the glowing face of the god
and the god's dissembling words—and Helen's gown
and the veil adorned with a yellow acanthus border.

   But above all, tragic Dido, doomed to a plague   850
about to strike, cannot feast her eyes enough,
thrilled both by the boy and gifts he brings
and the more she looks the more the fire grows.
But once he's embraced Aeneas, clung to his neck
to sate the deep love of his father, deluded father,   855
Cupid makes for the queen. Her gaze, her whole heart
is riveted on him now, and at times she even warms him
snugly in her breast, for how can she know, poor Dido,
what a mighty god is sinking into her, to her grief?
But he, recalling the wishes of his mother Venus,   860
blots out the memory of Sychaeus bit by bit,
trying to seize with a fresh, living love
a heart at rest for long—long numb to passion.
                                      Then,
with the first lull in the feast, the tables cleared away,
they set out massive bowls and crown the wine with
    wreaths.   865
A vast din swells in the palace, voices reverberating
through the echoing halls. They light the lamps,
hung from the coffered ceilings sheathed in gilt,
and blazing torches burn the night away.
The queen calls for a heavy golden bowl,   870
studded with jewels and brimmed with unmixed wine,
the bowl that Belus and all of Belus' sons had brimmed,
and the hall falls hushed as Dido lifts a prayer:
"Jupiter, you, they say, are the god who grants
the laws of host and guest. May this day be one   875
of joy for Tyrians here and exiles come from Troy,
a day our sons will long remember. Bacchus,
giver of bliss, and Juno, generous Juno,
bless us now. And come, my people, celebrate
with all good will this feast that makes us one!"   880

With that prayer, she poured a libation to the gods,
tipping wine on the board, and tipping it, she was first
to take the bowl, brushing it lightly with her lips,
then gave it to Bitias—laughing, goading him on
and he took the plunge, draining the foaming bowl,   885
drenching himself in its brimming, overflowing gold,
and the other princes drank in turn. Then Iopas,
long-haired bard, strikes up his golden lyre
resounding through the halls. Giant Atlas
had been his teacher once, and now he sings   890
the wandering moon[14] and laboring sun eclipsed,
the roots of the human race and the wild beasts,
the source of storms and the lightning bolts on high,
Arcturus, the rainy Hyades and the Great and Little Bears,
and why the winter suns so rush to bathe themselves in
     the sea   895
and what slows down the nights to a long lingering crawl . . .
And time and again the Tyrians burst into applause
and the Trojans took their lead. So Dido, doomed,
was lengthening out the night by trading tales
as she drank long draughts of love—asking Aeneas   900
question on question, now about Priam, now Hector,
what armor Memnon, son of the Morning, wore at Troy,
how swift were the horses of Diomedes? How strong was
     Achilles?

     "Wait, come, my guest," she urges, "tell us your own story,
start to finish—the ambush laid by the Greeks, the pain   905
your people suffered, the wanderings you have
     faced.
For now is the seventh summer that has borne you
wandering all the lands and seas on earth."

> Books Two and Three involve a lengthy flashback in which
> Aeneas narrates the fall of Troy and his subsequent travels
> around the Mediterranean. These books make it very clear
> that Aeneas is bound by fate for Italy, a fact that Dido
> seems not to heed, whether because she fails to "read" Ae-

neas's tales correctly or because she is too assailed by love
to do so. The story of Dido and Aeneas resumes in Book
Four.

BOOK FOUR (ALL)

But the queen—too long she has suffered the pain of love,
hour by hour nursing the wound with her lifeblood,
consumed by the fire buried in her heart.
The man's courage, the sheer pride of his line,
they all come pressing home to her, over and over.   5
His looks, his words, they pierce her heart and cling—
no peace, no rest for her body, love will give her none.

A new day's dawn was moving over the earth, Aurora's
    torch
cleansing the sky, burning away the dank shade of night
as the restless queen, beside herself, confides now   10
to the sister of her soul: "Dear Anna, the dreams
that haunt my quaking heart! Who is this stranger
just arrived to lodge in our house—our guest?
How noble his face, his courage, and what a soldier!
I'm sure—I know it's true—the man is born of the gods.   15
Fear exposes the lowborn man at once. But, oh, how tossed
he's been by the blows of fate. What a tale he's told,
what a bitter bowl of war he's drunk to the dregs.
If my heart had not been fixed, dead set against
embracing another man in the bonds of marriage—   20
ever since my first love deceived me, cheated me
by his death—if I were not as sick as I am
of the bridal bed and torch, this, perhaps,
is my one lapse that might have brought me down.
I confess it, Anna, yes. Ever since my Sychaeus,   25
my poor husband met his fate, and my own brother
shed his blood and stained our household gods,
this is the only man who's roused me deeply,
swayed my wavering heart . . .

The signs of the old flame, I know them well.   30
I pray that the earth gape deep enough to take me down
or the almighty Father blast me with one bolt to the
    shades,
the pale, glimmering shades in hell, the pit of night,
before I dishonor you, my conscience, break your laws.
He's carried my love away, the man who wed me first—   35
may he hold it tight, safeguard it in his grave."

    She broke off, her voice choking with tears
that brimmed and wet her breast.
                                    But Anna answered:
"Dear one, dearer than light to me, your sister,
would you waste away, grieving your youth away, alone,   40
never to know the joy of children, all the gifts of love?
Do you really believe that's what the dust desires,
the ghosts in their ashen tombs? Have it your way.
But granted that no one tempted you in the past,
not in your great grief,   45
no Libyan suitor, and none before in Tyre,
you scorned Iarbas and other lords of Africa,
sons bred by this fertile earth in all their triumph:
why resist it now, this love that stirs your heart?
Don't you recall whose lands you settled here,   50
the men who press around you? On one side
the Gaetulian cities, fighters matchless in battle,
unbridled Numidians—Syrtes, the treacherous Sandbanks.
On the other side an endless desert, parched earth
where the wild Barcan marauders range at will.   55
Why mention the war that's boiling up in Tyre,
your brother's deadly threats? I think, in fact,
the favor of all the gods and Juno's backing drove
these Trojan ships on the winds that sailed them here.
Think what a city you will see, my sister, what a kingdom   60
rising high if you marry such a man! With a Trojan army
marching at our side, think how the glory of Carthage
will tower to the clouds! Just ask the gods for pardon,
win them with offerings. Treat your guests like kings.
Weave together some pretext for delay, while winter   65

spends its rage and drenching Orion whips the sea—
the ships still battered, weather still too wild."

   These were the words that fanned her sister's fire,
turned her doubts to hopes and dissolved her sense of
      shame.
And first they visit the altars, make the rounds,   70
praying the gods for blessings, shrine by shrine.
They slaughter the pick of yearling sheep, the old way,
to Ceres, Giver of Laws, to Apollo, Bacchus who sets us
      free
and Juno above all, who guards the bonds of marriage.
Dido aglow with beauty holds the bowl in her right hand,   75
pouring wine between the horns of a pure white cow
or gravely paces before the gods' fragrant altars,
under their statues' eyes refreshing her first gifts,
dawn to dusk. And when the victims' chests are splayed,
Dido, her lips parted, pores over their entrails,[15]   80
throbbing still, for signs . . .
But, oh, how little they know, the omniscient seers.
What good are prayers and shrines to a person mad with
      love?
The flame keeps gnawing into her tender marrow hour
by hour and deep in her heart the silent wound lives on.   85
Dido burns with love—the tragic queen.
She wanders in frenzy through her city streets
like a wounded doe caught all off guard by a hunter
stalking the woods of Crete, who strikes her from afar
and leaves his winging steel in her flesh, and he's unaware   90
but she veers in flight through Dicte's woody glades,
fixed in her side the shaft that takes her life.
                                             And now
Dido leads her guest through the heart of Carthage,
displaying Phoenician power, the city readied for him.
She'd speak her heart but her voice chokes, mid-word.   95
Now at dusk she calls for the feast to start again,
madly begging to hear again the agony of Troy,
to hang on his lips again, savoring his story.
Then, with the guests gone, and the dimming moon

quenching its light in turn, and the setting stars   100
inclining heads to sleep—alone in the echoing hall,
distraught, she flings herself on the couch that he left
    empty.
Lost as he is, she's lost as well, she hears him,
sees him or she holds Ascanius back and dandles him on
    her lap,
bewitched by the boy's resemblance to his father,   105
trying to cheat the love she dare not tell.
The towers of Carthage, half built, rise no more,
and the young men quit their combat drills in arms.
The harbors, the battlements planned to block attack,
all work's suspended now, the huge, threatening walls   110
with the soaring cranes that sway across the sky.

    Now, no sooner had Jove's dear wife perceived
that Dido was in the grip of such a scourge—
no thought of pride could stem her passion now—
than Juno approaches Venus and sets a cunning trap: 115
"What a glittering prize, a triumph you carry home!
You and your boy there, you grand and glorious Powers.
Just look, one woman crushed by the craft of two gods!
I am not blind, you know. For years you've looked
    askance
at the homes of rising Carthage, feared our ramparts.   120
But where will it end? What good is all our strife?
Come, why don't we labor now to live in peace?
Eternal peace, sealed with the bonds of marriage.
You have it all, whatever your heart desires—
Dido's ablaze with love,   125
drawing the frenzy deep into her bones. So,
let us rule this people in common: joint command.
And let her marry her Phrygian lover, be his slave
and give her Tyrians over to your control,
her dowry in your hands!"
                            Perceiving at once   130
that this was all pretense, a ruse to shift
the kingdom of Italy onto Libyan shores,
Venus countered Juno: "Now who'd be so insane

as to shun your offer and strive with you in war?
If only Fortune crowns your proposal with success!   135
But swayed by the Fates, I have my doubts. Would Jove
want one city to hold the Tyrians and the Trojan exiles?
Would he sanction the mingling of their peoples,
bless their binding pacts? You are his wife,
with every right to probe him with your prayers.   140
You lead the way. I'll follow."
                         "The work is mine,"
imperious Juno carried on, "but how to begin
this pressing matter now and see it through?
I'll explain in a word or so. Listen closely.
Tomorrow Aeneas and lovesick Dido plan to hunt   145
the woods together, soon as the day's first light
climbs high and the Titan's rays lay bare the earth.
But while the beaters scramble to ring the glens with nets,
I'll shower down a cloudburst, hail, black driving rain—
I'll shatter the vaulting sky with claps of thunder.   150
The huntsmen will scatter, swallowed up in the dark,
and Dido and Troy's commander will make their way
to the same cave for shelter. And I'll be there,
if I can count on your own good will in this—
I'll bind them in lasting marriage, make them one.   155
Their wedding it will be!"
                         So Juno appealed
and Venus did not oppose her, nodding in assent
and smiling at all the guile she saw through . . .

    Meanwhile Dawn rose up and left her Ocean bed
and soon as her rays have lit the sky, an elite band   160
of young huntsmen streams out through the gates,
bearing the nets, wide-meshed or tight for traps
and their hunting spears with broad iron heads,
troops of Massylian horsemen galloping hard,
packs of powerful hounds, keen on the scent.   165
Yet the queen delays,[16] lingering in her chamber
with Carthaginian chiefs expectant at her doors.
And there her proud, mettlesome charger prances
in gold and royal purple, pawing with thunder-hoofs,

champing a foam-flecked bit. At last she comes,   170
with a great retinue crowding round the queen
who wears a Tyrian cloak with rich embroidered fringe.
Her quiver is gold, her hair drawn up in a golden torque
and a golden buckle clasps her purple robe in folds.
Nor do her Trojan comrades tarry. Out they march,   175
young Iulus flushed with joy.
Aeneas in command, the handsomest of them all,
advancing as her companion joins his troop with hers.
So vivid. Think of Apollo leaving his Lycian haunts
and Xanthus in winter spate, he's out to visit Delos,   180
his mother's isle, and strike up the dance again
while round the altars swirls a growing throng
of Cretans, Dryopians, Agathyrsians with tattoos,
and a drumming roar goes up as the god himself
strides the Cynthian ridge, his streaming hair   185
braided with pliant laurel leaves entwined
in twists of gold, and arrows clash on his shoulders.
So no less swiftly Aeneas strides forward now
and his face shines with a glory like the god's.

     Once the huntsmen have reached the trackless lairs   190
aloft in the foothills, suddenly, look, some wild goats
flushed from a ridge come scampering down the slopes
and lower down a herd of stags goes bounding across
the open country, ranks massed in a cloud of dust,
fleeing the high ground. But young Ascanius,   195
deep in the valley, rides his eager mount
and relishing every stride, outstrips them all,
now goats, now stags, but his heart is racing, praying—
if only they'd send among this feeble, easy game
some frothing wild boar or a lion stalking down   200
from the heights and tawny in the sun.
                                        Too late.
The skies have begun to rumble, peals of thunder first
and the storm breaking next, a cloudburst pelting hail
and the troops of hunters scatter up and down the plain,
Tyrian comrades, bands of Dardans, Venus' grandson
     Iulus   205

panicking, running for cover, quick, and down the
   mountain
gulleys erupt in torrents. Dido and Troy's commander
make their way to the same cave for shelter now.
Primordial Earth and Juno, Queen of Marriage,
give the signal and lightning torches flare   210
and the high sky bears witness to the wedding,
nymphs on the mountaintops wail out the wedding hymn.
This was the first day of her death, the first of grief,
the cause of it all. From now on, Dido cares no more
for appearances, nor for her reputation, either.   215
She no longer thinks to keep the affair a secret,
no, she calls it a marriage,
using the word to cloak her sense of guilt.[17]

   Straightway Rumor flies through Libya's great cities,
Rumor, swiftest of all the evils in the world.   220
She thrives on speed, stronger for every stride,
slight with fear at first, soon soaring into the air
she treads the ground and hides her head in the clouds.
She is the last, they say, our Mother Earth produced.
Bursting in rage against the gods, she bore a sister   225
for Coeus and Enceladus:[18] Rumor, quicksilver afoot
and swift on the wing, a monster, horrific, huge
and under every feather on her body—what a marvel—
an eye that never sleeps and as many tongues as eyes
and as many raucous mouths and ears pricked up for
   news.   230
By night she flies aloft, between the earth and sky,
whirring across the dark, never closing her lids
in soothing sleep. By day she keeps her watch,
crouched on a peaked roof or palace turret,
terrorizing the great cities, clinging as fast   235
to her twisted lies as she clings to words of truth.
Now Rumor is in her glory, filling Africa's ears
with tale on tale of intrigue, bruiting her song
of facts and falsehoods mingled . . .
"Here this Aeneas, born of Trojan blood,   240
has arrived in Carthage, and lovely Dido deigns

to join the man in wedlock. Even now they warm
the winter, long as it lasts, with obscene desire,
oblivious to their kingdoms, abject thralls of lust."

    Such talk the sordid goddess spreads on the lips of men,   245
then swerves in her course and heading straight for King
    Iarbas,
stokes his heart with hearsay, piling fuel on his fire.

Iarbas—son of an African nymph whom Jove had raped—
raised the god a hundred splendid temples across
the king's wide realm, a hundred altars too,   250
consecrating the sacred fires
that never died, eternal sentinels of the gods.
The earth was rich with blood of slaughtered herds
and the temple doorways wreathed with riots of flowers.
This Iarbas, driven wild, set ablaze by the bitter rumor,   255
approached an altar, they say, as the gods hovered round,
and lifting a suppliant's hands, he poured out prayers to
    Jove:
"Almighty Jove! Now as the Moors[19] adore you, feasting
    away
on their gaudy couches, tipping wine in your honor—
do you see this? Or are we all fools, Father,   260
to dread the bolts you hurl? All aimless then,
your fires high in the clouds that terrify us so?
All empty noise, your peals of grumbling thunder?
That woman, that vagrant! Here in my own land
she founded her paltry city for a pittance.   265
We tossed her some beach to plow—on my terms—
and then she spurns our offer of marriage,
she embraces Aeneas as lord and master in her realm.
And now this second Paris . . .
leading his troupe of eunuchs,[20] his hair oozing oil,   270
a Phrygian bonnet tucked up under his chin, he revels
in all that he has filched, while we keep bearing gifts
to your temples—yes, yours—coddling your reputation,
all your hollow show!"
                        So King Iarbas appealed,

his hand clutching the altar, and Jove Almighty heard   275
and turned his gaze on the royal walls of Carthage
and the lovers oblivious now to their good name.
He summons Mercury, gives him marching orders:
"Quick, my son, away! Call up the Zephyrs,
glide on wings of the wind. Find the Dardan captain   280
who now malingers long in Tyrian Carthage, look,
and pays no heed to the cities Fate decrees are his.
Take my commands through the racing winds and
     tell him
this is not the man his mother, the lovely goddess,
     promised,
not for this did she save him twice from Greek attacks.   285
Never. He would be the one to master an Italy
rife with leaders, shrill with the cries of war,
to sire a people sprung from Teucer's noble blood
and bring the entire world beneath the rule of law.
If such a glorious destiny cannot fire his spirit,   290
if he will not shoulder the task for his own fame,
does the father of Ascanius grudge his son
the walls of Rome? What is he plotting now?
What hope can make him loiter among his foes,
lose sight of Italian offspring still to come   295
and all the Lavinian fields? Let him set sail!
This is the sum of it. This must be our message."

     Jove had spoken. Mercury made ready at once
to obey the great commands of his almighty father.
First he fastens under his feet the golden sandals,   300
winged to sweep him over the waves and earth alike
with the rush of gusting winds. Then he seizes the wand
that calls the pallid spirits[21] up from the Underworld
and ushers others down to the grim dark depths,
the wand that lends us sleep or sends it away,   305
that unseals our eyes in death. Equipped with this,
he spurs the winds and swims through billowing clouds
till in mid-flight he spies the summit and rugged flanks
of Atlas, whose long-enduring peak supports the skies.
Atlas: his pine-covered crown is forever girded   310

round with black clouds, battered by wind and rain;
driving blizzards cloak his shoulders with snow,
torrents course down from the old Titan's chin
and shaggy beard that bristles stiff with ice.
Here the god of Cyllene landed first,   315
banking down to a stop on balanced wings.
From there, headlong down with his full weight
he plunged to the sea as a seahawk skims the waves,
rounding the beaches, rounding cliffs to hunt for fish inshore.
So Mercury of Cyllene flew between the earth and sky   320
to gain the sandy coast of Libya, cutting the winds
that sweep down from his mother's father, Atlas.[22]

                                                   Soon
as his winged feet touched down on the first huts in sight,
he spots Aeneas founding the city fortifications,
building homes in Carthage. And his sword-hilt   325
is studded with tawny jasper stars, a cloak
of glowing Tyrian purple drapes his shoulders,
a gift that the wealthy queen had made herself,
weaving into the weft a glinting mesh of gold.
Mercury lashes out at once: "You, so now you lay   330
foundation stones for the soaring walls of Carthage!
Building her gorgeous city, doting on your wife.[23]
Blind to your own realm, oblivious to your fate!
The King of the Gods, whose power sways earth and sky—
he is the one who sends me down from brilliant Olympus,   335
bearing commands for you through the racing winds.
What are you plotting now?
Wasting time in Libya—what hope misleads you so?
If such a glorious destiny cannot fire your spirit,
[if you will not shoulder the task for your own fame,]   340
at least remember Ascanius rising into his prime,
the hopes you lodge in Iulus, your only heir—
you owe him Italy's realm, the land of Rome!"
This order still on his lips, the god vanished
from sight into empty air.

                                     Then Aeneas   345
was truly overwhelmed by the vision, stunned,
his hackles bristle with fear, his voice chokes in his throat.

He yearns to be gone, to desert this land he loves,
thunderstruck by the warnings, Jupiter's command . . .
But what can he do? What can he dare say now   350
to the queen in all her fury and win her over?
Where to begin, what opening? Thoughts racing,
here, there, probing his options, turning
to this plan, that plan—torn in two until,
at his wits' end, this answer seems the best.   355
He summons Mnestheus, Sergestus, staunch Serestus,
gives them orders: "Fit out the fleet, but not a word.
Muster the crews on shore, all tackle set to sail,
but the cause for our new course, you keep it secret."
Yet he himself, since Dido who means the world to him   360
knows nothing, never dreaming such a powerful love
could be uprooted—he will try to approach her,
find the moment to break the news gently,
a way to soften the blow that he must leave.
All shipmates snap to commands,   365
glad to do his orders.
                              True, but the queen—
who can delude a lover?—soon caught wind
of a plot afoot, the first to sense the Trojans
are on the move . . . She fears everything now,
even with all secure. Rumor, vicious as ever,   370
brings her word, already distraught, that Trojans
are rigging out their galleys, gearing to set sail.
She rages in helpless frenzy, blazing through
the entire city, raving like some Maenad
driven wild when the women shake the sacred emblems,   375
when the cyclic orgy, shouts of "Bacchus!" fire her on
and Cithaeron echoes round with maddened midnight cries.

    At last she assails Aeneas, before he's said a word:
"So, you traitor, you really believed you'd keep
this a secret, this great outrage? Steal away   380
in silence from my shores? Can nothing hold you back?
Not our love? Not the pledge once sealed with our right
    hands?
Not even the thought of Dido doomed to a cruel death?

Why labor to rig your fleet when the winter's raw,
to risk the deep when the Northwind's closing in?   385
You cruel, heartless— Even if you were not
pursuing alien fields and unknown homes,
even if ancient Troy were standing, still,
who'd sail for Troy across such heaving seas?
You're running away—from me? Oh, I pray you   390
by these tears, by the faith in your right hand—
what else have I left myself in all my pain?—
by our wedding vows, the marriage we began,
if I deserve some decency from you now,
if anything mine has ever won your heart,   395
pity a great house about to fall, I pray you,
if prayers have any place—reject this scheme of yours!
Thanks to you, the African tribes, Numidian warlords
hate me, even my own Tyrians rise against me.
Thanks to you, my sense of honor is gone,   400
my one and only pathway to the stars,
the renown I once held dear. In whose hands,
my guest, do you leave me here to meet my death?
'Guest'—that's all that remains of 'husband' now.
But why do I linger on? Until my brother Pygmalion   405
batters down my walls? Or Iarbas drags me off, his slave?
If only you'd left a baby in my arms—our child—
before you deserted me! Some little Aeneas
playing about our halls, whose features at least
would bring you back to me in spite of all,   410
I would not feel so totally devastated,
so destroyed."
                        The queen stopped but he,
warned by Jupiter now, his gaze held steady,
fought to master the torment in his heart. At last
he ventured a few words: "I . . . you have done me   415
so many kindnesses, and you could count them all.
I shall never deny what you deserve, my queen,
never regret my memories of Dido, not while I
can recall myself and draw the breath of life.
I'll state my case in a few words. I never dreamed   420
I'd keep my flight a secret. Don't imagine that.

Nor did I once extend a bridegroom's torch
or enter into a marriage pact with you.
If the Fates had left me free to live my life,
to arrange my own affairs of my own free will,   425
Troy is the city, first of all, that I'd safeguard,
Troy and all that's left of my people whom I cherish.
The grand palace of Priam would stand once more,
with my own hands I would fortify a second Troy
to house my Trojans in defeat. But not now.   430
Grynean Apollo's oracle says that I must seize
on Italy's noble land, his Lycian lots say 'Italy!'
There lies my love, there lies my homeland now.
If you, a Phoenician, fix your eyes on Carthage,
a Libyan stronghold, tell me, why do you grudge   435
the Trojans their new homes on Italian soil?
What is the crime if we seek far-off kingdoms too?

    "My father, Anchises, whenever the darkness shrouds
the earth in its dank shadows, whenever the stars
go flaming up the sky, my father's anxious ghost   440
warns me in dreams and fills my heart with fear.
My son Ascanius . . . I feel the wrong I do
to one so dear, robbing him of his kingdom,
lands in the West, his fields decreed by Fate.
And now the messenger of the gods—I swear it,   445
by your life and mine—dispatched by Jove himself
has brought me firm commands through the racing winds.
With my own eyes I saw him, clear, in broad daylight,
moving through your gates. With my own ears I drank
his message in. Come, stop inflaming us both   450
with your appeals. I set sail for Italy—
all against my will."
                Even from the start
of his declaration, she has glared at him askance,
her eyes roving over him, head to foot, with a look
of stony silence . . . till abruptly she cries out   455
in a blaze of fury: "No goddess was your mother!
No Dardanus sired your line, you traitor, liar, no,
Mount Caucasus fathered you on its flinty, rugged flanks

and the tigers of Hyrcania gave you their dugs to suck!
Why hide it? Why hold back? To suffer greater blows?   460
Did he groan when I wept? Even look at me? Never!
Surrender a tear? Pity the one who loves him?
What can I say first? So much to say. Now—
neither mighty Juno nor Saturn's son, the Father,
gazes down on this with just, impartial eyes.   465
There's no faith left on earth!
He was washed up on my shores, helpless, and I,
I took him in, like a maniac let him share my kingdom,
salvaged his lost fleet, plucked his crews from death.
Oh I am swept by the Furies, gales of fire! Now   470
it's Apollo the Prophet, Apollo's Lycian oracles:
they're his masters now, and now, to top it off,
the messenger of the gods, dispatched by Jove himself,
comes rushing down the winds with his grim-set
     commands.
Really! What work for the gods who live on high,   475
what a concern to ruffle their repose![24]
I won't hold you, I won't even refute you—go!—
strike out for Italy on the winds, your realm across the sea.
I hope, I pray, if the just gods still have any power,
wrecked on the rocks mid-sea you'll drink your bowl   480
of pain to the dregs, crying out the name of Dido
over and over, and worlds away I'll hound you then
with pitch-black flames, and when icy death has severed
my body from its breath, then my ghost will stalk you
through the world! You'll pay, you shameless, ruthless—   485
and I will hear of it, yes, the report will reach me
even among the deepest shades of Death!"
                                        She breaks off
in the midst of outbursts, desperate, flinging herself
from the light of day, sweeping out of his sight,
leaving him numb with doubt, with much to fear   490
and much he means to say.
Catching her as she faints away, her women
bear her back to her marble bridal chamber
and lay her body down upon her bed.
                                        But Aeneas

is driven by duty now. Strongly as he longs   495
to ease and allay her sorrow, speak to her,
turn away her anguish with reassurance, still,
moaning deeply, heart shattered by his great love,
in spite of all he obeys the gods' commands
and back he goes to his ships.   500
Then the Trojans throw themselves in the labor,
launching their tall vessels down along the beach
and the hull rubbed sleek with pitch floats high again.
So keen to be gone, the men drag down from the forest
untrimmed timbers and boughs still green for oars.   505
You can see them streaming out of the whole city,
men like ants that, wary of winter's onset, pillage
some huge pile of wheat to store away in their grange
and their army's long black line goes marching through
    the field,
trundling their spoils down some cramped, grassy track.   510
Some put shoulders to giant grains and thrust them on,
some dress the ranks, strictly marshal stragglers,
and the whole trail seethes with labor.

    What did you feel then, Dido, seeing this?
How deep were the groans you uttered, gazing now   515
from the city heights to watch the broad beaches
seething with action, the bay a chaos of outcries
right before your eyes?
                    Love, you tyrant!
To what extremes won't you compel our hearts?
Again she resorts to tears, driven to move the man,   520
or try, with prayers—a suppliant kneeling, humbling
her pride to passion. So if die she must,
she'll leave no way untried.
                        "Anna, you see
the hurly-burly all across the beach, the crews
swarming from every quarter? The wind cries for canvas,   525
the buoyant oarsmen crown their sterns with wreaths.
This terrible sorrow: since I saw it coming, Anna,
I can endure it now. But even so, my sister,
carry out for me one great favor in my pain.

To you alone[25] he used to listen, the traitor,   530
to you confide his secret feelings. You alone
know how and when to approach him, soothe his moods.
Go, my sister! Plead with my imperious enemy.
Remind him I was never at Aulis,[26] never swore a pact
with the Greeks to rout the Trojan people from the earth!   535
I sent no fleet to Troy, I never uprooted the ashes
of his father, Anchises, never stirred his shade.
Why does he shut his pitiless ears to my appeals?
Where's he rushing now? If only he would offer
one last gift to the wretched queen who loves him: 540
to wait for fair winds, smooth sailing for his flight!
I no longer beg for the long-lost marriage he betrayed,
nor would I ask him now to desert his kingdom, no,
his lovely passion, Latium. All I ask is time, blank time:
some rest from frenzy, breathing room   545
till my fate can teach my beaten spirit how to grieve.
I beg him—pity your sister, Anna—one last favor,
and if he grants it now, I'll pay him back,
with interest, when I die."
                              So Dido pleads and
so her desolate sister takes him the tale of tears   550
again and again. But no tears move Aeneas now.
He is deaf to all appeals. He won't relent.
The Fates bar the way
and heaven blocks his gentle, human ears.
As firm as a sturdy oak grown tough with age   555
when the Northwinds blasting off the Alps compete,
fighting left and right, to wrench it from the earth,
and the winds scream, the trunk shudders, its leafy crest
showers across the ground but it clings firm to its rock,
its roots stretching as deep into the dark world below   560
as its crown goes towering toward the gales of heaven—
so firm the hero stands: buffeted left and right
by storms of appeals, he takes the full force
of love and suffering deep in his great heart.
His will stands unmoved. The falling tears are futile.
                                              Then,   565
terrified by her fate, tragic Dido prays for death,

sickened to see the vaulting sky above her.
And to steel her new resolve to leave the light,
she sees, laying gifts on the altars steaming incense—
shudder to hear it now—the holy water going black   570
and the wine she pours congeals in bloody filth.
She told no one what she saw, not even her sister.
Worse, there was a marble temple in her palace,
a shrine built for her long-lost love, Sychaeus.
Holding it dear she tended it—marvelous devotion—   575
draping the snow-white fleece and festal boughs.
Now from its depths she seemed to catch his voice,
the words of her dead husband calling out her name
while night enclosed the earth in its dark shroud,
and over and over a lonely owl perched on the rooftops   580
drew out its low, throaty call to a long wailing dirge.
And worse yet, the grim predictions of ancient seers
keep terrifying her now with frightful warnings.
Aeneas the hunter, savage in all her nightmares,
drives her mad with panic. She always feels alone,   585
abandoned, always wandering down some endless road,
not a friend in sight, seeking her own Phoenicians
in some godforsaken land. As frantic as Pentheus[27]
seeing battalions of Furies, twin suns ablaze
and double cities of Thebes before his eyes.   590
Or Agamemnon's Orestes[28] hounded off the stage,
fleeing his mother armed with torches, black snakes,
while blocking the doorway coil her Furies of Revenge.

    So, driven by madness, beaten down by anguish,
Dido was fixed on dying, working out in her mind   595
the means, the moment. She approaches her grieving
sister, Anna—masking her plan with a brave face
aglow with hope, and says: "I've found a way,
dear heart—rejoice with your sister—either
to bring him back in love for me or free me   600
of love for him. Close to the bounds of Ocean,
west with the setting sun, lies Ethiopian land,
the end of the earth, where colossal Atlas turns
on his shoulder the heavens studded with flaming stars.

From there, I have heard, a Massylian priestess comes   605
who tended the temple held by Hesperian daughters.
She'd safeguard the boughs in the sacred grove
and ply the dragon with morsels dripping loops
of oozing honey and poppies drowsy with slumber.
With her spells she vows to release the hearts   610
of those she likes, to inflict raw pain on others—
to stop the rivers in midstream, reverse the stars
in their courses, raise the souls of the dead at night
and make earth shudder and rumble underfoot—you'll
       see—
and send the ash trees marching down the mountains.   615
I swear by the gods, dear Anna, by your sweet life,
I arm myself with magic arts against my will.
                                    "Now go,
build me a pyre in secret, deep inside our courtyard
under the open sky. Pile it high with his arms—
he left them hanging within our bridal chamber—   620
the traitor, so devoted then! and all his clothes
and crowning it all, the bridal bed that brought my doom.
I must obliterate every trace of the man, the curse,
and the priestess shows the way!"
                                    She says no more
and now as the queen falls silent, pallor sweeps her face.   625
Still, Anna cannot imagine these outlandish rites
would mask her sister's death. She can't conceive
of such a fiery passion. She fears nothing graver
than Dido's grief at the death of her Sychaeus.
So she does as she is told.
                                    But now the queen,   630
as soon as the pyre was built beneath the open sky,
towering up with pitch-pine and cut logs of oak—
deep in the heart of her house—she drapes the court
with flowers, crowning the place with wreaths of death,
and to top it off she lays his arms and the sword he left   635
and an effigy of Aeneas, all on the bed they'd shared,
for well she knows the future. Altars ring the pyre.
Hair loose in the wind, the priestess thunders out
the names of her three hundred gods,[29] Erebus, Chaos

and triple Hecate, Diana the three-faced virgin.   640
She'd sprinkled water, simulating the springs of hell,
and gathered potent herbs, reaped with bronze sickles
under the moonlight, dripping their milky black poison,
and fetched a love-charm ripped from a foal's brow,
just born, before the mother could gnaw it off.   645
And Dido herself, standing before the altar,
holding the sacred grain in reverent hands—
with one foot free of its sandal, robes unbound—
sworn now to die, she calls on the gods to witness,
calls on the stars who know her approaching fate.   650
And then to any Power above, mindful, evenhanded,
who watches over lovers bound by unequal passion,
Dido says her prayers.

                The dead of night,
and weary living creatures throughout the world
are enjoying peaceful sleep. The woods and savage seas   655
are calm, at rest, and the circling stars are gliding on
in their midnight courses, all the fields lie hushed
and the flocks and gay and gorgeous birds that haunt
the deep clear pools and the thorny country thickets
all lie quiet now, under the silent night, asleep.   660
But not the tragic queen . . .
torn in spirit, Dido will not dissolve
into sleep—her eyes, her mind won't yield tonight.
Her torments multiply, over and over her passion
surges back into heaving waves of rage—   665
she keeps on brooding, obsessions roil her heart:
"And now, what shall I do? Make a mockery of myself,
go back to my old suitors, tempt them to try again?
Beg the Numidians, grovel, plead for a husband—
though time and again I scorned to wed their like?
What then? Trail the Trojan ships, bend to the Trojans'   670
every last demand? So pleased, are they, with all the help,
the relief I lent them once? And memory of my service past
stands firm in grateful minds! And even if I were willing,
would the Trojans allow me to board their proud ships—
a woman they hate? Poor lost fool, can't you sense it,   675
grasp it yet—the treachery of Laomedon's breed?[30]

What now? Do I take flight alone, consorting
with crews of Trojan oarsmen in their triumph?
Or follow them out with all my troops of Tyrians   680
thronging the decks? Yes, hard as it was to uproot
them once from Tyre! How can I force them back to sea
once more, command them to spread their sails to the
    winds?
No, no, die!
                You deserve it—
                        end your pain with the sword!
You, my sister, you were the first, won over by my tears,   685
to pile these sorrows on my shoulders, mad as I was,
to throw me into my enemy's arms. If only I'd been free
to live my life, untested in marriage, free of guilt
as some wild beast untouched by pangs like these!
I broke the faith I swore to the ashes of Sychaeus."   690

     Such terrible grief kept breaking from her heart
as Aeneas slept in peace on his ship's high stern,
bent on departing now, all tackle set to sail.
And now in his dreams it came again—the god,
his phantom, the same features shining clear.   695
Like Mercury head to foot, the voice, the glow,
the golden hair, the bloom of youth on his limbs
and his voice rang out with warnings once again:
"Son of the goddess, how can you sleep so soundly
in such a crisis? Can't you see the dangers closing   700
around you now? Madman! Can't you hear the Westwind
ruffling to speed you on? That woman spawns her plots,
mulling over some desperate outrage in her heart,
lashing her surging rage, she's bent on death.
Why not flee headlong?   705
Flee headlong while you can! You'll soon see
the waves a chaos of ships, lethal torches flaring,
the whole coast ablaze, if now a new dawn breaks
and finds you still malingering on these shores.
Up with you now. Enough delay. Woman's a thing   710
that's always changing, shifting like the wind."
With that he vanished into the black night.

Then, terrified by the sudden phantom,
Aeneas, wrenching himself from sleep, leaps up
and rouses his crews and spurs them headlong on: 715
"Quick! Up and at it, shipmates, man the thwarts!
Spread canvas fast! A god's come down from the sky
once more—I've just seen him—urging us on
to sever our mooring cables, sail at once!
We follow you, blessed god, whoever you are—   720
glad at heart we obey your commands once more.
Now help us, stand beside us with all your kindness,
bring us favoring stars in the sky to blaze our way!"

Tearing sword from sheath like a lightning flash,
he hacks the mooring lines with a naked blade.   725
Gripped by the same desire, all hands pitch in,
they hoist and haul. The shore's deserted now,
the water's hidden under the fleet—they bend to it,
churn the spray and sweep the clear blue sea.
                                             By now
early Dawn had risen up from the saffron bed   730
of Tithonus, scattering fresh light on the world.
But the queen from her high tower, catching sight
of the morning's white glare, the armada heading out
to sea with sails trimmed to the wind, and certain
the shore and port were empty, stripped of oarsmen—   735
three, four times over she beat her lovely breast,
she ripped at her golden hair and "Oh, by God,"
she cries, "will the stranger just sail off
and make a mockery of our realm? Will no one
rush to arms, come streaming out of the whole city,   740
hunt him down, race to the docks and launch the ships?
Go, quick—bring fire!
                       Hand out weapons!
                                          Bend to the oars!
What am I saying? Where am I? What insanity's this
that shifts my fixed resolve? Dido, oh poor fool,
is it only *now* your wicked work strikes home?   745
It should have then, when you offered him your scepter.
Look at his hand clasp, look at his good faith now—

that man who, they say, carries his fathers' gods,
who stooped to shoulder his father bent with age!
Couldn't I have seized him then, ripped him to pieces,   750
scattered them in the sea? Or slashed his men with steel,
butchered Ascanius, served him up as his father's feast?
True, the luck of battle might have been at risk—
well, risk away! Whom did I have to fear?
I was about to die. I should have torched their camp   755
and flooded their decks with fire. The son, the father,
the whole Trojan line—I should have wiped them out,
then hurled myself on the pyre to crown it all!

    "You, Sun, whose fires scan all works of the earth,
and you, Juno, the witness, midwife to my agonies—   760
Hecate greeted by nightly shrieks at city crossroads—
and you, you avenging Furies and gods of dying Dido!
Hear me, turn your power my way, attend my sorrows—
I deserve your mercy—hear my prayers! If that curse
of the earth must reach his haven, labor on to landfall—   765
if Jove and the Fates command and the boundary stone is
    fixed,
still, let him be plagued in war by a nation proud in arms,
torn from his borders, wrenched from Iulus' embrace,
let him grovel for help and watch his people die
a shameful death! And then, once he has bowed down   770
to an unjust peace, may he never enjoy his realm
and the light he yearns for, never, let him die
before his day, unburied on some desolate beach!

    "That is my prayer, my final cry—I pour it out
with my own lifeblood. And you, my Tyrians,   775
harry with hatred all his line, his race to come:
make that offering to my ashes, send it down below.
No love between our peoples, ever, no pacts of peace!
Come rising up from my bones, you avenger still unknown,[31]
to stalk those Trojan settlers, hunt with fire and iron,   780
now or in time to come, whenever the power is yours.
Shore clash with shore, sea against sea and sword

against sword—this is my curse—war between all
our peoples, all their children, endless war!"

    With that, her mind went veering back and forth—   785
what was the quickest way to break off from the light,
the life she loathed? And so with a few words
she turned to Barce, Sychaeus' old nurse—her own
was now black ashes deep in her homeland lost forever:
"Dear old nurse, send Anna my sister to me here.   790
Tell her to hurry, sprinkle herself with river water,
bring the victims marked for the sacrifice I must make.
So let her come. And wrap your brow with the holy bands.
These rites to Jove of the Styx that I have set in motion,
I yearn to consummate them, end the pain of love,   795
give that cursed Trojan's pyre to the flames."
The nurse bustled off with an old crone's zeal.
                                           But Dido,
trembling, desperate now with the monstrous thing afoot—
her bloodshot eyes rolling, quivering cheeks blotched
and pale with imminent death—goes bursting through   800
the doors to the inner courtyard, clambers in frenzy
up the soaring pyre and unsheathes a sword, a Trojan
    sword
she once sought as a gift, but not for such an end.
And next, catching sight of the Trojan's clothes
and the bed they knew by heart, delaying a moment   805
for tears, for memory's sake, the queen lay down
and spoke her final words: "Oh, dear relics,
dear as long as Fate and the gods allowed,
receive my spirit and set me free of pain.
I have lived a life. I've journeyed through   810
the course that Fortune charted for me. And now
I pass to the world below, my ghost in all its glory.
I have founded a noble city, seen my ramparts rise.
I have avenged my husband, punished my blood-brother,
our mortal foe. Happy, all too happy I would have been   815
if only the Trojan keels had never grazed our coast."
She presses her face in the bed and cries out:

"I shall die unavenged, but die I will! So—
so—I rejoice to make my way among the shades.
And may that heartless Dardan, far at sea,   820
drink down deep the sight of our fires here
and bear with him this omen of our death!"

     All at once, in the midst of her last words,
her women see her doubled over the sword, the blood
foaming over the blade, her hands splattered red.   825
A scream goes stabbing up to the high roofs,
Rumor raves like a Maenad through the shocked city—
sobs, and grief, and the wails of women ringing out
through homes, and the heavens echo back the keening
     din—
for all the world as if enemies stormed the walls   830
and all of Carthage or old Tyre were toppling down
and flames in their fury, wave on mounting wave
were billowing over the roofs of men and gods.

     Anna heard and, stunned, breathless with terror,
raced through the crowd, her nails clawing her face,   835
fists beating her breast, crying out to her sister now
at the edge of death: "Was it all for this, my sister?
You deceived me all along? Is this what your pyre
meant for me—this, your fires—this, your altars?
You deserted me—what shall I grieve for first?   840
Your friend, your sister, you scorn me now in death?
You should have called me on to the same fate.
The same agony, same sword, the one same hour
had borne us off together. Just to think I built
your pyre with my own hands, implored our fathers' gods   845
with my own voice, only to be cut off from you—
how very cruel—when you lay down to die . . .
You have destroyed your life, my sister, mine too,
your people, the lords of Sidon and your new city here.
Please, help me to bathe her wounds in water now,   850
and if any last, lingering breath still hovers,
let me catch it on my lips."
                                    With those words

she had climbed the pyre's topmost steps and now,
clasping her dying sister to her breast, fondling her
she sobbed, stanching the dark blood with her own gown.   855
Dido, trying to raise her heavy eyes once more, failed—
deep in her heart the wound kept rasping, hissing on.
Three times she tried to struggle up on an elbow,
three times she fell back, writhing on her bed.
Her gaze wavering into the high skies, she looked   860
for a ray of light and when she glimpsed it, moaned.

     Then Juno in all her power, filled with pity
for Dido's agonizing death, her labor long and hard,
sped Iris down from Olympus to release her spirit
wrestling now in a deathlock with her limbs.   865
Since she was dying a death not fated or deserved,
no, tormented, before her day, in a blaze of passion—
Proserpina had yet to pluck a golden lock from her head[32]
and commit her life to the Styx and the dark world below.
So Iris, glistening dew, comes skimming down from
     the sky   870
on gilded wings, trailing showers of iridescence shimmering
into the sun, and hovering over Dido's head, declares:
"So commanded, I take this lock as a sacred gift
to the God of Death, and I release you from your body."

     With that, she cut the lock with her hand and all
     at once   875
the warmth slipped away, the life dissolved in the winds.

> In Book Five, Aeneas and his men continue on to Sicily,
> then at the beginning of Book Six they land at last in Italy,
> at Cumae on the Bay of Naples. Here they encounter the
> oracular priestess known as the Sybil, who leads Aeneas
> into the Underworld so he can speak with his father and
> gain knowledge of future Romans. While he is in the Un-
> derworld, he sees Dido in the lugentes campi, the "fields of
> mourning."

BOOK SIX (6.450–476)

And wandering there among them, wound still fresh,
Phoenician Dido drifted along the endless woods.
As the Trojan hero paused beside her, recognized her
through the shadows, a dim, misty figure—as one
when the month is young may see or seem to see   525
the new moon rising up through banks of clouds—
that moment Aeneas wept and approached the ghost
with tender words of love: "Tragic Dido,
so, was the story true that came my way?
I heard that you were dead . . .   530
you took the final measure with a sword.
Oh, dear god, was it I who caused your death?
I swear by the stars, by the Powers on high, whatever
faith one swears by here in the depths of earth,
I left your shores, my Queen, against my will. Yes,   535
the will of the gods, that drives me through the shadows
    now,
these moldering places so forlorn, this deep unfathomed
    night—
their decrees have forced me on. Nor did I ever dream
my leaving could have brought you so much grief.
Stay a moment. Don't withdraw from my sight.   540
Running away—from whom? This is the last word
that Fate allows me to say to you. The last."

Aeneas, with such appeals, with welling tears,
tried to soothe her rage, her wild fiery glance.
But she, her eyes fixed on the ground, turned away,   545
her features no more moved by his pleas as he talked on
than if she were set in stony flint or Parian marble rock.
And at last she tears herself away, his enemy forever,
fleeing back to the shadowed forests where Sychaeus,
her husband long ago, answers all her anguish,   550
meets her love with love. But Aeneas, no less
struck by her unjust fate, escorts her from afar
with streaming tears and pities her as she passes.

OVID,
HEROIDES
7 (DIDO TO AENEAS)

Translated from the Latin by
Erika Zimmermann Damer

This poem comes from Ovid's Heroides, *one of his early collections of poetry. In these poems, Ovid makes the heroines of Greek and Roman mythology speak, often to their lovers who have abandoned them. Many of the women who speak are connected to heroes of the Trojan War, from Ulysses to Paris. Ovid has clearly crafted this poem as a clever response to Vergil's* Aeneid. *Where Vergil gave us Aeneas's perspective on their love affair in Books One and Four, Ovid's response is purely Dido's perspective. Throughout the poem, Ovid clarifies ambiguities in Vergil's narrative and elaborates on Dido's powerful agency, first as queen of Carthage, and then as a woman who boldly chooses her own tragic fate.*

Ovid has proceeded in the Heroides *in a reverse chronological order of the Trojan War. He begins with Penelope's letter to Odysseus, and ends the Trojan War poems with Paris's and Helen's letters, whose affair would begin the war. Dido stands as the seventh poem.*

Dido is the queen of Carthage, in what is now Tunisia, and has just lost her lover, her second husband, Aeneas, the leader of the Trojan refugees. Having fled persecution in Tyre, in Phoenicia (what is now Lebanon), she has settled in Africa and founded the city of Carthage, where she wel-

comed the Trojan refugees and offered to make Aeneas
her consort. Aeneas, ordered by the gods, leaves her and
Carthage to head for Italy. Ovid imagines her writing to
Aeneas in the moments before she dies.

Like this, when death calls, the white swan drops
to wet
    Grass and sings by the banks of the Meander.[1]
I don't address you because I hope my prayer will move you—
    We set this in motion[2] with a god against us;
But when I've squandered my good deeds, my reputation,   5
    And my chaste body and soul, it's easy to squander words.
Still, are you sure you will go and leave Dido wretched?
    Will the same winds take your sails and your promise
    away?
Are you sure, Aeneas, once you set sail and break your pact,
    You'll reach Italian realms? You don't know where
    they are!   10
Does not new Carthage touch you, nor these rising walls,
    Nor the highest power handed over to your scepter?
You flee what you have done, you seek what you must do:
    Find another land across the world, though you have found
    one.
If you do discover this land, who will give it to you to hold?   15
    Who will yield their own fields for strangers to rule?
No doubt another love and another Dido await you—
    And more promises to give and break again.
When are you likely to found a city as great as Carthage
    And to see your people from high atop your citadel?   20
If it all turns out well, if your wishes do not delay you,
    Where will a wife be who will love you like this?[3]
I am on fire, like waxed torches smeared with sulfur,
    Like pious incense added to smoking altar fires.
Aeneas always clings to my waking eyes;   25
    Night and rest bring Aeneas back to my mind.
He is truly ungrateful and deaf to my gifts—

I'd wish, were I not so foolish, to be without him.
Still, I don't hate Aeneas, though he thinks ill of me;
   I lament the faithless man, and that makes me love
   him worse.[4]   30
Venus, spare your son's wife! Embrace your harsh brother,
   Brother Love—let him serve in your camps![5]
As for me, since I began this love affair (I think it not
unworthy),
   Give him to me, as reason for my worries!
I am deceived, and in my delusion[6] that fantasy flits
before me—   35
   He is at odds with his mother's nature.

Stones and mountains[7] and hard oak born on lofty cliffs,
   And savage wild beasts gave birth to you,
Or the sea, which you see is now churned by the winds,
   Where still you prepare to go, though waves oppose you.   40
Where do you flee? Winter blocks you. May winter's grace
help me!
   Look at how Eurus stirs the rolling waters!
What I'd rather owe to you, let me owe to the winds;
   Wind and waves are more just than your spirit.
I am not so important—why are you not judged unfairly?—   45
   That you should die while fleeing me across far seas.
You practice a costly hate, one won at great price,
   If, to be free of me, you think it cheap to die.
Soon winds will rest, waves will be smooth and even,
   Triton will ride his sea-blue horses through the sea.[8]   50
I wish you were as changeable as the winds!
   And you will be, unless your hardness rivals oak.
Why, as if you don't know what raging seas can do,
   Do you trust the water that has so often brought
   you risks?
Suppose you unmoor the ship when the sea invites
travel—   55
   Still the wide ocean holds many sorrows.
It isn't good for those attempting the sea to break
vows:
   That place exacts punishments from the faithless,

Especially when love is wounded, because Love's mother
    Was born nude, they say, from Cytherian waters.[9]   60
I fear that, if destroyed, I will destroy, or harm who
harms me,[10]
    That my enemy, shipwrecked, will drink the salty sea.
Live, I beg! That way I can bring you ruin finer than death.
    Better that you be called the cause of *my* demise.
Come, imagine you are caught in a rapid tornado   65
    (May this not bring you bad luck!)—wat then would you?
At once you'll recall your false tongue's broken promises.
    And Dido, forced to die by your Phrygian treachery.[11]
Before your eyes will stand the image of your cheated wife,
    Sad and bloodstained, her hair flowing around her.   70
What's so important to make you say, "I'm guilty! Forgive
me!"
    And to make you think hurled lightning fell against you?
Grant a short space for the sea's rage, and yours, to abate:
    A safe voyage will be the great reward for delay.
If you do not care about this, let young Iulus be spared![12]   75
    It's enough for you to be the cause of my death.
How is young Ascanius, how are the Penates guilty?
    Will waves destroy the gods snatched from Troy's fires?
But you don't bear them with you, nor, though you boast of it,
faithless man,
    Did those relics or your father press upon your shoulders.   80
You lie about it all! Your tongue did not begin its lies
    With us—I'm not the first woman you've hurt.
If you want to know where lovely Iulus' mother is,
    She died, left alone by her harsh husband![13]
You told me all this, warned me well! Burn me—I'm guilty!
    My punishment will be less than my blame.
My mind has no doubt that your gods will condemn you:
    Seven winters have tossed you through land and sea.
I welcomed you, cast from the waves, in a safe harbor.
    I shared my realm, though I'd scarce heard your name.   90
Still, I wish I had been content with those kind deeds,
    That the rumor of our affair had been buried!
That day undid me, when a dark rain storm drove us
    Into a sloping cavern to escape the sudden waters.[14]

Then I heard a voice; I thought the nymphs were crying out,   95
    But it was Furies giving signals for my doom![15]
Take vengeance,[16] wounded chastity, my marriage bed's
violated rights,   97a
    And the reputation I failed to keep till I was ash.   97b
And you, my ghost, and the soul and ash of my Sychaeus,[17]
    To whom I come, wretched and full of shame.
There is a statue of Sychaeus, sacred to me, in a marble shrine;
    Leaves lie before it and white wool covers it.   100
From here, I heard a familiar voice call to me four times—
    It was him, saying softly, "Elissa, come!"[18]
I do not delay. I am coming, your wife, bound to you,
    Though I come slowly from my shame.
Forgive my crime! A credible man deceived me;   105
    He removes the ill intent from my offense.
His divine mother and aged father, the pious burden of
his son,
    Gave me hope he would remain my lawful husband.
If I had to stray, my straying had good reasons.
    Think too of his promises, then there is no need for
    regrets.   110
My fated course persists, from my early days to my last,
    Following me to the final mome of my life.
My husband died, slain, before the altars in our house,
    And his brother now holds the rewards of such crime.
I am driven into exile, leaving my husband's ashes and my
homeland,   115
    Borne through uncertain paths as my enemy pursues.
I land at these shores, escaping my brother and the sea,
    And I acquire the shore I gave you, faithless man.
I have founded a city, and I have established wide-stretching
    Walls, the envy of neighboring lands.   120
Wars are brewing that threaten me, a foreign woman,
    And barely can I prepare the city's gates and defenses.
I pleased a thousand suitors, who allied in their complaint
    That I chose a nobody instead of their beds.
Why do you hesitate to hand me over in chains to Gaetulan
Iarbas?   125
    I would offer my arms to your wicked deed.

There is also my brother. His impious hands are stained
    With my husband's blood and cry out to be stained
    with mine.
Put down your gods and the relics your touch profanes!
    Your impious hand cannot worship the gods well.   130
If you were to worship them, snatched from the flames,
    Then your gods regret to have escaped the flames.
And you leave Dido when I may be pregnant, wicked man!
    A part of you may lie hidden in my body.
The wretched baby will share its mother's fate,   135
    And you will cause the death of your unborn child,
And when Iulus' brother will die with his mother,
    A single punishment will carry us off two entwined.

"But a god orders me to go." I wish he had forbidden you to
come,
    That Punic soil hadn't felt the press of Teucrian feet![19]   140
Was this the god who led you when you were storm-tossed,
    While you wasted so much time on the raging seas?
You would hardly have sought out Troy with such effort,
    If it were as great as it was while Hector still lived.
You don't seek your native Simois, but Tiber's waves.   145
    When you reach where you wish to be, you will be a
    stranger.
And since Italy hides, and hidden, avoids your ships,
    You'll grow old searching, and scarcely reach it then.
Better accept these people as your dowry, ceasing your
wanderings,
    And the wealth of Pygmalion I brought here.   150
You will have better luck resettling Ilion in this Tyrian city.[20]
    Have a king's wealth and sacred scepter here!
If your mind is eager for battle, or if Iulus seeks a war
    From which to gain a triumph for himself,
We will offer him a foe to conquer. He'll miss nothing!   155
    This place offers the peace's laws and war's arms.
Now, you, by your mother and your brother's arrows,
    And by the Dardan relics,[21] the gods, companions
    in your flight—

May they survive, along with any of your people fierce
    Mars saves! May that be the end of your losses,   160
May Ascanius happily live out his allotted years,
    And may the bones of elderly Anchises rest softly![22]
I beg you, spare my home, which gives itself for you to hold!
    What crime can you call mine beyond loving my people?
I am not from Phthia,[23] nor sprung from great Mycenae,   165
    Nor did my husband and father oppose you.
If it shames you to call me wife, I'll be your host, not your
bride.
    So long as she is yours, Dido will bear being anything.
The straits beating the African shore are known to me—
    At fixed times they grant travel and deny it.   170
When the breeze allows travel, then offer your sail to
the winds.
    Now slippery seaweed holds back your stranded ship.
Send me to watch for the right time—you'll go more surely,
    And I will not let you remain, even if you want to.
Your men demand rest too, and your mangled ship,   175
    Half-repaired, demands a brief delay.
In return for my good deeds and what I may owe
you still,
    In return for my marriage hopes, I seek a little time,
Till the straits and our love grow milder, till with time
    And practice I can bravely learn to bear sorrows.   180

Otherwise, I intend to pour out my life!
    You cannot be cruel to me for long.
If only you could see how this writer looks!
    As I write, your Trojan sword is in my lap,
My tears slip down my cheeks onto your drawn sword.   185
    Soon it will be stained by my blood, not my tears.
How well your gifts suit my doom!
    You equip my tomb at such a small expense.
This is not the first time my heart is pierced with a weapon:
    It already has a wound of savage love.   190
Anna, sister, sister Anna, sad aide to my wrongdoing,
    Soon you will give the final gifts to my ashes.

When consumed by the pyre, I'll be inscribed as
ELISSA, WIFE OF SYCHAEUS—
   this will be the brief poem on my marble tomb:
AENEAS OFFERED BOTH THE REASON
AND THE SWORD FOR MY DEATH.   195
DIDO FELL, STRUCK BY HER OWN HAND.

LAVINIA, REGENT OF LAVINIUM

Lavinia appears right at the beginning of Rome's legendary history. In Vergil's *Aeneid*, she is the daughter of King Latinus and becomes (through no fault of her own) the cause of war between two men, Turnus and Aeneas, who fight for her hand. It is not clear which of the two Lavinia herself wants to marry, since Vergil gives her no words to speak. She will ultimately be the bride of the victorious Aeneas, who founds a city, Lavinium, naming it after her. This small town will be the humble beginning of the Roman Empire of Vergil's own day.

Livy, born just over a decade after Vergil, takes up Lavinia's story, though briefly, at the start of his monumental *History of Rome*. She is a rare positive example of a woman holding power in Rome, albeit in service to the patriarchal line of her husband and his son.

LIVY,
THE HISTORY OF ROME

1.3

Translated from the Latin by
Stephanie McCarter

Ascanius, the son of Aeneas,[1] was not yet old enough to hold power, yet power was kept intact for him until he came of age. In the interim, it was under a woman's guardianship (for so great was Lavinia's natural ability) that the Latin state and the realm of his father and grandfather stood strong for the boy. By no means will I debate (for who could prove as certain something so ancient?) whether it was this Ascanius or an elder brother, the Iulus from whom the Julian family derives its name, who was born to Creusa while Troy was still intact.

This Ascanius (wherever he was born and whoever his mother was—it is certain that he was Aeneas's son) left Lavinium to his mother—or his stepmother—since the city was wealthy and flourishing in population, according to the standards of the day. He himself founded another new city near the Alban Mount, which was called Alba Longa since its site was spread along the mountain's ridge. There was a period of about thirty years between the foundation of Lavinium and the settlement of the colony at Alba Longa.

Yet wealth had grown so much, especially once the Etruscans were dispersed, that neither Mezentius and the Etruscans[2] nor any other neighbors dared to make an attack, not even when Aeneas died nor during the woman's guardianship nor at the very beginning of the boy's reign. They had agreed to peace on the condition that the river Albula, which people now call the Tiber, would be the border between the Etruscans and the Latins.

PART THREE

HISTORICAL QUEENS

ARTEMISIA I,
QUEEN OF CARIA

Artemisia (5th c. BCE) acceded to power upon the death of her husband, whose name has been lost. She ruled in the Carian region of Asia Minor, her realm including the city of Halicarnassus. Halicarnassus had been established as a Greek colony, and Artemisia's background was likewise Greek. The territory she ruled, however, had been a Persian satrapy since the middle of the sixth century BCE. When the Persian king Xerxes marched his massive army on Greece in 480 BCE, she joined him as an ally, contributing five ships to his navy and taking part in the Battle of Salamis, a key Greek victory.

We know of Artemisia primarily from Herodotus, the fifth-century BCE historian whose *Histories* documents the Persian invasion and its subsequent defeat by the allied Greeks. Herodotus was himself from Halicarnassus, which may explain both his spotlighting of her and his sympathetic portrait of her. He casts her in the role of the wise—yet ultimately ignored—advisor to the Persian king. Though a woman, she exemplifies *andreia*, "manly courage." She fights with Xerxes's forces, which Herodotus characterizes as slavish, yet she exemplifies independence and free speech. Like Halicarnassus itself, she occupies a blurred line between Greek ideas of west and east, male and female, free and unfree, while also giving voice to Greek ideals of gender, attributing the Persian loss to their failure to live up to normative masculinity.

HERODOTUS, *HISTORIES*

(SELECTIONS)

Translated from the Greek by
Daniel Holmes

7.99

*Herodotus catalogs Xerxes's fleet, giving Artemisia the
prominent final position.*

I need not recall the other squadron commanders, except for
Artemisia, at whom I particularly marvel because she, a woman,
fought against Greece. After her husband had died, she ruled
alone as tyrant[1] and, though she had a fully grown son—and
so was under no compulsion—she herself fought because of her
own manly spirit and courage. Her name was Artemisia and
she was the daughter of Lygdamis; on her father's side she was
Halicarnassian, on her mother's Cretan. She was leader of the
Halicarnassians, the Coans, the Nisyrans, and the Kalymnians,[2]
providing five of her own ships. After the Sidonians, these were
the most famous of the entire fleet; and of all the allies the advice she gave Xerxes was best.

8.67–69

*Xerxes seeks advice about whether to engage the Athe-
nians in a naval battle off the coast of Salamis.*

When the rest of the fleet arrived at Phaleron, Xerxes went himself down to the ships wanting to meet with the commanders and hear what they thought. On his arrival he sat on his throne. Already present were the tyrants of the various nations and the commanders of the squadrons that he had summoned. They sat there in the order of honor he had given them: first was the Sidonian king, after him the Tyrian, and so on for the rest. When they were sitting there in their respective ranks, Xerxes sent Mardonius[3] to sound out each one by asking whether he should engage in a naval battle. After Mardonius had finished going around asking the question, beginning with the Sidonian, all the rest were found to be unanimous in their opinion, bidding him to engage in a naval battle. Artemisia, however, had this to say:

"'Please tell the king that this is what I have to say—I who proved to be among the best at the naval battle off Euboea[4] and displayed great prowess: 'Master, it is therefore right that I now offer to you my advice, because what I happen to be thinking is in fact what is best for this situation of yours. This is what I say: save your ships and do not engage in a naval battle. For their men are as far superior to your men at sea as men are to women. Why should you run a further risk at sea at all? Do you not have possession of Athens,[5] which was the very reason you were eager to make your campaign? Do you not have possession of the rest of Greece? No one is standing in your way. Those who did have rightly been removed.

"Let me tell you how I think things will turn out for the enemy now. If you do not hastily press to engage in a naval battle, but keep your ships here close to land, then by waiting here or even progressing into the Peloponnese, you will easily accomplish what you came here for. The Greeks are not able to withstand you for a sustained period; rather, you will scatter them and each will flee back to their own cities. I have heard reports that they do not have food on the island they are now on and that it is likely that those who have come from the Peloponnese—if you march your ground forces against their territory—will not just remain there or continue to be interested in fighting at sea on behalf of the Athenians. But if you do hastily press to fight a naval battle, I fear that the defeat of your naval force will also bring destruction upon your ground forces.

"'Furthermore, King, consider this: there is a tendency among human beings that the good have bad slaves, and the bad have good slaves. So you, who are the best of men, have bad slaves who are said to be counted among your allies—Egyptians, Cypriots, Cilicians, and Pamphylians—but who are absolutely useless.'"

When Artemisia had said this to Mardonius, those who were sympathetic to her thought the speech would bring her trouble and that she would be punished by the King, because she was against a naval battle; but those who were resentful and jealous of her high position of honor among the allies were delighted at her counter-response, thinking it would mean her downfall. When, however, their opinions had been returned to Xerxes, he was extremely pleased with Artemisia's advice, and though he previously believed she was a person of importance he now acclaimed her even more. Nevertheless, he commanded that the majority opinion be followed.

8.87–88

Artemisia employs clever tactics at the Battle of Salamis.

I am not able to describe in detail how other barbarians or Greeks contended in the battle, but as regards Artemisia, this is what happened, as a result of which she was yet more esteemed by Xerxes.

At the critical point where the Persian side reached utter confusion, Artemisia's ship was being pursued by an Athenian ship. When she was not able to break free of it since her own allied ships were in front of hers and enemy ships were pressing close behind, she decided on an action that proved beneficial. As she was being pursued by the Athenian ship, she rammed an allied Calyndian ship with Damasthimus, their king, himself in command. I cannot say whether this incident occurred because of some lingering quarrel she had against him from their time at the Hellespont. Did she do this on purpose or did that ship just happen by chance to be in the way?

Anyway, when she had rammed and sunk the vessel, taking advantage of this stroke of good fortune, she went on to gain a double reward. When the commander of the Athenian ship saw Artemisia ramming a barbarian ship and so thought she was either a Greek ship or one defecting from the barbarians and helping to defend him, he gave up the pursuit and turned his attention elsewhere. Such was the first break that went her way—she escaped and did not perish.

The second resulted in her being especially honored by Xerxes, even though the incident harmed his cause. The story goes that Xerxes was watching and noticed that her ship was attacking. Then someone said to him: "Master, do you see how well Artemisia is fighting and has sunk one of the enemies' ships?" He then asked those around him whether it was truly Artemisia's doing. They replied that they clearly recognized her ship's markings and felt sure that the sunk ship was Greek. As I said, everything turned out to her favor, especially because no one from the Calyndian ship survived to bring forward an accusation. It is said that Xerxes' response to this information was: "My men have become women, and my women men." This is what they say he said.

8.100–103

After the Persian defeat in the naval battle at Salamis, Mardonius tries to raise Xerxes's spirits and urges him to concentrate on his land forces. He offers Xerxes two courses of action: (1) to continue on himself with his army or (2) to withdraw with much of his army, but leave Mardonius and three hundred thousand picked troops to conquer Greece.

When Xerxes heard Mardonius' speech, he was gladdened, given his present despondency, and pleased. He told Mardonius that he would seek out advice before he decided which of the two options he would pursue. So, he took counsel with his chosen Persian counselors, but also determined to send for Artemisia to join him because previously she alone proved to understand what actions were called for. When she arrived, Xerxes sent away all the rest, both the Persian counselors and his bodyguard, and spoke as follows:

"Mardonius is urging me to stay here and make an attack on the Peloponnese, arguing that my Persians and the other ground forces are not to blame for our suffering, but in fact would be glad to have a chance to prove themselves. So, he urges me either to give them this chance, or to let him choose 300,000 picked troops from the army and use them himself to deliver to me Greece enslaved. He urges me, too, to march back with the remainder of the army to return to my old life. Because you gave such good advice regarding the naval battle and were against it, so now advise me which of these two options is the better recommendation."

So, Xerxes asked for her advice, and she said: "When asked for advice, it is difficult to come up with what is best to say; but it is my opinion, given the current circumstances, that you should march back, but leave Mardonius here—if he is willing and eager to do so—with the troops he wants. If he subdues all he promises to and if all his avowed plans succeed, that success is yours, master. But even if it turns out just the opposite of what Mardonius intends, it will be no great disaster, so long as you survive, along with all of your own family's affairs. For if both you and your house survive, the Greeks will still many times have to risk their lives in contending with you. If something befalls Mardonius, it makes no difference. Even if the Greeks are victorious, they will have no real victory, since they will only have destroyed your slave. But you will go home having achieved the very object of your expedition—you torched Athens."

Xerxes was pleased at her advice. For in her speech, she came up with just what he was thinking. In my own opinion, not even if everyone—men and women—advised him to remain, would he have done so. That was how shaken with fear he was. He then thanked Artemisia and sent her to take his sons to Ephesus, for some of his illegitimate children were tagging along with him.

SALOME ALEXANDRA, QUEEN OF JUDEA

Alexandra, whose Hebrew name was Shelamzion, ruled Judea from 76–67 BCE. She was part of the Hasmonean dynasty, a family that reigned in Judea from 140–37 BCE. She is the only known queen to rule independently during this period, having inherited power upon the death of her husband Alexander Jannaeus. She was sixty-four years old at the time.

Our main source for Alexandra is the Jewish historian Josephus (ca. 37–100 CE), who initially opposed the Romans but eventually defected to Rome and acquired Roman citizenship. Writing in Greek, he recounts her reign in both *Jewish War* and *Jewish Antiquities*. His assessment of her is highly ambivalent. On the one hand, he regards her as a capable and pious administrator, while on the other she seems overly ambitious and easily swayed by the Pharisees, whose influence grew under her reign. Josephus ultimately suggests that rule by a woman was to blame for the loss of Judean sovereignty, a judgment that may have arisen as Josephus adopted hostile Roman attitudes toward women in power.

Following Alexandra's death, her son Hyrcanus succeeded to the throne but was driven from power by his brother Aristobulus. The brothers undertook a war of succession that weakened the dynasty, leaving it susceptible to the Romans. The Hasmonean dynasty came to an end when Herod, backed by the Romans, captured Jerusalem in 37 BCE and installed himself as client king to Rome.

JOSEPHUS

(SELECTIONS)

Translated from the Greek by
Stephanie McCarter

JEWISH WAR 1.107–19

Alexander left the kingdom to his wife, Alexandra. He believed that the Jews would especially submit to her since she had won over the people by lacking his cruelty and by opposing his transgressions. His hope did not fall short, for the little lady[1] ruled the kingdom through her reputation for piety. She was exact in the nation's customs and expelled from office those who offended against the holy laws. Of her two sons with Alexander, she appointed the elder, Hyrcanus, as chief priest both because of his age and because he was too slow-witted to be troubled with the whole. She confined the younger, Aristobulus, to a private station due to his fervor.

Arising alongside her reign were the Pharisees, a contingent of Jews that were thought to be more pious than others and more exact in interpreting the laws. Alexandra deferred to them too much in her zeal for the divine, and by gradually exploiting the woman's sincerity they soon became the administrators of the whole, banishing and recalling, freeing and jailing whomever they liked. In general, the advantages of sovereignty belonged to them, the costs and troubles to Alexandra. But she was skillful at administrating key matters and doubled the size of the military through constant enlistment, even marshaling foreign mercenaries. The result was that she not only strengthened the state domestically but also became fearsome to foreign powers.

She ruled others, but the Pharisees ruled her. Indeed, they put to death Diogenes, a prominent man who had become a friend to Alexander, calling him the mastermind behind the king's crucifixion of the eight hundred.[2] And they urged Alexandra to slay others who had provoked Alexander against those men. And since she complied due to her religiosity, they killed whomever they liked. The elite among those imperiled fled to Aristobulus, who persuaded his mother to spare them on account of their rank, or to eject them from the city if she did not believe them to be innocent. Their safety granted, they dispersed across the country.

Alexandra sent the army to Damascus, citing as pretext Ptolemy's constant oppression[3] of that city, but it returned having accomplished nothing worthy of comment. And when Tigranes, the king of Armenia, was encamped before Ptolemais and besieging Cleopatra,[4] she drew him away with treaties and gifts. Yet the initiative in leaving was actually his since there was trouble at home with Lucullus' attack on Armenia.

When Alexandra became ill, her younger son, Aristobulus, seized the moment. Along with his associates (and there were many, all drawn to his fervor) he took control of all the strongholds, then used the funds in them to recruit mercenaries and appoint himself king. When Hyrcanus bewailed over these events, his mother pitied him and imprisoned Aristobulus' wife and children in Antonia. This was a garrison adjacent to the north side of the temple. In the past, as I mentioned, it was named Baris, but it later received the other name when Antony took power, just as Sebaste and Agrippias were named after Augustus[5] and Agrippa. But Alexandra died before she could take measures against Aristobulus for deposing his brother. She held power for nine years.

JEWISH ANTIQUITIES 13.428–432

*Josephus's account in this later work is more hostile, depicting Alexandra as something of a power-hungry queen (*basilissa*), though he simultaneously offers her some praise.*

The following selection comes at the end of the account and gives an assessment of Alexandra's accomplishments, character, and legacy.

The Jewish elders and Hyrcanus came to the queen and begged for her advice about the present circumstances. For Aristobulus was already master of nearly everything since he had taken control of so many strongholds. But it was not their place to make plans on their own while she was still alive, even if she was very sick. Yet the danger was imminent. She told them to do whatever they deemed expedient, that she had left them many resources, a formidable nation, military might, and funds in the treasuries. She had little concern now, she said, for state affairs since her body was failing.

Not long after saying this, she died. She ruled nine years and lived a total of seventy-three, a woman endowed with none of the weakness of her sex. Becoming immensely skillful in her ambition, she showed through her deeds the effectiveness of her intellect and the witlessness of those men who always stumble in exercising power. She valued the present over the future and considered all else second to authoritative rule, and because of this she paid little attention to what was noble or just. Indeed, she brought so much misfortune to her house that not long afterwards, due to her desire for things that do not concern a woman, the sovereignty acquired through great dangers and hardships was lost. This was because she held the same judgment as those hostile to her family[6] and had left the realm without anyone to care for it.

Even after her death, she filled the palace with misfortunes and upheaval that sprang from how she governed in life. But although she ruled in this way, she kept the nation at peace. This is the end of what concerns Alexandra.

CLEOPATRA VII, QUEEN OF EGYPT

Cleopatra is the most famous woman from classical antiquity, and we are still debating her identity and legacy. She remains in many ways an enigma, largely because what we know of her is the work of Roman propaganda—even in her own lifetime she became a character formed in the minds of her enemies.

She was the last of the Ptolemaic rulers in Egypt, a dynasty that went back to Ptolemy I Soter, a Macedonian Greek who had been one of the commanders of Alexander the Great. Her father was Ptolemy XII, but a firm identity for her mother has not been established. Cleopatra is at the end of a long line of powerful Ptolemaic queens who reigned as consorts of royal husbands. These women all held the names of Arsinoe, Berenice, or Cleopatra—our Cleopatra is in fact the seventh of that name. As power became concentrated in the hands of a single family, these women were key players both within the Ptolemaic household and within the Egyptian state.

After her father's death in 51 BCE, she acceded to power alongside her brother Ptolemy XIII, with whom she quickly came into conflict, resulting in her expulsion from Alexandria. When Julius Caesar came to Alexandria after Pompey the Great was killed there, she sneaked into the city (as legend now has it, rolled in a rug) in order to seek his alliance. The two began an affair, and Cleopatra became pregnant with his son, Caesarion, in 48 BCE. When Ptolemy XIII was killed in 47 BCE,

Cleopatra reigned as co-ruler with her twelve-year-old brother (and ostensible husband), Ptolemy XIV, whom Cleopatra later would allegedly poison in order to install her son Caesarion as her co-ruler. Cleopatra went to Rome on at least one occasion and had to flee the city when Julius Caesar was assassinated on the Ides of March 44 BCE.

Cleopatra next becomes known to us as the lover and ally of Mark Antony, a Roman who would himself be embroiled in civil war with Octavian, later Augustus, the first emperor of Rome. Despite the fact that he was married to Octavian's sister, Octavia, Antony spent much time with Cleopatra in Egypt, and together they had three children, twins named Alexander Helios and Cleopatra Selene II, and a son named Ptolemy Philadelphus. In 32 BCE Octavian declared war on Cleopatra, and in 31 BCE she and Antony were defeated in a naval battle at Actium. They retreated back to Alexandria, with Octavian marching on the city the following year. Antony was the first of the two to die by suicide, by falling on his sword. Cleopatra, according to our sources, preferred to die rather than be marched in a Roman triumph, and so also took her own life—most likely with poison, though the Romans have given us the sensational story that she used asps, a version that has subsequently become a canonical part of her legend.

It is clear that Cleopatra herself was an intelligent, strategic leader whose alliance with Roman men was politically motivated to shore up her country's power. She promoted herself to her Egyptian subjects by learning their language and presenting herself as a pharaoh or as the goddess Isis. Abroad and on coinage, she depicted herself as a cosmopolitan Greek. It is, however, the Roman version of Cleopatra that has inspired much of her subsequent representation. The following selections were key to shaping Cleopatra as an exotic femme fatale eager to enslave Rome and its men.

LUCAN,
CIVIL WAR

10.53–171

Translated from the Latin by
Matthew Fox

*Lucan's epic was written during the tumultuous years of
Nero's rule, and his composition of it ended abruptly when
he was forced by the emperor to die by suicide in 65 CE.
The epic tells the story of Julius Caesar's civil war with
Pompey the Great, ending as Caesar is in Egypt during the
buildup to the Alexandrian War against Ptolemy XIII. It is
profoundly hostile to Caesar's imperial ambitions; whereas
Vergil's* Aeneid *had recounted the myth of the empire's rise,
Lucan offers, to quote Gian Biagio Conte, an "anti-myth of
Rome, its inexorable decline."[1]*

*Prior to Lucan, few writers had mentioned Julius Caesar's
affair with Cleopatra, most likely because Augustan writers
had wanted to present Augustus's deified adoptive father in
a positive light and focused instead on her degradation of
Mark Antony. In Lucan's hands, Julius Caesar is similarly
taken in by her charm, luxury, and corrupting influence.*

Coming up from the Nile's Pelusian mouth,   65
the boy king[2] had by now allayed the angers
of his unwarlike people; as a hostage of peace
Caesar was safe inside the Pellaean palace—

when Cleopatra, in a little bireme,
bribed the guard to relax the chains of Pharos[3]   70
and got herself inside the Emathian halls
without Caesar knowing.
                         Egypt's disgrace,
to Latium a lethal Fury, her unchastity damaged
Rome as much as the Spartan's harmful face and figure[4]
battered Argos and knocked down the homes of Ilium,   75
so much did Cleopatra swell Hesperia's frenzies.[5]
She terrified the Capitol with her sistrum[6]
(can it be?), and with her unwarlike Canopus
sought Roman standards to stage Pharian triumphs
with Caesar as captive. And in the gulf off Leucas[7]   80
there was a dangerous chance that she, a woman—
not even one of our own—would rule the world!

    Such daring spirit she got from that first night
when our own generals lay wrapped up in bed
with Ptolemy's incestuous daughter.[8] Who   85
will not forgive your raving love for her, Antony,
when fire even consumed the hard heart of Caesar?
In the midst of all the madness and fury,
with Pompeian shades inhabiting the halls
and drenched in blood from Thessaly's massacre,   90
he committed adultery, let Venus join his cares,
confused the arms of war with unlawful couches,
and fathered offspring that were not his wife's.[9]
What shame! Forgetting Magnus,[10] he gave you, Julia,
a brother from a filthy mother, permitting   95
the partisans he had routed to regroup
in Libya's distant kingdoms while he chose
to give away Pharos, not conquer it for himself. . . .

    Trusting her beauty, Cleopatra came to him,
sad but not in tears, decked out in false grief   100
(which suited her well), her hair disheveled
as though it were torn, and began her speech like this:
"If there is anything, O most mighty Caesar,

in noble birth, I—a most illustrious child
in the line of Lagus[11] and the founder of Pharos—   105
am exiled, outcast forever from my father's scepter,
unless your right hand raise me up, restore me
to my former fate.
                    "I, a queen,
embrace your feet. You have come to us
as a fair star of support unto our nation.   110
I will not be the first woman to possess
the cities of the Nile. Pharos has learned
to have a queen—sex makes no difference here.
Read my father's final dying words—
he gave me an equal share of royal power   115
and marriage with my brother. The boy loves me,
his sister, if only he were free. But his affections—
and his swords—are under the sway of Pothinus.[12]
I do not ask for any of my father's power.
Just free our house from the deep shame of its error,   120
remove the deadly arms from his attendant
and order the king to rule! How that servant
struts around, his mind so puffed with pride!
The severed head of Magnus—he's already menacing you
with that (but may the Fates keep this far off).   125
Dishonor enough, to you and the world, Caesar,
that Pompey was murdered, and Pothinus took the credit!"

     She would have tried to tempt the stubborn ears
of Caesar in vain, but looks support her prayers
and, summing up, her figure closes her filthy speech.   130
She reaps a night too wicked to speak of, spent
corrupting her judge with bribes.

                              Once her peace
was born with the chief, bought with monstrous gifts,
they consummated their pleasures in such grand affairs
with a feast, and Cleopatra rolled out   135
in great commotion her own display (not yet
exported into Roman life and times)

of lavish luxuries.
                The place itself
was like a temple, any age more decadent
could hardly build one like it. Coffered ceilings   140
vaulted their riches, the beams hid thick with gold.
No thin veneer of choicest marbles gleamed
encasing the house's walls: freestanding agate
was put to good effect, and royal porphyry,
and spread throughout the hall to walk upon   145
is onyx; vast doorposts are wrought of ebony
from Meroë (not cheap wood overlaid with it),
not just for looks but holding up the house.
Ivory decks the entryways, and hand-dyed shells
of Indian tortoise rest upon the doors,   150
their mottled knobs all adorned with emerald.
Jeweled couches flash and furnishings
of yellow jasper. All the coverlets glitter—
most of them long cooked and not just once
in vats of Tyrian dye, absorbing its full force,   155
some embroidered with radiant plumes of gold,
others on fire with crimson, the threads laced
in the Pharian style together on the loom.

     Then there were the servants, a mob in number,
an entire population of attendants helping,   160
some distinct in color and blood, some by age,
some with Libyan hair, still others so blond
that Caesar says in all the fields along the Rhine
he never saw such ruddy locks. Some with dark skin
had heads tortured into shape[13] and wore their hair   165
pulled far back off the brow. Unlucky boys
were those whom steel had rendered delicate
and soft, their manhood cut off. Standing opposite
were stronger youths whose chins, despite their age,
had yet to darken with the slightest fuzz.   170

     Reclining there were kings and a greater power,
Caesar. And with her harmful beauty painted on

excessively, not satisfied to hold her scepter
or with her brother as husband, loaded down
with the Red Sea's spoils, around her neck   175
and in her tresses Cleopatra wears her riches,
and labors under refinement. Her white breasts[14]
are clearly shining through the Sidonian fabric
(a Nilotic needle loosened the compact threads
of Chinese weave and then relaxed the texture   180
by stretching out the cloth).
                On snow-white tusks
they set down wheels, hewn from an Atlantic forest,[15]
the likes of which did not meet Caesar's eyes
even when Juba was conquered.[16]
                   What blind desire
for favor, what senseless frenzy of ostentation,   185
to reveal their own riches to a man engaged
in civil wars, to set on fire the mind
of a guest who comes in arms!
                Even supposing
it wasn't that man full ready for wicked war
and hunting for resources in the world's rubble,   190
put ancient leaders in, names from poverty's age,
Fabricius or grave Curius, have him lie down,
bring in that consul, dusty[17] from Etruscan plowing—
he will pray to lead such a triumph for his country!
They pour out dishes on gold, things that earth and air   195
and sea and the Nile had given, things that luxury,
raving to show its vanity, hunted the world over
though no hunger demands it. Many birds and beasts
they served were gods of Egypt.[18] Over their hands
crystal pours Nile waters, and gemstone goblets   200
take ample shares of wine, not from the grapes
grown on Lake Mareotis, but famed Falernian,[19]
which Meroë takes untamed and with a few years
of age compels to ferment. They put on crowns
woven with flowering nard along with roses   205
that never fail, and drench their hair with cinnamon
whose strength had not yet faded in foreign air

nor lost its native land's aroma, and cardamom
picked fresh and carried in from nearby farms.

    Caesar is learning to waste the rich resources   210
pillaged from the world, and feels ashamed
for waging a war with his poor son-in-law,
and prays for causes for war with Pharos' peoples.

PLUTARCH,
ANTONY

25.3–27.5

Translated from the Greek by
Daniel Holmes

The biographer Plutarch (46–119 CE) describes the first meeting of Antony and Cleopatra at Tarsus (in modern Turkey) in 41 BC. Though Cleopatra was at first reluctant to accept his summons, she ultimately, according to Plutarch, used this as an opportunity to display her power and to bring the Roman statesman under her sway. Plutarch throughout considers the source of Cleopatra's seductive power, arguing that it was not her beauty but her overall presence and intellect.

For [Caesar and Pompey] knew [Cleopatra] when she was still a girl and without experience in public affairs, but she was about to visit Antony at that very age when women are most stunning in their beauty and at their peak in intellect. So, she gathered together many gifts, much money, and adornments such as one would expect her to bring from all her extensive resources and thriving kingdom, but what she really put her hopes in when she arrived was her own self—the spells and beguilements of her very presence.

She received many letters of invitation both from Antony and from his friends, yet she so disdained and derided the man that she sailed up the Cydnus River on a barge fitted with a gold cabin, billowing purple sails, and a crew of rowers pulling at silver oars to the music of flutes accompanied by pipes and lyres. She herself was reclining under a canopy inwoven with gold, done up like Aphrodite in a painting, with boys, like painted Cupids, on either side fanning her. Similarly, her most beautiful slave girls—decked out like Nereids or Graces—were employed along the ship at the helm or near the mast. Wondrous fragrances emanating from numerous incense burners filled the banks. As soon as she stepped from the river, some of the inhabitants gathered about her and accompanied her on her way, while others came down from the city for the spectacle. The crowd which had been in the marketplace was now pouring out, until finally Antony found himself abandoned, all alone, sitting at his seat of office. The word on everyone's lips was that Aphrodite had come to cavort with her Dionysus for the good of Asia.

So, Antony sent for her, inviting her to dinner. But Cleopatra thought it better that he come to her. He wanted to show how easygoing and friendly he was, so he immediately assented and went to see her. He found there an opulence beyond words, but what particularly astounded him was the vast number of lights. They were suspended, it is said, in great quantities and were lit up on all sides at once; they also had been arranged in such interrelated angles and positions, whether in rectangular or circular patterns, that it was far and away one of the most remarkable and beautiful sights to see.

On the next day, Antony gave her a feast in return. He was competitively keen to outdo her in splendor and in attentiveness to detail, but he was outdone and beaten in both respects, yet was the first to make fun of his own preparations for their cheapness and vulgarity. Seeing in Antony's crude jokes the characteristics of a military and coarse man, Cleopatra treated him in a like fashion, though now with neither restraint nor caution.

As others have said, her beauty taken by itself was not altogether incomparable nor such as to astound those who saw her. But just her presence held you in an irresistible grip. Her demeanor together with the eloquence of her conversation and her character—which somehow pervaded her every interaction—all produced a certain stinging excitement. There was also a sweetness in the sound of her speaking; and her tongue, like a many-stringed instrument, she effortlessly turned to whatever language she wished, so she rarely met with foreigners needing any translation at all, but for the most part made her replies solely by herself—whether they were Ethiopian, Trogodyte, Hebrew, Arab, Syrian, Mede, or Parthian. She is said to have learned the languages of many other peoples, though the previous kings had refused to take up even the native Egyptian language.

CASSIUS DIO,
ROMAN HISTORY

50.4–5

Translated from the Greek by
Daniel Holmes

Cassius Dio (ca. 155–232 CE), born and raised in Bithynia, was a Roman senator and historian. His monumental history of Rome was written in Greek and consisted of eighty books that only partially survive. He here describes the reaction in Rome when the alleged contents of Antony's will were made public, revealing that he recognized Caesarion as Julius Caesar's legitimate heir, had bequeathed large gifts to his children with Cleopatra, and planned to be buried beside her in Egypt. This leads many in Rome to denounce him and begin preparing for war, ostensibly against Cleopatra.

Because of this the Romans grew angry and now believed the other reports that had been bandied about—namely that, if he gained power, Antony would grant Cleopatra their city as a gift and would transfer the center of power to Egypt. They became so angry that not only did Antony's enemies and those neutral in the conflict severely rebuke him, but so did his close friends. They were greatly alarmed at what they had read and began to worry that Caesar[1] might suspect them too and so were repeating what everyone else was saying. The Romans then stripped Antony of the consulship to which he had been elected as well as all the rest of his authority. They did not formally denounce him as an enemy, fearing that thereby they might make his companions who did not renounce him their enemy too; but by their action they clearly showed their opinion of him. Though they voted to pardon and praise those of Antony's friends who renounced him, against Cleopatra, nevertheless, they proclaimed outright war. They even changed into their military cloaks as though Antony were close at hand, then went to the temple of Bellona and performed all of the customary pre-war rituals with Caesar serving as Fetialis.[2]

These activities were ostensibly directed at Cleopatra, but in fact were particularly aimed at Antony. She had so enslaved him that she had persuaded him even to become gymnasiarch[3] of the Alexandrians; she was also called "Queen" and "Mistress" by him and had Roman soldiers in her personal bodyguard who inscribed her name upon their shields. She used to go to the market-place with him, joined him in arranging major festivals and determining cases of law, and rode on horseback beside him in the cities. Sometimes she would be conveyed by chariot while Antony followed her on foot with the eunuchs. Furthermore, he used to call his command post "the palace" and sometimes wore a Persian sword. His mode of dress was far from that customary to his fatherland, and he used to be seen in public on a gold couch or seat. He was depicted with her in painting or statue form—saying that he was Osiris or Dionysus, she Selene or Isis. It was because of this especially that he was thought to have lost his mind through some magical power of hers. She had so bewitched and enchanted not only him, but also those who had any influence over him, that she hoped that she would rule even the Romans; and, whenever she made an oath, her strongest pledge was "to give judgements on the Capitol."

PLINY THE ELDER, *NATURAL HISTORY*

9.119–121

Translated from the Latin by Stephanie McCarter

Prudence Jones well summarizes this famous story of Cleopatra's decadence from Pliny the Elder (23–79 CE): "Cleopatra sacrifices her pearl as a vivid reminder that she surpasses Antony not only in wealth, but in cleverness and power as well."[1]

The two largest pearls in history were both owned by Cleopatra, the last queen of Egypt, passed down to her through the hands of Eastern kings. As Antony was bingeing at one of their sumptuous daily banquets, she, with a haughty yet flirtatious arrogance that befits a queen-whore, belittled his elegance and pomp. When he asked what more magnificence could possibly be added, she answered that she could spend ten million sesterces on a single feast. Antony yearned to learn how, but did not think it was possible. And so, they made a wager.

On the following day, when judgment was to be rendered, she placed before Antony a feast that elsewhere would be magnificent, for a special occasion, but to him was daily fare. He laughed, disparaging the cost. But she asserted that this was just an extra, that the dinner would use up the whole sum—

that her portion alone would be worth ten million sesterces. She then called for dessert.

At her command, slaves placed before her a single glass of vinegar, the acidity and strength of which could dissolve pearls. Upon her ears she wore extraordinary, unparalleled works of nature. As Antony eagerly awaited what she would do, she took one off, put it in the liquid, and once it had melted, drank it down. Lucius Plancus, the wager's judge, threw his hand on the other pearl, just as she was preparing to swallow it in the same way, then declared Antony the loser—an omen that proved true. Another story accompanies this, that, after the queen who had won the contest was captured, the mate of this pearl was cut in half, so that Venus in the Pantheon at Rome might wear half of that dinner on each of her ears.

VERGIL, *AENEID*

8.675–731

Translated from the Latin by
Stephanie McCarter

Vergil's Aeneid, *although it focuses on Rome's mythical foundation, nevertheless contains several key prophecies that reveal the future ascendency of Augustus, prophecies that have been termed "history in the future tense."[1] In the following scene, the narrator describes the images on the shield of Aeneas, which Venus has persuaded her husband, Vulcan, to manufacture. The very center of the shield features an elaborate portrayal of the Battle of Actium, with the gods and generals of Rome arrayed against Antony, Cleopatra, and their Egyptian gods.*

Visible in its midst were ships of bronze—   675
Actian battle. You could see Leucate
ablaze with war, the gleam of golden waves.
Caesar Augustus here leads forth Italians,
with senate, people, gods of home and state.
On the tall stern he stands, his joyous temples   680
spewing twin flames, his father's star above him.[2]
Elsewhere Agrippa,[3] winds and gods propitious,
leads forth, on high, his troops. His temples gleam,
beaked with a naval crown, proud badge of war.
Here, with barbarian wealth and motley troops,   685
Antony, victor from Dawn's lands and blushing

shore, escorts Egypt, eastern strength, and distant
Bactra, as his Egyptian wife (sin!) follows.
All rush together, and the whole sea foams,
battered by rowing oars and three-pronged beaks.   690
They seek the deep. You'd think the Cyclades,
uprooted, swam, that peaks crashed into peaks,
in such a mass do men attack the ships.
Their hands hurl hempen flames as iron spears
go flying. Neptune's fields turn red with blood.   695
The queen, amid this, signals with her sistrum,
not seeing yet the twin snakes at her back.
All sorts of monstrous gods and barking Anubis
fight armed with Neptune, Venus, and Minerva.
And in the conflict's center rages Mars,   700
engraved in iron. From the sky, sad Furies
advance, and Discord, joyous, clothed in rags,
trailed by Bellona with her bloody whip.
Actian Apollo bends his bow, observing
on high. In terror, each Egyptian flees,   705
each Indian, Arabian, and Sabaean.
The queen herself appears to call the winds
as she unfurls her sails, the ropes now slack.
Amid the gore, the flame-lord made her pale
at looming death as wind and waves conveyed her.   710
Across, great-bodied Nile, in mourning, spreads
his arms, his whole robe welcoming the conquered
into his sea-blue bays and hidden streams.

But Caesar, borne to Rome in triple triumph,[4]
pays the Italian gods immortal vows: 715
three hundred massive temples through the city.
Streets roar with gladness, games, and cheers as matrons
throng every temple, each with its own altar;
before the altars, slain calves strew the ground.
He sits upon bright Phoebus' white threshold,[5]   720
reviewing nations' gifts, fixed to proud posts.
In a long line, the conquered peoples march,
varied in language, dress, and arms. Here, Vulcan
forged Nomads and unbelted Africans,

Leleges, Carians, arrow-armed Geloni,   725
Euphrates (waves now soft), far-flung Morini,
the two-horned Rhine, the Dahae (still untamed),
and the Araxes, outraged by his bridge.[6]

Amazed at Vulcan's shield, his mother's gift,
Aeneas savors scenes he cannot grasp,   730
then shoulders his descendants' fame and fates.

HORACE,
ODES

1.37

Translated from the Latin by
Stephanie McCarter

*This Horatian ode (23 BCE) celebrates the defeat and death
of Cleopatra. Horace's portrait of her is famously ambivalent. On the one hand, she is a dangerous, out-of-control
woman who threatens to enslave and corrupt Rome and its
men, while on the other she is a worthy adversary for Augustus, who significantly appears at the very center of the
poem and who defeats her in much the same way a hero
might defeat a mythical monster.*

Now we must drink, now pound upon the earth
with a free foot. Now it is past the time
    to ornament the couches of the gods
        with banquets of the Salii,[1] my comrades.

Before, it was a sin to bring Caecuban[2]   5
out of ancestral cellars, while the queen
    was plotting for the Capitol insane
        destruction and a funeral for the empire,

alongside her polluted herd of men
foul with disease. She had no self-control   10

to check her hopes, and on sweet fortune she
        was drunk. But having scarcely just one ship

safe from the flames diminished all her madness.
Her mind, diluted by Egyptian wine,
        was made to face the terrifying truth   15
            when Caesar, as she flew from Italy,

chased after her with oars, just as an eagle
pursues soft pigeons or a speedy hunter
        a hare within the open fields of snowy
            Thessaly, so that he could put in chains   20

the deadly monster. She, desiring
to die more nobly, neither like a woman
        grew frightened at the sword nor came ashore
            at hidden beaches with her speedy fleet.

She even dared to view her toppled palace   25
with a serene face and was brave enough
        to handle scaly serpents so she might
            drink into her own body their black poison,

fiercer because of her deliberate death—
begrudging to the cruel Liburnians[3]   30
        that she, a queen no longer, be paraded
            (no lowly woman!) in a pompous triumph.

PROPERTIUS, *ELEGIES*

3.11

Translated from the Latin by
Stephanie McCarter

In this complex poem, Propertius (ca. 50–15 BCE) connects the world of his elegiac verse to that of his contemporary Rome. The elegiac lover regularly depicts himself as metaphorically "enslaved" to his dominating mistress, and as a parallel for Cynthia's immense feminine power, Propertius cites a number of examples of famous Eastern women from both history and myth, including Medea, Penthesilea, Omphale, Semiramis, and especially Cleopatra. The poem ends, however, with a celebration of Augustus's masculine power. He becomes the sole male figure who can not only withstand emasculation by a woman like Cleopatra but also dominate her in turn.

Why marvel that[1] a woman dominates my life
    and drags beneath her laws a man enslaved?
Why falsify base charges that I am a coward
    since I can't break my yoke[2] and burst my chains?
The sailor better forecasts how the winds will blow.   5
    From wounds the soldier knows to be afraid.
I too was full of swagger in my bygone youth—
    now you should learn to fear from my example.
The Colchian yoked[3] fire-breathing bulls with adamant
    and sowed arms-bearing battles in the ground;   10

she closed the guardian dragon's furious, gaping jaws
   so Jason could take home the Golden Fleece.
Once, fiercely shooting arrows from her horse, Maeotic
   Penthesilea fought against Greek ships,
and when she stripped the golden helmet from her brow,   15
   her glowing grace subdued her male subduer.
Omphale garnered such great honor for her grace,
   a Lydian girl who bathed in Gyges' lake,[4]
that he, who'd set up pillars in the conquered world,[5]
   would use his hardened hand to spin soft wool.   20
Semiramis built Babylon, the Persian city,
   raising the solid structure from baked bricks,
so that two chariots could pass each other by
   atop the walls, unscratched by passing axles;
she led Euphrates through the citadel she founded,   25
   and to her empire she made Bactra bow.
For why should I cast blame at heroes, why at gods?
   Jove brings himself[6] and his own house reproach.
And what of her,[7] who recently disgraced our army,
   that woman worn out even by her slaves,   30
who, as the price for her vile marriage, sought Rome's walls,
   and to enslave the senate to her realm.
Destructive Alexandria, land rife with tricks,
   and Memphis, often bloodied by our woe,
there where the sand robbed Pompey of a triple triumph[8]—   35
   no day, Rome, shall remove your mark of shame!
Better had you met death on the Phlegraean field,
   or had displayed your own neck to your in-law![9]
No doubt, the whore queen of promiscuous Canopus,
   lone mark of shame burned into Philip's blood,[10]   40
dared to oppose our Jove with the barking god Anubis,
   to force the Tiber to endure Nile's threats,
to drive off Roman trumpets with her rattling sistrum,
   to rout Liburnian warships[11] with her barge-poles,
to wrap Tarpeia's rock[12] in foul mosquito nets,   45
   and to give laws near Marius' arms and statues![13]
What would have been the use of breaking Tarquin's axes,[14]
   whose proud life marked him with a matching name,
if a woman had to be endured?[15] Sing, Rome, in triumph,

and, safe, pray that Augustus will live long.   50
Yet *you*—you fled[16] to swollen Nile's meandering streams,
   nor did your hands lay hold of Roman chains.
You watched as sacred serpents bit into your arms,
   as your limbs drained a secret path of sleep.
"No need to fear me, Rome, with such a citizen!"   55
   she said, drowning her tongue in ceaseless wine.
The city, tall with seven hills, which rules all earth,
   [stands, not to be knocked down by human hand].[17]   58
These walls the gods set up; these too the gods preserve.   65
   With Caesar safe, Rome hardly need fear Jove!   66
Now where is Scipio's fleet,[18] the standards of Camillus,   67
   or, Bosporus, those Pompey's hand just seized?   68
Hannibal's spoils?[19] The monument of conquered Syphax?
   Pyrrhus' glory broken at our feet?   60
By closing chasms, Curtius built his monument;[20]
   Decius charged his horse, bursting the battle.
A street bears witness to the shattered bridge of Cocles,
   and one man took his surname from a crow.   69
Leucadian Apollo will record[21] the routed lines: 70
   one day concluded so much work of war.
But, sailor, whether you seek harbor or embark,
   remember Caesar through Ionian waves.

CASSIUS DIO, *ROMAN HISTORY*

51.14

Translated from the Greek by
Daniel Holmes

Cassius Dio describes Cleopatra's death, which took place inside her own tomb, already built in Alexandria. She had taken two enslaved women and a eunuch into the tomb with her, and they also die by suicide.

No one knows exactly how she died, for there were only light puncture marks found upon her arm. Some say that she used an asp brought to her in a water jar or even among some flowers. Others say that she used a pin with which she tied up her hair, smeared with a certain poison that did not harm the body unless it came into direct contact with even the smallest amount of blood, but then it would kill very quickly and painlessly. She regularly used to wear this poison pin in her hair, but this time she pierced her arm a little and stuck it directly into her blood. So in this way, or very like it, she died with her two slave women; but her eunuch, as soon as she was being arrested, delivered himself up voluntarily to the snakes and, once he had been bitten, rushed straight into the coffin that had been prepared for him.

When Caesar[1] heard of her end, he was dumb-struck. Indeed, he viewed her body and tried to use medicines and Psylli tribesmen to see if they might revive her. Now, these Psylli are males (there are no female Psillae), and they are able to suck out the poison of any snake, then and there, before someone dies. Even if they themselves are bitten, they suffer no harm. Psylli can only be begotten of other Psylli, and they test their offspring either by immediately throwing them among snakes or by throwing their swaddling-clothes among them. Then, in the one case, the child is not harmed, or, in the other, the snakes are numbed by the clothing. At any rate, when Caesar was not able to revive Cleopatra by any means, he stood in both wonder and pity of her, and was himself deeply grieved— as though he had been deprived of all glory for his victory.

AMANIRENAS,
QUEEN OF KUSH

The title "kandake" was given to the queens of the realm of Kush in ancient Nubia. As Solange Ashby points out, Kush in fact refers to three successive kingdoms: Kerma (2700–1500 BCE), Napata (800–300 BCE), and Meroë (300 BCE–300 CE).[1] Amanirenas was a queen during the last of these periods, ruling from ca. 40–10 BCE—that is, during the same period when Egypt, to the north, fell to Roman control. Amanirenas herself engaged in a war against the Romans as they endeavored to extend their rule into Nubia. Her troops attacked several Roman fortifications but were eventually repelled by the Roman general Petronius. After a series of battles, Augustus and Amanirenas came to a peace treaty that extended Rome's southern border to Qasr Ibrim but left Meroë independent and exempt from Roman taxation. Unlike Cleopatra's Egypt, Amanirenas's Kush never became a Roman province.

STRABO,
GEOGRAPHY

17.1.54

Translated from the Greek by
Daniel Holmes

Strabo (64 BCE–24 CE) focuses on the major events involved in the war between Rome and Meroë (which he designates using the blanket term "Ethiopians"), offering only one tantalizing glimpse of Amanirenas herself, referring to her as Candace, i.e., her title rather than her name. One detail is of particular interest. Strabo reports that, upon taking the Roman forts at Syene, Elephantine, and Philae, Amanirenas's troops toppled Augustus's statues. In 1910 excavations in Meroë uncovered a statue head belonging to Augustus buried beneath a temple. Now in the British Museum, this head is widely believed to have belonged to one of these toppled statues.

The Ethiopians, overconfident because part of the [Roman] force in Egypt had gone with Aelius Gallus to wage war against the Arabians, attacked the Thebaïs and the base of the three cohorts in Syene. They struck fast, taking Syene, Elephantine, and Philae, reducing them to slavery and toppling the statues of Caesar. But Petronius counterattacked, with fewer than five thousand infantry and eight hundred cavalry against thirty thousand men. First, he forced them to flee to Pselchis, an Ethiopian city, then sent an embassy to demand back what they had seized and ask their reasons for starting the war. They said that the nomarchs had treated them unjustly, but Petronius replied that these were not the rulers of that land—Caesar was. They requested three days to deliberate but were just stalling. So Petronius attacked and forced them to engage in battle. They were soon put to flight because they were both outmaneuvered and ill-equipped for battle. Their oval shields were huge and made of raw leather. For weapons they had axes, though some had pikes and swords. Some were driven into the city, others fled into the desert, while others made it to a nearby island, crossing at that part of the river largely free of crocodiles because of the swift current. Among this group were the generals of Queen Candace, who in my own time ruled the Ethiopians, a manly woman, blind in one eye.

Petronius, sailing after these generals in skiffs and ships, captured them all alive and immediately sent them to Alexandria while he attacked and took Pselchis. Judging by the number of men who died or were captured in this battle, those who escaped this attack turned out to be very few. From Pselchis, crossing those sand dunes where Cambyses' army was buried by a sudden sand-storm,[1] he came to the fortified city of Premnis.[2] With the first onset of his attack he took the stronghold and then set off for Napata.

This was Candace's capital and here too was her son. She herself was living somewhere nearby. She sent envoys brokering peace and also gave back those captured in Syene as well as the statues, but nevertheless Petronius attacked, captured, and— since her son escaped—utterly demolished Napata. Once he had enslaved all, he judged that going farther would be difficult, and so he turned back with his spoils.

He erected better walls in Premnis, put in a guard-post and enough food to last four hundred men two years, then left for Alexandria. Some of the captives he sold off for money, but sent one thousand to Caesar, who had just returned from Cantabria. Diseases dealt with the rest.

In the meantime, Candace attacked the guard-post of Premnis with countless thousands of men. But Petronius set off to help and reached the city first, securing the place in all manner of ways. Envoys came to him, but he told them to make their appeal to Caesar. When they claimed not to know Caesar or how to reach him, he gave them personal escorts. They reached Caesar in Samos where he was preparing for his journey to Syria and his send-off for Tiberius to Armenia. The envoys got everything they asked for, plus Caesar removed the taxes he had earlier imposed.

BOUDICCA, QUEEN OF THE ICENI

Boudicca—whose name is also spelled Boudica, Boadicaea, and Buddug (in Welsh)—was the queen of the Iceni, a Celtic tribe living in Britain at the time of the Roman occupation in the mid-first century CE. Her husband, Prasutagus, had ruled as a client king on behalf of the Romans for many years. Upon his death, soldiers in the Roman army took over the palace and badly mistreated the king's family. As a result, Boudicca staged an uprising in 60/61 CE that represents one of the most successful revolts against the empire in all of Roman history. Her forces, however, were ultimately defeated by the Roman general Paulinus, after which Boudicca died either due to self-inflicted poisoning (Tacitus) or due to sickness (Dio).

TACITUS, ANNALS

15.31–35

Translated from the Latin by Paige Graf and Christopher M. McDonough

What follows is from the account given forty years after the revolt by the historian Tacitus of events immediately following Prasutagus's death and of Boudicca's speech encouraging rebellion. Although Tacitus would have known this story from his uncle, Julius Agricola, who served in Britain at the time and was later governor of the province, it is likely that the speech the historian gives to Boudicca is a work of fiction, depicting what he imagines the queen might have said on the occasion.

The king of the Iceni, Prasutagus, was widely known and extraordinarily rich. At the end of his life, in hopes of preserving his kingdom and family from danger, he had named both Caesar and his two daughters as heirs in his will. This plan, however, turned out disastrously.

After Prasutagus died, the Roman centurions ravaged his kingdom while their slaves treated his household as a prize of war. The king's wife, Boudicca, was whipped and his daughters were violated and raped. The ancestral properties of other Icenian nobles were plundered and the king's relatives were forced into slavery. Previously the Iceni had felt that they were free. But now, they understood they were nothing more than a province.

After this atrocity, and fearing still worse, the Iceni resorted to arms. The Trinobantes were likewise moved to rebel. Other tribes whose spirits had not yet been broken by slavery all swore a secret oath to recover their freedom. The former Roman soldiers were especially despised—already the city of Camulodunum had been colonized by them, and now they were acting as though the rest of the region was theirs for the taking. These veterans were displacing people from their homes, driving them from their fields, and labeling the native peoples as "captives" and "slaves."

> *Tacitus outlines the progress of the rebellion, including the Britons' destruction and pillaging of three Roman cities: Camulodunum (modern Colchester), Londinium (modern London), and Verulamium (near modern St. Albans). He then describes the violence the Britons inflicted on the Romans, subjecting them to the same punishments the Romans themselves regularly used against the enslaved:*

It is agreed that around seventy thousand citizens and allies died in the places I have mentioned. There was no capturing or selling or any other trade of war, but rather slaughter, gallows, burnings, and crosses—as if they were rushing to take vengeance ahead of time for the punishment they would inevitably pay.

> *The Britons and Romans now prepare for a final clash. Tacitus attributes a famous speech to Boudicca before the Britons head into battle, after which she is defeated and dies by suicide by poison:*

Boudicca, riding with her daughters before her, approached each tribe in her chariot. Often, she told them, Britons had gone to war under a woman's leadership. "But," she continued, "I do not come to you as a member of the nobility for the sake of a kingdom and wealth. Instead, I come as one of the people. I want vengeance for the freedom which they have taken. I want vengeance for my body which they have whipped. And I want vengeance for my daughters whom they have raped. Roman lust has gone so far that they leave nobody untouched, not the old nor even the virgin young.

"The gods themselves stand beside us in our justified vengeance. The legion that dared to start this war has already been destroyed. The rest of them are hiding in their camps or are looking for escape. They will not withstand the sound of our soldiers' war-cries, never mind the force of their attack! Think about the sheer numbers of arms involved, and then think about the causes of this war. We either must win on the battlefield, or we must die.

"That is *this* woman's determination. You men may continue to live, and be slaves!"

TACITUS, *AGRICOLA*

16.1–2

Translated from the Latin by
Stephanie McCarter

Tacitus gives a much more condensed version of the revolt in the Agricola, *one that emphasizes the brutality he deems characteristic of barbarians.*

Incited, one after another, by things of this sort,[1] they all collectively took up war—and a woman, Boudicca, was their leader[2] (for they do not differentiate between the sexes when it comes to military commands). After they had chased down the Roman soldiers scattered among the forts and stormed the garrisons, they attacked the colony itself,[3] considering it the seat of slavery. In their wrath and victory, they omitted no kind of brutality found among the barbarians. If Paulinus had not rushed in to help after learning of the disturbance in the province, Britain would have been lost.

CASSIUS DIO, *ROMAN HISTORY*

62.3–7

Translated from the Greek by Daniel Holmes

The account of Boudicca's revolt found in Cassius Dio (ca. 155–235 CE) is from one of his books that did not survive in its original form but instead comes from the eleventh-century CE epitome penned by Byzantine writer Ioannes Xiphilinus, who likely condensed the text. Whereas Tacitus's version of Boudicca's speech comes at the end of the revolt, before she goes off to her final defeat, Dio's version comes as the uprising is getting underway. Dio, furthermore, offers much more gruesome details about the rebellion itself, though it is generally agreed that his account, written more than a century later, is historically unreliable.

Just prior to this speech, Dio gives a memorable description of Boudicca's appearance: "She was towering in stature and grim in appearance; her look was fierce and her voice was rough. She had full red hair¹ which fell below her waist and, around her neck, she wore a great golden torc. Clothed in a colorful embroidered tunic, she wore a cloak fastened around her." Her looks are a stark contrast to the conventions of feminine dress among the Romans. With her streaming hair and golden torc, she is the very embodiment of the barbarian, perhaps of Britain itself.

"You have now been convinced—through actual experience—how much greater freedom is than slavery. Even if some of you previously were ignorant of this due to your lack of experience and were deceived by the seductive promises of the Romans, now that you have tried each, you know just how wrong you were when you preferred a foreign master to your native way of life. You have also learned how far superior poverty without a master is to wealth with slavery. Is there any degrading or painful thing that we have not suffered since the Romans appeared in Britain? Have we not lost all of our abundant and most precious possessions? If anything is left to us, are we not taxed on it? Do we not also pasture and cultivate all of our land for them? And then every year bring them what they exact from our bodies' labor? Would it not be far better to be sold off once and for all, rather than every year to make payments in the name of some empty freedom? Would it not be better to have been slaughtered and killed than to live a life constantly subject to taxation? Yet not even this is true. For with them our deaths, too, are a source of income. You know the taxes we pay for our dead. In the rest of human society, death frees even the slave, but among the Romans alone the dead still live for their profit. And how is it that, even though none of us has any money—where could we get it from?—we are despoiled and picked over like murder victims? Will they temper their treatment of us in the course of time? But it is only at the very beginning that people care for what they've captured, even wild animals.

"We are the ones responsible for all of our problems, to speak plain truth. We initially allowed them to set foot on our island. We did not, as we did with Julius Caesar, immediately drive them out.[2] We did not, as we did with Augustus and Gaius Caligula, make sure that they kept their distance and feared even to attempt the crossing. This is why our island[3]—an island so large, like a continent surrounded by the sea, like a world of our own, separated by the ocean from all others, so separate that some of them, even the most learned, believed we inhabit a different earth and sky, and had not until recently correctly learned our name—this is why we have been despised and trampled on by people who know nothing but greed. But although we did not act sooner, now is the time, citizens, friends, and kin—and I do consider you all my kin, who share this single island as our home and are called by a single name—now is the time to act and to do our duty while we can still remember freedom, so we can leave our children both the word and the reality of freedom. For if we entirely forget the thriving vigor in which we were brought up, what could they do who were brought up in slavery?

"The goal of this speech is not to rouse hatred in you for what you now suffer (for hatred is already in you) nor to rouse fear for what may come (for fear too is in you), but to praise you because you are already willingly doing what you have to do, and also to thank you because you are readily taking up my cause and yours.

"Don't fear the Romans at all. They are neither more numerous nor braver than you. Here is proof: they cover their bodies in helmets, breast plates, and greaves; they build stockades, walls, and trenches in their worry about enemy raids. They do this out of fear, whereas we act as each present moment demands. Our exceptional bravery means that we consider our tents to be more secure than their walls and our shields more effective than their entire suit of arms. And so, when we have the upper hand in battle, we capture them; but when we are under pressure, we can escape. If we choose to retreat, we can disappear into marshes and mountains and not be detected or captured. But, because of the very heaviness of their gear, they can neither pursue nor flee. If they do run off, they flee to certain predesignated places where they are caught in a trap like animals.

"Their inferiority is also shown in their inability to withstand hunger and thirst, cold and heat—unlike us. They must have shade and shelter, bread rolls, wine, and olive oil. If even one of these is lacking, they're done for. Whereas for us, any plant or root is our food, any juice our olive oil, any water our wine, and any tree our house. Furthermore, we know this land like a friend and ally, but for them it is unknown and hostile. We swim across the rivers naked; they can barely cross them with boats. So let's take them on with great confidence in our good fortune. Let's show them that they are hares and foxes trying to rule dogs and wolves."

At this, she let loose a hare from her dress as a form of augury.[4] When the hare ran to the side of good omen, the entire crowd shouted aloud in delight. Boudicca stretched her hands up to the sky and said: "I give thanks to you, Andraste,[5] and call upon you, woman to woman. I do not rule slavish Egyptians like Nitocris did,[6] nor merchant Assyrians like Semiramis—and it is from the Romans that we have learned about such people—nor do I rule Romans, as Messalina once did,[7] and then Agrippina, and now Nero who, though he may be called a 'man,' is in fact a woman—his singing, lyre-playing, and use of makeup clearly attest to this.

"No, I rule men of Britain—men who know not how to work in the fields nor ply a trade, but who have rigorously learned combat in war; who believe that everything they have is a common possession of all, even their children and women—and this means that their women have the same prowess and courage as their males. As queen of such men and such women, I pray and implore you, Andraste, for victory, deliverance, and freedom from men who know neither honor nor justice nor satiety nor reverence—if, indeed, we ought to call 'men' people who bathe in warm water, eat contrived delicacies, drink unmixed wine, daub themselves with perfumes, sleep on soft beds with young men (and some not so young) and who are now slaves to a lyre-player—and a bad one at that. May this Neroess, this Domina-trix[8]—please may she no longer be queen over us. Let her sing and be slavemaster of Romans—and don't those who put up with such a tyrantess deserve to be enslaved to such a woman? But for us, Mistress Andraste, may you ever be our only commander."

After giving a speech such as this to her people, Boudicca led her army against the Romans, who happened to be without a leader since their commander Paulinus was making war on Mona, an island[9] off the coast of Britain. Because of this, she ransacked and pillaged two Roman cities,[10] unleashing (as I have said) an unspeakable massacre. There is no kind of atrocity that was left undone to those they captured. Their most atrocious and brutal deed was this: they stripped and strung up the most noble and illustrious women, then cut off their breasts and sewed them onto their mouths so that it looked like they were eating them. After this, they impaled them on sharp stakes driven lengthwise through the whole body. And as they did all this, they performed sacrifices and feasted and committed abuses in all of their own shrines, especially in the grove of Andate—this was their name for Nike,[11] and they revered her most highly.

ZENOBIA,
REGENT OF PALMYRA

Zenobia (ca. 240–274 CE) ruled in Palmyra, Syria, coming to power after the assassination of her husband, Odaenathus. She ruled as regent for her son, Septimius Vaballathus. The Palmyrenes were nominally subordinate to Rome, but in 270 CE Zenobia rebelled, taking over Egypt and areas of Asia Minor. Her rebellion was put down by the Roman emperor Aurelian in 272–273 CE, who sacked Palmyra, took Zenobia captive, and marched her in triumph in Rome in 274 CE.

HISTORIA AUGUSTA,
"THE THIRTY PRETENDERS"

30

Translated from the Latin by
Stephanie McCarter

The so-called Historia Augusta *(4th c. CE), a collection of biographies of Roman emperors, offers the primary Roman literary evidence for Zenobia, though conflicting Arab versions of her reign exist. The* Historia Augusta *unsurprisingly offers ambivalent testimony, attributing to her qualities that are stereotypical of female rule while also characterizing her as a worthy adversary of Rome.*

Now all shame was squandered, and the state became so enervated that, while Gallienus conducted himself[1] appallingly, even women ruled most effectively. In fact, a foreigner named Zenobia, about whom much has been said already, who boasted that she was descended from Cleopatra and the Ptolemies, wrapped the imperial cloak around her shoulders after the death of her husband, Odaenathus, dressing like Dido and even accepting a diadem. She ruled in the name of her sons Herennianus and Timolaus longer than the female sex should be endured. Indeed, this proud woman served as regent while Gallienus was still ruling the state as well as while Claudius was busy battling the Goths.[2] Finally, she was just barely conquered by

Aurelian,[3] and yielded to Roman authority after being marched
in a triumph.

A letter of Aurelian still exists that gives testimony about
this woman's captivity. For when certain people reproached
him since he, the mightiest of men, had marched a woman in
triumph as if she were a general, he sent a letter to the senate
and the Roman people, defending himself on these grounds: "I
hear, senators, that I am criticized for the unmanly deed of
marching Zenobia in triumph. But those who fault me could
never praise me enough if they knew what kind of woman she
is, how wise in her counsel, how resolute in her plans, how im-
pressive to her soldiers, how generous when need demands,
how strict when austerity demands. I can say that it was due to
her that Odaenathus conquered the Persians and routed Sapor,
advancing as far as Ctesiphon. I can assert that this woman so
terrified the peoples of the East and of Egypt that the Arabians,
the Saracens, and the Armenians made no trouble. I would not
have kept her alive if I had not known her to have aided the
state greatly while she was preserving power for herself or for
her growing children. And so, let those who cannot be pleased
keep the venom of their tongues to themselves. For if it is not
seemly to have conquered a woman and marched her in triumph, what do they say of Gallienus, in contempt of whom
this woman ruled well? What of divine Claudius, that holy and
reverend general, who, because he was busy attacking the Goths,
is said to have let her rule? And he did this thoughtfully and
wisely, so she could guard the empire's eastern border while he
fulfilled his aims." This speech shows Aurelian's high opinion
of Zenobia.

They say she was so chaste she would not even have sex
with her own husband unless they were trying to conceive. She
would sleep with him a single time, then abstain until she was
due to menstruate, when she would learn if she was pregnant.
If not, she would grant him another opportunity to try for
children.

She lived in regal grandeur. She was worshipped in the Persian manner, and banqueted like Persian kings. But she marched
helmeted like a Roman general to assemblies, while wearing a
purple-striped stola[4] with gems dangling from its hem, pinned

in the middle with a jewel rather than a woman's clasp, and her arms were regularly uncovered. Her face was brown, dark in its complexion, and her black eyes were unusually full of life. Her spirit was godlike, and her charm beyond belief. Her teeth were so bright that most people thought they were pearls, not teeth. Her voice was loud and masculine. She had a tyrant's austerity, when need demanded, and the mercy of good emperors, when piety required it. She was generous, but with restraint, and thrifty with treasure more than is normal for a woman. She would ride in a two-wheeled carriage, rarely in a four-wheeled matron's wagon,[5] and more often she went on horseback. They say she regularly would walk alongside the infantry for three or four miles. She hunted with the zeal of the Spanish. She drank with the generals but otherwise was sober. She also drank with the Persians and Armenians in order to overpower them. At banquets, she used golden goblets covered in gems, even ones that belonged to Cleopatra.

She kept mature eunuchs on her staff, but girls very rarely. She ordered her sons to speak Latin, and consequently they spoke Greek infrequently and with difficulty. She herself was not entirely fluent in Latin, yet she would repress her embarrassment and speak it. She spoke Egyptian perfectly. She was such an expert in the history of Alexandria and the East that she is said to have written an abridgment of it. But she read Roman history in Greek.

After Aurelian took her captive and brought her into his presence, he asked her, "Why, Zenobia, did you dare to insult Rome's emperors?" She is said to have answered: "I recognize that *you* are an emperor, for you are a conqueror, but I did not think Gallienus and Aureolus and the rest were. Trusting that Victoria was similar to me,[6] I hoped we could join our realms, if the distance between our lands allowed." And so, she was led in triumph with such splendor that the Romans thought nothing could be more magnificent. First, she was adorned with enormous gems and struggled under the weight of her adornments. The woman, though very strong, reportedly stopped often, saying she could not bear the gems' weight. Her feet were shackled with gold, her hands with golden fetters, and there was a golden chain around her neck, which a Persian jester carried in

front of her. Her life was spared by Aurelian, and she is said to
have lived, along with her children, in the manner of a Roman
matron on an estate given to her at Tibur that even today is
named "Zenobia." It is not far from Hadrian's Villa or that
place known as Concha.[7]

Notes

PART ONE: THE WOMAN-RUN STATE

1. **"defeated, by men":** See "Amazons," *Oxford Classical Dictionary*, 4th ed. (Oxford: Oxford University Press, 2012).

STRABO, *GEOGRAPHY* 11.5.1–4

1. **In fact, Theophanes:** Mytilenean (and later a Roman citizen) who accompanied Pompey the Great on his Third Mithridatic War (73–63 BCE). He wrote a history of Pompey's campaigns.
2. **Metrodorus of Scepsis and Hypsicrates:** Scepsis is in northeast Anatolia, in the Troad region. Metrodorus (mid-early first century BCE) wrote a variety of works including a geographical treatise. Little is known of Hypsicrates. He likely lived circa first century BCE and is perhaps from a Greek colony (Amisus) on the Black Sea.
3. **the long hammer:** The *sagaris*, a long-shafted weapon with a metal axe-like or hammer-like head. Used especially by horse-riding peoples such as the Scythians.
4. **the light shield:** The *pelte*—it was made of wicker and covered with leather, unlike the heavier wood and metal shield carried by Greek hoplites.
5. **area from Themiscyra:** This is the original legendary city of the Amazons, normally located in the Pontic region of Asia Minor.
6. **Ephesus, Smyrna, Cyme, and Myrina:** Cities in Asia Minor popularly believed to have been founded by Amazons.
7. **Cleitarchus says that:** Greek historian (fl. around 300 BCE) who was the source of what is now known as the "vulgate tradition" of Alexander the Great. Ancient critics generally viewed him as unreliable.

DIODORUS SICULUS,
LIBRARY OF HISTORY 2.45–46

1. **acquired its name:** See Introduction, p. xiv.
2. **the river Tanais:** The modern Don in Russia.
3. **to Artemis Tauropolos:** Artemis the "bull-tamer."

HERODOTUS, *HISTORIES* 4.110–118

1. **fought the Amazons:** This probably refers to Hercules's expedition to steal the war belt of Hippolyta.

DIODORUS SICULUS,
LIBRARY OF HISTORY 4.16

1. **Aëlla was the first:** Her name means "storm wind."

PLUTARCH, *THESEUS* 26–28

1. **Eupatrids in Athens:** The name simply means "well-born" and refers to the ancient Athenian nobility.
2. **month of Boëdromion:** This was the last month of the Athenian summer.
3. **celebrate the Boëdromia:** A festival for Apollo Boëdromios—"he who runs to one's aid" in difficult times.
4. **struck by Molpadia's spear:** Molpadia would be the name of an Amazon.
5. **across to Chalcis:** A town on the island of Euboea.
6. **called the Amazoneum:** This would have been a site of Amazon tombs, and cult worship likely took place there.
7. **died around Chaeronea:** A town in the Greek region of Boeotia.
8. **Phaedra and this son:** Phaedra would fall in love with Hippolytus, her own stepson. When he rebuffs her, she dies by suicide after penning a letter falsely accusing him of raping her. Believing her, Theseus curses Hippolytus to his own father, Poseidon, who sends a bull from the sea to kill him. The best-known version of these events is the tragedy *Hippolytus* by Euripides.

QUINTUS OF SMYRNA,
POSTHOMERICA 1.574–674

1. **son of Peleus:** Achilles.
2. **loud-thundering son:** Achilles and Ajax were cousins, both grandsons of Aeacus, the king of Aegina. The island takes its name

from Aeacus's mother, Aegina, whom Zeus kidnapped in the form of an eagle and thereupon raped, making her pregnant with Aeacus.

3. **both of us:** Ajax and Achilles.
4. **flowing Xanthus:** One of the chief rivers in the plain around Troy.
5. **that Chiron forged:** Chiron was the wisest of the horse-man centaurs. He mentored a number of heroes, including Jason and Achilles.
6. **for slaying Argives:** "Argive" was a general term for the "Greeks."
7. **well-crowned Cypris:** Aphrodite, goddess of erotic love and sexuality. She was traditionally married to Hephaestus, the god of fire, but famously had an affair with Ares, the war god.

QUINTUS CURTIUS, *HISTORY OF ALEXANDER* 6.5.24–32

1. **bordering Hyrcania:** Hyrcania was a region in modern-day Iran. Alexander's conquests extended across the Achaemenid Persian Empire and into South Asia.

ARISTOPHANES, *ASSEMBLYWOMEN*

1. **O splendid brilliance:** The translation is based on the text of Jeffrey Henderson in the Loeb Classical Library (Cambridge, MA: Harvard University Press, 2002). The notes are indebted to the commentaries of Alan H. Sommerstein, *Ecclesiazusae* (Warminster, UK: Aris & Phillips, 1998) and Robert G. Ussher, *Aristophanes: Ecclesiazusae* (Bristol: Bristol Classical Press, 1998).
2. **your birth and fortunes:** Praxagora is offering a parody of a hymn or prayer, which involves formulaic components, such as mentioning the story of the god's birth and various offices.
3. **at the Skira:** Also known as the Skirophoria, the Skira was a religious festival in Athens. Little is known about it, but it seems to have involved women-only rites and thus would have afforded women a rare opportunity to leave the domestic sphere and to convene in the absence of men.
4. **Pyromachus, if you recall:** The joke here is unclear, but Pyromachus seems to have made a slip of the tongue when addressing the Assembly, perhaps saying "courtesans" (*hetairai*) when he meant to say "comrades" (*hetairoi*). Praxagora may hint at both meanings here, which I have tried to capture with "bedfellows."
5. ***rowed* me on the bed:** Salamis was an island well-known for contributing rowers to the Athenian fleet.

6. **at leisure, from her husband:** The joke here is probably that her husband is impotent.

7. **Here's mine, by Hecate:** Hecate was a goddess associated with the crossroads, magic, and the moon, and this was a common women's oath. Women often swear on female goddesses, and this feature of women's speech is something they must overcome as they practice for the Assembly.

8. **nicer than Epicrates':** Epicrates was a politician known for his long beard.

9. **executioner in business:** This is another difficult joke to decipher. In mythology, Argos was the hundred-eyed guardian of Io. He would perhaps have held a staff and worn a tattered leather shepherd's coat, or perhaps the coat refers to his own skin, dotted with eyes. As Sommerstein explains, "we expect the sentence to end with 'Io,' but instead it ends with the public executioner. . . . 'Lamius', it may be hoped, will soon be providing (becoming) a day's work for the executioner."

10. **some woolwork done:** Woolwork was done exclusively by women and thus would have given them away.

11. **bare any skin:** As commentators note, carding wool required women to sit with their skirts raised and one leg propped up. On the one hand, Praxagora does not want the women to card wool *during* the Assembly in case they accidentally flash someone. On the other hand, she does not want the women to work wool while waiting for the Assembly to begin in case they have trouble finding a seat and inadvertently flash someone while trying to climb across the crowd.

12. **exposing her Phormisius:** Another politician known for his hairiness.

13. **once a woman:** It is unknown who Pronomus was, but clearly the joke is about Agyrrhius's lack of virility and likely a suggestion that he has played the passive role in sexual acts with men.

14. **these garlands down:** These were also for practicing since speakers in the Assembly wore garlands.

15. **beards on roasted cuttlefish:** A joke based on the associations of women with paleness. A cuttlefish is light in color, and its being "roasted" refers to the suntans of the women.

16. **carry round the cat:** A reference to the sacrifice made prior to the start of the Assembly. This normally would have been a pig, but the women are practicing with a cat.

17. **wear this garland:** Garlands were also worn at symposia, "drinking parties," to which wives were not normally invited.

18. **between your legs:** Praxagora tells them to lean their "frame" (*schema*) on their walking stick. *Schema* was also a slang term for female genitalia.

19. **Back in the day:** Prior to the introduction of pay for attending the Assembly, a recently instituted change that Agyrrhius seems to have championed.

20. **What's more, this League:** Commentators note that this could be two possible anti-Spartan alliances, either an alliance with Thebes in 395 BCE or a slightly later one also involving Corinth, Argos, and others.

21. **Hieronymus is wise:** Hieronymus was an Athenian general. The point is that both he and the people of Argos made similar proposals, but the fickle Assembly had divergent reactions to them.

22. **Thrasybulus gets angry:** He was a famous naval commander who advised the Assembly not to accept a peace treaty with Sparta. Praxagora implies he did this because he was not put in charge of it.

23. **common interest flails:** Aesimus was an important politician and ambassador. Praxagora suggests that he was known for being unsteady, either on his feet or mentally.

24. **In the displacements:** It's not entirely clear what period of displacement she means, but the most likely possibility was in the aftermath of the Athenian defeat at Aegospotami in 404 BCE.

25. **what if Cephalus:** An orator and politician. He seems also to have been involved in the manufacture of pottery.

26. **Athens go to pot:** As Sommerstein notes, *kerameuein* means both to "make a pot" (cf. the English word "ceramics") and to mishandle public affairs. I follow his translation of the pun.

27. **rheum-eyed Neocleides:** Otherwise unknown, but mentioned as a politician numerous times in Aristophanes's later plays.

28. **one knob the richer:** A *pattalos* is literally a "clothespin," but it was also a slang term for a penis.

29. **made this vow:** I have tried to keep my line numbering of the choral odes as close as possible to Henderson's.

30. **have the runs:** Cinesias was a dithyrambic poet at whom Aristophanes frequently takes aim, accusing him more than once of having bouts of diarrhea.

31. **The pear Thrasybulus:** This exact reference is unknown, but Sommerstein suggests that perhaps "Thrasybulus asserted that one or another Spartan or Persian demand was blocking the path to peace as firmly as a wild pear blocks up the bowels."

32. **O reverend Ilithyia:** She is the goddess of childbirth.

33. **to mark the circle:** This dye-smeared rope was used to round people into the Assembly. The laughter here probably arose from the fact that the Assembly was over before it usually began.
34. **just like shoemakers:** Because they worked indoors, their skin would not have been tanned by the sun. Pale skin was commonly associated with women, who similarly would have spent much time indoors.
35. **Antilochus, mourn not:** This is a quotation from the tragedy *Myrmidons* by Aeschylus, except that "my three obols" has been inserted for "my dead comrade." In the tragedy, Achilles laments the loss of Patroclus.
36. **Nausicydes could have funded:** According to Xenophon (*Memorabilia* 2.7.6), he was a wealthy miller.
37. **image of Nicias:** Most commentators understand this Nicias to be the grandson of the famous general of the same name, which would make him about twenty years old at the time of the play.
38. **"tightened Spartan reins":** Praxagora is probably quoting a line of tragedy here, using "reins" to refer to the straps of her husband's Spartan sandals.
39. **All has been done:** Lines 514–19 are in catalectic anapestic tetrameters, a significant metrical shift from the predominantly iambic rhythms that have preceded. To capture this change, I have switched to dactylic pentameter, which has similar rhythms.
40. **baby was a boy:** In acting as a midwife, Praxagora could expect extra payment for assisting the birth of a boy.
41. **Off with delay:** This line returns us to the anapestic tetrameter seen already in 514–19, which I again render in English dactylic pentameter. This meter will continue throughout the debate between Praxagora and Blepyrus.
42. **his poopermint scent:** Aristophanes puns on *kalaminthes* ("mint") and *minthos* ("poop"). The joke is that he licks anuses.
43. **stoas for banquets:** Literally "as *androne.*" An *andron* was the public "male" space (*andra* = "man") in the house that was used for symposia. Citizen wives and daughters would not normally be present in such spaces.
44. **We won't allow:** The English meter here changes to three dactylic feet to reflect the shorter anapestic lines of the Greek.
45. **Now say if:** This line returns us to the regular iambic meter.
46. **Come here, my sieve:** The Neighbor playfully collects his possessions as if he were orchestrating a mock Panathenaic Procession, a major Athenian religious festival in which offerings were carried up to the Acropolis as dedications to Athena. He is giving

these orders to two enslaved men, Sicon and Parmenon, whom he names below.

47. **More than Callias:** He was known for having squandered much of the fortune he had inherited.

48. **to copper coins:** This probably refers to silver-plated bronze coins minted at the end of the Peloponnesian War, a time when Athens was in financial crisis. These coins were withdrawn after just a few years.

49. **five hundred talents:** This tax was most likely meant for the building of a new fleet.

50. **licking clean the women's bowls:** A joking reference to cunnilingus.

51. **Geron is there:** His name means "old man," and he seems to have reverted to youth. The rejuvenation of the old is a recurring comic motif.

52. **Converse with *this*:** It is unclear to what the old woman refers, but Sommerstein suggests she may be pointing to her anus, giving her the middle finger, or holding up a dildo.

53. **blow job queen:** The Greek literally says that she is a "lambda, like the Lesbians." This joke doesn't work in English at all since the connotation of "lesbian" has changed drastically. In Greek antiquity, it was associated with performing fellatio.

54. **except for Mr. Oldman:** The Greek calls this man Geres, which means "old."

55. **_here's_ the entrance:** The Greek word for "door" was a common euphemism for a vagina.

56. **hammer at the moment:** My translation plays on "hammer" as in "to knock" and "hammer" as in the tool. The Greek plays on *krouseis* ("knock") and *krêsera* ("colander").

57. **urns that hold the dead:** I.e., Death. He is suggesting that Death would mistake her for a corpse.

58. **gonna be Procrustes:** Procrustes was a mythical figure who tied travelers to his bed and either cut their limbs or stretched them out to make them fit it. Theseus subjected him to this same procedure. Aristophanes also puns on the word *prokrouein*, "to fuck first," which appeared twice in the women's decree.

59. **one of my demesmen:** In the classical period, Attica was subdivided into about 139 demes, or districts, and all male citizens would have been officially registered in one of them.

60. **one bushel's value:** In reality, this was a restriction on women in the Athens of Aristophanes's day.

61. **decline on oath:** Such an oath was sworn by someone who could not take up a public office due, for instance, to sickness.

62. **to be a merchant:** Because merchants were exempt from military duty, Epigenes hopes this would exempt him from this sexual duty too.

63. **A Diomedean must:** A reference to an obscure proverb. Sommerstein connects this to a story about Odysseus and Diomedes and defines such a "must" as "a situation in which one has to obey orders or die." An ancient scholiast suggests this refers to another Diomedes, who forced passersby to sleep with his daughters.

64. **a bed of marjoram:** Epigenes describes preparations for a funeral—his own.

65. **a funeral spray:** These lines play on bridal and funeral imagery. The "bouquet" the old woman has just mentioned is in Greek the "garland" worn by a bride. Epigenes says that he will buy her one made of wax—wax garlands were often placed on the heads of the dead at funerals.

66. **giant blood blister:** An Empusa was a shapeshifting female monster. The blood blister is probably a reference to the old woman's rouge.

67. **now must pound:** Cannonus's decree stated that anyone accused of "injuring the Athenian people" had to be bound during their trial and held by two guards.

68. **bowl of bearded oysters:** Literally, a bowl of plant bulbs (*bolbôn*), which commentators take to be a fortifying aphrodisiac. But *bolbôn* can also mean "vulvas," while "bowls" are frequently mentioned in reference to cunnilingus. Nowadays, oysters are considered aphrodisiacs, while "bearded oyster" is a slang term for a vulva.

69. **that one there:** Probably Old Woman C.

70. **finished with hot wings:** This menu list is one long word in the original—the longest surviving word in ancient Greek!

SEMIRAMIS, QUEEN OF BABYLON

1. **all the way to India:** For the similarity, see Iris Sulimani, "Myth or Reality? A Geographical Examination of Semiramis' Journey in Diodorus," *Scripta Classica Israelica* 24 (2005): 45–63. Sulimani writes that "the Persian kings, Alexander's predecessors, had also toured most of these countries, as had the Hellenistic kings and Roman leaders, his successors."

DIODORUS SICULUS, *LIBRARY OF HISTORY* 2.4–20 (SELECTIONS)

1. **a city, Ascalon:** Present-day Ashkelon lies on the coast of Israel about thirty miles south of Tel Aviv.

2. **Syrians call Derceto:** Usually called Atargatis by the Greeks.
3. **mountain called Bagistan:** This mountain in western Iran is now known as Behistun (also spelled Bisotoun, Bisotun, or Bistun).
4. **pleasure garden:** The Greek is *paradeisos*, from which we get the word "paradise."
5. **had etched upon it:** This is the famous Behistun Inscription—made by Darius, King of Persia, and here wrongly attributed to Semiramis.
6. **mountain called Zarcaeus:** The Zagros Mountains in western Iran.
7. **then reached Ammon:** This is the famous oracle at Siwah, where Alexander also consulted the god.
8. **all of her satrapies:** These are the provinces of various Near Eastern empires, and they were ruled by governors known as "satraps."
9. **Ctesias of Cnidus:** A fifth-century BCE Greek historian from Caria in Asia Minor.
10. **Romans and their Libyan elephants:** Perseus was the final Antigonid king of Macedon, ruling from 179–168 BCE. He was defeated by the Romans at the Battle of Pydna.

OVID, *HEROIDES* 9.53–118 (DEIANIRA TO HERCULES)

1. **Meander, frequent roamer:** A river (the modern Büyük Menderes) in Lydian Asia Minor known for its "meandering" course.
2. **wears as covering:** Hercules's first labor was to kill the Nemean lion, whose pelt the hero then famously dons.
3. **white poplar suits:** The white poplar was sacred to Hercules, and he is sometimes described as wearing a crown of its leaves.
4. **mares with human flesh:** Diomedes was a Thracian king who fed the flesh of murdered guests to his rabid mares. Hercules in turn fed him to the mares.
5. **But had Busiris:** Busiris was an Egyptian king who sacrificed guests. He prepared to sacrifice Hercules too, but the hero escaped and killed him.
6. **shamed at submitting:** Antaeus was a son of Poseidon and the Earth, and he was invincible so long as his body remained in contact with his mother. He would challenge passersby to a wrestling contest, pinning them to the ground and killing them. Hercules defeated him by holding him off the ground and crushing him in his arms. The word *succumbuisse* ("to submit") has a clear sexual suggestion here since it can be used of submitting to

sexual penetration. Conquest is thus figured in sexual terms, and Antaeus feels feminized by having been conquered by such a feminized hero.

7. **famous mistress' share:** An enslaved woman might be assigned a *pensum*, a weighed allotment of wool, to spin each day.

8. **You lay before:** The text of this couplet is considered spurious and omitted by most editors.

9. **your infant hand:** When Hercules was a newborn baby, Juno/Hera sent snakes to kill him. Instead, he strangled and killed them.

10. **mauled the earth:** One of Hercules's labors was to capture the Erymanthian boar alive.

11. **skulls nailed up:** Diomedes, after feeding his mares human flesh (see note 4 on line 68 above), would nail the victims' skulls up in his palace.

12. **that triple marvel:** Geryon was a three-bodied monster killed by Hercules. The hero had to steal his cattle as one of his labors.

13. **with hissing snakes:** Another labor of Hercules was to capture Cerberus, the guard dog of the Underworld. Cerberus often had three heads, with snakes intertwined in his fur.

14. **by her own loss:** The Hydra was a monster with multiple serpent heads. If one head was cut off, two would grow back in its place. Hercules defeated her by cauterizing the necks to keep them from regenerating.

15. **were strangling him:** The identity of this victim is not clear.

16. **the equine troop:** The centaurs, whom Hercules fought and defeated en route to capture the Erymanthian boar. As the centaur Pholus was hosting him in his cave, the other centaurs smelled the wine Pholus opened for his guest and attacked.

17. **your Sidonian garb:** Sidon was famous for the rich purple dye produced from the murex shellfish.

18. **with Lerna's poisons:** After killing the Lernaean Hydra, Hercules poisoned his arrows by dipping them into her blood.

OVID, *FASTI* 2.303–358

1. **to his mistress:** Omphale, mistress of the "Tirynthian youth," Hercules.

2. **vines of Tmolus:** Tmolus was a mountain in Lydia, but it was also the name of Omphale's husband, the Lydian king, after whose death she came to sole power.

3. **his dusky steed:** Hesperus is the god of the evening. Ovid imagines him riding a dark horse across the sky.

4. **dyed Gaetulian purple:** Gaetulia was a North African region known for its luxurious purple dye.
5. **the vine's inventor:** Bacchus.

APOLLONIUS OF RHODES, *ARGONAUTICA* 1.607–914

1. **1.607–904:** These are the line numbers for the original Greek, although the line numbers for Poochigian's English translation are given throughout the selection.
2. **the venerable Sintians:** This was traditionally the name of the inhabitants of Lemnos.
3. **handcrafts of Athena:** The spinning and weaving of wool.
4. **Maenad cannibals:** Maenads were female devotees of Dionysus, the god of wine. It was thought that they would enter an ecstatic state and perform a *sparagmos*, a "tearing-apart," of a wild animal, then consume the raw flesh (*omophagia*). This is probably what the narrator has in mind when he calls them "cannibals" since there were myths that involved them performing a *sparagmos* on human beings.
5. **his father Hermes:** The messenger god, and thus suitable to be the father of a messenger.
6. **tide of Acheron:** Acheron was a river in the Underworld and often stood for the Underworld as a whole.
7. **change homes endlessly:** Aethalides would experience a cycle of death and reincarnation. Because he remembered everything, he had the ability to recall his past lives.
8. **sought out the Minyans:** This was another name for the Argonauts.
9. **vivid-purple mantle:** Thus begins the most significant ekphrasis in the *Argonautica*. Such *ekphraseis*, or descriptions of works of art, were a standard feature of epic going back to Homer's *Iliad*, where the shield of Achilles is described. Apollonius offers an ekphrasis not of armor but of a cloak, highlighting the fact that Jason's success comes not from battle prowess but personal attractiveness. Much ink has been spilled on how to interpret the individual scenes on the cloak, but no consensus has been reached. What is clear is that the cloak bestows Jason with a radiant beauty that gives him a starlike quality.
10. **Pallas had given:** Pallas was another name for Athena, who works on Jason's behalf. She was the goddess of war, handcrafts, and weaving.
11. **The Cyclopes:** These are the one-eyed giants best known from Homer's *Odyssey*. They are also craftsmen who fashion accoutrements for the gods, often toiling in the workshop of Hephaestus.

12. **Zethus and Amphion:** These twin sons of Zeus and Antiope were credited with the construction of Thebes's walls. While Zethus toiled to hoist the rocks, Amphion simply charmed them into place with his lyre.

13. **thickly braided Cytherea:** Aphrodite, who here gazes at her reflection in the shield of Ares, her lover.

14. **to win the herd:** Electryon was a king on the Greek Argolid, and the Taphians were descendents of his brother, Mestor. The Taphians came to claim Electryon's kingdom and, when he rebuffed them, drove off his cattle. Electryon's sons then fought against the Taphians to retrieve the cattle, with all but one man dying on each side.

15. **pair of chariots:** This is the chariot race between Pelops and Oenomaus, who was the king of Pisa in the Greek region of Elis. Pelops wanted to marry Hippodamia, Oenomaus's daughter, but the king refused unless Pelops could defeat him in a chariot race. Pelops won by bribing Myrtilus, Oenomaus's charioteer, to remove the linchpins from his chariot, causing him to wreck.

16. **at giant Tityus:** Tityus was shot by Apollo and Artemis when he attempted to rape their mother, Leto. He is traditionally one of the eternally punished sinners in the Underworld, being strapped to a fiery wheel that spins through the air. Tityus's father was Zeus and his mother the mortal Elara, whom Zeus hid in the earth so Hera could not find her. Elara was killed by the sheer size of Tityus during pregnancy, and he was subsequently born from the earth instead.

17. **Phrixus the Minyan:** He and his sister Helle were the children of the Boeotian king Athamas and the nymph Nephele. The children escaped their hostile stepmother Ino by flying away on the back of a golden-fleeced ram sent by Nephele. As they crossed the Hellespont, Helle fell off and died (thus giving the crossing her name), and Phrixus continued until he reached Colchis. It is this ram's fleece that the Argonauts are en route to acquire.

18. **spear that Atalanta:** Atalanta was an Arcadian huntress.

19. **plot of Cypris:** Cypris is another name of Aphrodite.

20. **son of Aeson:** Jason.

STATIUS, *THEBAID* 5.1–498

1. **like loud flocks:** Statius does not identify the birds, but the simile is based on two earlier ones by Homer (*Iliad* 3.1–3) and Vergil (*Aeneid* 10.264–66) that describe cranes.

2. **on bare Haemus:** A mountain in Thrace.

3. **the chief Adrastus:** He is the king of Argos and the father-in-law of Polynices. The foremost of the Seven, he is, like Hypsipyle, a figure who values piety and loyalty—and, as such, he seems quite out of place in the world of this particular epic.

4. **Aegean Nereus circles Lemnos:** Aegean Nereus is the Aegean Sea. Nereus was a sea god and stands metonymically here for the sea itself.

5. **tired of fiery Etna:** Vulcan's forge was often placed on Sicily beneath the powerful volcano of Mount Etna.

6. **in ancient Paphos:** Site of her chief sanctuary on Cyprus.

7. **drove Idalia's birds:** Doves, Venus's sacred birds.

8. **the infernal sisters:** Furies.

9. **Hymen grows hushed:** He was the god of marriage.

10. **Phrygian pipes and 'Euhan' heard on peaks:** Phrygia was an area near Troy in Asia Minor. The worship of Bacchus was associated with the East, and thus the Bacchants use Eastern instruments. "Euhan" was a ritual cry associated with Bacchus.

11. **has Lucina witnessed:** Lucina was the goddess of childbirth.

12. **one Greek father:** Danaus, who came into conflict with his brother, Aegyptus. Marrying his fifty daughters to Aegyptus's fifty sons, he ordered them to slay their bridegrooms on their wedding night. All but one did so, and now the forty-nine are punished in the Underworld—they must eternally try to fill a sieve with water.

13. **the Thracian wife:** Procne. After her husband, Tereus, the tyrant of Thrace, raped her sister Philomela and cut out her tongue, Procne took vengeance by killing her own son, Itys, and feeding him to his father.

14. **their father thrilled:** Their father was commonly thought to be Ares/Mars, the god of war.

15. **Martial Enyo and nether Ceres:** Enyo was a goddess of war, and nether Ceres is Proserpina, the goddess of the Underworld. The Stygian goddesses that follow this are the Furies.

16. **battles near Strymon:** A river in Thrace. Haemus and Rhodope are Thracian mountains.

17. **The Sisters, joyous:** The Furies.

18. **Lapith feasts on chilly Ossa:** This is a reference to the Centauromachy, the battle between the Lapiths and the centaurs (the "Cloud-Born") that ensued after the centaur Eurytion tried to kidnap the bride at the wedding feast of Hippodamia and Pirithous.

19. **Thyoneus appeared to us:** Thyoneus is another name for Bacchus, who is the father of Thoas.

20. **Lucifer drives off:** Lucifer, "the light-bringer," is the planet Venus, the morning star.

21. **sated, the Eumenides:** The Furies, given the apotropaic designation "kindly ones."

22. **The Pelian ship:** The *Argo.*

23. **think Ortygia moved:** The island of Delos.

24. **Thracian Orpheus leans:** Orpheus was the mythological singer par excellence.

25. **blocked by Clashing Rocks:** The Symplegades were located at the Bosporus. They crashed together, crushing any ship that went through. The *Argo* was the first ship to make it through, after which the rocks became stationary.

26. **Telamon and Peleus:** The sons of Aeacus, king of Aegina. They will later be the fathers of Ajax and Achilles, respectively.

27. **sons of Aeacus:** Hypsipyle offers a mini-catalogue of key Argonauts, who traditionally numbered fifty young men. These are the foremost heroes of the generation preceding the Trojan War.

28. **Ethiopians' homes and shores:** As far back as Homer, the gods had a special relationship with the Ethiopians (a term that encompassed a wide geographical region of Africa, from Sudan to areas within sub-Saharan Africa), with whom they regularly feasted. My translation of *rubentum* (literally "red" or "blushing") as "sunkissed" is indebted to Sarah Derbew's translation of similar words in *Untangling Blackness in Greek Antiquity* (Cambridge: Cambridge University Press, 2022).

29. **Marathon's proud savior:** For slaying the Marathonian bull.

30. **sons of Aquilo:** Calais and Zetes, the sons of the north wind Aquilo/Boreas.

31. **master of ungrudging Phoebus:** Apollo (also known as Phoebus) had to endure a period of servitude to Admetus as punishment for killing a Cyclops.

32. **Nereus' son-in-law:** "Calydon's heir" is Meleager, and "Nereus's son-in-law" is Peleus.

33. **The Spartan twins:** Castor and Pollux.

34. **my own will or crime:** Hypsipyle accuses Jason of having raped her, a very different version from what is presented in Apollonius's *Argonautica.*

35. **rouse different loves:** This is a clear reference to Medea, whom Jason will seduce into helping him once he arrives in Colchis.

VERGIL, *AENEID* (SELECTIONS)

1. **314–56:** These are the line numbers for the original Latin, although the line numbers for Fagles's English translation are given throughout the section.

2. **or Thracian Harpalyce:** She was the daughter of Harpalycus, king of the Amymnaeans. Her father was expelled from power, whereupon he raised her in the woods, teaching her to hunt and fight.

3. **high-laced hunting boots:** Venus here sports cothurni, the boot worn for hunting but also famously by tragic actors. Many have seen here a foreshadowing of the tragic tale of Dido that will unfold.

4. **Byrsa, the Hide:** *Byrsa* is the Greek word for oxhide, a word the Greeks connected to *Bosra*, the Phoenician word for Carthage's citadel.

5. **exploring its features:** The temple of Juno in Carthage is decorated with scenes from the Trojan War. Since these are meant to celebrate the goddess, then they must ostensibly be celebrating the Greeks' triumph over Troy. This is not, however, how Aeneas reads the scenes; he sees them instead as a lament for Troy's fall. This passage offers a powerful illustration of Vergilian ambivalence, for both ways of reading the temple are simultaneously true. The sympathy that Vergil detects in the scenes finds expression in Dido's welcoming of the Trojans to her land.

6. **Rhesus' men betrayed:** This scene depicts the so-called "Dolonea" from *Iliad* 10, in which Diomedes and Odysseus sneak into the camp while the soldiers are sleeping and butcher them.

7. **Troilus in flight:** Troilus was a young Trojan prince killed by Achilles as he was fetching water outside Troy's walls. There had been a prophecy that if he grew to twenty years of age, Troy would not fall.

8. **the Trojan women:** In *Iliad* 6, Trojan women take a robe to Athena/Minerva in the hopes of placating her, but she rejects their offering.

9. **body off for gold:** A reference to Priam's ransoming of Hector's body from Achilles in *Iliad* 24.

10. **and silent Latona:** Diana's mother, known in Greek as Leto.

11. **the Dardan people:** The Trojans. Dardanus was the founder of Dardania, near Troy.

12. **Teucer came to Sidon once:** This is not the Trojan king Teucer but the Greek Teucer, son of the Telamon who ruled Salamis. Teucer was the half brother of Ajax. Telamon exiled Teucer for not preventing Ajax's suicide during the Trojan War. Coming to Phoenicia, he allied himself with Belus against Cyprus. Belus, victorious, allowed Teucer to settle there, and he founded a new Salamis.

13. **hurled against Typhoeus:** Typhoeus was an earthborn giant Jupiter had to fight in his rise to power. The idea that Love could break the thunderbolt is found in ancient art and literature; see

for instance *Greek Anthology* 16.250. And it is Vergil, after all, who coined the phrase *omnia vincit Amor* ("Love conquers all") at *Eclogues* 10.69.

14. **the wandering moon:** Bards play a key role at feasts going back to Homer. This song, by a bard named Iopas, has been much discussed by scholars. He sings of topics that in antiquity would have been designated as natural philosophy—the sort of philosophy a poet such as Lucretius wrote about in his Epicurean *De Rerum Natura*, written not long before the *Aeneid*. Like Lucretius, Iopas suggests that the gods are not involved in natural forces, an idea that seems to conflict with the gods' involvement in the events of Book One. Julia Hejduk has even written an influential article suggesting that Dido shows several characteristics of Epicureanism. See "Dido the Epicurean," *Classical Antiquity* 15, no. 2 (1996): 203–21.

15. **pores over their entrails:** One type of augury, haruspicy, involved the reading of divine signs on the entrails, especially the livers, of slaughtered animals.

16. **the queen delays:** This is one of several key instances of delay in the poem that mark dramatic moments—and fateful choices.

17. **sense of guilt:** This translates the tricky Latin word *culpa*, which can mean "sense of guilt" but also a "fault" or "wrongdoing," especially a sexual one. The key interpretive issue here is whether the word *culpa* is focalized through the narrator or Dido. Is this his appraisal or hers alone?

18. **Coeus and Enceladus:** A Titan and a Giant, each born from the Earth.

19. **as the Moors:** These are the inhabitants of ancient Mauretania, located in what is now Morocco and northern Algeria.

20. **troupe of eunuchs:** Iarbas lodges a barrage of Eastern stereotypes against Aeneas, essentially casting him as effeminate and luxurious. He sees him as a "second Paris" because, as Iarbas views it, he is stealing the woman he desires to wed.

21. **calls the pallid spirits:** Mercury is the "psychopomp" that leads souls to and from the Underworld.

22. **mother's father, Atlas:** Mercury's mother was Maia, the daughter of Atlas.

23. **doting on your wife:** The Latin word is *uxorius*, meaning that Mercury accuses Aeneas of being in the power of his *uxor*, "wife." The adjective reflects how the relationship between Antony and Cleopatra was represented in Roman propaganda.

24. **ruffle their repose:** This furnishes another suggestion that Dido is something of an Epicurean. The Epicureans did not believe that the gods intervened in human affairs but instead embodied perfect

mental tranquility. By espousing such Epicurean principles, Dido
clearly questions Aeneas's claim that his quest has been given to
him by the gods.

25. **To you alone:** There seems to be in the background here a different version of the story, one in which it was Aeneas and Anna,
not Aeneas and Dido, who became lovers. The late antique com-
mentator Servius, for instance, records that this was a version
known to the Roman writer Varro.

26. **never at Aulis:** This is where the Greek ships gathered before sailing to Troy.

27. **As frantic as Pentheus:** A figure familiar from the *Bacchae*, a
tragedy by Euripides, Pentheus was a king of Thebes who denied
the divinity of Dionysus/Bacchus. In retaliation, the god drove
him mad, causing him to see "two suns" and "two Thebes" (*Bacchae* 918–19).

28. **Or Agamemnon's Orestes:** In Euripides's *Eumenides*, Orestes is
hounded by Furies for the murder of his mother, Clytemnestra.

29. **three hundred gods:** The number three and its multiples were
common in magical rites.

30. **treachery of Laomedon's breed:** The Trojan king Laomedon was
famous for his treachery. For instance, he promised the gods
Neptune and Apollo a reward if they helped him build Troy's
walls, but afterward he refused to pay them. Dido associates the
Trojans as a whole with such deceit.

31. **avenger still unknown:** Hannibal, Carthage's general during the
Second Punic War (218–201 BCE).

32. **lock from her head:** This tradition is not known elsewhere, though
commentators connect it to the practice of cutting hair from sacrificial victims.

OVID, *HEROIDES* 7

1. **banks of the Meander:** Dido opens her final words by comparing
the poem to a swan song, the most beautiful song a swan will
sing as it knows it is dying. The Meander is a very winding river
in Turkey, near Troy, in ancient Phrygia.

2. **We set this in motion:** I have taken this plural, Latin *movimus*,
as a true plural, not the royal "we." Dido gives Aeneas credit for
their tragic love affair here.

3. **Where will a wife be:** Here Dido alludes to Aeneas's future bride
in Italy, Lavinia, who is a character without a voice in the
Aeneid.

4. **love him worse:** I can't read Ovid here without hearing Purcell's Dido (1688). I've shifted toward a more archaic style in verses 27–30.

5. **serve in your camps:** Venus is the goddess of love, and Aeneas's mother. Through Aeneas, she becomes the founding mother of the Roman people. Amor, or Cupid, is her other son.

6. **in my delusion:** Ovid responds to Vergil's story that Venus drove Dido mad with burning love for Aeneas.

7. **Stones and mountains:** Scorned lovers in Latin literature often curse their exes by saying they are the children of wild animals or dangerous parts of the natural world.

8. **Triton will ride:** Triton is the god of the sea.

9. **from Cytherian waters:** Venus was born near Cythera, so she is called Cytheria, or Cytherian Venus.

10. **who harms me:** Ovid piles on the repetition and variation here, calling attention to what comes, the first mention of Dido's suicide in the poem at line 64.

11. **your Phrygian treachery:** Aeneas and other Trojans are sometimes called Phrygians, after the Phrygians, another group of people who live in Western Asia.

12. **let young Iulus:** Aeneas's son is called both Iulus and Ascanius. As Iulus, he will give his name to the Roman patrician family of the Julii. Julius Caesar and Augustus will both claim their ancestor is the goddess Venus through Iulus.

13. **her harsh husband:** Iulus's mother was Creusa, Aeneas's Trojan wife who died during the fall of Troy.

14. **escape the sudden waters:** Ovid's poem recalls a famous moment in the *Aeneid*. A sudden fierce rainstorm separates Aeneas and Dido from the rest of a hunting party. They take shelter in a cave and make love. According to Vergil, "Dido calls it marriage."

15. **signals for my doom:** The Furies are Greek and Roman goddesses of revenge.

16. **Take vengeance:** The text here is difficult to determine. As lines 97a and b, I've translated the text offered by Peter Knox, *Ovid, Heroides: Select Epistles* (Cambridge: Cambridge University Press, 1995). Line 97b does not appear in four of the principal manuscripts.

17. **ash of my Sychaeus:** Sychaeus was Dido's husband, and king, in Tyre. Her wicked brother Pygmalion murdered him to claim the throne for himself. Dido fled Tyre to escape from her brother.

18. **softly, "Elissa, come!":** Dido's Phoenician name is Elissa.

19. **of Teucrian feet:** Dido refers to Carthage as Punic soil because she and her colonists are from Phoenician Tyre. Teucrian is another name for Trojan.

20. **Ilion in this Tyrian city:** Ilion is another name for Troy. Ovid's line imagines the complexities of Dido's new city, one she hopes will be multiethnic, founded by a Phoenician refugee from Tyre, built in Africa, and where she invites Aeneas's Trojans refugees to settle as well.
21. **Dardan relics:** Dardan = Trojan.
22. **Anchises rest softly:** Anchises is Aeneas's father and onetime partner of Venus.
23. **not from Phthia:** Phthia is where Achilles is from in the Greek world; Mycenae is where Agamemnon is from. Achilles is the greatest warrior in the Trojan War; Agamemnon is the chief king leading the Greek army at Troy.

LIVY, *THE HISTORY OF ROME* 1.3

1. **Ascanius, the son of Aeneas:** In Vergil's *Aeneid* he is the son of Creusa, Aeneas's Trojan wife, and flees from Troy along with his father and grandfather. He confusingly has two names, Ascanius and Iulus, and it is the latter that allowed the Julian family to claim descent from him. Livy reveals that there was disagreement about whether Ascanius and Iulus were the same person, and about whether it was Lavinia rather than Creusa who was Ascanius's mother.
2. **Mezentius and the Etruscans:** In the *Aeneid*, Mezentius is an Etruscan king who fights alongside Turnus against Aeneas.

HERODOTUS, *HISTORIES* (SELECTIONS)

1. **alone as tyrant:** The term "tyrant" need not have the negative connotations it acquired later—though it can. In its broadest sense it means simply one-person rule.
2. **and the Kalymnians:** Cos, Nisyros, and Kalymnos were islands off the coast of Caria.
3. **Xerxes sent Mardonius:** Mardonius was one of Xerxes's commanders and closest advisors.
4. **naval battle off Euboea:** The Battle of Artemisium, a narrow Persian victory.
5. **possession of Athens:** After the loss at Thermopylae, the Athenians withdrew from the city and took refuge to Salamis, leaving the city open to the Persians, who destroyed much of the city, including many of the old buildings on the Acropolis. The Persians withdrew after the defeat at Salamis, and the Athenians were able to return.

JOSEPHUS (SELECTIONS)

1. **the little lady:** The Greek word is to *gynaion*, a diminutive of "woman," *gyne*. The tone is hard to gauge here since the word ranges from a term of endearment to a contemptuous insult.

2. **crucifixion of the 800:** In 88 BCE, Alexandra's husband Alexander crucified eight hundred Pharisees who had rebelled against him.

3. **Ptolemy's constant oppression:** Ptolemy (son of Mennaeus) was the tetrarch of Iturea and was making inroads against Damascus. In *Jewish Antiquities*, Josephus reports that the army sent by Alexandra was under the command of her son Aristobulus.

4. **Ptolemaïs and besieging Cleopatra:** This is Cleopatra Selene, the daughter of the Egyptian rulers Ptolemy VIII and Cleopatra III. She married three successive Syrian kings, Antiochus VIII, Antiochus IX, and Antiochus X. The last was killed in war with the Parthians in 88 BCE, whereupon Cleopatra Selene stationed herself at the city of Ptolemaïs. Tigranes II of Armenia besieged her at Ptolemaïs in 69 BCE but had to rush back to Armenia, where he lost a horrible defeat to the Roman general Lucullus.

5. **named after Augustus:** Herod renamed Samaria as Sebaste in honor of Augustus, whose Greek name was Sebastos (which, like "Augustus," means "revered").

6. **those hostile to her family:** The Pharisees.

LUCAN, *CIVIL WAR* 10.53–171

1. **its inexorable decline:** Gian Biagio Conte, *Latin Literature: A History*, trans. Joseph B. Solodow (Baltimore: Johns Hopkins University Press, 1994), 445.

2. **the boy king:** Ptolemy XIII. Julius Caesar is at this point trying to broker a peace deal between him and Cleopatra, who has been driven from the city and now sneaks back in to meet with Caesar.

3. **chains of Pharos:** This probably refers to some sort of chain that blocked the harbor between Alexandria and Pharos Island.

4. **Spartan's harmful face and figure:** This refers to Helen, who supposedly "caused" the Trojan War when Paris stole her away from her husband, Menelaus.

5. **swell Hesperia's frenzies:** Hesperia was another name for Italy.

6. **Capitol with her sistrum:** A sistrum was a sort of rattle associated with Eastern religious rites. The Capitol is the Capitoline Hill in Rome.

7. **gulf off Leucas:** A reference to the Battle of Actium, in which Cleopatra and Antony would later be defeated by Octavian.

8. **Ptolemy's incestuous daughter:** The Ptolemies practiced endogamy, and Cleopatra was likely nominally married to both Ptolemy XIII and Ptolemy XIV, her brothers.

9. **not his wife's:** Caesar's Roman wife was Calpurnia.

10. **Forgetting Magnus:** I.e., Pompey the "Great."

11. **line of Lagus:** Lagus was the father of Ptolemy I Soter.

12. **sway of Pothinus:** Since Ptolemy XIII was underage when he and Cleopatra came to power, the eunuch Pothinus headed his regency council. It was supposedly Pothinus who ordered the beheading of Pompey.

13. **tortured into shape:** The translator takes this as a reference to head molding, whereas earlier translations took it as a reference to hairstyle.

14. **Her white breasts:** Paleness was regularly a mark of femininity in ancient thought, but the word *candida* here might describe not so much Cleopatra's skin tone as her radiant beauty. The word suggests less whiteness than brightness, unlike the "snow-white" tusks of line 181, which uses a different word, *niveus*, that clearly denotes the color of snow.

15. **an Atlantic forest:** This refers here to a Mauretanian forest, suggesting citron wood.

16. **Juba was conquered:** A Numidian king defeated by Caesar in 46 BCE.

17. **that consul, dusty:** A reference to Cincinnatus. He, along with Fabricius and Curius, were heroes of the Roman Republic. Lucan suggests that Cleopatra's wealth likely would have corrupted them too.

18. **gods of Egypt:** Egyptian gods often took the form of animals. Anubis, for example, was regularly depicted as a jackal, Apis a bull, and Bastet a cat.

19. **but famed Falernian:** Cleopatra does not here drink Egyptian wine from Lake Mareotis, but wine grown from Italian Falernian grapes, which have been exported to the Kush kingdom of Meroë to be fermented and aged.

CASSIUS DIO, *ROMAN HISTORY* 50.4–5

1. **worry that Caesar:** "Caesar" became a title for all the Roman emperors. Cassius Dio uses it here for Octavian (the future Augustus).

2. **Caesar serving as Fetialis:** Octavian himself served as the priest from the college of Fetiales. This priest sanctioned treaties after they had been made, but also, as here, outlined the causes for war before a formal declaration was issued.

3. **to become gymnasiarch:** The supervisor of the public gymnasia, a position that was clearly prestigious and occupied by the wealthy.

PLINY THE ELDER,
NATURAL HISTORY 9.119–121

1. **Prudence Jones well summarizes:** "Cleopatra's Cocktail," *Classical World* 103, no. 2 (Winter 2010): 210.

VERGIL, *AENEID* 8.675–731

1. **"history in the future tense":** See the opening lines of the poem "Secondary Epic," by W. H. Auden.
2. **father's star above him:** In 44 BCE, a comet appeared, which the Romans took as a sign that Julius Caesar had been deified.
3. **Agrippa:** Marcus Vipsanius Agrippa, the chief general of Octavian/Augustus. He would marry Augustus's daughter Julia, and from them would descend the future emperors Caligula and Nero.
4. **in triple triumph:** In 29 BCE, Octavian/Augustus celebrated a triple triumph for victories in Actium, Illyricum, and Egypt.
5. **bright Phoebus' white threshold:** The shield seems to conflate Augustus's triple triumph with his dedication of the Temple of Palatine Apollo in 28 BCE.
6. **outraged by his bridge:** The Araxes was a river over which Augustus, like Alexander the Great before him, had built a bridge, taken here as a symbol of domination.

HORACE, *ODES* 1.37

1. **banquets of the Salii:** The Salii were priests of Mars known for their exuberant dancing.
2. **to bring Caecuban:** A native Italian wine.
3. **the cruel Liburnians:** The warships used by Octavian/Augustus at Actium.

PROPERTIUS, *ELEGIES* 3.11

1. **Why marvel that:** The manuscripts of Propertius are vexed, and I have followed here the text of G. P. Goold, *Propertius: Elegies,* Loeb Classical Library 18 (Cambridge, MA: Harvard University Press, 1990).

2. **break my yoke:** Propertius has in mind here the Roman practice of "subjugation," whereby conquered peoples were forced to pass beneath a yoke to signify their enslavement.

3. **The Colchian yoked:** This is Medea, who is from Colchis on the eastern shore of the Black Sea, in present-day Georgia. She uses her knowledge and magic to help Jason perform a series of labors. First, Medea gives him an ointment to protect his skin from fire-breathing bulls that he must yoke in order to plow a field. Second, she tells him to defeat warriors sown from dragon's teeth by casting a stone into their midst to make them turn against each other. Third, Medea lulls to sleep the dragon that guards the Golden Fleece so that Jason can retrieve it.

4. **bathed in Gyges' lake:** This likely refers to the river Pactolus near Sardis, thought to have gold flowing in its waters.

5. **pillars in the conquered world:** The "Pillars of Hercules" were associated with the Strait of Gibraltar.

6. **Jove brings himself:** The god Jupiter is famously subjected to the force of love, though of course this regularly leads him to dominate others through rape.

7. **what of her:** Cleopatra is never named directly by Augustan poets.

8. **robbed Pompey of a triple triumph:** After his defeat at Pharsalus, Pompey fled to Egypt, where he was killed and decapitated by Ptolemy XIII. Pompey's three triumphs would have been over the Marians in Africa, over Sertorius in Spain, and over Mithridates in Pontus.

9. **neck to your in-law:** Propertius cites two other times Pompey faced death, once during a sickness in Naples (the "Phlegraean field") and again after his defeat by Julius Caesar, his father-in-law.

10. **burned into Philip's blood:** Cleopatra was descended from Philip of Macedon.

11. **rout Liburnian warships:** These were the warships used by Octavian (the future Augustus) at the Battle of Actium.

12. **wrap Tarpeia's rock:** A citadel in Rome from which condemned criminals were hurled as execution.

13. **Marius' arms and statues:** These would have been on the Capitoline in Rome.

14. **breaking Tarquin's axes:** Tarquinius Superbus ("Tarquin the Proud") was the last king of Rome, expelled after his son Sextus raped the Roman matron Lucretia.

15. **woman had to be endured:** Propertius uses the Latin word *patienda* ("had to be endured"), which frequently suggests sexual

penetration. Cleopatra thus threatened to make Roman men sexually submissive to her.

16. **Yet you—you fled:** Propertius now addresses Cleopatra directly.

17. **stands, not to be knocked down:** This line is corrupted in the manuscripts, and I therefore translate a suggestion by F. H. Sandbach, "Some Problems in Propertius," *Classical Quarterly* 12, no. 2 (November 1962): 264.

18. **where is Scipio's fleet:** Propertius now includes a list of famous Roman accomplishments that dim in comparison with Augustus's defeat of Cleopatra. Scipio Africanus sailed his fleet to North Africa, where he won against the Carthaginian general Hannibal. Camillus crushed the Gauls and recovered the Roman standards they had taken. Pompey defeated Mithridates near the Bosporus.

19. **Hannibal's spoils:** Propertius names three enemies of Rome. Hannibal unsuccessfully led Carthage against Rome in the Second Punic War. Syphax was a Numidian king defeated by Scipio in 203 BCE. Pyrrhus was the king of Epirus in Greece and was defeated by the Romans in 275 BCE.

20. **Curtius built a monument:** Propertius now includes a series of legendary Roman heroes from the Republic. Curtius, heeding an oracle, rode his horse into a chasm that appeared in the forum in order to ensure Rome's glory. The three men named Decius Mus (a grandfather, father, and son) each on different occasions charged on horseback directly into enemy lines, allowing the Romans to gain victory. Cocles single-handedly defended a bridge against the Etruscans until the Romans were able to destroy it. Marcus Valerius Corvinus fought against the Gauls in 348 BCE, miraculously aided by a crow. His cognomen "Corvinus" comes from the Latin word *corvus*, "crow."

21. **Leucadian Apollo will record:** A temple of Apollo on the island of Leucas, from which the Battle of Actium would have been visible.

CASSIUS DIO, *ROMAN HISTORY* 51.14

1. **When Caesar:** That is, Octavian (later Augustus).

AMANIRENAS, QUEEN OF KUSH

1. **three successive kingdoms:** Solange Ashby, "Priestess, Queen, Goddess: The Divine Feminine in the Kingdom of Kush," in *The Routledge Companion to Black Women's Cultural Histories*, ed. Janell Hobson (London: Routledge, 2021), 23.

STRABO, *GEOGRAPHY* 17.1.54

1. **sudden sand-storm:** Described at Herodotus 3.26.
2. **city of Premnis:** Qasr Ibrim.

TACITUS, *AGRICOLA* 16.1–2

1. **things of this sort:** Tacitus has just reported the various opinions among the Britons in favor of war.
2. **woman, Boudicca, was their leader:** The Latin words *femina duce* ("woman leader") would have recalled to the Roman mind Vergil's use of the same words (*dux femina*) to describe Dido at *Aeneid* 1.364. The phrase would later become associated with a different British queen, Elizabeth I, after the defeat of the Spanish Armada.
3. **the colony itself:** Camulodunum (modern Colchester).

CASSIUS DIO, *ROMAN HISTORY* 62.3–7

1. **full red hair:** Boudicca is famous for her red hair, but the color Dio uses is *xanthos*, a word hard to pin down and often used as a generic hair color. It had a wide range from bright blonde to deep brown, but normally with a reddish or coppery glow.
2. **"drive them out":** Julius Caesar's invasions into Britain never reduced the island to the status of a province but instead helped to establish a system of client kings. Augustus and Caligula prepared invasions against Britain that were ultimately called off. The conquest of Britain got underway in earnest during the 40s CE, in the principate of Claudius.
3. **"why our island":** Boudicca here offers a geography of Britain that is quite fanciful. In the words of Eric Adler, *Valorizing the Barbarians* (Austin: University of Texas Press, 2011), her description "stems from a Greco-Roman perspective, not a Celtic one" (p. 149).
4. **form of augury:** Although this form of augury would seem strange to Dio's Roman readers, the Romans too had pre-battle forms of divination that in turn appear odd to us. Compare the Roman use of "sacred chickens"—if the chickens ate, the omens were auspicious for battle; if the chickens did not eat, the omens were unlucky.
5. **"Andraste":** A warrior goddess of the Britons.
6. **"like Nitocris did":** Nitocris was a female pharaoh of Egypt, but her historicity has been questioned.
7. **"Messalina once did":** Boudicca here suggests that it was the wives and mothers of the emperors who have really been in charge in Rome. Messalina was the third wife of Claudius, whom

he later had executed for conspiracy. Agrippina is likely Agrippina the Younger, the fourth wife of Claudius and the mother (with Gnaeus Domitius Ahenobarbus) of the emperor Nero.

8. **"Nero-ess, this Domina-trix":** Maybe alluding to Nero's aunt Domitia, but the point here is that Nero is a female *dominus*, "slavemaster" or "enslaver."

9. **Mona, an island:** Modern Anglesey.

10. **two Roman cities:** This conflicts with Tacitus's account, which specifies three cities.

11. **name for Nike:** The goddess of victory.

HISTORIA AUGUSTA,
"THE THIRTY PRETENDERS" 30

1. **Gallienus conducted himself:** Gallienus was emperor from 253–268 CE; he is characterized as a bad emperor in our sources.

2. **battling the Goths:** Claudius Gothicus was emperor from 268–270 CE.

3. **conquered by Aurelian:** He came to power in 270 CE.

4. **purple-striped stola:** Literally, she wore a purple *limbus*, which was the stripe on the bottom edge of a woman's stola. The stola was the primary garment associated with matrons in the Roman world. The purple stripe also suggests the clothing of Roman magistrates, so Zenobia's dress is, as is she herself, a blend of masculine and feminine.

5. **four-wheeled matron's wagon:** Modes of transportation could have gender associations. Zenobia's preferred carriage was a *carpentum*, which was two-wheeled and drawn by mules. In the earlier periods of Rome, it could be used by powerful women such as the Vestal Virgins and female members of the imperial family. Yet as Jared Hudson notes in *The Rhetoric of Roman Transportation: Vehicles in Latin Literature* (Cambridge: Cambridge University Press, 2021), it had by Zenobia's day become a "general term for a carriage" (p. 58). Zenobia tellingly avoids the *pilentum*, a four-wheeled carriage with strong associations with matrons.

6. **"Trusting that Victoria":** Victoria was the widow of the Gallic emperor Victorinus, so Zenobia here imagines an alliance of a powerful queen in the east and a powerful queen in the west.

7. **that place known as Concha:** This would have been near Hadrian's Villa near modern Tivoli, Italy.

Metamorphoses

Winner of the 2023 Academy of American Poets Harold Morton Landon Translation Award

The first female translator of Ovid's epic into English in over sixty years, Stephanie McCarter addresses accuracy in translation and its representation of women, gendered dynamics of power, and sexual violence in the classic. The *Metamorphoses* holds up a kaleidoscopic lens to the modern world, one that offers the opportunity to reflect on contemporary discussions about gender, sexuality, race, violence, art, and identity.